CONTRACTED TO HIM

CATHY WILLIAMS

ANNIE WEST

MILLS & BOON

First published in Great Britain 2024
by Mills & Boon, an imprint of HarperCollins*Publishers* Ltd,
1 London Bridge Street, London, SE1 9GF

www.harpercollins.co.uk

HarperCollins*Publishers*, Macken House, 39/40 Mayor Street Upper,
Dublin 1, D01 C9W8, Ireland

Contracted to Him © 2024 Harlequin Enterprises ULC

Royally Promoted © 2024 Cathy Williams

Signed, Sealed, Married © 2024 Annie West

ISBN: 978-0-263-32010-7

06/24

Cathy Williams can remember reading
Mills & Boon books as a teenager, and now that
she's writing them she remains an avid fan. For
her, there is nothing like creating romantic stories
and engaging plots, and each and every book is a
new adventure. Cathy lives in London. Her three
daughters—Charlotte, Olivia and Emma—have
always been, and continue to be, the greatest
inspirations in her life.

Growing up near the beach, **Annie West** spent lots
of time observing tall, burnished lifeguards—early
research! Now she spends her days fantasising
about gorgeous men and their love-lives. Annie
has been a reader all her life. She also loves
travel, long walks, good company and great food.
You can contact her at annie@annie-west.com
or via PO Box 1041, Warners Bay, NSW 2282,
Australia.

ROYALLY PROMOTED

CATHY WILLIAMS

MILLS & BOON

CHAPTER ONE

'YOU'RE WET. WHY? Why are you soaking wet? You're also late.'

The door to Malik's office had been pushed open with its usual vigour and there she was, dripping on his pale-grey carpet, her blonde hair clinging to her in strands as she did her best to wring it out into semi-dried submission. He sat back in the leather chair, steepled his fingers and looked at his secretary with his head tilted to one side.

Lucy Walker, who had been working for him for a little over three years, was a force of nature. She was petite and curvy, with curly, bright blonde hair that had a will of its own, and a dimpled smile that had a disconcerting tendency to throw Malik off-track when he was taking her to task.

Right now was an excellent example.

Malik had long stopped asking himself how it was that she had stayed the course for as long as she had when, in every way, shape and form, she was precisely the sort of PA who normally wouldn't come close to being short-listed for the high-powered role she occupied.

But she had shown up for the interview, impressed him with her in-depth knowledge of negotiating the stock market, informed him that there was nothing she couldn't turn her hand to, smiled that dimpled smile and challenged him to set any task so that she could prove her worth.

Malik had duly given her ten minutes to work out projections for investing several million over several companies. She'd proven her worth in half the time. She was outspoken to a fault and was impressively immune to what, Malik knew, was a forbidding side to him that made most people think twice about saying anything of which he might disapprove. In every single walk of life, he was respected and feared in equal measure. But not by her.

She rid herself of her waterproof, which she dumped on the chair she occupied when in his office. The coat, too, was dripping onto his expensive carpet.

'Can you believe this weather, Malik? It's a disgrace. Why don't those overpaid people ever get the forecast right? No mention of a storm this morning when I switched on the telly—sunshine and showers!'

'Perhaps you should have paid more attention to the *showers* part of the weather report. It's after nine-thirty.'

'I would have texted, but my phone was low on juice. Still, I'm here now and ready to go! Lots of thoughts about that IT company you're looking to get hold of, by the way.'

'You need to go and get into some dry clothes.'

Lucy grimaced. 'That would involve a trip to the shops. I took the spare stuff I keep here back with me a couple of weeks ago and I completely forgot to replace them. I was bored of blues and greys. I thought that, with Christmas just round the corner, more festive colours might be in order.'

'We're in September.' Malik sighed heavily and sat back in the chair to look at her in brooding silence, before buzzing through to one of his other employees, who scuttled in at speed to stare with badly disguised laughter at his dripping secretary.

'Sir?'

'You need to go and get some dry clothes for Lucy,' he said, looking at Julia, who was secretary to one of the guys who worked for him. 'I don't care where. Put it on Robert's company card and be quick.'

'Malik…'

Malik looked at Lucy with an impatient frown. 'I need you here right now. I can't spare you for an hour hunting down a replacement outfit.'

'Duly noted.'

'Get one of the towels from the cloakroom and wrap it around you. I can't afford to have you off work with flu.'

'Trust me, flu is the last thing I want to have.'

Julia had hurried out, breathlessly promising to be back in under half an hour, which made Malik wonder how it was that his own secretary could be as stubborn as a mule when a snap of his fingers had every other person on the face of the earth jumping to attention.

'Off you go, Lucy. I have things to discuss with you of some importance, and time's moving along.'

Lucy ignored him to sit on the chair, causally pushing the wet waterproof off it and onto the ground.

'First, you deserve an explanation or else you're going to be in a grumpy mood with me all day.' She dimpled. 'I thought I'd walk in this morning. It was so lovely and sunny, not a hint of those showers Carol on the telly mentioned at seven when I left home—and, actually, I need the exercise, if I'm honest with myself. I don't get nearly enough fresh air these days and—'

'Cut to the chase, Lucy.'

'So I headed off. Normally, it would have taken forty-five minutes, but then it clouded over, and forget about *showers*; this was a deluge. To top it all, the Tube drivers are on strike, which meant no Tube, and the buses were all packed out. Wasted nearly half an hour waiting at the bus stop. In the end, I had no option but to try and be as quick as I could on foot, but with the aforementioned deluge… You want to see the streets out there, Malik. They've turned into canals. We could be in Venice.'

'Did it occur to you at all to buy an umbrella?' He sincerely did not want to be amused.

'Not really, no. I kept thinking it would blow over. Anyway, it was all a bit chaotic.'

'I don't pay you handsomely to be chaotic.'

'Point taken.' She stood up, grimaced as she looked down at her wet outfit and told him that she'd be a minute, that the towel was a good idea and might warm her up.

'Can I get you a coffee on my way back?' she asked brightly.

'Just get yourself dried off, and you might just as well wait for Julia to get back with whatever she's got for you.' He dismissed her with a wave of his hand but continued to look at her as she hustled out of his office, closing the door behind her with a smart click.

This was not how he had anticipated starting the morning. Indeed, the entire day had kicked off to an unpredictable and nightmarish start, with his mother calling him at a little after four in the morning to inform him that his father had been rushed to hospital with a heart attack.

As usual, she had delivered the news coolly, calmly and without emotion. The only hint as to what was going on beneath the surface was the slight tremor in her voice when, after a moment's hesitation, she had told him that the doctors had been unable to confirm whether he would pull through. It was going to be a long night ahead.

'I'll come immediately,' Malik had said, already thinking ahead to the repercussions of his father's situation now staring him in the face.

They were not inconsiderable. Malik, at thirty-two, returned to his country of birth on a reasonably infrequent basis. Here in London, he ran the family house, where the vast wealth of his family was invested with military precision by a team of highly trained hedge-fund managers and investment bankers. He oversaw the lot of them, whilst handling his own pet projects: investments into green energy and property that would had made him a billionaire in his own right, regardless of his vast family fortune.

He liked it this way. Returning to Sarastan, where his parents lived in palatial splendour as dictated by their royal status, always came with the down side of their tacit disapproval about his marital status—or lack thereof. In their eyes, time was running out for him to continue the family name.

It was just the way it was.

Here in London, though, he could shove that inconvenient truth to the back of his mind. But now…?

He scowled as he waited for Lucy to return.

His father had been rushed to hospital and Malik knew exactly what that meant. His time for relaxing was over. Yes, he would still be able to live in London, with perhaps more frequent trips back to supervise the running of the various arms of the family businesses, and make sure the oil was still pumping and still being exported as it should be—not to mention all the other concerns that sheltered under the Al-Rashid umbrella. But the time to take a wife had come.

He wondered whether his mother would address the elephant in the room head-on, given the circumstances. She was a cold and regal woman, not inclined to indulge in conversations of a personal nature, always preferring him to get whatever message she wanted to convey via a combination of telling silence and disapproving asides.

His father was hardly any more communicative. Duty and obligation lay at the forefront of their rigidly controlled lives. With his father in hospital and facing an uncertain outcome, the weight of duty and obligation that they shouldered was bearing down fast on Malik, and he knew that he was stsanding at a crossroads, like it or not.

Lost in a sequence of unpleasant thoughts, he looked up to see his secretary framed in the doorway of his office, as dry as could be expected and in a different outfit: a thick grey skirt, a white blouse and a grey V-necked jumper.

Julia, he surmised, had been intentionally mischievous in the purchase and had managed to get hold of precisely the sort of clothes her friend would have made a point of shunning.

'Sit.'

'You're not still annoyed over my late arrival, are you?'

Malik watched as she tugged at the skirt and shoved up the arms of the jumper.

'Consider it forgotten, just so long as there isn't a repeat performance. You might want to check if the Tube is running next time you decide to walk to work and, while you're at it, you could also look at the weather forecast.'

'I'll definitely do the former but I won't bother with the latter. As I told you, no one mentioned a storm, and I could have happily coped with a light shower. You have a point, though. I might invest in an umbrella.'

She sat down, settled her laptop on the desk so that they were facing one another, flipped it open and proceeded to scrutinise him over the lid.

She had truly amazing eyes, cornflower-blue and fringed by the thickest, darkest lashes that contrasted spectacularly with the vanilla-blonde of her hair. She was intensely pretty, an impression that was compounded by the generosity of her curves and the way she dimpled whenever she smiled.

'You'll be impressed to hear,' she was saying now, 'That not only have I sorted out all those back reports you gave me on Friday, but I've also managed to get through to the bio-fuel company you're looking at reaching out to and persuaded them to forward me their latest balance of accounts. That's in addition to the tech company you're thinking of acquiring.'

'You spent the weekend working?'

'A couple of hours, that's all. No need to thank me.'

Malik hesitated.

That was the first inkling Lucy had that the day was not going to go to plan.

Staring at him, at the sharp lines of his incredibly beautiful face, she felt momentarily disconcerted because hesitation really didn't feature in his database.

She had been working for him for three years and she could say, in all honesty, that she had never met anyone as focused, as single-minded, as crazily sharp or as utterly self-assured as the guy sitting opposite her. He could be ruthless, forbidding and cold but, for Lucy, those traits were eclipsed by other, more compelling ones.

She knew that he scared a lot of people but, oddly, he didn't intimidate *her* and he never had—even when she had walked into his office all those years ago, having made it through the gruelling preliminary interviews, to face the final hurdle for the job she had hoped to secure.

He had thrown her a challenge, something to do with the stock market, and she had met the challenge in half the allotted time, tempted to ask him if he had anything harder up his sleeve. Just as she was leaving, he'd asked her why she thought she deserved the job when there were more qualified candidates desperate for it. She hadn't batted an eyelid. She'd smiled and told him that that was a question that wouldn't even cross his mind in a year's time because she would have long since proved herself.

Lucy knew that, whether he would ever agree with her or not, her ability to answer him back and speak her mind went a long way to earning his respect...*whether she had a university degree or not.*

Speaking her mind was something that came naturally to her. Sandwiched between four sisters, speaking her mind was the only tool she'd had ever been able to use to get heard.

As the only non-graduate in her entire family, and that included her parents, she'd had to find her voice from very early on to make sure she wasn't squashed by her much more academic sisters with their strident opinions, all of whom wanted to be one step ahead of the others.

A sprawling family of girls had come with other disadvantages, along with the amazing up sides, but being invisible had never been one of those disadvantages.

'You're looking at me as though you want to tell me something but can't figure out how,' she said now, direct as always, even though just voicing those thoughts made her feel a little uneasy. 'You're not about to sack me, are you?'

'I'm not about to sack you.'

'Thank goodness. I couldn't face jumping back into the job market. It's a shark pit out there.'

'I had a call very early this morning, Lucy. My mother telephoned to tell me that my father has been rushed to hospital—his heart. He's had a triple bypass, and they're waiting overnight to see whether the operation has been successful.'

'Oh. My. Goodness…' She half-stood, hesitated, then sat back down. She knew that she was emotional, but her boss was not, and a hug was the last thing he would welcome.

Thinking about it, hugging him was also something that made a curious tingle feather up and down her spine.

'I'm so sorry, Malik,' she said with genuine sympathy. 'You must be devastated. How is your mother taking it?'

'As well as can be expected.'

'You'll want to think about going over, I suppose. Do you want me to arrange a flight for you?' Her voice was uncharacteristically subdued.

'Yes. I'll have to return, and possibly for a matter of several weeks. I'll have to see how the land lies, and naturally I'll be returning to London, but in the interim arrangements will have to be put in place while my father recuperates—and that is if there's no worst-case scenario.'

'Worst-case scenario?'

'If he doesn't pull through,' Malik said bluntly and was unsurprised when she paled.

She was as transparent as a pane of glass and generous when it came to expressing her feelings. After months spent dissuading her from that weakness, because emotionalism frankly got on his nerves, he had now given up. Maybe he'd just got used to it, but it didn't get on his nerves in her case.

'Oh, don't even think of going there, Malik. The most important thing you can do now is remain positive. It's called the laws of attraction. At least, I think that's what it's called. It's all about positivity making good outcomes. What can I do? I'm so, so sorry.'

'These things happen, Lucy,' he said flatly. 'And, for the record, I'll dispense with the mumbo-jumbo nonsense. I'm a realist and I know that preparations will have to be made for all eventualities. However, we won't dwell on that. Let's return to the fact that I'm going to be out of the country for quite some time.'

'Yes, let's.' Lucy was trying to work out how the place would run without him there but, then again, he was a master at delegation and had the sort of well-oiled, high-level team that could march onwards without supervision, such was their level of excellence and the depth of their loyalty to their paymaster.

Which begged the question…*where did she fit in to all of this?*

Which instantly brought her back to that moment of hesitation she had seen shadow his face earlier. He might not be sacking her, but was he going to give her a little reduced-pay time off? Lucy sincerely hoped not. Despite being surrounded by high powered sisters, she was on a par with them earnings-wise, and had been furiously putting money aside to get her own place.

She knew she was proving a point because she had no degree. Proving that she could be a success at what she did, because everyone had had their say when she'd ditched university without warning. One minute her bags had been packed for Durham, and the next minute they'd been unpacked and she'd turned her back on what her entire family had expected of her. Goodbye maths and economics course, hello technical college in Exeter, as far from the family home in leafy Surrey as she'd been able to get.

No one could fathom the reason why, and she hadn't confided, because she had never been more alone than at that very point in time in her lovely, noisy family.

How could she have told any of them about the fool she had been? How could she have admitted that she had fallen head over heels for a smooth-talking charmer who had turned her head, strung her along and then ditched her the minute she'd told him that they'd made a very costly mistake?

How could she ever have borne the mortification of telling any of the family that she had accidentally fallen pregnant? Two of her sisters were married with kids. Their pregnancies had been meticulously planned. Noisy debates had abounded over the years about girls who had unplanned pregnancies.

How on earth did that happen?

How hard was it to get hold of the pill?

A week after she'd been ditched, she had miscarried. She'd barely been pregnant and yet the pain had been immense. She'd turned her back on all the expectations lying on her shoulders and she'd started walking down a different road. She hadn't regretted it. It had led her to the most interesting job imaginable, working for the most interesting man imaginable, with a stupendous pay cheque and none of the constant stress her sisters seemed to face in their chosen fields of medicine and law.

A pay cheque she had grown accustomed to. At the moment she rented, which was very expensive to do in London, even where she lived in her small box on the third floor of a mansion block, the saving grace being the fact that it was in an okay part of North London.

So, with Malik departing for faraway shores for an indeterminate length of time… Well, from where she was sitting, the future was beginning to look far from rosy. All the managers there had their own dedicated secretaries. The intense nature of their jobs demanded it. Was she about to be tacked on to someone else's desk, fetching cups of coffee while Malik disappeared on a one-way ticket to Sarastan?

She was highly imaginative and now, as she stared at him, for once in complete silence, her imagination was hurtling in free fall. She was further dismayed by that hesitation on his face again and, instead of doing what she would normally have done, instead of flatly asking him what was going on, she found herself biting her lip. Sometimes to ask a question risked getting an answer you didn't particularly want to hear.

'It's inevitable, I'm afraid, and not at all welcome.'

'I can imagine, although I'm sure your parents will really enjoy having you back with them. I'm confident your dad will be released from hospital and be fighting fit in no time at all.' She wondered what it would be like, not waking in the morning to the thought of going in to work, where Malik would be waiting with a list as long as his arm of things for her to do. Her heart skipped a beat at a sudden sense of loss.

Malik raised his eyebrows. 'Positivity, yes. I got it the first time. No need to revisit the theme. You'll no doubt be wondering where you fit into this picture.'

Lucy reddened. 'It's a tough time for you,' she said gruffly, 'And where I fit in isn't important. The most important thing is for you to be out there for your family. They need you.'

'A generous sentiment. Here's where you fit in—I will have a great deal of work to do out there. Naturally, I'll make sure that everything is in place here to cover my absence, and remote work is largely trouble-free, but I will still have to devote considerable time to making sure everything over here ticks along without any hitches. Not just this office, but as you know there are a lot of ongoing deals at the moment, and taking my eye off the ball isn't going to do.'

'I suppose not, although…'

'Although…?'

'I could do my best to keep things ticking over if you assign someone to temporarily take your place. You know how good I am at self-motivating and I know most of those deals going through like the back of my hand. Ask me any question about any of them and I'll be able to give you an answer. I'm obviously not saying that as a *long-term* solution it would work—that would be crazy. But in the short term, I could do my best.'

'I hate to break this to you, Lucy, but, good as you are, I am irreplaceable.'

Lucy's eyebrows shot up. 'You have a very high opinion of yourself.' She dimpled and Malik returned the smile with raised eyebrows and one of his own.

He'd been wired since his mother had called him. Yes, he was concerned for his father's health, but beyond that the unravelling ramifications of what had happened had initiated a series of conclusions, none of which were particularly pleasant and all of which would have to be dealt with.

But here, with Lucy, he felt himself relax. The woman was a tonic, with her breezy irreverence. That was something he reluctantly had to concede.

'How well you know me,' Malik drawled but the half-smile left his lips as quickly as it had appeared and he stood up and strolled towards the window.

Lucy's eyes followed him.

He was a thing of beauty, she mused. It never failed to impress her. Everything about him was stunning, from the chiselled perfection of his harsh, arrogant features to the grace and symmetry of his long, muscular body.

He was six-four and there was not an ounce of wasted fat to be seen. He was all sinew, muscle and well-honed physical perfection. If all else failed, a career in modelling awaited.

He was intensely private and, despite the fact that Lucy had worked for him for over three years, she had in fact only ever met one of his girlfriends, a judge, and, she had later learnt, the youngest woman ever to have taken silk.

From that one encounter, Lucy had formed a picture in her head of the sort of women he favoured: tall, elegant, career-driven beauties who had powerful jobs and dressed in snappy, sharp designer clothes that were immaculately tailored and never prone to mundane things like creasing or the occasional coffee stain. Women who definitely wouldn't go with festive colours in September.

He was a guy who liked sophistication, beauty and could easily get both. Why had he never married? She had no idea, but rich guys played the field...didn't they?

And he wasn't old by any means, so he had years left in him to play in whatever fields took his fancy.

He might be a million light years away from the nightmare she had once dated, but Lucy knew that, however seriously sexy he was, and however often her disobedient eyes were inclined to stray in his direction, she could never consider him anything other than her gorgeous boss, because he was a guy who couldn't commit.

Heartbreak, and the loneliness and disillusionment that had come with it, had taught her that the one thing in life she wanted in a man was commitment. She didn't care about anything else because nothing else mattered. The guy who was willing to commit was the guy who was willing to give his heart, and without that what was left was some chump happy to use a woman for as long as it suited him before dumping her by text.

That would never be Malik's style. She knew him well enough by now to know that. But he still wasn't into long-term commitment. So she allowed her eyes to stray, and now and again her imagination went for the ride, but that was as far as it would ever get.

Which was all moot anyway, because he would never spare a glance her way. She idly thought of her friend Helen, now happily married to her billionaire boss and just expecting their first baby, and had to reluctantly concede that at times the exception proved the rule.

Her mind drifted. Helen was contained and *mysterious*. They had been out many times together, and Lucy had always noticed the way guys had surreptitiously glanced at her friend, sizing her up and taking her in. Of course, Helen never seemed to notice, but at first she had still been wrapped up in memories of George and her own disappointment there, and then without even realising it wrapped up in the whole business of falling for her boss.

Unlike her friend, Lucy was the opposite of mysterious. There was no room for mystery when she'd grown up in a family of vocal, assertive people. Mystery, in the environment in which she had grown up, would have been the equivalent of disappearing. Her dad often joked that he had to make an appointment to get a word in edgeways, which made her think of Malik and his dad, and how calmly and coolly he'd relayed the facts about his hospitalisation.

'Are you paying a scrap of attention to what I am saying, Lucy?'

Lucy blinked and surfaced to find her boss frowning at her. He was backlit by the thin, fading, last-of-the-summer sun filtering through the windows, a dark, looming silhouette that momentarily took her breath away.

'Sorry, I was a million miles away.'

'You need to focus. I'm talking about your immediate future and how what's happened is going to have an impact on you.'

Lucy straightened, suddenly tense. She tucked her unruly blonde hair behind her ears and stared down at the desperately boring clothes her work colleague had decided to choose for her. She liked bright colours. It seemed appropriate that she was now wearing drab-as-dishwater clothes for an occasion like this, one in which she was obviously going to find the comfortable course of her life thrown off-course for reasons that had nothing to do with her.

'I'm focused,' she said quietly. 'You know I'm good at focusing even if it may not always seem that way.'

'I will have to leave immediately—probably by tomorrow evening. I've arranged a board meeting with my ten top guys to fill them in.'

'And me?'

'This is where it may be a bit tricky.' He raked his fingers through his hair and again that off-putting hesitation was back on his face.

'I wish you'd just say what you have to say,' Lucy finally said with her customary forthrightness. 'Since when do you make a habit of holding back? I'm a grown woman. I can take it. You told me I'm not going to get the sack because you have to return to Sarastan, so where does that leave me? Am I about to be demoted to office junior, is that it? Wearing a uniform, sweeping the floors and making sure the place is locked last thing?'

Malik ignored her flight of imagination, which he was used to. 'The favoured option is for you to accompany me, Lucy. I won't be able to get hold of anyone who will be able to work as efficiently alongside me as you. You're familiar with multiple takeovers, and you know the ropes when it comes to dealing with clients.'

'You want me to come with you?'

Malik tilted his head to one side and strolled back towards his desk.

'I appreciate,' he said gravely, 'That this is going to be massively inconvenient for you, and I'll naturally ensure that you are compensated accordingly.'

Lucy stared at him in silence as her brain shifted gear and began travelling down an altogether different route.

'You said you had no idea how long you would be away,' she reminded him slowly.

'It's a tough call. My father, presuming he pulls through this, might recover quickly or it might go slower than expected. I can't put a timeline on it for obvious reasons, which makes it even more inconvenient for you. I've given this thought, and I'll formally sign a contract that allows you to bail should you find the conditions onerous.'

'Conditions onerous… The mind boggles.'

'You have an active life here,' Malik said bluntly. 'You'll lose that immediately should you accept my offer.' He paused. 'I'm not entirely sure whether that active life involves a boyfriend,' he mused, narrowing his eyes and staring at her. 'Does it? And, if so, would that be a temporary loss you would be willing to endure? Like I said, I don't know for sure how long my presence will be required in Sarastan. It's not just being there while my father recovers but in terms of sorting out my family's business affairs. I'm hoping it's weeks rather than months, and of course I'll be going to and from London, I imagine, but I can't give you a precise timeline. Right now, everything is up in the air.'

'I… I…'

'I'd like to give you time to consider my proposition, Lucy. I know this has been thrown at you out of the blue. But, in this instance, time is of the essence. I would propose you make arrangements to join me within the week.'

'Within the *week*?'

'If you rent, all rent would be covered until you return so that you don't jeopardise where you live. If you own, all mortgage payments will be handled. All bills will be met. Additionally, as compensation, I'll treble your pay for the duration of your time in my country.'

'*Treble?*'

'You're parroting me.'

'Can you blame me? My thoughts are all over the place.'

'Moving along, you'll also find your bank account substantially increased to cover incidentals such as appropriate clothing, shopping, beauty treatments...or whatever else it is that you do with your money.'

'Does it look as though I spend lots of money on beauty treatments?' Lucy said absently, while her mind continued to somersault. 'If I did, my hair would know how to do what it was told.'

'You haven't answered my question, Lucy. Is there a man in your life? Someone who might prevent you from disrupting your routine here?'

'Possibly,' she said airily. 'However, I should say that, were there such a man, I would never allow him to dictate how I chose to handle my life.'

'Patient guy, were such a man to be in your life.'

'In this day and age, Malik, men don't decide what women do. It's all about equal partnership.' She saw that he was smiling, amused, yet something in her shivered at the thought of this big, powerful man being protective of his woman. 'What if I choose not to go out there?'

'Naturally, your job would be safe,' Malik said briskly. 'But in all honesty there wouldn't be much for you to do here, as this is an intense group of people with dedicated PAs. Of course, you could while away the hours sweeping floors, as you say, but actually you would be put on temporary leave of absence until such time as I returned to London. Obviously, after a certain period of time full pay may no longer be appropriate, which we can discuss, but you would still be compensated adequately and your job would be held for you, unless I decide to limit my time in London and take up full residence in Sarastan.'

'What's the likelihood of that?' She paled as a void opened up at her feet.

'Who knows?' Malik shrugged. 'I can speculate but there's no reliable crystal ball to hand.'

There was an ominous note to that suggestion that sent chills down Lucy's spine. She knew that she got away with a lot when it came to her brilliant, charismatic boss but the truth was, there was an iron fist concealed within the velvet glove, and she was getting the uneasy impression that there were definite limits to how much he would indulge her.

Theirs was a healthy trade-off. He allowed her outspoken irreverence and, in return, she gave him the benefit of her amazing talent, which involved not only the number-crunching she was exceptionally good at but a real gift at communicating with people, so that he could leave many jobs involving important clients for her to handle at her discretion. She worked very hard, not to mention over and beyond without question.

Trade-offs, however, were not set in stone. And what would she be sacrificing if she accompanied him to his country for a few weeks? Lots of stuff with her family... movies, dinners out and pub lunches now and again with her friends...

'But where would I stay?' she asked with genuine curiosity. 'Would there be some sort of routine there? How would it all work? What would I do in my spare time?'

'A routine will be established when we get there. On the work front, with some disturbances given the situation, things will mirror what happens here. The scenery might change, Lucy, but the job will remain the same.' He smiled wryly. 'Trust me, Sarastan is an extremely wealthy country and I am an extremely wealthy man within it. I'd go so far as to say that my family are...of much elevated status. As such, you will find that your life will lack nothing when it comes to creature comforts.'

'Much elevated status? What does that mean?'

'Of royal lineage,' Malik expanded. 'On a more practical front, you may have to adapt your dress code to accommodate the heat and…' he paused '…you might find that my family…my parents…are painfully reserved. It may take a while for them to become accustomed to your, er, ebullience…'

Lucy got the message loud and clear and she burst out laughing…because fair was fair.

'I'll do my best to curb my enthusiasm.' She grinned.

'You can be your usual exuberant self when you're with me,' Malik conceded wryly. 'In fact, it would be odd dealing with a *quiet* you. So, what's it to be, Lucy?'

'Okay. I'll come. Is that all there is I need to know?'

Now that she had made her decision, she was already thinking ahead to what would be a wonderful adventure, a few weeks away from the pleasant predictability of her life. She wouldn't start extrapolating to anything beyond that. There was no point trying to cross bridges that weren't even on the horizon yet.

'I'll email you with the details of what you'll need to know, pack, and expect, for that matter.' He frowned and then, as he was about to return to the business of work, said, 'Just one more thing I suppose you should know…'

'What's that?'

'The time has come for me to marry. Finding a wife will probably be something else on the agenda whilst I am over there.'

CHAPTER TWO

WHAT? A WIFE? You're going to be finding a wife? Wait! What?

In receipt of that shocking postscript casually tacked on to the end of the conversation, Lucy's jaw dropped to the ground.

She had a million and one questions to ask him but, before she could get the first one out, he held up his hand, turned his attention to his computer and informed her that there was a hell of a lot to get through before he left, and three hours of valuable working time had already been squandered because of her late arrival.

'Yes, but...'

'But...?'

'You have to find a *wife*, Malik? As in, see what's available at the nearest department store? Maybe have a look in the cosmetics department? Who *does* that?'

In response, his eyebrows had shot up and he had said, wryly, 'Actually, Lucy, that aspect of my trip back to Sarastan will be the one that affects you the least. I only mentioned it because you'll obviously be around and there's no point having you indulge in colourful guessing games, should you be confronted with the situation as it unfolds.'

'The situation *as it unfolds*? Will you be conducting interviews for the post?'

'I haven't given much thought to the how the process will be negotiated. Now...back to those reports on Thompson and the bio-fuel company I have my eyes on...'

And that was that.

She spent the remainder of the day eaten up with curiosity.

Why was he looking for a *wife*? He could have anyone he wanted. One snap of his fingers, and there would be a queue of eligible women forming down the road. So, why go to the trouble of practically interviewing, for want of a better word, for the role? Whatever had happened to love?

It occurred to her that she knew precious little about Malik's family and personal life. While she made a habit of saying exactly what was in her head, he was careful with what he revealed, which, when she thought about it, was precious little.

By the end of the very long day, during which she barely had time to break for lunch, Lucy was spent, partly from working non-stop and partly because being eaten up with curiosity was an exhausting business and took a lot of energy.

'Right; enough. I think we've covered all we're going to be able to cover for the day.' This from Malik as he appeared at her desk to stare down at her as she furiously flicked through various open screens on her laptop, linking multiple reports and working at breakneck speed to cover the workload he had left her to get through in record time.

Lucy sat back and looked up and up and up at him.

'Very good.'

'I beg your pardon?' She arched her eyebrows and looked directly into amused dark eyes.

'You've done very well today. One hundred percent focus, even though I know you must have many questions to ask.'

'I hardly know where to begin with them, now that you mention it.'

'I'm sure, and they'll all be answered. It's…' he glanced at his watch '…a little after six. Why don't I take you somewhere for an early dinner and you can ask away? It's a temporary lifestyle change for you but it's a significant one. You need to get to Sarastan with a clear head and as little apprehension as possible.'

'Right now?'

Malik frowned. 'Right now, what?'

'Dinner.'

Lucy stood up, glanced down at her disorganised desk, stuck a pen in the flowerpot she used as a container and decided that further work to neaten her work area would have to wait for another day.

'Right now, Lucy.'

'I can't.'

'Why not?'

'I hate what I'm wearing and I refuse to be seen in it anywhere, unless it's on a bus heading back home, preferably behind dark shades and wearing a wig. Remind me to think up something clever to get back at Julia for this little trick of hers.'

Malik shook his head, looked to be on the verge of saying something and then raked his fingers through his hair.

'Lucy, it's now or never. I have things to do and I haven't got time for you to go back to wherever you live and change into something you feel more comfortable wearing. Besides, those colours… Believe it or not, those are the colours largely worn by the working population in the City.'

'All very dismal, boring people.' She grinned. 'With the exception of everyone working in these offices. Okay, could you at least give me ten minutes to freshen up? And it's in Swiss Cottage, by the way.'

'What is?'

'Where I rent.'

'Ten minutes. I'll meet you in the foyer on the ground floor.'

Malik watched as she began gathering her various belongings. She was right. There was a vibrancy about her that didn't work well with greys, blacks and navy-blues although, in fairness, they did work when it came to providing contrast with the bright-vanilla blonde of her hair which had now dried into a waterfall of corkscrew curls falling over her shoulders, almost to her waist.

The women he dated tended to be tall, angular and brunette with controlled hair and, yes, a predilection for all those colours his secretary had scorned. Just for a fleeting moment, he narrowed his gaze to look at her and was caught by the softness of her skin, the way her hair fell in its unruly tangle as she bent to reach for her bag, which had been dumped on the ground next to her chair, and the swing of heavy breasts just about outlined under the top Julia had decided to buy for her colleague, tongue no doubt very firmly in cheek as she'd made her choice.

Then he turned away with a dark flush and began heading for the door that led out to the main open-plan office with its towering greenery, carefully positioned glass partitions, sleek wood and metal desks.

* * *

Lucy spotted him as soon as the lift disgorged her and
its other eight occupants into the grand marble foyer that
housed Malik's elite, high-powered workforce. They occupied two floors of a towering glass building in the City.
Two floors where the elite of the elite handled more billions than anyone would ever come close to guessing.

He was sitting on one of the grey chairs clustered
round a circular glass table and was frowning at whatever he was reading on his phone. His long legs were
stretched out and he had undone the top three buttons of
his white, hand-tailored shirt.

She stopped dead in her tracks and stared for a few
seconds. Her heart picked up speed. She had signed up
to going away with this guy for weeks and she had no
real idea what that was going to entail, aside from the
fact that it would, supposedly, work as usual.

With the small technicality of him interviewing a suitable wife. So, in other words, not really *working as usual*,
was it? Because, as he had pointed out, she was going to
be around, so whatever fascinating interview techniques
he got up to, presumably she would be in the vicinity with
a bird's eye view of what was going on.

Maybe he foresaw these interviews being conducted
during working hours. She pictured herself scurrying
around with cups of tea and coffee for an array of women
sitting outside his office, sprucing up their CVs and anx-
iously rehearsing answers to possible questions.

He glanced up suddenly and she blushed, fussed with
her skirt and made her way over to him as he simultaneously rose to his feet, six foot four of sinful perfection.

'Right. Ready for me to answer those tons of questions
you have?' He smiled.

'I should have made a list.'

'I can't imagine you need a list to fire away, Lucy. I've phoned ahead and there's a table waiting for us at the French bistro a couple of streets away. I've made sure to ask them to sit us somewhere relatively quiet.'

'Don't you need to reserve that place months in advance?' Lucy fell into step, very much aware of him next to her as they left the glass building and emerged onto streets that were busy with after-work crowds keen to make the most of whatever fine weather was left of summer, which wouldn't be much.

Where was she going to live? Was she even going to like it there? What if she ended up lonely and miserable, hiding away in her bedroom?

'I can hear you thinking, Lucy,' Malik murmured with wry amusement, leaning down so that she could feel the warmth of his breath against her ear which made her shiver.

'Can you blame me?'

'I'd be surprised and disappointed if you didn't have anything to ask.'

Lucy was frowning and going through a veritable hornet's nest of scenarios which had been noticeably absent when she had airily accepted his offer a few hours ago.

The adventure aspect was beginning to nudge elbows with the fear factor, but she reminded herself that it was hardly going to be a life change set in stone, signed in blood and lasting years. Furthermore if she *did* end up feeling miserable and lonely—which was highly unlikely, because why would she?—then she could always leave. She wasn't going to be manacled to the office desk, after all.

The bistro was already heaving by the time they got

there but they were ushered to a quiet table at the very back of the room.

'I've never been here before.' She looked around her appreciatively. It was very modern with clean lines, a black-and-white tiled floor and interesting framed black-and-white photos on the walls of places and people she didn't recognise but felt she probably should.

Her mind was pleasantly diverted from her rising stress levels until her gaze landed squarely on the guy sitting opposite her, at which point she remembered that this was the very guy she had agreed to accompany abroad for an indefinite period of time.

'Wine?'

When Lucy looked, it was to find that a bottle of Chablis had been delivered to the table, along with some nibbles in a pewter dish.

'Sure.'

'Shall we order before the inquisition begins?'

'It's not going to be an inquisition.'

'I reserve judgement. The fish is extremely good here. How is it you've never been when it's ten minutes away from the office?'

'Perhaps you haven't checked the prices,' Lucy said kindly. 'Slightly out of my price range for a quick bite after work.'

'You're extremely well paid, Lucy. I personally handle all your salary increases and bonuses.'

'Yes, well...'

'And, in case I've never told you, you deserve every penny of those salary increases and bonuses.'

'Thank you, Malik. I appreciate that.'

Malik grinned. 'Now.' He sat back and flung his arms wide without taking his eyes off her face. 'Fire away.'

'What's it like?'

'What's what like?'

'Sarastan. Where you live. What's it like?'

'Relatively small and extremely wealthy.'

'Is that it?'

'It's largely desert, but there is some truly exquisite scenery and the surrounding sea is beautiful. We have breath-taking skyscrapers, world-class restaurants, luxury shopping malls and awe-inspiring houses.'

'Why did you leave?'

'Come again?'

'If it's so fantastic, why are you living in dreary London with its grey skies and pollution?'

Malik's gaze cooled. 'Not pertinent to your temporary posting over there, Lucy. You need to stick to the brief.'

Lucy reddened, a retort springing to her lips, but then it hit her that he was absolutely right.

This was an unusual situation, which didn't mean that she wasn't still his employee, paid by him to do a job. She was here to ask practical questions that would be relevant to her life over there, not delve into his personal thoughts on anything. Boundary lines existed between them for a very good reason and she would have to make sure that they didn't get crossed. What Malik's private life looked like was none of her business any more than it hers was his business.

'Where will I be living?' She changed direction, and then took time out to inspect the menu which had been brought to their table, quickly making a choice, although she hardly paid attention to what was there.

'I'll make sure that something very comfortable is sorted out for you.' He looked at her pensively. 'I usually stay with my parents when I'm over there,' he mused, thinking aloud. 'But, given the circumstances, I think I'll change that routine. In fact…'

'In fact…?' Lucy sat back as a basket of bread was brought to the table along with some very interesting-looking butter. She hesitated and, when she glanced at him, he waved at the bread and told her to tuck in.

'I won't, actually,' Lucy said politely. 'I'm not a bread person.' It occurred to her that this was the first time she had ever been to dinner with Malik on a one-to-one basis. Yes, they had shared a meal on the run, something brought to the office when they'd happened to be working late on a deal with a deadline, but dinner at a fancy place like this? Never.

Suddenly self-conscious, she primly placed her hands on her lap and sat back.

'Really? That flies in the face of the many baguettes you've bought from the deli on the corner at lunchtime.'

Lucy was suddenly stung by that remark. What did he really think of her, she wondered, apart from being a whizz at what she did? Did he find her too talkative, too mouthy? An open book without any interesting nooks and crannies? She was hardly an enigma, was she?

Out of nowhere, she thought of her sisters. They'd all followed in the footsteps of their dad, while she never did as she was told, feet firmly planted in the footsteps of their mum. She'd taken that break-up all those years ago so hard, and she had never really forgotten it, had never forgotten the trauma of that early miscarriage and the horror of being ditched like a sack of old junk that had seen better days. It had wreaked havoc with her self-confidence, and at the time had made her look in the mirror and wonder if she was as awful as she felt.

'You're upset,' Malik said quietly. 'I'm sorry if I offended you with that remark.'

'Offended? Me?' Lucy loosed a brittle laugh but she had to desperately blink back the urge to cry. 'As if. Where are you going to put me when I come over? You still have to answer that.'

Malik looked at her in silence for a few seconds, long enough for her to squirm, but she maintained eye contact, her chin tilted at a defiant angle.

She was saved by the arrival of her fish course, which allowed her to break eye contact and focus on the turbot on her plate. Her heart was thudding inside her. He'd apologised; he had seen the way she had reacted to his perfectly innocent, amusing banter and that, somehow, felt worse than if he hadn't said anything.

Did he pity her, feel sorry for her? Lucy knew that her imagination was playing tricks on her and she breathed in deeply and began to nibble at the food.

What did it matter what Malik thought of her? The most important thing was that she impressed him with her ability to do the job she was paid to do.

Did it matter whether he saw her as a *woman* or not? No!

She eyed him surreptitiously from under her lashes and accepted that anyone as beautiful as he was would really be unable to see her as anything other than the woman who worked for him. Guys who could have any woman they desired weren't the sort of guys who'd give her a second glance.

She forced a smile and made a few noises about the excellent quality of the food.

'So? You were saying?'

Malik finally picked up the thread of the conversation

as he dug into the food on his plate. 'I think I'll use one of the family properties to house us.'

'Sorry?' Fork on the way to her mouth, Lucy froze as she digested this.

'It would make sense.'

'On what planet would it make sense?' The words were out before she could take time to think about it. 'Malik, I'm not sharing *a house* with you!'

'Why not?'

'Because…because I'm *not*!'

'You shock me,' Malik murmured, looking down as he calmly carried on eating. 'What's there not to like about the idea? We'll be working together, and it would certainly do away with the aggravating chore of making our way into the capital every day.'

'That's not going to work, Malik. No way.'

'I'm very well trained in all domestic settings,' Malik told her mildly. 'Despite my privileged background, I find I'm generally capable of tidying up after myself in the absence of anyone else to do it for me and, at a push, have actually created one or two edible meals for myself.'

'Forget it!'

Her cheeks were hot and her pulses were racing. Disturbing images were flying through her head at dizzying speed. They involved the two of them in close quarters, bumping into one another in search of the kitchen late at night for a glass of water, sharing dinners, lunches and breakfasts, settling down to watch telly in the living room…

Her heart was on the verge of packing up altogether when she slowly noticed that he was finding it hard to control his laughter.

'What?' Lucy snapped, blinking her way back to reality.

'Calm down, Lucy,' he said gently. 'I know what's going through your head, and there's nothing to get over-excited about here. The family residence is a palace of quite sizeable proportions. It'll be convenient, because it's close enough to my parents' place for me to visit regularly to check my father's progress as and when. It'll also be big enough for you to have your own quarters, which will be in a completely different wing to where I will be staying. You'll even have your own garden where you can relax any time you want. I already have various rooms kitted out for office purposes, and naturally there will be staff on hand to take care of all our daily requirements. You'll find that you won't have to lift a finger.

'If it's any consolation, I've used the place hundreds of times for conferences that have involved people from different countries having to power-work on something and needing a place to stay for a few days at a time.'

Lucy stared at him and tried to sift through this baffling array of information, finally settling on, 'Palace? We'll be staying in a palace? When you say *palace*…?'

'You'll get the picture soon enough.'

'And when you say *staff*…?'

'You won't have to cook or clean or generally think about doing anything aside from working and relaxing.'

'I can't see myself relaxing in a place where I won't know anyone.'

'You'll know me.'

'You're my boss, Malik. It's completely different.'

'Is this your way of telling me that you're having second thoughts?'

'No. I said I'd come and I will. I'm just voicing a few perfectly valid concerns. A girl has to be prepared...'

'I could introduce you to some of my relatives who are your age.'

'You have brothers? Sisters?'

'I have cousins.'

'But no siblings.'

'We seem to be going a little off-piste here,' Malik murmured.

'No wonder you're eaten up with anxiety,' Lucy said sympathetically. 'Must be awful having to bear the burden of this on your own.'

'I find I'm managing just fine. Believe it or not, in the absence of siblings you tend to develop quite robust coping mechanisms. Moving on...'

'You *are* super self-contained, now that you mention it. Well, I guess when your dad returns home—and return home he will,' Lucy stressed, 'It might be a bit frantic and chaotic.'

Malik said nothing.

'Frantic and chaotic' were not words he would ever have associated with his highly organised, utterly controlled parents and he was sure that, whatever the circumstances at the moment, nothing at all was going to be frantic or chaotic within those palace walls. His mother had broken the news of his father with her usual cool, emotionless restraint and he was under no illusions that things would be in place at the palace for his father's eventual return there for recuperation. A calm, well-run, highly efficient household would be on offer, as it always had been from the day he'd been born.

His parents had had an arranged marriage and he had

never spied anything within it that could even be loosely described as 'passion'. Which, he reflected now, mouth tightening, was actually no bad thing. Bitter experience had long taught him that, however stultifying his once-youthful self had found his parents' marriage, it was a damned sight better than the alternatives that lay out there, like steel traps in wait of the unwary.

'I'll naturally make sure that photos of where you'll be staying are emailed to you and you'll be given ample opportunity to approve it. You can trust me on this, Lucy— we won't be under one another's feet. I will retreat to my own quarters when the working day is done, and you'll be free to do whatever you want to do in your spare time. I could have arranged for a PA over there, to spare you the ordeal of this situation, but no PA would be able to get up to speed with all the complex deals in progress that you're currently handling. And also, of course, as you've said, you can't sit in a vacuum for weeks at a stretch.'

'I get it, Malik, but back to the end of the working day situation... How I can build a personal life for myself over there?'

'There's a wealth of very comprehensive tourist blurb on the place. I'll also make sure you're emailed with information on things you might be interested in. Obviously, there might be one or two things you'll simply have to accept as quite different to what you're accustomed to.'

'Name a few.' She relaxed into a smile, mind soothed by what he had said about their living arrangements.

'Pubs: not really many of those, although there are some magnificent hotels with excellent nightlife. Public transport is sparse.' He smiled. 'Your hair might go grey-whilehunting for the nearest Tube. Taxis, however, are cheap and plentiful and, most importantly, air-conditioned. There's the coast and a wealth of museums and galleries and, of course, it's a vibrant hub should you want to fly out to visit any of the surrounding cities or countries. The family jet will be on standby, as will any number of drivers. A fleet of cars is always available for use.'

'A fleet of cars...what luxury.'

Malik remained silent. It would be interesting to see how she dealt with what would await her in his country. She would be exposed to a level of luxury that might come as a shock. How would she react?

He was surprised to feel a certain amount of tension at what could be an unfortunate outcome, but didn't he have experience in that particular area? And wasn't it wise to expect nothing and therefore never court disappointment?

He looked at her in brooding silence but his mind was elsewhere, playing with memories of the woman he had foolishly fancied himself in love with at the tender age of eighteen, when he had been at university in London. She had been as bedazzling as any woman he had ever met in his life before.

He had boarded from the age of thirteen, a tremendous place on the outskirts of Paris where he had learned to speak French fluently. But during those years he had spent all his holidays in Sarastan, where he had become accustomed only to meeting girls from the same social circle as his—girls who had been born knowing their place in the world and the extremely privileged status they enjoyed. Most of them had never strayed beyond the confines of a very rarefied social circle.

Sylvie had defied all those stereotypical images he had grown up with. Slight, and as graceful as a ballerina with green eyes and long red hair, he had met her in his first week and it had been lust at first sight. At the age of eighteen, love and lust had been immediate bedfellows and he hadn't fought any of it. He'd fallen hard for the girl, who'd worked in a hip, vintage record shop. With knowing eyes and raucous laugh, she was a girl with three earrings in each ear and a tiny, interesting tattoo just below her belly button.

She'd known how deep his pockets were. He hadn't tried to conceal his wealth. She had accepted the gifts with open arms and over the course of time had changed from the carefree girl he'd fallen for to a woman who had begun to see the people around her as less than her. She'd learnt arrogance. She'd felt it her right to complain to the people who served her in restaurants. Petulance had kicked in if she didn't get her own way. She'd become demanding.

Maybe those traits had always been there, but Malik had been left bitterly disillusioned, and even more so when, at the end of their disastrous relationship, she had laughed in his face and told him that she'd been fooling around behind his back the entire time.

Maybe she had. Maybe she'd concocted something to hurl at him because he had dumped her.

There was no *maybe* about the fact that he'd been a complete fool. He'd allowed himself to lose control of his emotions and had paid the price. He'd taken lessons with him from that experience. Never again would he trust emotions. They'd let him down once; he wasn't going to risk them letting him down ever again.

Avoiding those pitfalls? Easy. He dated women who were single-minded in their careers and weren't interested in long-term relationships. He'd been honest with each and every one of them from the very start; had told them that, if they were in search of Mr Right, then they should look somewhere else. He'd had fun but he'd decided, somewhere deep inside, that when it came to marriage he would choose as his father had—with his head and not with his heart.

It would be an arranged marriage with a woman who came from the same background as his and would be unimpressed with the magnificent riches that accompanied him. She would understand the value of spreading wealth around those less fortunate who lived in the country, and promoting all those causes that furthered infrastructure in Sarastan, as his parents had over the course of their marriage. With money and power came responsibility.

He wondered whether Lucy would have her head turned by the treasures she would find at the end of the rainbow. When he thought of that, something inside him twisted. Time would tell.

'Actually,' he surfaced to hear her say, dimpled smile back in place, 'Who needs a fleet of cars? If I had just the one, I would have been in work on time today. No, scratch that—I would still have decided to walk in. Exercise is essential. Although, thinking about it, it *was* a very ambitious walk. So…well… I probably would have arrived at exactly the same time, because I would have ended up trying to grab a Tube train that was never going to show up.'

'Thank you for that wealth of information.' Malik looked at her, still caught up wondering what she would think of what was awaiting her. 'You should get a car. I have no idea how anyone can survive without one.'

'You probably have no idea how anyone could survive without lots of things,' Lucy returned drily. 'A car being the least of those things.'

'Maybe you have a point.'

* * *

He smiled slowly. Flustered by that lazy smile, Lucy drew in a sharp, unsteady breath. Sprawling palace or no sprawling palace, she felt a shiver of thrill, excitement and quaking panic all rolled into one. The roof might be huge but they were still going to be living together under it.

Her heart sped up. She would be in 'her own quarters', whatever that meant, but she would still be *aware* of him in the same place as her, within the same palace walls. Hardly the same as when she headed off to her box in Swiss Cottage.

'Are you going to tell me about this interviewing for a bride thing?' she asked quickly.

'I'm not sure I specified an *interview*   and, for the record, there's nothing much to tell, Lucy. It's something that will most probably happen while I'm out there. An arrangement will be cemented.' He shrugged. 'With my father's health quite possibly permanently compromised, succession becomes more important. It's not crucial at this juncture, but it's desirable.'

'And…does that mean you get married and live out there?'

'It means the future holds what the future holds.'

'And the future holds an arranged marriage…'

'Like I told you,' Malik said patiently, 'This is not something you need to concern yourself with. Your duties over there will be very straightforward.'

'One last question on the subject…'

Malik called for the bill.

She was curious and, considering she was being asked to put up with what might turn out to be quite a bit of upheaval in her life, she deserved to have some of her questions answered.

Knowing her as well as he did, he would have been shocked if she had accepted his offer without an A4 sheet filled with questions. That said, he would have to curtail her curiosity. Her role would be vital on the work front but negligible everywhere else. She would possibly meet his family now and again—it would be downright bizarre if she didn't, given the circumstances—but largely she would be invisible.

When Malik thought of her meeting his formidable, cold and ultra-traditional parents, he drew a blank. *Best not* were the words that sprang to mind.

'Will I be involved in the interviewing procedures? Not that you want to use the term *interviewing*, but I can't think of any other word to use.'

Malik burst out laughing and flashed her a glance as he settled the bill.

'What's so funny?'

Malik opened his mouth to quip that involvement from her would probably result in all interviewees fleeing for the hills in terror, but then he remembered the way she had looked at him with huge, hurt eyes when he had teased her about her penchant for baguettes and thought again.

'You can use whatever word you like,' he said gently. 'And, no, Lucy, your talents won't be called on when it comes to my choosing of a wife. I've never involved you in my personal life and I won't be starting now.'

For a few seconds, their eyes tangled and she was the first to look away.

That'll teach me, she thought.

They worked well together, and they had the easy familiarity of two people who shared a lot of time on a daily basis. He appreciated her talents and, she liked to think, she had a healthy ability to speak her mind without being cowed or awed.

But that was it. Beyond that, all doors were firmly locked and, if she hadn't known it before, he had just made very sure to remind her.

All good; no room for annoying, drifting thoughts. She would have a job to do and she would make sure that it would be a job well done.

CHAPTER THREE

BETWEEN PACKING, PANICKING, texting loads of people and conference-calling her entire family—each of whom had way too much to contribute on her sudden departure—plus sorting out stuff with the flat, Lucy still managed to devour everything she could get hold of on the Internet about Sarastan.

True to his word, Malik had personally emailed her a PDF with facts and figures about his country, and had listed things that she might like to do while she was there. She did a lot of hectic cross-checking and decided that, yes, there would be a lot to do while she was there, which helped eradicate fears about rattling around in a palace like a spare part the second her work duties were done for the day.

She realised that she had managed to omit quite a number of practical questions, but she reckoned she could sort that all out once she reached the place. In the meantime, she spent a busy week tying up all manner of loose ends in the office, and co-ordinating files that needed to be accessible should the need arise for one of the partners, whilst deciding what to pack.

Malik had opened an account for her and deposited a vast sum of money which he told her was to 'equip herself with suitable clothing'. She had taken that to mean 'suitable clothing' for a very hot country, and hopefully not suitable clothing designed to ensure she didn't stick out like a sore thumb. She liked bright colours and felt that, under hot, sunny skies, bright colours would be just the ticket. If it turned out that she stood out too much, then she would revisit her choices.

For the moment...nerves decided to put in a long-over-due appearance. The novelty of her upcoming adventure had sunk in, as had the guilty pleasure of her spending spree accompanied by two of her sisters, Alice and Jess.

She would have been anxious at the airport, with a wildly different future only a matter of hours away, but she was distracted by the novelty of flying first class and luxuriated in a couple of glasses of champagne before promptly nodding off.

It wasn't a long flight. Now, here she was with the plane descending, and suddenly it was all too real. Her stomach knotted as she strapped her seat belt, and she closed her eyes as the plane screeched to a shuddering stop on the Tarmac.

A driver would be waiting for her. She should exit the terminal and look for a long, sleek black Bentley. The journey to where they were staying would take under an hour. Malik would meet her at the house. Those were his instructions. He had also given her the registration number, although he had said Bentleys were few and far between. In fact, his family owned all five of them.

Lucy emerged from the uber-modern, crazily clean terminal in record time. Her case looked mournfully in-adequate, hobnobbing with far more expensive luggage on the carousel, and she trolleyed it out into blistering early evening heat.

Every piece of literature had said that it was hot, yet

nothing quite prepared her for the sauna intensity of the sun beating down on her as she screeched to a stop outside the glass doors and looked around her. The long, wide strip of road outside was lined with palm trees and, beyond the airport bustle, a distant vision of desert brought home to her just how far out of her comfort zone she was going to be here.

Lucy had done some travelling in her life: family holidays to Europe. With so many of them, money had been stretched. They had rented houses in France and been to more camp sites than she could shake a stick at.

But this felt wildly different.

Thankfully, the flowery dress she had chosen to wear for the flight, sticking to her like glue as it was, seemed acceptable. Tourists, pink-faced and sheltering under hats, were climbing into black taxis or else looking around them for their lifts, and there were locals, some in Western clothing, some in traditional robes.

Excitement momentarily displaced nerves until she spotted the Bentley and, as she hurried towards it, pulling both her cases, a driver leapt out of the car to relieve her of them. Her instinct was to launch into polite chatter, but it was clear that he was there to do a job and, after greeting her, he stepped back and spun round to head for the door.

From behind privacy glass in the splendid luxury of his car, Malik watched Lucy as she tripped behind his driver, head swinging left and right as she did her best to take everything in.

He originally hadn't planned to meet her at the airport. With his father back from hospital, and a million things to do with the various family business concerns which had practically gone into panicked meltdown at his father's sudden health shock, time was in short supply.

The ship had to be steadied. Many thousands depended on the stability of the Al-Rashid family, which was involved in every part of the country's economic infrastructure. His father was an expert when it came to handling the complex network of companies. Malik handled much of the family billions, but from the London hub. Returning to Sarastan, he had quickly realised that there would be a lot of ground to cover to get up to speed with the way the vast machinery of his family's businesses were handled here.

The thorny business of ship-steadying was going to take time. Yet, he had thought about Lucy arriving and had suddenly become restless to see her.

He'd missed her. He'd missed her input. Missed her being his right-hand helper. God knew he'd needed it over here, where rules of engagement weren't quite the same as they were in his well-oiled set-up in London.

He opened the door and vaulted out, leaning against the car as the heat struck him with the force of a sledgehammer.

He smiled. She was wearing a flowing, bright, flowery dress buttoned all the way up. The flowers were huge and in wildly energetic colours and the dress was cinched in at the waist with a matching cloth belt. Lifting his reflective sunglasses to look at her, he absently wondered how it was that he had never noticed quite what an hourglass figure she had.

But, then again, this dress seemed designed to show it off, even though the actual style was really quite modest: below the knee, sleeves, little dainty collar...

The smile turned to a grin. For the first time in a week, he felt some of the tension oozing out of him.

'Lucy,' he drawled as she slowed her pace and looked at him from the opposite side of the car as his driver rushed to open the door for her. 'Good flight? You look hot.'

Lucy hadn't expected him.

Her mind had been drifting this way and that as she'd followed the driver. Her eyes, likewise, had been taking everything in. She'd also been sweltering and idly wondering what would happen if she fainted from the heat.

So she had the shock of her life when Malik stepped out of the car. In the space of a week, she'd somehow managed to forget just how beautiful he was. His raven-black hair was swept back and curled slightly at the collar of his shirt, a white short-sleeved shirt with an almost invisible white embroidered monogram on the front pocket. Maybe it was being out here in the blazing sun for a week, but he seemed a shade more bronzed.

And taller—which she knew was an optical illusion. Baking heat didn't make a person grow a couple of inches. Still, she stopped dead in her tracks and, for a few seconds, her heart slowed, the heat was forgotten and breath caught in her throat.

He had shoved his sunglasses up and was looking at her with lazy amusement.

'What are you doing here, Malik?'

She ducked into the back seat; what bliss…it was *cold*. She closed her eyes for a couple of seconds, then turned to look at him as he followed suit, slamming the door after him.

She breathed him in and felt a little unsteady.

'I wasn't expecting you,' she tacked on a little lamely. 'But, now that you're here, how's your dad doing? It's just brilliant that he's back from hospital, and thanks for filling me in. Hospitals...awful places.'

'You speak from close personal experience?'

'Not at all, but I've seen enough hospital dramas.'

'Which makes perfect sense.'

Hell, he'd missed this. There was a lot to be said for her conversational twists and turns, excellent distraction. Only now did he truly realise just how much stress he'd been under since he'd returned.

'And how is your mother dealing with it? I know you said she's fine, but I'll bet she's not. Probably making sure to keep a stiff upper lip because she doesn't want you to get too worried. My mother is very much like that. My father, come to think of it, not at all. He's excellent at feeling sorry for himself when he's under the weather.'

'It's all under control, Lucy. Best team of medics, best consultant, best after-care.'

'Best of everything—I'm getting the message. But still...there's more to recuperation than the best of everything.'

'Indeed there is,' he replied gravely, dark eyes flicking across her face, still flushed from the heat outside.

His eyes dropped to her mouth, which had a perfect Cupid's bow. And then drifted lower, to the cling of her dress across her full breasts. Something kicked in and his mouth tightened as he quickly looked away from a sight that was suddenly a little too tempting for his own good.

'Sticking to business, however...part of the reason I came here is to fill you in on anything you might want to find out now that you're actually here.'

* * *

Lucy would rather have delved into a few more questions about his family. It had been such a huge and presumably traumatic event and she marvelled that he could remain as cool as a cucumber. One of her sisters had broken her leg three years previously and Lucy had been distraught. She paled when she thought of either of her parents going into hospital.

'It's hotter than I expected,' she said, focusing on the guy looking at her with brooding attention.

'It shouldn't be. I sent an encyclopaedia worth of information, including details about the weather.'

'And that was extremely helpful.' She'd tied her hair back into something that should have been a bun, but it had gradually unravelled over the course of the day, and she helped things along now by yanking off the elastic tie and shaking her head.

The car was beautifully cool and her hair wasn't accustomed to being restricted. She failed to notice the sudden tension that rippled through Malik's body as he took in her carefree gesture. Failed to notice the way his eyes narrowed and his nostrils flared before he controlled his expression.

'Questions?' he reminded her, voice terser than intended.

'Here's one. Should I have my hair chopped off? I'm not sure this heat is going to agree with it. English heat is very different to this.'

'Up to you. Not the sort of question I had in mind, however.'

Lucy rested her head back, half-closed her eyes and dimpled at him.

'I know. I was just thinking out loud.'

'Well?'

'Are you happy to be back here?'

'Yet another question I didn't have in mind.'

Lucy half-opened her eyes and looked at him in silence for a few seconds.

She was tempted to probe. He was a very private guy. She knew that: knew it from the way he never, ever gave any hint of a life outside the walls of his very expensive office in London. The place was stuffed with other super-bright, highly ambitious and driven individuals, and yet even these bright and driven men occasionally talked about their partners. Some even went so far as to daringly have a few photos on their desks, which always made her smile.

But Malik was a closed book and now, out here in these circumstances, she realised that he was even more closed a book than she had imagined.

What stirred under that ridiculously gorgeous, utterly impenetrable exterior? she wondered. And not for the first time. Although sitting in this car, with him so close to her, her curiosity felt sharper. Was it because just being here, in the place where he'd been born, opened a door to the background she knew nothing about?

'Questions, questions, questions...' she mused, while her mind threatened to break its leash and run off.

'Focus, Lucy,' Malik said drily. 'You look as though you're a million miles away.'

'It's been a long day,' she said, not untruthfully. 'If I think about practical stuff, Malik, I do have a few questions, as it happens.'

'Spit them out.'

'Eating.'

'Come again?'

'I know my working hours are going to be the same as they are in London, but I'm not going to be heading back on the Tube for dinner in my box.'

'Your box?'

Malik frowned and inclined his head.

'That's where I live. It's a nice enough box. But, now that I'm here, what happens about breakfast and lunch and dinner...?' Her mind played with the alarming thought of sharing those times with him then she told herself that that would actually be the last thing he would want. That dinner he had taken her to before he'd left had been a one-off for purely practical reasons. Making a habit of it wasn't going be on the agenda—thank goodness.

'They'll be provided for.' His voice bordered on bewildered. 'My place isn't in the centre of the city. Of course, I have a suite of rooms there, but where we'll be staying is on the outskirts. You won't be able to stroll in for a baguette every lunchtime.'

'I wouldn't expect there to be baguettes for lunch, Malik.'

'I have staff. They'll be in charge of everything. They take care of everything to do with the palace and personal chefs handle the food. Some work will be done on the premises, of course, and as I've said everything is in place in that regard.'

Outside, the car was eating up the miles. Questions could wait a while. He nodded to the city as they approached it and began giving her some historic information about it. Lucy listened and stared out at a flashing panorama of soaring glass skyscrapers and pavements so clean she could probably have eaten her dinner off them.

'I know a bit about the history of the area,' she said,

more to herself than to him, because she was squinting outside into fast-fading light.

'You do?'

'One of my sisters studied history at university, and Sarastan was one of the countries she focused on.'

Silence fell, which Lucy only noticed as they city began disappearing behind them, consumed by vast open space and the darkness of dunes as mysterious as the ocean.

'What does said sister do now?' Malik asked mildly. 'Lecturer?'

'Gosh, no. That's my mum. Jess became a lawyer.' She stifled a yawn. 'I'm beginning to feel the toll all this travel has taken,' she murmured, closing her eyes. 'I'm not accustomed to this. All far too exciting for me.'

'And what about your other sisters?'

'Law, accountancy, medicine… My dad's a doctor.'

Lucy was barely paying attention to what she was saying. Exhaustion was settling over her like a cloud, stifling her thoughts and making her limbs heavy and lazy.

Her sharp consciousness of him next to her was fading under the weight of her own tiredness.

'And you?' Malik asked softly. 'Never tempted by university?'

Lucy's eyes flew open. She straightened and looked at him.

Just like that, the sun seemed to explode into sunset and then disappear into darkness. She was gazing out of the window, and his dark, deep voice was actually quite lulling as he told her about his country. Her body felt slack and the coolness inside the car was making her drowsy.

When he began to explain about his centuries-old culture, it was natural to confide that her sister had mentioned some of it to her on their shopping spree. Jess had been fascinated and envious and had asked her to try and get hold of some souvenirs. She was half-smiling at the memory of the conversation as she chatted to him. But his question shook her right out of her drowsiness. 'Sorry?'

'All your sisters went to university, so why not you? I don't believe you ever told me.'

His dark eyes glittered, and Lucy could feel hot colour creep into her cheeks.

She thought about her broken heart. She thought about the pain of everything that had happened that had made her walk away from the life that had been set in stone for her.

'Well?' Malik prompted. 'Don't tell me it's because you're not as clever as the rest of your family. I know what you're capable of.'

'I don't have to tell you anything, Malik.' Lucy's voice was sharp and cold.

Even in the dark, she could see his astonishment at the sharpness of her voice. It was so uncharacteristic of her. For once, she felt the true gaping differences between them. She might joke but she worked hard. She might challenge him but always within limits, and she was always ready to back away should she, as he sometimes told her, 'go beyond her brief'.

This tone of voice was a first. She had no idea how to break the impasse as the silence stretched between them to breaking point. One thing was for sure—she wasn't going to delve into this slice of her past. Not with him, not with anyone. It was her dark, sad secret and not one to be shared.

Would she ever share it? Maybe one day. Maybe if she found someone she could trust.

'You…you never said…' She cleared her throat and gathered her scattered wits. 'How does your father feel about returning to…er…work? Is he as much of a workaholic as you are? You, well, you never said…'

For a few seconds, she wondered whether he was going to answer. She could feel his lazy, intent stare burning a hole through her composure. She had to fight the urge to babble on about something and nothing just to put an end to the charge that had suddenly gathered in the space between them.

He did her a favour when he lowered his eyes.

'Nothing has been determined on that front,' he murmured. 'Early days, as you must know, having seen so many hospital dramas. The consultant, the recuperation, the bracing words of advice…you're probably better equipped than I am to predict what's going to happen next.'

The mood suitably lightened, Lucy relaxed and burst out laughing. 'I *am* quite knowledgeable on a range of various situations and their outcomes.' She grinned.

'I'm sure you are.'

They chatted. Questions of a practical nature were temporarily put on hold. However, Malik's antennae were on red-alert: so open, so transparent…a woman with nothing to hide. Or so he had thought.

But he'd hit a nerve and, having hit that nerve, he was suddenly keen to discover more.

This time, when he looked at her from under thoughtful, brooding lashes, his gaze was laser-sharp. She had the body of a siren. A guy would have to be blind not to notice lush curves like the ones she had. Something about that dress had managed to reveal just enough to tease— enough for distant alarm bells to start ringing.

And now…there was a story lurking behind the fact that she'd not been to university. What?

Malik had never indulged in curiosity when it came to women. That was a road that either led to exploring a past they might wish to share in which he had little interest, or to a future about which they might wish to conjecture but in which he had even less interest. He was a guy who preferred the enjoyable business of living in the present when it came to his relationships. Back in that distant time when reason had been lost to insanity, in the first flush of love and lust he'd actually contemplated what a future with Sylvie might look like, fool that he'd been then.

Never again. But now…he wondered.

'There.'

He pointed ahead of them and Lucy blinked at the impressive spectre of a palace slowly materialising in the distance. Darkness had fallen and out here, with the city lights behind them, it was deep and velvety, blanketing everything. The rolling sand dunes were interspersed with patches of trees but, as they drew closer to the palace, those dunes were replaced by carpets of grass, and the palm trees that clustered here and there were planted in rigid lines to form an avenue through which they now drove.

She fell back and stared. When he had told her that he lived in a palace, she had instantly conjured up something reasonably contained with multiple turrets. She could distinctly remember something of the sort in the cartoons she used to watch as a kid: tall and ivory-pale with small windows and lots and lots of turrets, often containing witches.

This was on a different scale altogether. It was illuminated and, against a backdrop of utter darkness, there was something ethereal about the sight. It sprawled, embracing a courtyard in front which was as vast as a park. Pillars and columns dissected a procession of windows, and gracing the centre of the structure was a multiple-domed rotunda. It was a thing of elegance and beauty.

'That's *yours*?'

'It belongs to the Al-Rashid family. I did tell you that there was no risk of us crowding one another. Now you can see how it can be used for accommodation and work-space for a substantial amount of people.'

'It's huge, Malik.'

'Indeed,' he agreed. 'I've never done a room count, but I'd say a minimum of twenty-five bedrooms, excluding various suites. So, yes…substantial.'

'Well, that's an understatement if ever there was one.'

She dragged awe-struck eyes away to look at him. Maybe for the first time she truly appreciated the depth of his wealth and the extreme privilege in which he had been raised. For the first time, she could see why he would consider an arranged marriage to a woman of equally noble standing.

'I get it,' she said quietly.

Leaning against the seat, legs spread, hands resting loosely on his thighs, Malik returned that pensive gaze with a speculative one of his own.

'Tell me what you get.'

'I get why you would want an arranged marriage,' she said slowly. 'All of this…' she gestured to the magnificent, pale spectacle nearing them '...would be too much for anyone ordinary. You would have to marry a woman who was accustomed to it.'

'You think so?' Malik murmured. 'Point of order, I agree with you, but even so...you don't think an *ordinary* woman would be able to cope?'

'I don't think any ordinary woman would want to!' She broke the sudden serious silence with a burst of laughter. 'Personally? Give me a two-up, two-down any day of the week!'

She looked away, just in time to see the imposing front door opened by a man in uniform and from behind him came more of the same.

When her cornflower-blue eyes briefly turned to meet his, they confirmed what she had just said: *no ordinary woman would want this.*

CHAPTER FOUR

MALIK WONDERED...

No ordinary woman would want this? Palaces, wealth beyond most people's wildest dreams, a life in which every need was met and every whim within easy reach... really?

Lucy's amused, heartfelt declaration that she couldn't be less interested in stuff like that, that no ordinary woman would be, had buried in his head like a burr and had been churning around there for the past week, even though no more had been said on the subject.

Instead, he had focused on work, on familiarising Lucy with the layout of where they were staying and on introducing her to a routine with which she felt comfortable. It was up to him to ensure she settled in. He was very much aware that she was here at his request and would probably feel like a fish out of water for the first few days or even weeks.

He thought long and hard about how to ease the temporary transition and decided to stick to a routine similar to the one they had shared in London. They discussed plans for the day over a breakfast brought to them at nine sharp in the conservatory that overlooked the manicured gardens at the back. By then, he had been working for at least two hours, catching up on his own business con-

cerns. As soon as she joined him, they dived into what
had to be done that day—it was not unlike discussing
plans for the day in his office in London, where she would
sit opposite him scrolling through her laptop and quickly
taking notes on what had to be packed in.

Twice, they had taken the Bentley to the headquarters
in the capital and spent a hectic day there. Things had
been well run under his father's eagle-eyed stewardship.
Concerns raised about what happened next now that Ali
Al-Rashid was recuperating had to be dealt with.

Accustomed to her input, the clever way she commu-
nicated with clients, her chattiness and constant upbeat,
vocal personality, a suddenly subdued Lucy had taken
some getting used to.

'Am I background enough?' she had asked four days
ago, on their return from the head office in Sarastan.
Then she had smiled and he had wanted to tell her that
'background' was the last thing he wanted her to be—
even though here it was exactly what she had to be.

'Perfect,' he had said instead, and she'd smiled a little more.

Then, head tilted, she'd said, 'Well, that's a shame. It's
very annoying not being able to chat. I don't think I was
ever this quiet even when I had laryngitis four years ago.'

Sitting here now, Malik glanced at his watch and immediately frowned at his lack of focus. His mother was
talking. His mind was elsewhere. He was thinking about
Lucy, thinking about how much he missed the free and
easy ebullience of her rapport with him.

He was absently wondering how he had managed to
become used to a working relationship with Lucy that
bore no resemblance to anything he had ever experienced
with a woman before. He didn't quite know at what point

he'd gone from indulging her enthusiasm for saying exactly what she thought about a thousand random things with long-suffering patience to actually expecting it and finally to enjoying it.

Was it because of the novelty of being in the company of someone who didn't tiptoe around him? Sylvie had been a novelty for him on the romantic front. She had knocked him for six because she had been a curiosity he hadn't been able to resist. After a diet of all the right food, she had represented something sweet and tempting but ultimately bad for him. The relationship had crashed and burned, and he would never go there again, but Lucy…?

This was completely different. She posed no threat to his peace of mind because he wasn't and never would be romantically involved with her. He could appreciate her outspokenness because it was something that he left behind when he shut the office door behind him at the end of play.

Malik was unaccustomed to his mind drifting. He shifted, tried to bring it back to heel and tilted his head to one side as his mother, in her usual perfectly well-mannered, utterly restrained way, updated him on what his father's consultant had said following his visit to the palace earlier.

'Of course,' she was saying, her voice cool and well-modulated, 'Jafna, the senior nurse he has allocated, is in charge of dispensing all the medication. It is a complicated regime, but I am assured, once your father is fully recovered, he will be able to halve the number of tablets he is currently on. We hope for a good outcome by the end of the month.'

He looked at her and marvelled at how rigidly contained she was. Nadia Al-Rashid was a beautiful woman.

Her dark hair was now lightly streaked with grey and tied back in an elegant chignon, and every inch of her was impeccably regal, from her finely chiselled features and haughty posture to the elegant, flowing gold-and-blue dress she wore that fell to the floor. She was not quite sixty, but her face was unlined.

She moved on from his father, who was resting upstairs, to Lucy, whom she had yet to meet.

'And this young lady you have brought with you, Malik—tell me what she is like before she arrives. You say she works well alongside you?'

'She knows the ropes,' Malik confirmed wryly. 'She's clever, quick and, as I explained, there's too much happening within my own companies to delegate to an outsider. Hence her presence in Sarastan.'

'I understand. Your father's secretary, Zahra… He has been upset that she will no longer have the job she has enjoyed for over two decades. She was a mature woman in her forties when your father took her on, ten years older than him, and he has much respect for her.'

Malik was startled at this piece of information because he knew next to nothing about the people in his parents lives, far less the ones who worked for his father.

He was also startled by the softening in his mother's voice.

'He can surely shift her to someone else?'

'It is not as easy as that. They have a very special working relationship because her mother was a cherished retainer in our household, and I am afraid Zahra might be too old now for a transfer. Perhaps it is the same with your employee?'

Malik shifted and thought about the shapely body that had made him sit up and take notice ever since she'd come to Sarastan. Maybe that was a little different from his father and Zahra, who was probably well into her sixties if he did the maths.

Yes…definitely a different scenario.

'Perhaps…'

He was about to return to the subject of his father when the door to the sitting room was quietly pushed open and Yusuf entered, who had been with his parents for what felt like a thousand years, bowing, his flowing white robes practically enveloping him. He was small and thin and as loyal an employee as it was possible to be.

Lucy's arrival was announced.

Malik rose to his feet.

She had been here a little over a week and this would be her first meeting with his mother. His father would not be making an appearance; that was fine—one out of two worked.

Out of the corner of his eye, he could see his mother sit up and prepare herself for the formality of entertaining a stranger.

Under normal circumstances, would she have been alarmed at the thought of them sharing the palace? Probably not. A secretary would pose no problem because, in his mother's eyes, Lucy was so far down the pecking order socially that she wouldn't contemplate her son being attracted to her.

Even more so now, because he had informed both his parents that, in view of changed circumstances, he was willing to wed a suitable bride. It had been one of those rare occasions when he had actually witnessed his mother reveal what was going through her head and he'd been amused at the pleased satisfaction on her face.

He stifled a grin now and wondered whether more

genuine emotion might be revealed on her face when she met Lucy who, guaranteed, was probably going to be nothing like any girl she'd met before.

He sat back in the plush, velvet and highly uncomfortably erect chair and waited for his secretary to be shown in.

Standing outside, Lucy adjusted her dress.

She'd spent the past few days doing her best to contain her naturally sunny disposition. She'd met quite a number of the people who worked in various capacities for the sprawling set of Al-Rashid companies.

Actually, for the first time in her life, she'd felt a little tongue tied in Malik's presence. Seeing him in his natural habitat had been…awe-inspiring. Of course, in London, he was the king of the jungle. He walked into a room and people fell silent. His youth was never seen as an impediment. If anything, it enhanced his status as someone formidable and gifted beyond his years. Since she'd been working for him, he had never, to her knowledge, lost money on any deal or misjudged the volatile money markets to his detriment. He issued orders and was obeyed without question.

Here…he walked into a room and people bowed. They were respectful not simply of his talent, business acumen and his crazy intelligence, they were respectful of his inherited status. He was of royal blood and what happened within his vast business concerns affected not just him but everyone in his kingdom.

Likewise, she had found herself taking a step back from being her usual effervescent self. She wasn't awkward around him but she bit her tongue when she got the urge to say something that might get under his skin, even though he'd always laughed when she'd done that. She'd stopped saying whatever popped into her head, no longer safe in the knowledge that she wasn't breaking any unspoken rules. Here, she felt she might be.

He hadn't changed, and yet she felt that she was seeing a different side to him—the side to the man who would marry for duty.

She hadn't asked him anything about the marriage plan and he'd said nothing. Were there women lined up for him? He was following in his parents' footsteps.

As she fussed with her dress, she wondered what his mother would be like. Would she set the benchmark for what a suitable bride for her son might resemble?

In accordance with the nerve-racking dinner that awaited her, she had done her best to dress for the occasion. The dress was the most formal in her repertoire. It was long, with a pattern of small flowers, and the sleeves, also long, were softly flowing, as was the rest of the dress. Lucy had bought it because, when she did a fast circle in it, she felt wonderfully light, as though she was a butterfly about to spread its wings and flutter away.

Which was a great feeling, because she certainly wasn't anything like a dainty butterfly in appearance. She breathed in deeply as the door was gently pushed open and a bowing Yusuf stepped aside to allow her to go past him.

The magnificent room into which she was shown brought her to an abrupt stop. It was richly decorated in blue and cream and the silk rug that covered most of the floor was absolutely enormous, the size of a football field. The palette of colours that adorned it was dizzyingly beautiful.

Lucy walked slowly inside and, for a few seconds,

couldn't resist casting her eyes around her as she admired the tapestry that hung on one of the walls, the vibrant, stylised paintings, the clusters of formal chairs and tables and then, at last…the woman looking at her in silence.

And sitting alongside her… Malik.

This wasn't a Malik she immediately recognised because he was formally dressed in the robes of his country. Loose black-and-gold silk fell to his ankles as he stood. He moved towards her and her heartbeat sped up until she thought her heart would actually jump out of her chest.

Her eyes widened, and they widened even further as he leant into her and whispered devilishly, 'Are you ready for me to make the introductions, Lucy, or should I see if I can find some smelling salts instead? Because you look as though you're about to faint.'

'Very funny.' But her heart was all over the place.

'It's a little grander than where we're currently staying.'

'You could have warned me.' Her eyes skittered beyond him to his mother, who was looking at them both with a guarded, unreadable expression.

She smiled a wavering smile.

'No point.' He straightened but his dark eyes were still amused. 'I very much like the outfit, by the way,' he murmured. 'It makes a change from all those muted colours you've been wearing since you got here. I was beginning to wonder whether the Lucy I've become accustomed to had been replaced with a clone.'

'I *did* bring lots of bright stuff. They're just in my wardrobe waiting for the right moment to make their grand entrance.'

She felt colour steal into her cheeks. The compliment might have been a throwaway one, but it still somehow had the capacity to make her feel all hot and bothered. Upon which she broke away and walked towards the austere and stunningly beautiful woman sitting upright on one of the chairs.

It was a struggle not to falter. Normally an instinctively good judge of character, she had no idea what the older woman was thinking. Was that cool look concealing boredom, curiosity, disapproval? Maybe she was planning dinner menus for the month.

She wanted to glance back to Malik for moral support but she reminded herself that she was well able to stand on her own two feet. Her boisterous family had prepared her to have a voice and to use it without fear.

She also reminded herself that, however terrifying this beautiful woman was, she was also a woman who had just recently had to cope with the shock of her husband having a heart attack, and at an age that was still relatively young.

Her natural warmth and empathy brought a smile to her face.

'Mother, this is my secretary, Lucy.'

Introductions were made. Lucy thought that 'Nadia' was a wonderful name. She wondered whether she should curtsey and decided that there was nothing to lose.

'Mrs Al-Rashid...or should I address you as something else? Your son never said. In fairness, I didn't get round to asking. Your Majesty...'

'Nadia will be fine, my dear, and please, there is no need for you to curtsey.'

'I just want to say how deeply, *deeply* sorry I was to hear of your husband's heart problems.'

'That is very kind of you to say so. He is, fortunately, in the best possible hands.'

'Yes, your son told me. How wonderful. It must be so reassuring to know that you have the very best that the medical world can offer.' She looked at her hostess earnestly whilst still in awe of just how stunningly beautiful she was. 'Sometimes it can all be a little hit and miss, at least in the UK.'

'Hit and miss?'

'Doctors rushed off their feet… Nurses in a tizzy running here, there and everywhere—amazing at what they do, but it's non-stop. I believe—I read.'

'Lucy, perhaps you'd like something to drink?'

Malik's voice from behind brought her sharply back to her feet and she reddened.

'You have a wonderful place here, Mrs… Your Majesty… *Nadia.*'

'Lucy…'

Malik emerged from behind to stand directly in front of her, a looming, six-four, ridiculously good-looking version of his striking mother.

'Why don't you sit? Tea will be served.'

Nadia's lips were twitching, moving to a smile.

'I apologise…er… Nadia…ma'am,' Lucy murmured, shuffling into one of the upright chairs and feeling vaguely mortified at her lack of finesse. 'I tend to talk a little too much when I've nervous.'

'But why are you nervous, my dear?'

'Well…'

'We are very relaxed and hospitable hosts, Ali and I, and of course it is a pleasure to meet the girl of whom my son has spoken so highly.'

'Has he?' Lucy glanced across to Malik from under her lashes and was surprised to find him looking a little off-kilter at the direction of the conversation.

'Well, he really should,' she said tartly. If sharing space with four sisters and her outspoken parents had done one thing, it was to have taught her that she had a voice and, just so long as she wasn't being mean, cruel or offensive, then it was there to be heard. 'Because without me—' she snapped her fingers, magician-style '—he just wouldn't know what to do when it comes to an awful lot of his deals. It's like that with all of us working behind the scenes.' Lucy dimpled. 'Our bosses don't know it, but we PAs actually are the ones who make the whole place run efficiently.'

Nadia smiled. 'I believe you, my dear.' The dark eyes twinkled. 'And I hope you make sure to tell him that often. Tea?'

Tea was brought and served and Lucy unwound, enjoying this regal woman with the dark eyes that lit up with amusement at some of the things Lucy said to her. Sitting to one side with a dainty cup balancing precariously on his thigh, Malik watched their interaction without giving away a thing on his face.

This man who was so devastatingly handsome in his formal robes, the robes of the man before whom people bowed, sprawled on a chair that was way too small for his towering frame, made her shiver with emotions she couldn't identify. He was the same and yet so incredibly different.

She thought of the easy familiarity they'd shared and in a heartbeat she realised how easy it would be for her to be completely over-awed by this new version of the guy she worked for. Seeing people bowing to her boss, it was hard for her not to slowly fall in line and put him on a pedestal where subservience became the norm.

It would be even easier for him to accept that, she was

sure. From everything she had seen, it was what he had grown up with—a life of unimaginable privilege where he was obeyed without fear of dissent. Had he ever had anything happen in his life to shatter that comfortable illusion?

The conversation moved back to Malik's father.

Lucy let her mind drift for a while as she nibbled some of the delicacies that had been brought in for them. They were delicious. She surfaced to a lull in the conversation and immediately filled it with sincere remarks about the nibbles.

'Thank you, Nadia, for inviting me here.' Lucy stood up, taking her cue from Malik. Nadia likewise stood up, as tall and slender as a willow, and Lucy impulsively hugged her.

'I really feel for you,' she confided, drawing back to look up at the older woman, who was smiling at her. 'Your son isn't great when it comes to talking about anything of a personal nature, but I just want to say how pleased I am that your husband is on the path to recovery. You know—and this is just my personal belief...'

She leaned forward, tilting up to look at her hostess and continued earnestly, 'You can sometimes get just scared stiff of small things after you've had a health scare. My aunt had a stroke a few years ago and it took her ages to get back to the things she'd grown fond of doing.'

'Lucy...' Malik tapped his watch. 'Time is moving along...'

'Hush, Malik, and let the child finish what she has begun to say.'

When Lucy looked at her boss, she was surprised at his dumbfounded expression and instantly rueful, feeling that she had maybe gone a step too far without realising it.

Was a hug a little too much? Because she had been excused from curtseying didn't mean that she was at liberty to drop all formalities. She blinked, suddenly skewered with doubt.

'I am afraid I do not quite understand you, my dear. Your aunt?'

Lucy mentally took a deep breath and carried on, because she was who she was, but she was inching ever so slightly back towards the door, conscious that Malik was ready to leave. 'Was very much into mountaineering.'

'Mountaineering?'

She stopped and thought of Aunt Maud, a proud spinster who was fond of preaching about the advantages of nature over men. Lucy had often thought cynically that she was preaching to the converted, after Colin and her broken heart. 'Loved it. She used to say that she was wed to nature because it would endure the test of time so much better than any marriage. She became quite hesitant about climbing after her health scare...'

'Lucy,' Malik said firmly, 'I'm really not convinced my mother is particularly interested in the ins and outs of mountaineering...'

Lucy reddened.

'But, Malik, I am keen to hear the rest of the story.' There was a distinct smile in Nadia's voice.

'But eventually,' Lucy concluded, looking over her shoulder to her brooding boss and saying sweetly to him in a rapid undertone, 'And I'm cutting this story as short as I can, Malik, believe me.

'Aunty Maud came to terms with the fact that life was there for living to the fullest and so she began taking small steps to overcome her fear. Of course, she never really could do the big mountains again, but she still enjoys exploring.'

'I understand what you are saying, Lucy, and of course we all hope that our beloved Ali returns to his duties as soon as possible.' Nadia smiled, a smile that softened the austere lines of her beautiful face. 'Although, as you wisely point out, some of his activities might have to be curtailed. He will tire. I hope, however, that his optimism remains tireless.'

'I would definitely discourage him from thinking about mountaineering.' Lucy grinned and, unexpectedly, Nadia laughed, a light, girlish laugh.

'I will certainly remember your aunt and her curtailed escapades, although Ali and mountains are not a natural mix.'

'Perhaps I can get to meet your husband some time,' Lucy said warmly.

'You certainly will, my child.'

Lucy was quite unaware of Malik's dark eyes resting coolly on her amid the polite farewells as they were ushered to the door. His mother fell back, allowing one of the staff to pull open the front door, and the still warm, humid night air wrapped around them. She'd been apprehensive about what to expect and had been pleasantly surprised, because the very limited picture Malik had painted had been of a couple who were so rigidly traditional that any stray word would have had her escorted to the nearest tower for instant beheading.

As soon as they were in the car, and still basking in the relief of not having made a fool of herself in front of his illustrious parent, Lucy spun to look at Malik with bright eyes.

'She's *nothing* like I thought she was going to be!' She

had tugged her hair over one shoulder and was playing with the ends of it.

'What do you mean?'

Malik was leaning back against the seat, legs splayed, his hands resting lightly on his thighs.

What had he expected of this brief social call? He didn't know. Perhaps a cool, polite visit, over before it had begun. As he had expected, tea had been exquisite. He had known that his father wouldn't be making an appearance and his mother, also as expected, had been her usual elegant, coldly beautiful self.

So far, so good.

He'd felt a little sorry for Lucy, landing in this place of well-bred civility, which he supposed would be a family dynamic which was the polar opposite of what she had grown up accustomed to.

He hadn't expected her to throw herself with gusto into their perfunctory visit. He couldn't remember the last time he'd seen his mother laugh and he hadn't seen her so relaxed since... Frankly, it escaped him. Had his father's illness softened her? Or had he just never looked deep enough to someone else behind the sophisticated, distant façade?

Along had come Lucy and drawn something out of his mother that he had never quite managed to get hold of and now Malik frowned, uncomfortable with that thought.

'You told me that your parents were extremely reserved.'

'They are.'

'I suppose when you said *traditional* that I was expecting something else.'

'Where is this conversation going, Lucy?'

'Does it have to go anywhere? I'm just saying how lovely I thought your mother was and not at all as I thought she was going to be. First off, she's really beautiful. I mean *really* beautiful. What does your father look like?'

'My father looks like a man recuperating after major heart surgery.'

'I can tell that your mother's worried sick about him and misses him—something in her eyes whenever she talks about him. But I have to admire her restraint, her poise. I suppose,' she said pensively, staring at Malik but not really seeing him, and definitely missing his frowning disapproval of the conversation, 'That's the sort of thing you would be looking for in this woman you'll be interviewing for the role of wife. I'd really love to meet your dad some time—'

'Enough, Lucy!'

Lucy blinked, focused and then frowned.

'Sorry?'

'I introduced you to my mother as an act of courtesy. You're staying with me at the palace, and of course there would come a time when it would be appropriate for you to meet her. That's now been done and dusted.'

'Done and dusted?'

Malik looked at her in brooding silence, lips thinned, wondering how to steer this conversation away from choppy waters. At any rate, choppy waters for *him*, because he was unsettled by what was beginning to feel like an invasion of his privacy.

This didn't happen. No woman had ever been introduced to any family member before and he had never been tempted to go there. Family introductions fell into the category of the sort of cosy arrangements that led to unrealistic expectations of the kind he didn't want. Whatever ground rules he'd laid down with the women he'd dated in the past, there had always been some who'd wanted more than he was ever prepared to give.

Of course, Lucy was in a different category, and meeting his mother had been a matter of courtesy more than anything else, but even so...

His reaction was an automatic, ingrained response to anyone trying to trespass into his private terrain, which was what this felt like. He reminded himself that Lucy was Lucy, that her interest was to be expected and that he had never tried to dampen down her natural exuberance or her intellectual curiosity, so why would he start now?

She would be confused. He'd introduced her to his mother, so why would he suddenly be tense at her responding to the visit with her usual outspoken candour?

'Of course, you may meet my father in due course.' He reined in his natural instinct to shut her down and protect a slice of private life that, he decided, honestly didn't need protecting from a woman who wasn't after anything. 'But, like I said, he's still very frail after his operation. He tires easily and spends much of the day resting. I hear from him in sound bites because it's vital I find out certain things on the business front.'

Sudden silence gathered between them and Malik shifted, annoyed with himself for being short with her, making a mountain out of a molehill.

She wasn't looking at him. She was staring straight ahead, and the angle of her head was proudly defiant, her expression tight-lipped. Something placatory seemed required. That said, it was important that he conveyed the important message that she shouldn't overstep his boundary lines, even inadvertently. That message was more important to him than smoothing ruffled feathers. Ruffled feathers would smooth over perfectly fine in due course.

'Lucy,' he said gently, 'As with my "interviewing a wife", as you insist on calling it, my family life is not a place you will be frequenting. Maybe, in passing, you might meet my father before you go but—'

'I get it.'

She swung round so that she was staring at him. Their eyes tangled and neither looked away.

She *did* get it, and she wanted to shout at him exactly what it was she *got*. She'd been so pleased when they'd left his mother's palace because all her apprehensions about meeting his mother had proved unfounded. It had been a fantastic visit and it had left her wanting more. She'd been greedy to see more of the life that had shaped her charismatic boss and that was a mistake. He'd obviously sensed something behind her effervescent responses and he'd backed off at speed.

Duty visit to meet the mother? Tick.

Any kind of encore? Not on the cards.

He was reminding her of her place in his life: an employee who was paid for doing a job and not someone who should get it into her head that she might be anything more just because she'd met his mother.

The Bentley slowed to circle the enormous courtyard, stopping in front of the magnificent palace.

'Tell me what you get,' Malik murmured. He circled his hand around her arm to stop her leaping out of the car as soon as it stopped and it was as hot as a branding iron. Lucy's thoughts scattered and she breathed in deeply, finding the will power from somewhere to manage a reply.

His touch…scorching her skin and shooting her body down pathways that were confusing and electric.

'I get it that you introduced me to your mother because you felt you had no choice, not really, but that's as far as it goes.' She was breathing heavily, and he hadn't moved his hand, which was making thinking difficult.

Ahead of them, the brightly illuminated palace shone, nestled amid its opulent greenery, the ocean of sand just dark shadows all around.

Malik stared. He could actually hear his own breathing but then fancied that he was imagining it.

Yet he was gripped by something that made the words still in his throat. He was driven to look at her breasts, heaving as she breathed fast, and had to grit his teeth to resist the urge. Her skin under his fingers was soft and smooth. Her tumbling vanilla-blonde hair tempted his fingers to explore. He released her abruptly and sat back but he knew that he was shaking.

'Spot on,' he said coldly. He raked his fingers through his hair, barely aware of his driver patiently waiting until the order was given for him to open the passenger doors. Malik duly rapped on the privacy glass separating them, and at once the driver leapt out to open Lucy's door.

'Back to the routine tomorrow, Lucy, but I'm glad we understand one another.'

He broke eye contact and pushed open his door to vault outside into the humid air, only taking a couple of seconds to breathe in deep and stamp down the unexpected surge in his libido that had taken a sudden battering ram to his self-control.

CHAPTER FIVE

HE WAS GLAD they understood one another?

Malik Al-Rashid might be a prince, but Lucy truly hoped that he wouldn't think what he had said would be conveniently forgotten. How was it a crime to have shown some interest in his parents? How had that been crossing his precious boundaries?

He'd politely introduced her to his mother and she'd politely given him some feedback. It was the first time she could recall him ever really knocking her back and it hurt. She resolved not to say anything more about it because, on reflection, it wouldn't get anyone anywhere, which didn't mean that she didn't spend the following day simmering.

Several times as she looked at him, reclining in the black leather swivel chair in the huge wing of the palace which had been adapted for use as offices, she had to bite down the temptation to have it out with him.

He was as cool as a cucumber. He'd said his piece and put it behind him, but he'd never reminded her of her status before, and she'd been an idiot to think that, because he never had, then it followed that he never would. It had been enough that she'd known which lines couldn't be crossed at home but, over here, the lines were blurred, she'd crossed them and his harsh reminder had been a slap in the face. Yes, of course he was her boss, and well within his rights to reprimand her for going beyond the brief, but surely they were more than boss and secretary, with all the formality that that implied?

Were they perhaps friends? Or had she got that completely wrong?

Shorn of her customary self-confidence around him, she worked more or less in silence for the duration of the day. She noticed that he didn't say a word about that, didn't once crack any jokes about her being practically mute. He would have done that in London. He would have teased her, coaxed her into telling him what was wrong. He might not have seen that as the strands of a friendship between them, but *she* had, and as the day drew to a close she wondered whether she'd spent years being a fool.

Had that easy familiarity between them just been a manifestation of him humouring her? Had he put up with her idiosyncrasies because she was a talented worker, and putting up with idiosyncrasies had just been him taking the path of least resistance?

Lucy was mortified to think that she'd somehow drifted into the trap of thinking that she occupied a special place in his life. He had his glamorous, clever women, but she had the guy who laughed at stuff she said, who stopped being the forbidding leader of the pack who was so good at intimidating the opposition.

She'd fancied that she'd somehow accessed the man not many people saw. Had that illusion fed the low-level attraction she felt towards him? Because there was no denying that she was attracted to him.

Well, *that* thought didn't exactly fill her with joy and rapture. Yet being near him was like being close to the creamiest chocolate: drool-worthy, but of course off-limits because it was bad for you.

He tempted her, an innocent temptation, and she could acknowledge that she enjoyed that temptation. It made the time she spent at work exciting and she liked that. In a way, she'd become almost addicted to it. Of course, she had lots of friends, and of course she'd dated guys on and off over the years, enjoying their company, but never enough for any of those relationships to develop into anything of significance. She was appalled to think that throughout all those pleasant enough but short-term relationships there had hovered a comparison between those men and her boss.

Ages ago, she had teased her best friend, Helen, that she had a crush on her boss. She knew now that she was guilty of the same weakness, although in Helen's case that crush had turned to love and had ended in a very happy place.

Her crush, if it could even be called that—and the jury was out on that one—was now revealed as a silly bit of nonsense and the guy in question actually thought a lot less of her than she'd imagined.

'You're quiet,' Malik said flatly, just as she'd slammed shut the lid of her laptop and was preparing to return to her quarters.

'Am I?' She tugged her hair over her shoulder and met his questioning dark eyes with a blank expression, and then forced herself to crack a polite smile. The offices where they worked were cold. Very efficient air-conditioning meant that it was vital that she wear a cardigan, and she now shrugged on the patchwork one she had thankfully brought with her.

'Going to tell me, or are we going to have a round-the-houses guessing game?'

'I have a headache,' Lucy told him, reaching down for her laptop and shoving it into the bright-orange vinyl case she'd bought for it.

'Why do you have a headache?'

'I really don't know, Malik. Once I complete my medical degree, maybe I'll work that one out.'

Malik tilted his head to one side and looked at her without saying anything. He'd been sitting behind his desk and now he vaulted upright to perch on the edge of it, where he continued his silent appraisal until she began to feel hot under the collar.

'What?' she eventually muttered under her breath as her heart began to do an annoying drum beat inside her.

She was in a riot of colours—loose yellow trousers and a black-and-white striped tee-shirt, which couldn't help but clash horribly with the patchwork cardigan she had made for herself during a short-lived knitting phase.

He, on the other hand, looked cool, elegant and irritatingly sexy in pale chinos and a white linen shirt which was cuffed to the elbows and hung loosely over the waistband of his trousers.

Why couldn't she stop being *aware* of him? she wondered helplessly? She was fuming at him for his ill-conceived remark the evening before, and yet her disobedient eyes were still drawn to him, as though the pull of his beauty was too compelling.

She was restlessly aware of a powerful urge to paper over her hurt feelings so that things could return to normal between them. It wasn't his fault that she'd seen what they had through different eyes. She'd had her horrendous experience, had had her heart broken and nursed her hurt in silence, but even after that her optimism about people, and love and life in general, had never dimmed.

She'd floated along imagining that, within the parameters of their working relationship, she and Malik had something just a little bit special and she felt that she'd been cruelly disabused of that illusion.

'I'll be heading over to see my father later,' he eventually said. 'I've repeatedly told him that he needs to be on bed rest, and definitely no stress whatsoever, but every day he gets a little stronger and a little more anxious about what's happening with the businesses. I've consulted his specialist who said that, as long as I keep it light and brief, it might be better than to force him into fretful silence. And, like I've said, I need to talk work with him anyway.'

He paused. 'My mother suggested that you come along but I told her that you had other plans. I got the impression that she took to you.'

'Thank her for the invitation,' Lucy said coolly. 'And please make my excuses.'

Of course he wouldn't want her getting too used to the notion that she might be part of his family. She was his secretary. She was the paid help.

'Is that all?' she asked politely and jumped when he slammed his fist on the desk and looked at her with simmering frustration.

'What the hell is going on with you?' he roared, leaping from where he'd been sitting to stride restlessly around the room, hand jerkily raking through his hair. He approached her in ever-diminishing circles until he was towering over her, scowling and as lacking in his usual rigid self-control as she had ever seen him.

'Headache.'

'Yes, and as soon as you get your medical degree you'll diagnose what's causing it and get back to me. Spit it out. You've been in a mood all day and it's really getting on my nerves. You're not a moody person so just tell me what's going on.'

Lucy breathed in deeply. Their eyes tangled and for a second she felt as if she was drowning in the depths of his fathomless dark gaze. She knew that she had to get past this. She couldn't be in a mood with him for the rest of their working lives. She would just have to swallow back any misplaced hurt and pick up where they had left off, but in her heart she knew that she would have to toughen up. She couldn't get hurt every time Malik said something unconsciously thoughtless.

It was disconcerting seeing him in a different light but reacting to it? Allowing him really to get under her skin? That wasn't going to do.

'Honestly, Malik, I really do have a headache.' Frankly, she was on the brink of getting one after this stressful conversation, so no lie there. 'It must be the heat.'

'What heat? This place is as cold as Siberia. We wouldn't be able to work otherwise. So you can ditch the *overheating* excuse. Talk to me, Lucy. It's not like you to bottle things up.'

'Meaning?'

'Meaning that it's not like you to bottle things up.'

'I'll be fine after I've had a shower and relaxed.'

'Is it the work?'

'What do you mean?'

'Am I working you too hard? It's pretty intense at the moment and especially when we're working here—there isn't the distraction of strolling out to see some shops and get away for an hour. It's something that's crossed my mind more than once, even though I made sure to point out the differences you would find living and working over here. So is it that? Are you beginning to feel constrained?'

'No. I'm not. I knew what I was letting myself in for when I came here. I'm fine catching up on emails and phone calls to my family when I take a lunch break. I don't need round-the-clock entertainment to survive.' She smiled stiffly. 'Maybe I wouldn't be able to do that for ever but, just while we're here, it's not a problem.'

'Come.'

He shifted his gaze and glanced across to the huge windows that overlooked the incongruously pristine green lawns, an oasis of emerald amid the tan of the sand dunes. There was a dark flush on his face when he returned his glance to her startled face.

'I beg your pardon?'

'I said what I had to say yesterday…made things clear between us…' He flushed darkly. 'But my mother specifically asked for you to come. So, come.'

'It's fine.'

'It's clearly not. I don't believe a word about a fictitious headache and, if it's not the workload and it's not boredom, then it's what I said to you last night.'

'I don't want to talk about that. There's no point. Of course we understand one another. Believe it or not, a little curiosity doesn't add up to me trying to worm myself into your family unit.'

'Why do you have to be so over-imaginative, Lucy? Did I mention anything about you trying to worm your way into my family?'

'I don't need reminding that I work for you. I know I work for you. I know you're my boss and I'm just your secretary.'

'So I'm guessing you were sulking about what I said.'

'You *hurt* me, Malik!'

The silence stretched between them. She was bright red and already regretting the outburst. Chatting about diet fads, her family and her preoccupation with house renovation shows on the telly was quite different from... *this*. Feelings wasn't a topic that had ever arisen between them. The conversation felt raw and dangerous, and her colour heightened.

'I apologise.'

'Do you? Are you really sorry that I was hurt by what you said? You don't want me to meet your father because...because what? Because I might get it into my head that...?'

A quagmire of things that shouldn't be said opened up at her feet and she gulped.

'That what, Lucy?'

'It doesn't matter. I just... I was hurt because you... I suppose you put me in my place and...' Her voice faltered.

'I'll finish what you started saying, shall I?' Malik prompted quietly and Lucy stared at him, licked her lips, and tried and failed to find something to say in response.

'I wouldn't want you to get it into your head that, because you've met my family...'

'I won't.'

'Sure about that?'

'One hundred percent.'

Malik smiled. 'Okay. Good. We'll let that go. Actually, there's another reason why it might not be such a good idea to tag along, at any rate not on a regular basis.'

'Why is that?'

Danger averted.

What if he had come right out and warned her not

to fall for him? Not to think that what they had was more than just a great working relationship? Her blood ran cold at the thought of him guessing just how attractive she found him. It ran even colder at the thought of him patiently telling her that meeting his parents wasn't 'meeting the parents', with all the connotations the latter implied.

She would brush past this and find her sunny side if it killed her. She raised her eyebrows and then resumed getting ready to leave, pointlessly straightening one or two things on her desk whilst inching away from him.

'My mother is in the process of arranging my suitable bride. Would you really be interested in joining in that particular conversation?'

'Is she?' Lucy momentarily parked her anger and her hurt, vaguely knowing that she would return to both in due course.

'It's an exciting time for her.'

'Are you being sarcastic?'

'There's some sarcasm there.'

'Is it an exciting time for you as well?'

'It's life. The inevitable arrived a little sooner than expected, but I can handle it.' Malik grinned, eased himself away, stretched and then turned to look at her, hands stuffed in his trouser pockets. 'As for *exciting*... Maybe not quite the adjective I would use on this occasion.'

'I just don't get it,' Lucy confessed, anger and hurt very firmly shoved aside now. 'Okay, maybe I *do* get the whole duty thing—*sort of*. Now that I've met your mother, I can see that life here for you is…a little different than it would be for a normal guy.'

'That's a lot of generalisations you're throwing around. What's abnormal about me?'

* * *

But Malik expelled a sigh of contented relief because this was more like it. This was more like the woman he knew—asking questions no one would dare ask and barging past barriers as though they didn't exist. He hated the thought of hurting her, even though he knew that it had been a conversation that had had to be had. Yet those bruised cornflower-blue eyes had cut him to the quick.

Something was going on between them. It was a feeling that came to him as fleeting as quicksilver, leaving before it could take hold. Was that indistinct feeling the *something* that had driven him to be blatant in warning her against getting too wrapped up in a family dynamic that wasn't her concern? Had he been reminding himself of something as much as he had been reminding *her?* At any rate, he was perfectly happy to let things get back to where they belonged now.

He strolled to one of the comfortable leather chairs, part of one of the informal sitting areas in the space. He pushed it back and stretched out his legs to the side, relaxing into the buttery leather, loosely linking his fingers on his stomach and looking at her with brooding interest.

Yes, *much* more like it.

'Where to begin? Seriously, Malik, how can you be so casual about marriage?'

'Because I'm not a romantic person who's on the hunt for fireworks. My approach to life is on a more practical level. Truth is, a woman who understands what comes with being my wife and what doesn't is what I need and what I always expected.'

'Well, you're right. I wouldn't want to get involved in any conversations with your mother or your parents about stuff like that. None of my business and, in fairness, I'm not sure they would welcome my input. Although, maybe knowing that I'm your very efficient secretary, they might ask me to sift through some CVs…weed out the ones I don't find suitable…'

'And who would those poor unfortunates be?'

'That's very egotistic. Some might say that the ones I sifted out would be the lucky escapees.'

'Let's ditch this conversation. It's all academic, at any rate. Tell me how you're going to spend your evening. I know you say that you're perfectly happy with arrangements here, but you could be here for another month, and I'm more than happy to put you in touch with some expat organisations. Might make a change from the four walls of this place.'

'Considerably more than four walls, Malik, and, like I've said, I'm enjoying the novelty of not doing anything at the moment. Life's usually so hectic. It's peaceful just catching up on reading and binge-watching series on my computer.'

Lucy realised that she didn't want him feeling sorry for her. She didn't want him thinking that he had to warn her over getting any ideas about her role in his life, and she didn't want him trying to sort out stuff for her here while he busied himself finding a wife.

What on earth was wrong with her? Why was she suddenly so sensitive around him? What was it she wanted from him that she hadn't before? She been bright and sparky as she'd teased him about his arranged marriage but underneath she'd been edgy.

The question lingered in her head, wispy, intangible and unsettling.

'I honestly don't need you to start feeling sorry for me,

Malik.' She laughed off the shortness of her remark but there was a breathlessness there that threatened to reveal that all was not as well as the picture she was desperate to paint.

The dark eyes resting on her were making her all hot and bothered and she wanted to fan herself again. Instead, she began backing towards the door.

She didn't want to find herself floundering in another inexplicable mood, taking things he said to heart because she'd lost her ability to brush them aside with her usual good humour.

'Have a nice evening!' she chirruped, backing away and then, before he could say anything else, she fled.

Having opened the door to the business of a wife, Malik knew that he was on a path that would quickly gather momentum. Lucy had asked him whether he was excited—it was a good question. He'd been honest with her and, as he'd stared into her puzzled, curious blue eyes, it had fleetingly crossed his mind—*what had he done? Was this really where he wanted to go with his life?*

It had been a fleeting thought, almost instantly overruled by the common-sense approach he had adopted over the years. An in-depth conversation had yet to be had but both parents had been relieved that he had initiated the process without having to be pointed in the direction.

'We are both, your mother and I, relieved that you have come to this decision, Malik.' His father had greeted the news some days previously. 'I could die, and an heir is needed to ensure continuity. Too much will rest on your shoulders and, should something happen to you, a lot will be lost. A grandson would hold everything in trust should you no longer be around.'

'Or granddaughter,' Malik had interjected, which had been met with a dubious nod—but a nod was a nod.

Now, here at the table with both his parents, he settled in for the detailed conversation he knew was necessary, even though part of his mind was preoccupied with Lucy and with her moodiness that had made him feel so restless and ill at ease.

An exquisite meal had been served and then cleared. Coffee was up. Both parents allowed a brief silence, and Malik smiled to himself, because he knew that they were preparing what they intended to say.

'I am sorry your lovely secretary could not make it, Malik. Ali…your father…would have enjoyed meeting her.'

Since he hadn't expected this, his eyebrows shot up. He thought of her hurt and killed the sudden appearance of a guilty conscience. He didn't want to talk about Lucy. He didn't want to think of those big, wounded blue eyes.

'Another time,' he said smoothly. 'But, now that we have covered various family issues within the company, shall we discuss what I know must be on both your minds—my impending nuptials?'

'We have some ideas.'

This was more like it. An arranged marriage was simply a business deal and he was excellent when it came to discussing business deals.

'No formal matchmaking,' his mother said, leaning to pour them all some more coffee from the ornate gold-and-sapphire china pot. His father met his eyes and for a second Malik was startled by a flash of amused camaraderie which was compounded when his mother smiled at him.

'You are not of our generation, Malik, so we decided

that bringing in a formal matchmaker would not be appropriate.'

'I didn't think they existed.'

'You do not live here.' His father actually stifled a grin. 'Some of the ladies would find it quite tricky to find a suitable partner without input from Mrs Bilal. Nadia, would you agree? Not every eligible young woman is a beauty queen.'

Malik burst out laughing as his mother lowered her lashes and tried not to laugh as well.

'Some names...'

'I'll leave it to you,' Malik said.

'But Malik, you cannot simply settle for who we find for you.'

'I trust you.'

'You will not be disappointed. A social gathering... something as befits your station...and, of course, should you not approve of any of the women, then we will not urge you to make a choice.'

Malik's mind was drifting. He would leave it to his mother because she would do a good job. His future was being discussed but it felt unreal, far more unreal than the trajectory of his thoughts, which kept returning to Lucy. But that was to be expected. Marriage to a woman whose face he couldn't conjure *was* going to feel like an out of body experience compared to the reality of the woman sharing his palace, with her outspoken opinions, sharp brain and, now, her somersaulting emotions.

So, a wife to be was a dimly shaped thought easily deferred for the moment. He knew the social pool from which she would be chosen. He didn't know quite what sort of social gathering his mother had in mind, but it would be what it would be.

He returned to a darkened palace a little after eleven. Under normal circumstances, he might have been tempted to work, catch up on what was happening with his own personal business interests scattered across various countries, but his mind refused to settle sufficiently for him to concentrate.

Lying in the silence of his magnificent bedroom, it dawned on him that niggling at the back of his mind was his secretary.

He thought about Lucy and he thought about his parents, and that brief glimpse of two people relaxed with one another, and more *human* than he'd ever noticed previously.

Had Lucy brought out something in his mother, some lightness that hadn't been visible before? Or was Lucy's presence here, in his country, making him see his parents through different eyes?

He would eventually have killed wayward thoughts by flipping open his computer and forcing himself to concentrate but he didn't have to do that. As distractions went, all wayward thoughts were dispelled the second the alarm signal flashed silently on his mobile.

Malik stilled.

He knew exactly where the intruder was. He had the option of immediately contacting the security team at the palace, who would respond within seconds, but he preferred the other option of confronting whoever had had the temerity to break in.

He slid quietly out of the bed, slung on a pair of drawstring joggers and stealthily made his way downstairs, bare-backed and bare-footed.

It was warm outside. Even in her loose tee-shirt and the cotton shorts she wore to bed, Lucy was still warm.

But it was beautiful. The sky was a black shroud covering everything, pierced with stars that shimmered like tiny jewels. No light pollution out here, and no noise pollution either. London could learn a lesson or two on that front, she thought.

Sitting on one of the rattan chairs, which she rarely used during the day because of the blistering heat, it was impossible not to think of paradise. The dunes were just about visible in the distance.

She hadn't been able to sleep because her mind had been too busy dwelling on how annoyed she still was with Malik, and how hurt she'd been when he'd warned her off getting too cosy with his family. As if she had some kind of hidden agenda! She might have earlier parked those emotions but, once the lights were off, they returned with renewed force.

She'd tiptoed her way through the palace a little after one in morning. It was a massive, bewildering place but she had managed to carve out a few familiar routes for herself. The one she took led down to the kitchens, where she fetched herself some water before heading outside so that she could sit back and let her thoughts wander until they'd covered all the ground they could possibly cover.

The sound behind her was so imperceptible that she was unaware of anyone behind her until she *felt* a presence. Heart beating madly, Lucy simultaneously spun round and shot out of the chair.

'Malik!'

They stared at one another while the silence gathered around them, dense and heavy.

Malik was lost for words.

He stared at her. He couldn't *stop* staring. Her hair was

all over the place, a riotous fall of caramel and blonde curls that pelted over her shoulders and down to her waist.

Even in the darkness, he could make out the quiver of her body, which only drew his attention to the swell of her lush breasts against the tee-shirt and the smooth length of shapely legs on show. His libido kicked into gear with painful force. He knew that, if he made the mistake of glancing down at himself, he would see the bulge of his erection distorting the light jersey of his joggers.

'What the hell are you doing out here?' His voice was uneven, sharp, a deflection from what was tearing through his body.

'I didn't realise I had to ask permission to come outside for ten minutes!'

'Got any idea of the time?'

'No! But I can check my phone and tell you!'

'Lucy...it's after one in the morning.'

'I couldn't sleep, Malik—and don't even try to tell me that it's dangerous for me to be out here. I haven't suddenly decided to go walking at midnight in a park in London.'

They stepped towards one another at the same time.

'How did you even know that I was out here?'

'Intruder alarm on my phone.' His erection was so painful he wanted to push it down or else do something else with it. His nostrils flared and he felt heat flare through his roused body. 'I'm alerted if anyone tries to break in...or, in your case, leave. I...' He shook his head, raked his fingers through his hair and shuffled. 'If a door or window is tampered with...opened... Hence I came down to find out what was going on.'

'Dressed like that?' Lucy wished she hadn't mentioned his state of undress because now she was riveted at the sight of his body, the hardness of his chest and the ripple of sinew and muscle in his arms. Her mouth went dry as she stared at the way the light joggers dipped low on his lean hips down to…down to…

Her heart stopped beating and her thoughts dissolved into frantic meltdown.

Was she mistaken? Surely Malik wasn't…*turned on*?

An electric charge roared through her and her body reacted with speed, her breasts swelling and liquid pooling hotly between her legs.

Her eyes flew back to his face but her voice was croaky when she said, 'Well, I'm safe and sound.'

'Why couldn't you sleep?'

'You know why.' She forced herself back in control, told herself that her eyes had been deceiving her. Obviously.

Breathe deep, count to ten and everything will be just fine.

'What I said earlier about… Jesus, tell me that's not still preying on your mind, Lucy.'

'I can't help it, Malik. It was so hurtful. How could you lecture me about not engaging with your family? About making sure I don't go getting any wrong ideas just because you've had no choice but to introduce me to them…her…your mum…? At least it wasn't a double whammy, with me meeting your dad as well and really upsetting the privacy apple cart!'

Lucy felt tears sting the back of her eyes. She wished she hadn't leapt out of the chair because now her legs felt like jelly. She'd said too much, put too much emotion on display. There was a difference between being talkative, challenging and good-natured with Malik and laying into him for something that wasn't his fault just because he'd upset her. But, with her thoughts all over the place, there was no room in her head for common sense.

'I apologised, didn't I? I'm sorry if I offended you.'

'You should know me better. You should *know* that I'm not the sort of person who would read anything… You should *know*…should just *know*…' She turned away but the tears were stinging the back of her eyes.

'You're right,' Malik muttered gruffly. 'I should. Lucy, it was just an instinctive reaction.'

'What's that supposed to mean?'

'I…it's just the way I am. With women…' He shook his head and raked his fingers through his hair, uncomfortable, edgy, yet urgent in his need to wipe her hurt away. 'I'm always upfront with them…and yet many times they read meaning behind something when there's none. It can lead to complications and I've never courted a complicated life.'

'That's different,' Lucy muttered. 'Those women— I'm not them.'

'Yes, it is different, and I'm sorry. I… I've missed you,' he said in a roughened undertone. 'Missed your laughter and your chat.' He moved towards her and brushed the tear from the corner of her eye with his thumb, then he left his hand there, cupping the side of her face.

Her skin was soft and smooth, and her rounded face was exquisitely feminine.

He traced her parted mouth with his finger and her eyes widened. Malik could feel the excited thrum of her body as she stepped towards him and, when he lowered his head to cover her mouth with his, she melted into the kiss, hands curving to the back of his head, tiptoeing to reach up to him.

Her breasts pushed against him and he stifled a groan of pure pleasure. He wanted this so badly, it was a physical ache. He'd never thought that desire could be so painful. He yearned to cup her sexy derriere in his hands; yearned to push beneath the baggy tee-shirt to feel the weight of her braless breasts; longed to strip her naked and take her right here where they stood.

He stepped back, but shakily. He stared down at her, breathing unevenly.

'Lucy...'

She'd leapt back and was now staring back at him in utter horror.

'No!'

'This is my fault.' He took the blame without reservation.

Lucy was in his country and it was up to him to protect her, not give in to some crazy urge to seduce her, even though he felt she had been more than up for the seduction. Looking at her, he could detect the flush of unrequited desire, desire that had temporarily got the better of them both.

'It won't happen again. You're here, in a different country, and probably feeling a little vulnerable...'

In receipt of that lifebelt, Lucy's mouth tightened and she folded her arms.

'Don't be ridiculous,' she refuted angrily. 'Don't you dare think that I'm such a silly, impressionable woman that a little bit of hot weather and a change of scenery is going to somehow make me forget how to behave!' She bristled. 'I *wanted* you to kiss me and I enjoyed kissing you back. It was a mistake, *yes,* but the mistake lies with *both of us.*'

Malik nodded. He should have been surprised but he

wasn't because this was Lucy, defiantly proud and honest to a fault.

They understood one another. A mistake had been made and recognised for what it was—a mistake never to be repeated.

He was here to sort out his family affairs and to find himself a suitable bride. Still, he hesitated.

'So, no more mention of this…?'

Lucy nodded and looked away. Her whole body was still on fire.

'Consider it forgotten.'

CHAPTER SIX

'SO, MALIK, EVERYTHING is in progress for you to meet some of the young ladies your father and I feel might be suitable choices for you.'

Having agreed to his arranged marriage, now that things were proceeding on that front, Malik couldn't help but think that for someone to have compiled a list of possible women for him to meet in this day and age felt a little weird.

Yet, why should it? No reason; relationships that were fuelled by emotion ran far more of a risk of failure, when he thought about it. He'd had his brush with the emotional stuff and had reverted to what he knew, which was the partnership his parents had, one that had been arranged and had stayed the course.

His family was all very traditional. Marriages had been arranged for the majority of them to the best of his knowledge. He could have gone for the love option. His parents wouldn't have objected. Only *he* knew the reason why he was content to let his head take the lead. And, if it pleased his parents in the process, then that was a bonus, even if it wouldn't have been his primary objective.

'Anyone on the list I might know?'

It was a little past four. Something had changed in the

family dynamic and, despite the formality of the conversation, he was more relaxed with both his parents than he could remember being in a long time. Tea had been brought, mint tea served in ornate jade and golden glasses, and he was balancing the glass on his thigh.

'Some, of course. A few attended the same school as you, although they would not have been in the same year. I have also spoken to a few of my own connections with some of our neighbours across the waters and your father and I have discussed possibilities.'

'Possibilities…hmm. Tell me, how was it for you?' He looked at them both. It was an impulsive, random question that suddenly felt important and his father was the first to smile.

'I saw her…' he shot Nadia a sideways look and made a *so-so* gesture with his hand '…and I thought, well, she will do.'

His mother laughed.

'Your father has a very poor memory,' she murmured, catching his gaze. 'I was the one who decided that I might just as well accept what was on offer, even though I knew I might have to get him ship-shape and house-trained.'

'So…what…? The arranged marriage was…?' Malik was almost shocked.

'It has worked well. That is what I will say.'

Malik fell silent. His remote parents, who had no highs or lows—or so he'd thought.

Was the road he had embarked upon the right one? He wasn't marrying in haste, but would he repent at leisure?

In the face of sudden doubts, Malik held steady. If he had underestimated the relationship between his parents, then that was his fault. The fact remained that their successful relationship was based on pragmatism, two young people sharing the same goals because they shared the same background. No room for error. It was what he wanted...wasn't it?

'So...what's the procedure for meeting these suitable women?'

He wondered what Lucy was up to. They had agreed their 'pretend we never touched' deal three days ago. Since then, Malik had discovered that some deals were tougher to stick to than others. He'd done deals that had made him a personal fortune but this deal, with no money involved, was crazily difficult to stick to.

She was fine, same as usual, nothing to see there. He'd kept looking. She'd smiled and chatted as she always had. He'd had to fight not to scowl at her continuing good humour. It hadn't really occurred to him previously, but it hit him now that Lucy would doubtless have to precede him back to London, were he to remain in Sarastan to discuss potential nuptials.

'I am arranging a ball. Nothing over the top, but a nice venue for you to circulate and meet whoever you wish to meet without the pressure of anything small and formally arranged. How does that sound to you, Malik?'

'It sounds...fine.'

'Naturally, Lucy, your secretary, would be invited. Perhaps she might wish to help with the arrangements, if that is what she is skilled at doing? We are more than open to suggestions.'

'Lucy?' Malik burst out laughing. 'No. I can't see that. She's more than a secretary, as it happens. She has a brilliant brain, and in fact takes on a lot of complex work more suited to some of my own hedge-fund analysts.

She...' He paused, realising that he was going off-piste with his description. He thought of that kiss, and the feel of her lush body pressed against his, and flushed. 'No, I don't see her wanting any input.'

'As soon as arrangements have been made, I will let you know the date, but certainly it will be within the next three weeks at most. And, son...?'

'Yes?' He looked at his strikingly handsome parents, his mother elegant and exquisitely dressed, his father gaunt from his health scare but still a commanding presence. He didn't see the coldness of an arranged marriage. He saw the warmth of two people who cared deeply for one another. How had he missed so much of that?

'Should you wish a different road for yourself...'

'A different road?' His expression cleared and he looked at them thoughtfully. 'No,' he said quietly. 'This is the right road for me. It worked for you both. It will likewise work for me.'

'We are all different, Malik,' his mother said. 'Your experiences have shaped you differently.'

He thought of the other road he had almost taken years ago and then the image of his secretary flashed into his head, confusing him. Emotional, big-hearted, exuberant Lucy... If on one side of the scales there was a suitable wife, then Lucy surely weighed on the opposite side of the scales?

All that emotion... The love and respect he had overlooked in his parents was evidence enough that head would always win over everything else. It would always be the trump card in the deck.

'This is what I want and what's needed,' he told them gently. 'And a ball sounds like an excellent idea. Just let me know that date.'

* * *

Lucy was eating in the kitchen when she distantly heard the slam of the front door, a heavy, muffled thud that barely travelled through the vast distance of the palace. She immediately tensed. As far as she'd understood, Malik had gone to his parents and then would be heading out to the city to have dinner with some of his business associates.

The horde of invisible staff had gone for the day and she'd looked forward to having the place to herself, cooking her own food in the kitchen, rather than having exquisite stuff prepared for her, and eating in front of her laptop so that she could catch up on the drama series she was currently binge-watching.

So, when she heard the slam of the front door, she could only hope that Malik would scamper up to his quarters rather than detour via the kitchen.

The kitchen might be the size of a football field but it would still be impossible to miss her at the ten-seater kitchen table, in front of a bowl of pasta with a glass of wine next to her, kitted out in old tracksuit bottoms and a voluminous tee-shirt with a logo of her favourite Disney movie on the front.

Fork hovering mid-air, she watched with a sinking heart as the kitchen door was pushed open and there he was, in all his sinful glory. He was wearing a pair of beige trousers, a black tee-shirt and loafers that would have cost the earth. He hadn't shaved and there was the darkening of stubble on his chin.

She'd spent the past three days with a smile pinned to her face, making very sure that her eyes didn't do anything reckless and disobedient—such as linger on him.

They'd kissed and her world had been turned on its axis but she knew that it was vital that she repositioned her skewered world back where it belonged, on the right trajectory, and carried on as normal.

Nothing had been harder.

'You're here.'

He was mildly surprised as he strolled into the kitchen, headed for the fridge to grab a beer, opened it and then sauntered towards her to inspect what she was eating, before settling in one of the chairs facing her.

'So are you,' Lucy was quick to respond. 'I thought you were going into the city after your parents'. How is your father doing?'

She self-consciously ate the pasta that had been on the way to her mouth before he'd interrupted her, and felt the flick of some wayward spaghetti and tomato sauce on her chin. She delicately wiped it off and proceeded to look at him with something close to accusation.

'My father is doing fine and, yes, that was the plan,' Malik agreed, drinking straight from the bottle and looking at her at the same time.

He'd breathed a sigh of relief the minute he'd returned from seeing his parents. With decisive plans underway for a marriage he had previously put off thinking about until necessity had brought it to his front door, Malik had suddenly felt hemmed in and constrained. That glimpse of his parents, the depth of their affection, had also thrown him.

A ball… Women he knew, and many he did not, would be at a glittering and impressive event and he would be able to converse with them, perhaps have his curiosity piqued by some of them...or else he would merely attend and assess the suitability of who was there.

He was going to be Prince Charming but without Cinderella, the glass slipper and the midnight cut-off. Something like that would certainly reduce the time spent looking. From a distant memory involving one of his cousins, he could remember an amusing but long-winded situation that had involved a matchmaker and a series of dates which had taken for ever, although in fairness had concluded in a positive result.

One fancy ball, a few dates and his fate would be sealed. The minute he had walked into the kitchen and seen Lucy at the kitchen table, he'd felt more settled. Looking at her was like looking at normality and he couldn't help but enjoy the view.

She was in a weird outfit. The tee-shirt looked as though it belonged to a kid—maybe it was of sentimental value—and the jogging bottoms were faded. But nothing could diminish the startling prettiness of her heart-shaped face and enormous cornflower-blue eyes, not even the fact that she was completely bare of make-up and there was a trace of tomato sauce on her chin.

Memory of that kiss shared surged through him like a sudden shot of potent adrenaline.

He should go.

He drained the bottle, dumped it on the table and remained where he was. The tee-shirt might be baggy, but he could still make out the shape of her breasts, big enough to more than fill his hands.

'That looks good,' he said huskily. 'What you're eating. What is it? I... I actually haven't had anything to eat tonight.'

Lucy tilted her bowl to show him what was left of her meal. 'It's spaghetti with tomato sauce from a bottle and some onions and garlic and cream, Malik. I won't be fronting my own cookery programme with the recipe. Why are you back here, anyway? You haven't said.'

'Any left?'

He stood up, edgy and restless, and peered into an empty saucepan on the cooker. There were two shining silver-and-black range-cookers in the kitchen, built into the marble and granite counter tops. He knew he would find something splendid, hand-prepared and delicious in the fridge. Instead, he helped himself to some water, a block of cheese and some bread, and resumed his place on the chair facing her.

'What have you got up to this evening?'

'You're looking at it.' Lucy half-lifted her laptop.

'You spent the evening on your computer? Tell me you weren't working.'

'Of course I wasn't working, Malik.'

'No need to be defensive.' He looked up from his plate of cheese and bread and grinned. 'But admit it, it's not the first time you've worked after hours.'

'It's impossible to do that here.'

'I'd have thought it was easy without the usual distractions.'

'Usual distractions?'

'Friends, family and pub crawls.'

'*Once.* I've been on a pub crawl *once* and woke up the next morning swearing I'd never do that again. Have *you* ever done something like that? Or is all your outside time taken up with work?'

'Seldom with work,' Malik murmured, and Lucy reddened, struck into immediate silence.

She rose to clear her plate and Malik told her to leave it. It would be taken care of in the morning when his staff arrived. She ignored him and began washing the dishes she had used.

'Some of us had to get on with the business of tidying up after ourselves,' she threw over her shoulder. 'In the absence of anyone around to tidy up after us. In my family there was a strict rota and woe betide anyone who decided to abscond.'

Malik pushed his plate to the side, angled his chair so that he could stretch out his legs and looked at her. Her hair was casually pulled back into a ponytail. Half of it had escaped to curl down her back in feathery tendrils. He could have sat there and watched her like that for ever, and he wondered whether it was because he had just come from having a conversation with his parents about the future that awaited him.

Did the promise of a suitable wife make him suddenly lust for the possibility of an unsuitable lover? Or had he opened a door that should have remained shut but, now that it was opened, continued to tempt him to go inside and discover what lay behind it?

He fidgeted. He could feel the rush of excited blood stiffen him. When she spun round and he noted the bounce of her breasts, he hardened yet further to a point where he was uncomfortable and over-conscious of his erection.

'You still haven't told me why you're back early. If I'd known you were going to show up, I would have...'

'Gone into hiding?'

'Of course not!'

'Then what? Would you rather I hadn't returned?'

'It's your house, Malik. You can come and go as you please.'

'That's not what I asked. You're disappointed to see me here. Scratch that,' he ground out. 'I cancelled the dinner. And it was with two of my father's business associates—an informal meeting to discuss rejigging some of the board members to deal with my father's early retirement. You can leave my plate, Lucy. You might be conditioned to tidy up after yourself, but you're not paid to tidy up after me.' He stood up, took his one plate and cutlery to the sink and, as an afterthought, washed it all and dumped it by the side of the sink, then he turned and perched against the counter to look at her.

'Wasn't in the mood for it after the visit to my parents,' he confessed.

'Should I ask how it went or will you remind me that it's none of my business?'

Once upon a time, she thought with dismay, she wouldn't have hesitated to ask him a question if it had been preying on her mind, but those days were gone, and in their place was this awkwardness…this *awareness*… that no amount of mental stain-remover had quite managed to remove.

She wanted to leave.

She didn't want to leave.

And so she dithered.

Their eyes clashed and she felt her heart pick up pace. Under the tee-shirt, her nipples tightened into stiff, hard bullets jutting against the soft cotton. Between her legs, a dampness was spreading, making her giddy with heat and the burn of desire which she had tried so hard to ignore.

'Have a nightcap with me,' Malik invited huskily. 'I'm in no mood for my own company.'

'And I'm a last resort?' Her voice was breathless, and the teasing jibe fell flat.

'Far from it.'

Lucy hesitated, antenna on full alert, because retreating to the cosy room that overlooked the sprawling back lawns felt intimate—all her imagination, of course. She nodded and offered to make coffee, in a voice that was laced with doubt because the high-tech machine concealed behind one of the doors filled her with mild terror. The chef who prepared their meals was adept at handling it but she feared a mishap if she tried. With this prickly awareness zinging through her, she knew that the wise thing would be to politely decline and leave.

'Maybe a nightcap…'

'A liqueur? There are several available.'

'You choose. I don't know anything about liqueurs.' She watched him as he poured them something amber-coloured in two small, heavy crystal glasses and then, as they made their way out, she decided to give in to her curiosity.

'So…'

'So?' Preceding her, Malik half-turned to look at her with raised eyebrows.

'When you say you weren't in the mood…'

The airy sitting area was a wash of muted colours and silk hangings.

Malik sighed. He rested back against the mint-green sofa, waited until she had sat next to him, eyes alert, and pondered what to say. He reminded himself that this was his destiny and one to which he didn't object. He knew what his goals were and he wasn't a guy who had ever shied away from facing the inevitable. To be born in a certain place, within a certain family, came with expectations, but right now the expectations on his shoulders, the very ones he had volunteered to carry because the time had come, felt…too heavy to bear.

And with Lucy sitting there…with one leg tucked under her, leaning towards him, blue eyes round and unashamedly curious…

God, it felt as if she embodied a life without complication.

He closed his eyes briefly before opening them to gaze at her in silence. 'My future is hurtling towards me at pace,' he murmured, sipping the liqueur. 'Women have been sourced…plans have been made…the time is coming for me to choose a suitable wife.'

'"Women have been sourced"?' Her heart picked up pace; she felt painful, *hurt*. 'Malik, you make it sound as though you've suddenly been transported back to mediaeval times.'

'Not quite.' He closed his eyes and half-smiled. 'But not a million miles away, at least for me.'

'But you don't have to do anything you don't want to do, surely? You mother strikes me as a very reasonable woman.'

'She is.'

'So why do you have to do something you don't want to do?'

Malik smiled wryly. 'You're mixing me up for someone who allows other people to run his life for him. If I didn't want this arranged marriage, I wouldn't be doing it. I can't remember saying that marriage to a suitable woman was something I didn't want to do, do you?'

'I suppose not...'

'Were you really taken aback to see me?'

'It's your castle. You can come and go as you please.'

'Palace. It's my *palace*...and that's a non-answer.'

'A man's home is his castle. I admit you took me by surprise. I would have... I probably would have...'

'Been hiding away in your rooms? Admit it, I make you uncomfortable.'

'Don't be silly. Of course you don't. Since when have you ever known me to hide away from anything? Since when have I ever been uncomfortable around you? We work perfectly together. *Perfectly.*'

'We did. Until that kiss interrupted the smooth flow of things.'

'We weren't going to bring that up!'

'My apologies.'

'You don't sound very sorry. Malik...'

'Maybe I'm finding out that I'm no good when it comes to make-believe.'

'I don't know what you're talking about—and what has this got to do with you settling down with someone who ticks all the right boxes anyway?'

Danger threaded between them.

The silence stretched. Her mouth remained half-open, on the cusp of saying something, something that refused to be said.

'You're getting married, Malik...' Lucy reminded him jerkily. 'This shouldn't be happening between us!'

'Jesus, you think I don't know that? But... I'm finding

it very hard to fight my attraction. The past three days
have been torture.' His dark eyes pinned her to the spot,
burning with hot intensity. 'Is it just me?'

He didn't move an inch closer to her, and yet Lucy felt
his words as forcibly as if he'd reached out and touched
her.

'I can't believe you're lost for words, Lucy, but on this
occasion I think I like it,' he murmured and the effect
was devastating.

She trembled, her eyelids fluttered and the breath
caught in her throat.

He was getting married!

To let anything come of this searing desire to sleep
with a guy on the cusp of…whatever you wanted to call
it…wouldn't do.

But this was different…wasn't it? There was no woman
in his life, not even a name or a face, just a possibility.
Yes, he would marry, and he would be out of her reach
for ever, but right now this man was very much within
her reach…

In an instant, Lucy's mind flew ahead and a series of
events unravelled at supersonic speed.

A wedded Malik would mean the end of her job, whatever he said. He would surely have to spend a lot more
time in Sarastan and how would she fit into that scenario on a long-term basis? There was even a chance that
he might emigrate completely because, if he married an
aristocrat from there, would she want to up sticks and
move to London?

She was facing the end of her career as she knew it,
whether that end happened in a week, in a month or in
agonisingly slow motion over a period of time.

And then…she would never see this man again.

But she was seeing him *now*, wasn't she?

'Well, of *course* I'm lost for words.' Lucy bristled with vigour. 'This isn't a conversation I was expecting!'

'We could talk about work, if you'd rather?' he suggested unevenly and waited for her to take the bait, to come to him, to touch like he wanted her to touch.

'It would be a lot safer!'

'Do you want safe? Truthfully? Because, if you do, then safe is what you'll get.'

'I…'

'This is a time for honesty,' Malik said huskily. 'We're both adults. We're both free agents at this point in time. So, do you want…*safe*?'

At this point in time…

'No.'

'I like where this is going…'

Lucy edged towards him and, when their bodies touched, she hissed a long sigh and shuddered.

She lowered her lashes and the thrill of the unknown and the highly anticipated rushed through her with tidal wave ferocity. She could have turned away, held him at arm's length while she swooned in a suitably helplessly feminine fashion, but what would be the point?

This was their sweet spot and it was never going to happen again if she turned her back on it—and why shouldn't she take charge of her own emotions, her own responses? She'd been a helpless fool with Colin, had let romantic thoughts of love turn her misty-eyed and vulnerable, but she knew the score here and, really, hadn't her background geared her to go after what she wanted? She wanted *this*.

She could lose herself in a labyrinth of 'shouldn't's… She could think about risk and consequences. She could reduce everything to a balancing act, weighing up the pros and cons coolly and rationally, but this burning desire she felt wasn't cool and it wasn't rational. It was something overwhelming that needed to be sated and, whatever thought of consequences tried to push through her haze of longing, it didn't stand a chance against the thing inside her, that was telling her that to walk away from this would be a regret she would nurse for ever.

She curled her fingers into his shirt and tugged him towards her, tilted her face to his and unconsciously parted her lips.

'Not here,' Malik said gruffly.

'Malik…'

'Second thoughts?'

'No. Even though it's a terrible idea.' She laughed softly under her breath. 'Although terrible ideas can be fun now and again, I guess. Have you ever had a terrible idea and gone through with it?'

'Tell me you're not about to have a long, meaningful conversation now when I can think of a thousand better things to do that don't involve talking…'

His low, hungry groan was an invitation she couldn't resist but she still yelped and laughed when he stood up, swinging her up with him in one fluid movement and almost knocking over the table with the liqueur glasses in the process.

He carried her swiftly upstairs as though she weighed nothing, which was just excellent for her self-confidence. His dark eyes flicking down to her, glowing with desire, also did the trick with this gloriously handsome guy, she the object of his desire.

And he the object of desire for every red-blooded woman under the age of ninety on the planet, she thought as heat poured through her.

He occupied a magnificent wing of the palace that was kitted out for the guy who didn't like being too far away from work. She was dimly aware of a sitting area that included a table of boardroom size at one end and a stark arrangement of leather and chrome, so different from the furnishings everywhere else.

When he nudged open the door to one of the bedrooms, *his bedroom*, the breath caught in her throat and she stared around her, absorbing everything as he gently lowered her onto a bed the size of an Olympic swimming pool.

She saw dark colours…deep burgundies, rich velvets, glass, metal and silks….

Then, there was *him*.

She died and went to heaven as she watched him undress very slowly in the shadowy darkness. He stripped off the shirt first and she breathed in deeply at the sight of his muscular torso, the width of his chest, the dark hair shadowing it. She almost couldn't look as he stepped out of his trousers and then hooked his fingers under the waistband of his dark boxers.

'Enjoying the view?' Malik drawled with amusement.

'Very much so.' Her voice was a dry croak. She was sprawled on the bed, watching as he neared her, and then, when he was close enough, he eased off the boxers and she stopped breathing completely. Her eyelids fluttered and she propped herself up on unsteady elbows to shamelessly stare at his impressive, throbbing erection.

'Still okay with the view?' he asked huskily.

'Better than the Empire State Building…' She breathed.

'I'm in favour of that comparison. Your turn now.'

'My turn?'

'I get on the bed and watch you strip down to your birthday suit.'

'Uh…really…?'

Malik leant down, caging her in, and nuzzled the side of her neck and he didn't stand back as he looked at her with serious, dark eyes.

'Are you shy?'

'Reasonably. It's not that unusual.'

'You're beautiful.' He kissed her slowly and tenderly until she was melting from the inside out. 'But you don't have to do anything you don't want to, Lucy. And that includes doing a striptease for me, much as I would enjoy the view.'

He joined her on the bed and undressed her in the semi-darkness, respecting her shyness, and Lucy loved him for that.

She had never felt like this before, never felt such tenderness as the final piece of came off, joining his in a heap on the floor.

She sighed and forgot about thinking altogether as Malik began to explore her body. He kissed her until she wanted to explode, until she was pushing her body hard against his, squirming with her hand behind his neck, caressing and drawing him as close as it was possible for him to be.

It had been a long, long time and never like this. She

felt reckless and wanton. She wasn't the young, naïve girl who had once given her heart and her body to a guy who had ended up hurting her. She was a woman yielding to the sort of passion she had never dreamt possible. Daringly, she parted her legs so that he could sink between them, and she shivered at the bulge of his erection against her, the promise of penetration filling her with unbridled excitement.

She arched up as his big hands cupped her breasts and then shuddered with pure pleasure when he took one of her stiffened nipples into his mouth to suckle on it, his tongue darting over the bud, driving her crazy so that the sighs turned into moans and her body heaved under his.

'I want you...' She groaned.

'No more than I want you...'

He caressed her breasts, stopping now and again to take deep, steadying breaths, then he began to work his way down her body, which was smooth, rounded and soft under his hands. He raised her heavy breasts and licked the sensitive skin beneath them... He rubbed her nipples until they were tough under the pads of his fingers and, when he trailed his tongue along her rib cage and down to her belly button, it was unhurriedly, as if he had all the time in the world.

If his painfully throbbing erection was anything to go by, then time was definitely *not* on his side. But he wanted to please this woman, wanted to make sure nothing was rushed, wanted to take her gently and feel her body and his move as one. Wanted to watch the spread of a satisfied smile warm her face.

Jesus, he wanted to be *romantic*. It was a notion he

squashed just as soon as it appeared. Romance? No. This wasn't about romance. Romance was alien to him; it was something that was a recipe for disaster.

This was about *desire*. Desire fitted perfectly into his well-oiled world. It was something he could control. Were there risks attached? Fact was, they understood one another, so what would those risks be—what? Besides, at this point, he felt as though he was on a fast-moving train, something thundering along, carrying him on it, something from which, right at this very moment, it would be be impossible to dismount.

He dipped his tongue into her belly button and then went lower and felt her shudder helplessly against him. He nuzzled into the soft down between her thighs and, when he parted the folds of her womanhood, she cried out in a near sob and held her body still for a few seconds.

He flicked the sensitive bud and she tossed and writhed under him. Her fingers were curled into his hair and, yes, he could have brought her to a climax—he could feel her edging inexorably towards one—but he wanted and needed to be inside her.

He was so close to coming himself, as he straightened and hunted briefly for the pack of condoms he kept in his wallet, that he had to try and detach himself—difficult when she was naked on his bed, a vision of absolute perfection.

'Hurry up,' she urged, tossing and looking at him with hot, slumberous eyes.

'A demanding woman. I like it…and I'd like nothing better than to oblige.'

He entered her with a deep, steady thrust, felt her tighten around him, heard her rapid breathing and soft moans and he was filled with a sense of wellbeing and satisfaction.

He watched her as she came, watched the rise of colour flooding her cheeks, her parted mouth and her fluttering lashes, and only then did he allow himself to let go. And, when he did, it was...explosive.

The best thing he'd ever felt, as if he'd gone through a portal and, just for a while, had entered a completely different universe.

He was still on a high when, eventually, his orgasm subsided and he rolled off her and lay flat with one hand over his eyes. He felt her wriggle onto her side and then he could feel her eyes boring into him. He wondered whether regrets might happen. He hoped not.

'So...?'

Malik half-opened his eyes and slid a glance sideways, to look at her warily.

'So...?'

'No point pretending that this never took place.'

'That would be difficult,' Malik agreed.

'In which case we need to talk about it. I know that's probably not your thing, Malik.' Lucy propped herself up on her elbows and pinned him with steady, unflinching blue eyes. 'I can't picture you doing a lot of chat after sex. I might be wrong, granted—am I? Wrong?'

'You know me well...' he murmured in return.

'But this isn't going to go away if we ignore it, so here's what I suggest.'

'Lucy, maybe we could save the post-mortem for later?' He heaved himself up so their bodies mirrored one another and then he swept some of her long, tangled hair from her face. 'I could think of something a lot more interesting to do right now. Nothing too strenuous, but guaranteed satisfaction nevertheless.'

'That's very tempting, Malik. I really love the thought of guaranteed satisfaction, but I have a much better idea. I think you should maybe go and get us something to drink…tea or coffee or something…and then we can discuss what happens next.'

Post-coital conversation… He had never wandered that road before. He'd not even come close. The minute sex was done and dusted, Malik's thoughts invariably turned to work, at which point he would gently but firmly begin the process of removing himself from whatever bed he happened to be in. He should be irritated and impatient with this unwelcome detour. He wasn't a guy who lay in bed for hours chewing the fat with women he'd just made love to.

'I'll go for the *something* option,' he murmured. 'And don't move a muscle till I'm back.'

He began to slide out of bed but, beforehand, he dropped a kiss on her mouth and then hung around for a couple of seconds longer just because he wanted to taste a little bit more of her…

CHAPTER SEVEN

LUCY HAD FIFTEEN minutes during which she fought her way past hot thoughts of what had happened between them to the more prosaic business of what would happen next between them.

She knew what *she* wanted, and that was for a repeat performance or even several repeat performances. She was still flushed from love-making and her blood was still rushing through her veins while her emotions clamoured for more. Still, she slipped off the bed to retrieve her scattered clothes, which she put back on before sitting on the sofa by the window. Serious conversations were best had fully clothed and this was going to be a serious one. She wasn't about to drift into something unless she was in the control room. She wasn't going to let Malik start thinking that she might be a soft touch who was ready and willing to do whatever he asked.

And she wasn't going to let him ambush her good intentions by touching her, which seemed to scramble her common sense and turn her to mush. Malik was going to marry. He might not love the woman he would marry, but that woman would be wearing his ring on her finger, and when that happened all bets would be off when it came to her own future.

She had already worked out that a career change would

be on the cards. That was a bridge she would have to cross when it came and, even if Malik tried to reassure her that it wasn't going to happen, she knew in her heart that it would—as she also knew that she wouldn't try and hang onto to him by her fingernails, until he'd eventually have no option but to prise them off just to get rid of her.

Opening at her feet was a void and gut instinct told her that, if she peered down into that void for too long, she'd go mad. Because the thought of a life without Malik made her heart stop beating…made her want to moan in quiet despair.

It was nothing she couldn't handle. Yet, she had to grit her teeth and stop herself from spiralling. Truth was that the future and whatever it held was obliterated by what was happening right now, because what was happening right now was unstoppable and would be worth whatever consequences she'd have to deal with at a later date. She accepted that, in a part of her that was primitive and all gut instinct.

She was primly upright, hands on her lap, when Malik pushed open the door, with two brandy glasses in his hands.

'You've put your clothes on,' he drawled, briefly pausing to look at her narrowly, head tilted to one side. 'Why have you done that? I want to see you. Please don't tell me that you've decided to become prudish with me. Not after the mind-blowing sex we've just had.'

'The mind-blowing sex we *shouldn't* have just had,' Lucy countered truthfully. 'But now that we have…'

'And there's no point pretending we haven't…'

'Correct. Now that we have…and there's no point pretending that we haven't…well, that's a conversation I don't want to have in bed, because it's not lazy bed chat.'

'Brandy?'

Lucy grimaced but accepted the glass from him. He was in his boxers, and seemed in no hurry to follow her lead and put back on his clothes, but he did join her on the sofa, one hundred percent lean, mean, sizzling temptation.

'What happens next?'

Her eyes strayed to his burnished brown body, the width of his shoulders and the flex of sinew and muscle under the taut, smooth skin—way too delicious for her liking when she wanted to be serious.

And, seriously? Suitable wife on the horizon or no suitable wife on the horizon, Lucy knew that he was a guy who didn't do commitment, and whatever they'd just shared was never going to go anywhere. She didn't know whether his arranged marriage would require fidelity. Would that be part of the contract or would he be able to carry on as normal but with the status quo intact and an heir guaranteed?

She was someone who needed long-term commitment. So how did this fit into the picture? Of course, she knew: he was Fantasy Guy, the object of forbidden desire, and this was her one and only chance to decide whether she took what was temporarily on offer. Because it *was* on offer—she could see it in the flare of desire burning in his eyes as he sipped his brandy and watched her over the rim of the balloon glass.

'What would you like to happen next?' Malik asked softly. 'And, as an aside, have you covered up because you're scared that if you're not we might just end up touching instead of talking?' He grinned.

'Absolutely not.'

'And I absolutely don't believe you. I should tell you

that you're just as much of a turn-on with your clothes on as you are with them off.'

'I wish you wouldn't say stuff like that when I'm trying to have this conversation, Malik. It means a lot to me that we have this out.'

'Okay—you win. I don't want you to think that I'm trying to undermine something you take seriously and you're right, of course—we do need to have this conversation even though, from my perspective, the timing could be slightly altered.'

'Malik, neither of us saw this coming. It...' She lifted her shoulders helplessly. 'I really never thought that *these things happen,* at least not in my world, but we're here. I mean, we're here in Sarastan, probably for a few more weeks. Do you know how much longer, actually?'

'Three weeks, give or take.'

'Right, so we're here for three more weeks, and it's going to be very awkward if we start circling around one another.'

'Especially given the fact that we wouldn't be able to keep our hands off one another.'

Lucy went bright-red but had to admit to feeling heady at the flattery.

'So maybe this has been all so sudden and unexpected but maybe, now that it's happened...and I repeat it shouldn't have happened...we could...'

'Let me help you out here, Lucy, because you're going round and round in circles. Okay, maybe it shouldn't have happened. I, personally, beg to differ on that count. We're both adults, and who knows? Maybe there was a simmering attraction between us before we came here but coming here unlocked doors that had been locked before. What do you think of that theory?'

'It's certainly a theory.'

'But, now we're here,' Malik continued smoothly, 'Why not enjoy one another?'

Had he said out loud what she had been thinking? She wanted to have control over the situation. Was this the direction she wanted to explore?

'I don't like the thought of being anybody's temporary plaything.'

'You're not my temporary plaything, Lucy. You're my equal. I don't see you as a toy to be picked up and dropped. I'm not a toddler.'

Would he be picking her up and dropping her? Lucy wondered. Wouldn't she have to put herself in a position of helplessness for that to happen?

She looked at him steadily and what she saw was a guy who was being honest with her. She'd learnt about dishonesty, thanks to Colin. She valued honesty, and this was honesty—raw, unflinching honesty about a relationship that was here and now, to be enjoyed and then released. She'd wanted a serious conversation—she'd got it. She'd wanted to control the direction of her choices—this was what she was being offered.

'Does this all seem very weird to you?'

'That's what lust is all about. Doesn't always make sense and doesn't always obey what our heads are saying. So, if by that you mean *weird,* then I guess so. But weird can often be wonderful.'

Malik was watching her carefully, eyes trained on her heart-shaped face. Had no man actually ever swept her off her feet? Had she been saving herself for Mr Perfect, just casually dating until someone came along who excited her and shared her dreams about fairy castles and everlasting romance?

He was uncomfortable with the notion that somehow she might start to get the wrong ideas about this new twist in their relationship. Underneath that discomfort, though, was a treacherous satisfaction that he could have roused her in ways no man ever had. He was, however, practical and wary enough to kill that illicit thrill stone-dead. He had hurt her when he'd told her that interacting with his family wasn't going to become part of her life in Sarastan, however much his mother seemed to have taken to her. He didn't want to hurt her again by pointing out pitfalls, but he knew he had to.

'Word of warning, Lucy,' he said gently. 'I wouldn't want you to start thinking that there might be more to this than what's on the table.'

'Meaning?'

'Meaning, as we come together, we will also pull apart. It's just the way it is.'

'That's very poetic, Malik, but I can hear your ego talking.' She looked at him with steely cool. 'Do you honestly think that every woman you go to bed with is going to fall in love with you?'

'Things have a way of happening. God,' he said huskily, 'You're really sexy when you're in dominant mode.'

'You're trying to distract me, Malik.' Lucy blushed.

'I'm driven to honesty. Carry on—I'm listening. Despite the obvious distractions.'

'Malik, I know you're going to marry someone suitable, and in fact this leads me on to something else I want to say. When you get married, you're probably going to end up living here.'

'What makes you say that?'

'Common sense. A girl from here probably isn't going to want to put down roots and start a family so far away from her own family, her friends, everything she's accustomed to.' She paused for breath without allowing any interruption. 'Chances are you might end up splitting your time, at best. In which case, I don't fit in. I'm here on temporary loan to you, Malik, but I have my own life and my own family in England, and I wouldn't be able to hop from one continent to the other as your secretary.'

She drew in a deep breath and powered on. 'So we… we… Yes, we want one another, and it's all about lust and it's going to end, and let that time be when we return to London. Or when *I* return to London. I'll leave and start looking for another job and all I ask is that you give me a good reference.'

'You're giving me a timeline? I have no idea how you've managed to leap to so many conclusions, Lucy. You've married me off and, having married me off, you've now got me house-hunting for somewhere to live here because the woman I marry couldn't possibly have any interest in relocating to London.'

'Even if you *did* decide to return to London to work and live with whoever you've chosen to marry, then it still couldn't work out for us. For me working for you—I would feel awkward and terrible for your wife.'

'Marriages of convenience don't obey the same rules.'

'What does that mean?'

'Romantic attachments assume secondary importance to practical considerations. I give you my parents.' He frowned. 'Although, to be fair, maybe time mellowed what they had into something different. No matter; they would never have been like perhaps your parents were…

I'm guessing there was nothing arranged about their marriage…?'

'They fell in love at university. Met on the very first night at the freshers' ball and, five daughters later, they're still together, holding hands and having fun.'

'They're in love,' Malik murmured.

'It does happen, Malik—love and marriage and happy-ever-afters.'

'I'm sure.'

'But not for you.'

'Not for me,' Malik concurred with a shrug. 'I'm not cut from that cloth. You are, however, which is why it's important that we both accept the limitations of this… magical thing that's materialised between us.'

He reached out and stroked the side of her face and then trailed a lazy finger just underneath the neckline of her tee-shirt.

'Malik, I can't think when you're doing that.' She flicked at his finger, but half-heartedly, because what more was there to talk about? She wanted to feel him again, next to her, under her, on her and in her.

'Good. Thinking can be overrated.'

'We still have things to work through.'

'And we will—scout's honour. Let me undress you.'

She hitched a soft moan as he tugged at her tee-shirt and then his eyes darkened when she obliged and pulled it over her head.

'Let's get back into bed,' he coaxed, standing up and tugging her with a nod to a very tempting bed.

This time Lucy undressed before his lazy, intent, appreciative dark gaze. She didn't rush. By the time she was lying in blissful abandon on the sheets, she was wet and ready for him. He parted her legs with his hand and inserted two fingers into her, slip-sliding them over the wet crease that sheathed her clitoris.

Naked on the bed, she could see the swelling of his erection and she nearly passed out when, his fingers still moving inside her, his dark eyes locked to hers, he began teasing the throbbing bud of her clitoris.

She dearly wanted to finish what they had been talking about. There was a lot happening in her head and she wanted to put it all into neat, manageable categories. She'd always loved a list.

Her body had other ideas, though. Her eyelids fluttered and she sank down the bed in little wriggling movements. She pushed her breasts up to him and sighed with pleasure when he began to pay them some attention. *A girl could get dangerously used to this* was the thought that floated in her head as she gave in to physical responses that were a lot more compelling than the intellectual ones she knew she would have to return to.

She discovered that he was absolutely right when he'd said that satisfaction could be guaranteed without penetration—a lot of satisfaction for both of them, as it turned out. She was spent at the end of an hour of sensual exploration, and then was tempted into more than just 'satisfaction guaranteed, no penetration necessary' as she spasmed against his mouth.

She tortured him with feathery kisses everywhere… She took his bigness into her mouth and used her hand and tongue to drive him to the very same place he had taken her. Then, when neither of them could handle the heat any longer, she sensually eased on his contraception, straddled him and felt him swell and release just before she did the same.

She flopped next to him, utterly exhausted, hair everywhere, her body damp with perspiration.

'I feel like I've run a marathon.'

'I've discovered that there are times when it's very rewarding for someone else to take charge. You just proved that.'

Malik stared deep into her blue eyes in the darkness and something twisted inside him. What was she thinking? She talked the talk but could she really and truly walk the walk? She was deeply emotional and a romantic at heart and, while his head told him that they had both entered into this with their eyes wide open, his heart was struggling to follow suit.

'I don't want to hurt you,' he said gruffly.

Lucy shrugged but there was a sadness in her expression that Malik couldn't quantify.

'It's just that it's...complicated: my life...my choices... You know how it is for me.'

'That's fine.'

'It's far from fine if I hurt you.'

'You should stop banging on about that. You should stop treating me as though I'm breakable, like a piece of china. You could never hurt me. I could only be hurt if I was in love with you, and I'm not in love with you, and I never could be.'

'What do you mean?'

'It doesn't matter, Malik. I should head back to my bedroom. We marathon runners need our beauty sleep.'

'Stay with me tonight.'

He meant it. Never had he issued that invitation to any woman but he meant this. He wanted to share his bed with her for the night; wanted to reach out and feel her soft, sexy body as he slept; wanted to open his eyes to her sweetly pretty face in the morning.

Wanted the sadness on her face to go away.

'Talk to me, Lucy. You were hurt in the past. Talk to me about it...tell me...'

Lucy pulled away to stare up at the ceiling. Her eyes had become accustomed to the darkness and moonlight picked up the dark, circular shapes of the concealed spotlights, the shadow of the enormous tapestry that hung on one wall and the scattering of their clothes on the ground.

Was this where she had ever planned to end up—in bed with a guy because she'd been overcome with lust? Colin had changed the direction of her life and her heart. She had turned her back on anything she felt wasn't safe, and yet Malik couldn't be *more* unsafe.

Still, she wanted this so badly. She thought about her friend Helen, who had felt so protected against falling in love with her boss, and yet she had fallen in love with him. She wasn't going to be the same, was she? She was protected against that because of her past, wasn't she? She'd learned lessons.

That was what she told herself as she continued to stare at the ceiling. She reminded herself that she had volunteered for this. She'd wanted it.

But her thoughts were all of a jumble as the silence lengthened between them until he eventually said, 'I would never want to hurt you. You tell me I can't because there's no love between us, and I get that, but you're lying there and you're hurting all the same. For me, nothing about this feels sordid. It's not a case of picking you up and putting you down. Does this feel sordid for you? Do you feel *used*? For me, what we just shared felt…damn near beautiful, if you want the truth.'

'You're just saying that.' But she turned a little to look at him and her heart lifted a bit. She wanted to smile and nestle close to him. 'And, no, I don't feel used. Not at all.'

'Tell me who hurt you.'

'I never said anyone did. It's just that… I want love and marriage and kids, and all that stuff, and I could never, ever fall for someone who wasn't interested in any of that. Or, rather, someone who might be interested in all that but only if he can oversee the process and control it.'

'Marriage and children… I admit they form part of the plan, but love? No. That's a complication that doesn't feature on the menu.'

'Why not?'

'Maybe,' Malik murmured huskily, 'We all absorb what we've grown up with and a sense of duty and responsibility is what I've absorbed.' He paused. 'And that's why I felt I had to warn you against expecting more than what's on offer. You want love and you deserve it.'

'And it's important I make sure not to stupidly get tempted to look for it in your direction.'

'I'm being honest.'

'You're right. You're honest with me and that's why I can't feel used. We're honest with each other. But you're right about me being hurt in the past.'

Malik stilled and stopped stroking her, all his attention focused on her lovely, subdued yet defiant face upturned to him.

'Tell me.'

'I've never told anyone this before,' Lucy admitted, but then she added quickly, 'And the only reason I'm telling you is because I want you to realise that I really do mean it when I say that what we have…isn't something I'm going to want more of. That you don't have to start quaking with fear every time we make love because at the back of your mind you wonder whether I'm going to suddenly start trying to cling to you like a limpet.'

Malik grinned wryly. 'Your talent for exaggeration never fails to impress, Lucy.'

'I fell for a guy when I was eighteen and about to go to university. You asked me once how come I was the only one in my family not to go to university. Well, this guy… I thought it was the real thing. I trusted him. When I accidentally became pregnant, it turned out that, for him, what we had was about as real as a three-pound note. He dumped me fast, said he was never into commitment, didn't know what gave me the idea that he was. I miscarried very early on but…it was devastating, Malik.'

She shouldn't have gone down this road because now she could feel tears gathering and beginning to leak out of her eyes and she couldn't control them. She could also feel the gentle touch of his fingers wiping the tears away, which actually made her feel even sorrier for herself.

'Oh, Lucy…'

'I coped.' But her voice wobbled. 'I dumped university and headed out into the big, bad world.'

'And none of your family knew?'

'I couldn't deal with the sympathy fest. They would all have meant well, but it was just something I had to deal with on my own.'

'I get it.'

'Do you? Really?' She sighed, in control now after that shaky patch, although in fairness she still rather liked the feel of his fingers brushing her cheek. 'No matter. Put it this way, I came through the other side. More than that,

I realised that Colin had never been the one for me. I also realised that the one for me would always be someone who was into marriage and commitment, and nothing else would do when it came to an investment in my heart. So, you see, what we have here… I'll never want anything more than what it is because I could never invest my feelings in someone who wasn't into returning the favour. If this is all about sex for you, then it's the same for me.'

Malik wanted to hold her close, wrap her up tightly. He also wanted to beat the hell out of the guy who had broken her heart.

And something else was nudging inside him, something unsettling—a feeling of somehow being reduced by what she had said even though what she'd said had been spot on. This was all about the sex. There would be nothing more to come. Because he was that man she'd just described—the one who didn't do commitment, the one who had to oversee the process and control the outcome. He wasn't sure he liked the sound of that guy. That was an uncomfortable thought and one he discarded as fast as it appeared on the horizon.

'Music to my ears,' Malik said huskily, moving to take her in a gesture that was tender and sensual at the same time.

He wondered whether he should try and prise some more details about that guy from her: names, addresses… the lot. Years had gone by but wherever he was now, whatever job he held, he could still find himself paying for the wrong he had done to Lucy. Malik was a powerful guy. Jobs could be terminated with a word in the right ears.

He had hurt her—an eye for an eye and all that stuff.

He gritted his teeth and pushed past those thoughts of vengeance. What was all that about? As she'd said, what they had was about sex, without complications.

'There's something you should know about me as well, Lucy…'

Malik was astonished at the urge to trade confidences, but then why was that so surprising? She deserved to know, didn't she, why he was the man that he was and what had helped to shape him? If she didn't want him thinking that she might cling, then why would he not want her to realise why her clinging would never work? With all the facts on the table, there would be no room for misunderstandings, because she was right—the time left to them was limited. He would marry and, yes, at least to start with he would end up splitting time between Sarastan and London until everything was settled: until his new wife found her feet within the marriage sufficiently to commit to living in London full-time, always with the expectation of returning to Sarastan to live.

There was no point dodging what was probably inevitable. Also…being lumped into the same box as a commitment-phobic, lying snake of an ex who had strung her along and hurt her made Malik's teeth grind together with impotent fury. It was an insult!

'What?' She smiled. 'You don't have to tell me anything you don't want to. I know you for who you are—no surprises in store for me. I know the man I'm dealing with. You don't have to warn me off you.'

She stroked his tough, hard body, skimming her hand over his chest, but he stilled her hand.

'In a minute.'

'Sex *in a minute*? Should I diarise that, Malik? You're

the guy who's all about the sex. Right here and right now, no promises made, no questions asked.'

'Now you're making me sound shallow.'

'If the cap fits…'

'I've had my own share of crap,' he confessed gruffly. 'Not on a par with you, but I too met a woman who let me down, a woman who wasn't what she claimed to be. I met her when I was the same age as you were when you got your heart broken by that creep.' She was staring at him with her wide, cornflower-blue eyes and her mouth half-open. He should have felt uncomfortable breaking habits of a lifetime and telling her something he'd never told a soul but he didn't. He felt a sense of release.

'She hurt you.'

'She hurt my pride,' Malik corrected grimly. 'It was enough for me to realise that what my parents had was foolproof—no room for anyone getting hurt, and I'm not talking about myself. I'm talking about a woman getting into a relationship with me and wanting more than I feel capable of giving because, after Sylvie, there's no room in me for love and fairy tales—not that, looking back, love was part of what I felt for the woman. May have seemed so at the time, but in the final reckoning I believe it's an emotion that's alien to me.

'Like I said to you, we all bounce right back to what we've been exposed to. In your case, heartbreak didn't make you turn your back on love, because you look to your parents and want what they have. It just narrowed the pursuit. And for me? No broken heart but an experience that made me look over my shoulder to my parents' arranged marriage and admire it for what it was—and even more so now because I suspect, after all this time, that despite the practical nature of their marriage they opened a door to affection and possibly even love.'

'I'm really sorry, Malik. Sylvie…what a pretty name. Was she very beautiful? I'm imagining long, straight hair, big green eyes and an elfin figure…'

'This touchy-feely stuff really isn't me, and whether she was beautiful or not with an elfin figure is by the by,' Malik drawled in response, but there was a reluctant grin on his mouth. 'But it seemed fair to put all the cards on the table because…'

'You don't have to spell it out. I know why you told me, and it was more than just putting those cards on the table, wasn't it?'

'Life, for me, is in a state of flux and I would never ask you to put yourself out to accommodate me. Like you said, you have friends and family and a social life in England.'

'So you really think you'll end up living here?'

'I have no idea what that particular slice of the future holds for me, but you raised a good point when you said that there might be a need for anyone I marry to at least have a period of adjustment before heading to London to put down roots. However well-travelled and cosmopolitan a woman might be, there's a difference between seeing the world and settling down to live in a part of it you've never lived in before.'

'And while we both have this time together…'

'We can both accept that there's nothing beyond what we enjoy in the here and now and we both have our reasons. We understand one another. You wanted to reassure me that you weren't going to want more than I could give, and I wanted to let you know why there would be nothing more than what's on the table.' He paused. 'And what's on the table will be…spectacular.'

'Spectacular…'

'I'll leave you with memories to last a lifetime.'

Something uneasy feathered Lucy's spine but she brushed that aside, because the slate was clean, and what lay ahead would be pure, carnal bliss…and she wanted that so badly, it hurt. Desire was powerful enough to stampede every niggling obstacle that lay in its way. They both knew the ropes; lines had been drawn. This would work, this freedom to taste, sample and enjoy one another without guilt or regret, a chapter closed once their time was up.

She wound her arms around him and drew him close enough to feel his heart beating in tune with hers.

'Well, we might as well start with the memory box now, don't you think?'

'Oh, yes…' Malik growled. 'I very much *think*…'

CHAPTER EIGHT

MALIK GLANCED AT LUCY, who was staring out of the window of the four-by-four with a rapt expression.

'What's going through your head?'

Lucy dragged her attention away from the rolling sand dunes surrounding them. The sky was ablaze with the vibrant colours of twilight: oranges, indigos and silver. In half an hour, all those colours would be consumed by the sort of blackness she was only now becoming accustomed to.

Half an hour before, as Malik had driven away from the city and its outskirts into uninhabited terrain, she had glimpsed a group of camels lounging around under the shade of a clump of sparse, oddly shaped trees.

'I'm thinking that this is a one-off for me. Honestly, five days at an all-inclusive in Tenerife pales in comparison.'

'Was that your last holiday?'

'Last family holiday that we all took together? That was a couple of years ago. Rose was tying the knot and we wanted to do something together one last time. Do you remember I told you all about it afterwards?'

'How could I forget the bridesmaid falling in the fountain?' Malik quipped drily. 'Not to mention the pink dress with the frills you said you were made to wear against your better judgement but then ended up loving it when you saw the photos afterwards. Wasn't there also a last-minute panic about the weather...which turned out all right because the sun shone at all the right times?'

'You have an incredible memory, Malik.'

'So it would seem.' He slid a dark glance across to her and then tore them away with difficulty to focus on the hazardous road winding through the dunes.

'To be fair, I talk quite a bit, so it'd be impossible not to pick things up along the way. But, yes, that was the last big family thing.'

'Busy.'

'Like you wouldn't believe. When most parents were finding out that their adult kids don't fancy going on holiday with them, my parents were making hectic plans so that we could all be together. In fairness, they're always fantastic fun. We all contribute according to what we can afford and then pull straws to find out who's sharing a room with who.'

'Sounds like a nightmare.'

'Slow down, Malik! I can just about spot some more camels over there!'

She tapped him reprovingly on the arm. Malik half-smiled at the absent-minded gesture and obeyed.

Things had changed between them and it wasn't just because they were now lovers. Since he and Lucy had climbed into bed, free to enjoy one another in the most perfect, no-strings-attached situation he could ever have dreamt possible, everyone and everything that had been in the way of him touching her had been hard to bear.

Three days of having to go into the office to oversee complex transference of duties between various CEOs had been a pain. Looking at her as she'd dutifully done her job, head down, ignoring him, had made him fidget with impatience. He had found himself glancing at his watch even more than usual on his visits to his parents, counting the seconds until he could get back to his palace and bury himself in her body. He'd sit there, barely taking in things his mother was saying, surfacing only when it was time to go.

Right now, Lucy was waxing lyrical about camels.

'Have you ever ridden one?' she was asking.

Malik could feel her eager blue eyes on him. 'When you grow up with desert all around, it ends up being inevitable.' He smiled and glanced at her, wanting to let that glance linger, but the driving conditions were too hostile for that indulgence.

'Very exciting.'

'And occasionally smelly.'

She laughed and his smile widened. He enjoyed the sound of her laugh. Out of the blue, he wondered whether this was normal. Was it? Was it normal to miss someone the way he missed her whenever she happened to be somewhere else? Was it normal to think about *her*—not always think about the great sex they shared but instead to think about the pleasure of hearing her laugh?

Was he missing a trick here? Should alarm bells be sounding? No, surely not? She was as relaxed as he was, and no mention was ever made of when things would end between them. They were both living in the moment and of course there was nothing disturbing about that. He was accustomed to laying down ground rules with the women he dated. It was his comfort zone.

He decided that there was no cause for unease in this situation. Plans for the upcoming ball were moving quickly ahead. Malik knew that it was a subject he would have to raise with Lucy pretty soon but the back burner, for the moment, seemed a pretty good place on which to park those good intentions.

It was much more satisfying listening to her chat about this, that and nothing in particular while eagerly drinking in all the sights he showed her.

Such as right now: twilight, camels and sand dunes; what better? And she had no idea where he was taking her, so she was in for a pleasant surprise, and he couldn't wait to see her face when they got there.

'You still haven't told me where we're going.'

'I want to surprise you.'

'Who says you haven't done that already?'

'Have I?' There was a wicked smile in his voice. 'How? No…don't tell me. I can guess. Your body tells me how much I surprise you every time I touch it.'

'There's more to life than pleasant surprises between the sheets.'

Malik burst out laughing.

'You're right and we're heading to one of them right now. Look ahead—see those lights in the distance?'

Lucy followed his hand as the four-by-four gently contoured the dunes to approach the lights. They looked like stars twinkling against the black velvet of the night. Actually her mind was only half on the approaching sight which, as they got nearer, she realised was an elaborate set-up: a billowing tent, a small building and people busily tending to food, a table with white starched linen set for two.

An extravagant dining experience for the two of them. She should be fizzing with excitement but, somewhere inside, she felt flat. When she had told him how much he surprised her, she hadn't been talking about the fantastic things he did to her body, the wonderful way he had of making it come to life under his skilful touch.

No, she had been talking about small stuff. He surprised her in the little confidences he shared without realising, such as when he'd told her about going to see the headmaster at his uber-expensive boarding school because one of his friends had been so desperately homesick Malik had been worried about his mental health. Or when he'd said wistfully that he'd always wanted a dog, but that had been comprehensively banned. Or the way he had of always making sure she was okay, always slowing down to accommodate her so that he never, ever strode ahead. In a thousand ways, he was so much more the man she had only ever glimpsed during office hours.

Her heartbeat quickened. She'd gone into this with her eyes wide open, knowing what she wanted and needed from it, and determined not to let the past determine the present.

But, now, she was in deep. One minute she'd been happily paddling around in the shallow end, the next minute she couldn't see the bottom of the pool and, when she looked over her shoulder, there was nowhere safe to head to. The sides of the pool had disappeared, and she was floundering in an ocean of disaster. She'd fallen for this guy and just admitting it to herself made her whole body tingle with suffocating panic.

She was barely aware of the car rounding to a stop or the door being held open for her by one of the many staff there who were all dressed in identical white robes and sandals.

Malik joined her, neatly hooking her hand into the crook of his arm. 'Tonight you're going to be treated to the finest cuisine my country can offer, prepared and cooked by one of the top chefs in the kingdom.'

'Dining under the stars,' Lucy said, dutifully impressed, 'I hope they won't mind me taking a thousand pictures to send to my family. This is just the sort of thing they'd love.'

When had that happened and what was she going to do now?

'Sit. Tonight is your night and I want you to savour every second of it.'

She was wearing a light pashmina over her dress and Malik scooped it off her and handed it to someone who appeared from nowhere to relieve him of it. Despite the number of people all there to make this evening memorable, it still felt incredibly private and intimate.

Lucy was frantically thinking while she rustled up a smile and gazed around her appreciatively. *Okay, we're here and there's no going back. The main thing is... keep your feelings to yourself.* They'd laid their respective cards on the table and no way was she going to suddenly kid herself into thinking that anything more would come of this than what he'd said from the start.

'You're the first person I've ever done this with,' Malik confided.

'That's a shame. It's so beautiful out here. If I could think of anywhere comparable, then I'd say, but I honestly can't. In fairness, as you know, I don't have much credit in my holiday destination account. A few places in Europe, and here and there in England and Wales— nothing like this. The only sand I've ever experienced has been on a beach filled with people getting lobster-red.'

She loved him and she wanted him and, short of making up some excuse to leave the country, she was here for another couple of weeks. She'd always known that it wasn't going to last. She'd set the deadline herself!

'Can I say something?'

'Sure.'

Plates of nibbles were brought to them, along with iced water and iced champagne in a silver bucket. The cork popped, the bubbles fizzed and she took a sip and looked at Malik over the rim of her glass.

He was devastatingly handsome, in a white shirt and grey linen trousers. She tingled when she looked at him, couldn't bear to tear her eyes away.

'When you return to London, I think you should consider going to university.'

'Huh?'

'You've explained why you didn't go all those years ago and, when I think about that, I see red. But that was then. Now, you could climb any ladder you wanted with the right ducks in a row.'

'You mean a ladder up the money tree?'

'Nothing wrong with that.'

'Not really who I am,' Lucy said truthfully.

God, he was so beautiful. Her heart was already breaking but at the same time she was already deciding that a broken heart now was going to be the same as a broken heart in a couple of weeks' time, so why not enjoy what she had? Why not live in this moment and feast on what was on offer instead of trying to find ways to make a martyr of herself?

She relaxed. It was under-cover love… But, while she remained here, yes, she would have her fill of this beautiful man.

'Can I hold your hand?' she whispered, and looked

furtively over her shoulder. 'Or is that kind of thing out of bounds for VIPs like you?'

'Of course you can,' Malik said gently.

'Good.' She briefly linked her fingers with his and squeezed his hand. 'Great nibbles, by the way. Honestly, I'm going to return to London a thousand pounds heavier than when I came here.' She thought that reminding herself frequently about London and returning to it would be a good idea, would keep things a little in perspective and would stop her daydreaming about stuff that was never going to happen.

'Promise me you'll never go on a diet,' Malik said seriously. 'I like your curves.' He shot her a wolfish smile that made her go hot with a sudden urge to hold more than his hand.

'I'll have to see how that stacks up with the hunk waiting to meet me in a few months' time.'

'What hunk?'

'Haven't found him yet,' Lucy said airily, mentally crossing her fingers at the lie. 'But the search will definitely be on when I get back to cold, wet London. Maybe I'll set one of my sisters on it. They all fancy themselves as matchmakers.'

'Doesn't do to rush into anything.'

Lucy looked at him with an amused expression whilst thinking that *that* was rich coming from the guy who was about to rush into marriage with a woman he didn't know from Adam.

'I'm not getting any younger! Last thing I want is to end up playing Fun Aunty at the age of sixty to a thousand nephews and nieces.'

'I'm going to miss your talent for exaggeration.'

Then hold on to me!

Lucy killed that treacherous thought and sat back as more food was brought and glasses were refilled.

'I could help you.'

'Sorry?'

'You say you're not interested in money but who doesn't want to make the most of their potential? And you've got bags of that, Lucy. I would be honoured to fund you for whatever it costs for you to get back into the maths degree you walked away from. That could be returning to university or, more than that, I could easily sponsor you to work in a company while you do it so that you earn as you go with a guarantee of a brilliant job afterwards. What do you say?'

Lucy stuck one hand on her lap, balled it into a fist and focused on the food in front of her while she fought off a tidal wave of hurt. He meant well, and that was the worst of it. He wasn't going to be happy having her leave, but he'd already resigned himself to it, and was now wiping his conscience clean of any unwelcome post-affair stains by lending her a helping hand financially.

'What a tempting offer, Malik. I actually haven't given much thought to what I'll do once I get back to London, but once I leave here I don't think we should have any sort of continuing arrangement with one another.'

'Continuing arrangement?'

'You sponsor me to do something I'm not interested in doing… I keep in touch to fill you in on how it's going because you're the paymaster… You give me pep talks now and again… No; clean break when I leave.'

Malik flushed darkly. 'I would never want anything back from you. I would never consider myself your "paymaster".'

'I'm sorry. That was unfair of me. I guess all I'm saying is I don't think applying for a university place is going to be on the agenda.'

'Can I at least ask why?'

Lucy sighed. 'Those days have come and gone. I'm not bothered by getting a degree. I should be able to get by just fine with a good reference from you and my own ability to work hard. Remind me why we're wasting time talking about this?' She tried a wolfish smile of her own, but wasn't sure she quite managed to pull it off, because he certainly wasn't looking like a guy on the brink of dragging her off to the nearest secluded spot so that he could have his deliciously wicked way with her.

'Because it's something that needs to be discussed.'

'Why?'

She watched, eyebrows raised, as he raked his fingers through his hair and scowled.

'This isn't about lots of chat.' She purred, giving him a taste of his own medicine and taking perverse pleasure in it. 'This is about other, more interesting things…' She sat back and looked around her. 'Like me enjoying this incredible scenery because I probably will never set eyes on it again…and tasting every morsel of this food, even if it turns me into a beached whale after I've eaten the lot… And of course, when we get back to the bedroom, well…'

'Forgive me for trying to do what's good for you,' Malik responded tersely.

'Don't you worry your head about what happens to me when I leave Sarastan. What's good for me is for us to just have some fun with what time we have left.' There was enough sincerity in that remark for her voice to husk over with genuine emotion, and in return Malik sighed and shook his head, as though fighting against the need to dismiss a conversation he wanted to have.

* * *

She was stuffed by the end of the evening. They had enjoyed an array of starters, letting the darkness soak them up, and appreciating the studded starry sky above. For the various desserts and coffee, they retired under an elaborate tent that was complete with all mod cons.

Lucy was beginning to feel tired. It had been a long day, and there was something a little exhausting about being presented with spectacular sights, one on top the other, from the wide-open dunes to the roaring twilight, from the camels and the emptiness to the wonderful finale he had arranged for hcr. Everything felt like a memory in the making and, as they slowly drifted back to the car, which was to be driven back for them, she suddenly had to know how much time was left to them.

She was determined to enjoy what was left, determined not to let their last few moments be blighted by anxiety and trepidation about a future without him. She wanted to be in charge of her own narrative. Wasn't it a fact that the only stuff you ever regretted was the stuff you wanted to do but never did? She had embarked on this crazy, whirlwind, beautiful, invigorating affair because she would have regretted having walked away from it.

She wasn't going to regret a single minute of what they had shared, even if it left her with a broken heart. There was something to be said for that old chestnut about it being better to have loved and lost than never to have loved at all. Which wasn't to say that a little mental preparation for departure wasn't going to be in order.

'So…'

'I'm beginning to dread when you open a sentence with *so…*'

Lucy ignored the interruption. It was good that Malik wasn't doing the driving. She had his full attention.

'We've had our chat,' she said, 'About what happens once I return to London—and many thanks, incidentally, for the kind offer of giving me a leg up the career ladder.'

'You should seriously think about it. A maths degree could open a lot more doors for you.'

'Like I said, I'm perfectly happy living with those doors shut. But what I'd really like to know now is when I can start planning my return. I want to make sure everything is okay with my place for when I get back. I can arrange for one of my sisters to nip in and have a look and make sure that the fridge is stocked for when I get in.'

'You need notice to get someone to buy some milk for when you return?'

'It's not a joke, Malik. I might want to start arranging interviews for when I'm back in London, and I can't do that if I have no idea when that's going to be, can I?'

'There's really no need for you to start job-hunting immediately,' Malik ground out with a sudden, darkening frown. 'I'm not rushing you out of the door.'

'I know you're not,' Lucy returned equably. 'I know you'd never do that, but I don't see any value in hanging around with nothing much to do once I'm back in London. It's just not in my nature.'

'We really don't have to have this conversation at the moment. Do we?'

'I can't believe you're saying that, Malik,' Lucy said with a wry smile, 'When you're the guy who's said more than once that only fools put off for tomorrow what has to be done today.'

'Remind me to avoid sharing pearls of wisdom with you from now on,' he drawled, lounging against the seat and looking so sinfully sexy that Lucy was very tempted to do just as asked and ditch the uncomfortable conversation in favour of shamelessly staring at him.

'I won't be around for you to share them with,' she returned more sharply than she'd intended. 'So…'

'A week and a half, if I'm forced to put a timeline on it. As you know, the brunt of the work transferring responsibility to various other people within the company has gone better than expected, and thankfully my father has agreed to return on a limited basis because his recovery is going well, so any remaining transfers of duty can be handled by him.'

'Less time than I thought. Fair enough.' She breathed in thinly and forced a smile. 'Maybe your father thinks that he might end up bored stiff if he decides to stay at home, pruning the roses and playing golf.'

Malik burst out laughing and looked at her with warm, dark appreciation.

She was flushed and her blonde hair curled over her shoulders, a tangle of vanilla that always gave her an untamed, raw sexiness he knew she wasn't aware of. There'd been moments during the evening when he'd barely been able to restrain himself from cutting short the meal so that he could get her back to the palace and make love to her. He just had to think about the feel of her breasts in his hands and his pulses went into freefall.

He didn't want to talk about her returning to London, even though it had been on his mind. Of course, everything she'd said had made perfect sense, and he should have been grateful that she was adopting such a pragmatic approach to a future that wasn't going to conveniently disappear just because he wasn't quite ready for it to overtake him. Not just yet. Not when he still burned for her.

Malik was accustomed to taking the lead when it came to ending relationships. This time, he'd found himself acquiescing to someone else's common sense and he was finding that he had to grit his teeth through it. Was it selfish of him to want more of her? He had to remind himself that his life was now going down a different road, the only road he was prepared to go down.

He *would* marry a suitable woman. The time had come, and he *would* step up to the plate and do his duty without flinching.

Lucy was a ship passing in the night and, as they'd both admitted, what she wanted was out of reach with him, so all he could do was wish her well in her search for Mr Right.

It was annoying that a part of him was a little piqued at her easy acceptance of the situation. He was ashamed to think that that might just be his ego talking. The shoe was on the other foot and he didn't like it.

'I don't think my father would recognise a golf club if I put one in front of him,' Malik mused, feasting on her prettiness and feeling the stir of his body responding. He noted the way her eyes darkened as they tangled with his. When he lowered his gaze to her thighs, she blushed but didn't look away. 'Once upon a distant time, he used to be quite passable at polo.'

'Really? Isn't that said to be the sport of kings?'

'Not kings in their sixties who are recuperating from heart problems.'

'You can be pretty funny when you put your mind to it.'

'I do my best.'

'How will he spend all the free time he'll be finding himself with?'

'Both my parents do a considerable amount of charity work with various other countries and kingdoms in the area. They're very much into promoting clean drinking water, irrigation and schooling for outposts that are located far from the cities.'

'That's amazing.'

'Yes. Yes, it is.'

'Will you and your wife...er...continue with that tradition?'

'Lucy, I haven't even met this so-called woman who will be entering my life. How on earth could I have had discussions with her about what she would or wouldn't like to do?'

'Just asking.'

'This isn't how I envisaged the evening ending up.'

'That's because when you're with me all you think about is sex.'

'That's not true!' Malik said in a low, outraged voice. 'You and I have a hell of a lot more between us than *just sex*.'

'Do we?'

'What's going on with you, Lucy? Why are you suddenly determined to pick an argument with me after the fantastic evening we've just had?'

'It's not unreasonable to ask a few questions. I'm not going to just live in a vacuum until I wake up one morning to find that my suitcase has been pulled out of the wardrobe and my airline ticket is on the dressing table. A week and a half isn't very long. I can start putting things in place, if that's a definite timeline.'

Malik flung his hands in the air in an exasperated

gesture and glared at her. 'How is it possible to be one hundred perfect definite in this? How much time will your sister need to get to the corner shop for the pint of milk?' He looked at her with brooding intensity. 'Maybe I won't find anyone. Maybe this thing we have between us…isn't…'

'Isn't what?'

'You look at me and I burn for you,' Malik muttered, every word sounding as though it was being dragged out of him. 'When we first… I didn't expect the ferocity of this. Maybe I can delay the whole marriage thing for a while…'

'I don't think so, Malik.'

'What do you mean by that?'

'This isn't going to play out on your terms and your terms only.'

'Did I ever say that it would?'

'You know, growing up in a big family, you had to make yourself heard; you had to be able to stand up for yourself and not let other people make decisions for you. So, now?' Lucy sighed. 'I can't just hang around until you get me out of your system.'

Malik flushed darkly.

'I don't like the way that makes me sound.'

'But,' she said gently, 'You *are* a guy who's accustomed to getting his own way, aren't you? With women… in business…in life in general. You mentioned a ball; is there a date set for it?'

'It's next Saturday.'

'Hence the week and a half guideline,' Lucy said. 'Is that what tonight was all about?'

'What do you mean?' There was genuine bewilderment in his voice.

'Tonight…it really *was* wonderful, Malik, and some-thing I'll remember for ever…but was it your last hurrah?'

'No idea what you're talking about.'

'Was this the last big gesture before we wrap things up?'

'That's not why I did tonight. I… I wanted to show you my country…what it's like in the desert at night… and I wanted to do it in style.'

Malik stilled as he looked back at the evening they had spent together. He had arranged the whole thing himself, including arranging which chefs should prepare the food. The whole thing had smacked of romance, and for a few seconds he'd been taken aback by the sheer pleasure that afforded him.

Him, the guy who didn't do *romance*.

And now he was here, wanting more.

Habits conditioned over a lifetime kicked in with force, because he could remember the bitterness of realising the truth about life—that allowing emotions free rein was a recipe for disaster. Especially for a man in his position, where duty to his country and the responsibilities of his blood line were vital. He was a guy who, at all times, needed to put his head above emotion. But what he felt here, sitting in the back seat of his car, caught up in this conversation with a woman he couldn't get enough of… It made him *vulnerable* and that was not going to do. Just contemplating that sign of weakness was enough to make his blood run cold.

'But of course you're right,' he said coolly, back in a place of control. 'You need a deadline. My parents are expecting you at the ball. It will be a grand affair and a good opportunity for you to meet a lot of people who have considerable financial concerns in London. A great chance to network. I will do my bit, and you can put it in the bracket of giving you a good reference. Day after, I'll make sure that you're booked first class to return to London.'

They stared at each other in silence for a few seconds that seemed to go on for ever.

'Sounds good,' Lucy murmured, the first to look away. 'That will give my sister plenty of time to get the pint of milk in.'

CHAPTER NINE

IT WAS A curious mix of feelings: utter sadness, fierce determination to keep smiling, a powerful sense of inevitability and the promise of despair waiting just over the horizon. This was the swirl of emotions Lucy felt as she stared down at the dress on her bed, waiting to be worn to the ball that awaited her in less than an hour and a half.

The remaining time they'd had together had shot by. It was as though, having put a timeline to everything, the ticking hands of the clock had sped up, determined to make sure that nothing came in the way of the parting of their ways.

Work had been side-lined by both of them. Of course, they'd done what was necessary but, without any conscious agreement, life had taken on the tenor of a holiday.

Malik had showed her Sarastan. She'd been awed by the dunes but she'd discovered that there was much more to his beautiful country than the rolling, ever-changing hills of sand beyond the walls of his magnificent palace. The city was modern and vibrant. The hotels were amazing, and they'd gone for dinner and drinks at several of them, once staying overnight because the hot temptation of bed had proved too much at a little past eleven in the evening.

Lucy had told him that she'd never seen so much marble, hanging crystal and over-sized indoor plants before in her life when they'd dined at one of the five-star hotels in the heart of the bustling city.

He's taken her to the old town, where markets and bartering were very different from the high-end malls stuffed with designer goods. And they'd gone to the coast, which was empty, quiet and quite spectacular. The sea was warm, and Lucy had swum until she was exhausted; then they'd lain down, staring up at the turquoise sky, lost in their own private thoughts.

She'd been thinking that job hunting in London was going to be a painful ordeal after this. She'd glimpsed paradise, had tasted paradise, and nothing would ever compete.

She hadn't breathed a word about Malik to any of her sisters, but she *had* told Helen, even though she'd been loath to unburden herself when her friend had been all angst about giving birth in a fortnight. In due course, she would confess everything to her family, but only after she was on the road to recovery.

The sight of the dress on the bed brought her back to reality with a thump because she had under an hour to get ready. She would be chauffeured to his parents' palace.

Malik was already there, having gone ahead to start the process of mingling. She had forced herself not to pepper him with questions about what that entailed because she wasn't interested in hearing the answer. However, her imagination had not held back in painting very colourful scenarios that involved him being introduced to a mile-long queue of eligible beauties, all breathlessly excited at being chosen to be a princess by the knight in shining armour.

On the spur of the moment, she picked up the dainty sandals she had bought and flung one against the wall, which it hit with absolutely no force before dropping to the ground, and thankfully not falling apart, because there were no alternative options in her wardrobe.

She showered in record time, applied her make-up and did her hair—the little that could be done with it— before stepping into the gown she had bought on one of their trips to the city centre. It was a long, layered affair in shades of blues and greens. The neckline was modest, the dainty straps were very demure and it just *fell*, only clinging slightly under the bust.

Yet, as Lucy stood back to inspect herself in the full-length mirror, she felt as though it was all just a little bit *too much*. Her boobs looked enormous, for starters. She'd been seduced by the Grecian style of the long dress but now had to conclude that Grecian women clearly didn't have big bosoms.

Her hair… Well, it was too late to do anything with it, although on impulse she fished out a couple of pearly clips and strung some of it back so that only escaping tendrils fell across her face.

The driver was there and waiting by the time she made it down and half an hour later, as the black Bentley made its way up the familiar courtyard that formed an enormous circle outside the palace, her heart was beating like a sledgehammer. There were lots of cars and none of them were old bangers. There were also lots of people, in an array of clothing, from traditional white robes to designer suits—dashing men and women dressed to kill, draped in jewellery and sheathed in the finest silks.

The palace was lit up like a Christmas tree and there

were uniformed staff everywhere. All that seemed to be missing was a red carpet.

Malik had given her the option of just not coming.

'It's not a necessity,' he had told her gruffly, a few days ago as they'd lain in bed, wrapped round one another, bodies so entwined that they couldn't have slipped a piece of paper between them.

'Wouldn't your parents be a little surprised?'

'I'm sure they could survive the disappointment.'

'You think I'm going to be upset, don't you? Because there'll be all those hopeful beauties there, waiting for you to chat them up.'

'Won't you?'

'Not a bit of it,' Lucy had returned stoutly. 'I'll have my own queue of hopefuls desperate to be my Prince Charming when I get back to London.'

He hadn't said anything.

Truth was, she *knew* that he felt she'd find it hard to deal with the situation, whatever she said to the contrary. The mere fact that she'd come to that conclusion made Lucy all the more determined to show up, even if it damn well killed her.

There was also the bracing thought that seeing Malik in action, seeing him embrace this final chapter in their relationship, the chapter in which he moved on, was *necessary.* It would be a healthy dose of reality. She would see him chatting to the woman he would eventually marry, and any rose-tinted spectacles she might be wearing would very quickly be ripped off her.

'Right,' she muttered under her breath as the Bentley slowly circled the courtyard, coming to a gradual stop outside the imposing front door, which had been flung open. 'Show time.'

On either side was uniformed staff, several of them. Lucy edged her way out, took a deep breath and decided that the very first thing she would do was help herself to a little bit of Dutch courage...

Inside the ballroom Malik tugged at the black bow-tie and helped himself to his second glass of champagne. He had expected nothing less than perfection, and perfection was what had awaited him when he'd arrived at his parents' sumptuous palace a couple of hours earlier.

Yes, last-minute things were still being done, but the wing in which the party was being held had been kitted out in regal style. Purple and white flowers wound like ivy around the multiple white pillars in the room; stunted palm trees in golden pots had been lugged in for special effect and some poor souls had spent hours buffing the many chandeliers. Waiters circulated with a giddy array of canapés and there was no end to the champagne.

At a little past seven, the guests arrived thick and fast. Many of them were esteemed families, all known to Malik, as were their kids, whose ages more or less aligned with his, from early twenties to mid-thirties. He had played rugby with a few of the guys and catching up was good.

There would be no formal introductions, his mother had assured him. In a rare moment of physical affection, she had adjusted his bow-tie, stepped back and told him that he should just enjoy the evening. Malik had wryly thought that it was hardly what he would have described as a relaxing social event, but he had smiled, nodded and told her that he would do just that.

Was he relaxing? He sipped his champagne. From where he was standing, back to one of the walls, he had a wide-angled view. The ballroom led off to various other rooms, all buzzing. There were ample, plush seating areas. There were two billiard tables in another room, with a groaning bar behind which several uniformed waiters were ready and eager to pour drinks, and there were ornately dressed tables laden with the finest food money could buy, served by an army of waiters.

He'd been introduced to several women. To a fault, they had demurely pretended that theirs was a polite, perfunctory introduction rather than a targeted meet-and-greet that could lead to matrimony with the kingdom's most eligible bachelor. They were all dressed traditionally and ornately in silks of quiet, restrained colours, abundant amounts of jewellery, lavish but cleverly applied make-up and were groomed beautifully to within an inch of their lives.

They were beautiful, subservient women who would all make a fantastic wife for a man like him: powerful, wealthy, leading a high-octane, high-stress life laden with responsibilities. A man who would require a subservient wife, a wife whose soothing personality would ease away the tensions of the day.

Additionally, of course, a wife who would know the ropes because it would be what she had grown up with. Someone who would realise that his workload would always come first, be they in London or Sarastan, because much of it involved the livelihoods of many other people, employees in the hundreds who worked in the factories and businesses owned and run by the Al-Rashid family. She would not expect declarations of love or the heady excitement of romantic gestures.

Whoever he chose would be like his parents: practicality before impulse, head before heart. In short, the ideal woman would know that unreasonable demands would not be in the picture.

Malik wondered where the hell Lucy was. He didn't realise that his eyes were trained on the door until he saw her and then he straightened and sucked in his breath. For a few wild seconds, his thoughts were all over the place, making a mockery of the very reason he was at this event: to find a suitable wife with characteristics and traits he had already painstakingly bullet-pointed in his head only moments before.

She looked extravagantly pretty. Next to the highly polished perfection of the women he had met, she looked so natural that it took his breath away.

Her hair was a tumble of blonde curls, some of it tied back but still falling around her heart-shaped face. Her face was smooth, with just a bit of colour on her cheeks and her perfect, full mouth. The colour on her cheeks might have been accentuated by her clear discomfort as she stood still, looking around her hesitantly and clutching a small blue-and-gold bag with a chain strap.

Malik couldn't quite get himself to move as he continued to look at her. The dress was magnificent. She'd taken herself off shopping, laughing when he'd offered to go with her, telling him that she was actually clever enough to make her way through some shops and whether or not he liked what she tried on wouldn't determine what she bought. The dress was a gentle swirl of blues and greens and outlined the generous rounded breasts that he had only recently lost himself in. Her curves were lovingly outlined by the sheer fabric.

She looked like a goddess and, as fast as his libido started rising at speed, he told himself that this was not appropriate. Their time was at an end. This was always going to be nothing more than a fling. Her appearance here was the final piece of a jigsaw that should never have been started. But he would never bring himself to regret it.

He pushed himself from the wall and began weaving his way towards her, only stopping halfway when he felt a gentle hand on his arm and looked down to see one of the women he had previously chatted to smiling up at him.

What was her name... Irena?

'There's going to be dancing, Malik.'

'Huh?' Malik tugged the bow-tie looser and then frowned when she straightened it back into position.

'Dancing, in the conservatory. The band's going to be setting up in an hour.'

'Terrific.'

He smiled to be polite, but he was impatient to rescue Lucy from her awkward dithering at the edge of the crowd.

She usually appeared so confident, even though he had learned from knowing her that the confidence was usually only skin-deep. Right now, it was clear that she couldn't even muster up the skin-deep veneer of confidence.

It was his duty to rescue her. They might have said goodbye to their brief liaison but he was still her employer, still responsible for her and, it might be said, still caring and thoughtful enough to want to make her feel less ill at ease amongst this glamorous crowd of people.

Boosted by that positive thought, yet not wishing to offend anyone—least of all this very attractive girl who was gazing up at him with expectation—Malik murmured something and nothing at her coy request that he save the first dance for her.

'Isn't it the last dance that's supposed to be saved, according to the song?'

She gave him look, polite, still smiling but puzzled, and he agreed to do just that before hurriedly moving away before Lucy could do something stupid like take flight and disappear.

From across the room—trying hard not to look as though she was looking around her, because she was lost and wanted to turn tail and flee—Lucy's gaze finally alighted on Malik.

She stilled and could feel the slow burn of colour creeping into her cheeks. This was exactly what she wanted and needed, wasn't it? Just what she'd told herself was necessary—ripping those damn rose-tinted specs from her eyes. Seeing him in action at this event where his bride would be chosen.

Yet, her heart constricted and she wanted the ground to open up and swallow her. Love was a steady, painful thump inside her and she blinked, only to see that he had broken up talking to someone so that he could dutifully wend his way towards her.

Was the woman one of the many hopefuls? Even a quick glance around her was enough to tell her that the place was teeming with hopefuls, and the hopefuls were all so staggeringly beautiful that he would have to have been a fool not to find someone here that fitted the bill.

What fitting the bill might entail, exactly, she had no idea because it was a topic that had been very firmly on the list of things that were forbidden to talk about.

The woman in question was tall and slender and looked to be in her early twenties, with raven-dark hair artfully swept up into something very clever that was threaded with lovely glittering jewels. Her dress was a simple black-and-gold affair. And her skin was flawless.

Lucy wished she had had the foresight to apply some fake tan for the occasion, then told herself not to be utterly ridiculous.

'Lucy.'

Lucy looked up at a Malik, who took her breath away. He was in dark trousers with a white shirt and a bow-tie. Where the jacket of the tuxedo was, she had no idea—probably discarded somewhere.

The bow-tie would have meta similar fate, she was sure, had it not been for the solicitations of the dark-haired beauty he'd been chatting to who had helpfully put it back in place.

She watched with a jaundiced eye as he began to yank it off.

'Damn thing's strangling me.'

'Oh, dear. Still, it's a good ploy.'

'What do you mean?'

'I mean it's certainly a clever way to get the ladies here jumping over each other to straighten it out.'

A waiter swung by with a tray filled with glasses of champagne and Lucy quickly nabbed a flute and took a few sips, while glancing around her—anywhere but at Malik.

Her heart was beating so fast she could feel it trying to fly right out of her chest. She could breathe him in and his unique musky, woody, intensely masculine aroma made her nostrils flare.

'This is all very magnificent, Malik. Your parents must have slaved day and night to put this all together.'

'Or employed people who did. Are you okay?'

'Of course I am! Why shouldn't I be?' Her champagne glass seemed to be empty.

'You drank that pretty quickly. You're nervous. I don't blame you. Look, let me introduce you to a few people. You'll find that they largely all speak fluent English.'

He half-turned but she remained put and he raised his eyebrows in a question.

'You don't have to tear yourself away from your own party to show me around, Malik. I'm fine making my way through the crowds.'

'Don't be silly. You don't know a soul here.'

'I know your mother.'

'I thought that this might be a bad idea.'

'What are you talking about?'

'It's awkward for you, Lucy. I get that.' He raked his fingers through his hair and whipped off the bow-tie completely, shoving it in his pocket.

'Well,' Lucy was appalled to hear herself say, 'There goes *that* golden opportunity for an attractive woman to fiddle around with you...'

'Lucy!'

'I'm sorry. That was uncalled for. She's very beautiful and she looks incredibly sweet.'

'Are you jealous?'

'No,' she lied. 'Maybe just a little. But don't worry. It doesn't mean that I'm not going to have a good time while I'm here, and you won't have to be anxious that I've glued myself to a wall somewhere because I'm too timid to do the rounds.'

Malik looked at her in silence for so long that she began to fidget.

'Well...' She backed away and gave him an airy wave

of her fingers. 'I shall go and pay my respects to your parents and then disappear into the crowd.'

'I doubt you'll be able to pull off a disappearing act in that outfit,' Malik ground out.

For the first time since he'd come here, he felt *alive*.

He could barely remember what the woman who'd playfully adjusted his bow-tie had looked like because he only had eyes for the woman standing in front of him. And that was a weakness he did not want to indulge.

They'd done what they'd done, but they'd both set their parameters, and he wasn't going to let a little physical weakness lead him astray.

'Thanks a lot, Malik!'

Lucy began to spin away but he reached out and circled his hand around her wrist, stilling her.

'You don't understand what I mean by that,' he said in a roughened undertone.

'I know exactly what you mean! You mean that, alongside all these sophisticated beauties with pedigrees as long as your arm, I look like a fool!'

'The opposite, for God's sake!'

'What do you mean?'

'You know exactly what I mean, Lucy.'

'No. I don't!'

'I mean you stand there and everyone else is in the shade! No one can miss you because you look sexy as hell!'

He whipped his hand away and stood back but he couldn't tear his eyes away from her.

He'd meant every word, but none of those words should have been spoken because none of them was appropriate, given the circumstances.

'My mother is in the sitting area,' he said unevenly. 'Let me…let me take you there—introduce you to some of her friends…'

'I'm fine,' Lucy shot back, tilting her chin and taking two steps away from him. 'You go and do what you have to do!'

Lucy knew how to mingle. Coming from a big family, where every event seemed to involve half the neighbourhood and so many extended family members that elbow room had to be fought for, mingling came naturally to her. Plus, she wanted to make sure that Malik didn't see her skulking somewhere, nursing her hurt and her wounded heart.

No, not her *wounded* heart. Her utterly destroyed and broken heart. She comforted herself with what he'd said about her looking sexy, but then told herself that that meant nothing.

Out of the corner of her eye, she always seemed to have him in her line of vision, noticing the way people flocked to him, male and female.

This was his *home*, she thought miserably. This was where he *belonged*. London had just borrowed him for a moment in time and soon the beautiful woman who had done his bow tie, who seemed to be next to him whenever Lucy looked in his direction, would anchor him back in his heartland.

Her smile was glassy as she mingled with everyone. The food was exquisite, and she filled her plate and sat with a lovely group of people at one of the many circular tables, but she barely tasted a thing. She knew that she was operating on automatic. She heard herself laughing and asking interested questions. Champagne flowed in her direction until she was woozy…and more miserable.

And ever more aware of the young, smiling brunette with the fabulous slender body who had attached herself to Malik. Who knew what he thought about *that* situation? Was the brunette to be *the one*…while Lucy returned to his palace with her airline ticket waiting for her, all booked for two days' time?

At the stroke of midnight, with reckless abandon, Lucy weaved her way to thank his parents for having her and, that duty under her belt, she headed towards Malik.

Of course, she should thank him for asking her along. He'd offered to be the solicitous host and it wasn't his fault that she'd turned her back on that act of charity.

Thanks, but no thanks.

But thank him politely she would! She knew exactly when he spotted her because at that very moment the group around him, including the brunette, seemed to perform a convenient vanishing act.

One simple 'thanks, and hope to see you before I leave the country' and she'd be gone—out of his life for ever, with just one backward glance at a life left behind when she went to clear her stuff from the offices in London.

'Lucy.'

His deep, dark, familiar, outrageously sexy voice brought the glaze of tears to her eyes.

'You don't have to…' she heard herself say and, when he looked at her enquiringly, she added for good measure, 'Marry someone you don't want to marry. You don't have to do that.'

And there it was—out in the open. All the love and longing she felt for him.

She squeezed her eyes tightly shut and, honest to the

last, she breathed with heartfelt sincerity. 'I love you, Malik.'

She looked at him, appalled by what she could hear herself saying, but driven to speak her mind before she disappeared out of his life for ever. To hell with stupid consequences. What more could happen? It wasn't as though she'd have to face him across a desk any longer.

'Don't marry her. Marry me.'

She watched as he turned his head away. He clenched his jaw, and when he looked at her his dark eyes were blank of expression.

'Lucy…'

'No. Don't say anything.'

'I'm sorry.'

CHAPTER TEN

MALIK COULDN'T MOVE a muscle as he watched her swiftly disappear, eaten up by all the people still there, including Irena, who had dutifully hunted him out for the first dance she had insisted he save for her. When he'd glanced across the space that had been set up for the young people to dance, Lucy was nowhere to be seen.

He'd known what she was going to say before she'd uttered those three killer words. He'd seen it in her eyes and had been pole-axed. Should he have seen that coming? They'd made a pact but pacts were often broken. He should know all about that because it had happened before—women given boundaries, only for him to find that the boundaries had become too onerous for them somewhere along the way.

But for Lucy to tell him that she loved him…

He had pulled away at speed.

No! That had *never* been on the cards. He wasn't after that. He was after the sanity and practicality of a marriage based on cool reason, with a woman who would understand the life they were signing up to.

A woman like Irena.

He forced himself to remain at his own ball for another couple of hours, making sure to disentangle himself from making any arrangements to do anything with any woman. Time enough for those sorts of life-changing decisions! Meanwhile, he would have to let his blood cool in the wake of Lucy's confession.

He knew when she was leaving because he'd handled booking the ticket himself: first-class direct flight in two days, mid-morning.

In the meantime, he would do them both a favour and lay low, which was easy, given he had a suite of rooms in the city centre. By the time he returned to London, she would be gone. He knew when she intended to go to the office to clear her things. He would give her the chance and the privacy to do that without having to look him in the face.

She was proud and he imagined she would be embarrassed by what she'd confessed. He could tell her that it would have been the champagne talking, but why not spare them both the awkwardness of circling around one another, both sharing the same place until she left where memories of what they'd had would be everywhere?

He found himself drinking way too much for his liking for what remained of the evening, and had a thick head when he awoke the following morning in his apartment in the city. It was a different bed, different décor with no warm, yielding, sexy body to wrap his arms around, to breathe in, to caress.

He was still in bed at close to ten when his phone beeped, and when he looked it was to see a text from Lucy.

Changed my flight. Leaving in a couple of hours. I'll clear my stuff out of the office tomorrow evening. It's

Sunday and no one will be around. Take care and good luck with the rest of your life.

His eyes felt damp when he pressed his thumbs over them.

Of course they weren't tears—it was fatigue. And too much champagne, followed by whisky—an unfortunate combination. Why would he cry when this was exactly what he had planned from the outset?

Yet the pain was unbearable. All those years of telling himself that he was invincible when it came to his emotion washed away in a tide of suffocating sorrow.

What the hell had he done?

He knew exactly what he'd done. He'd bought into his own misconception that he was immune to love; that what he felt for Lucy was something he could control; that his head was always going to have the final say, because that was what he had stupidly decided would always be the best outcome for him.

Now, in the loneliness of his luxurious apartment, all he could feel was the misery of his own wrong turns and bad decisions. He'd been blind when he'd assumed that all he felt for her was lust. He'd conveniently forgotten the way she'd made him smile, the way she'd made him feel warm and satisfied inside. Love had spouted tentacles long before they'd slept together, but he just hadn't seen it, and now...

He pressed his thumbs to his eyes again and felt the dampness of heartache tearing through him, leaking from his eyes.

Time to fix this. Or was everything lost for ever?

Once back in London, Lucy felt as though Sarastan and everything that had happened there had been a dream.

A dream dreamt a thousand years ago when she'd been a different person from the one who now stood here, in her box in North London, unpacking her suitcase and gazing around her at surroundings that couldn't have been further removed from the one she had left behind.

She was really tired. She'd managed to change the flight without any trouble at all. Actually, they knew who had booked it, and she felt if she'd shown up at one in the morning the staff there would have found a private jet, such was the power of the Al-Rashid name.

Malik.

God. She couldn't believe what she'd told him. Was there *anything* to be said for acting on impulse?

And yet, telling him how she felt about him had been cleansing. She hadn't meant to; she had always planned to leave with her head held high and her love firmly under wraps.

But then…there, at the ball and in the moment…it had all been too much.

Love had burst the barriers. Seeing him in the life he was going to be leading, away from her for ever, hadn't been the salutary lesson she'd been hoping for. It hadn't set her on the straight and narrow. It had just been a cruel reminder of what she was about to lose—the only man she could ever see herself loving.

She'd maintained her stiff upper lip all the way back to the palace. The driver who had brought her to the ball had been waiting to return her to Malik's palace and the last thing she'd needed was to sob her way noisily all the way back.

But, as soon as she'd got back to her suite of rooms, the tears had come, a river of them, great, heaving sobs followed by horrible nausea, thanks to too much champagne.

Still, she'd woken the following morning and, despite the thick head, she had packed fast, taken a couple of tablets and phoned to change her flight. The thought of bumping into Malik had panicked her—no need, as it had turned out.

She'd been prepared to tiptoe her way down, but the place had been quiet and, out of curiosity, she'd tiptoed to his rooms to find that he wasn't there. He hadn't come back at all, and that had cut her to the quick, because where had he spent the night?

At his parents'? Or with someone else? With the brunette? Surely not? That would surely have been frowned upon, but then was she really up and running about how modern or not the women in Sarastan were? Who knew what they got up to, tradition or no tradition? They could hit the local pole dancing clubs when the sun set, for all she knew.

Which thought made her smile for a minute or two.

She would give all those summery, optimistic dresses to charity so that there were no visible reminders of her time out there, and then she would head to the office to clear her stuff. Sunday would be a brilliant day to do that because there would be no curious eyes, no questions. She'd be able to disappear without any fuss.

In the morning, she would do a food shop and then head in to the office—it would be safer in the evening. Hedge-fund managers in charge of billions often had an annoying habits of working at the weekend but no one worked on a Sunday evening. That was beyond the pale.

And yet…

It had been oh, so easy to be calm and collected from the safety of her box in Swiss Cottage. Broken hearts

were so much easier to nurse when there were no reminders around.

Just heading in on the Tube was a reminder of the familiar route she would be leaving behind. Her feet slowed
as they approached the impressive, towering building that
housed Malik's elite task force. The sun had set and it
was very quiet. Groups and couples were drifting along,
heading for who knew what restaurant, bar or evening
dinner party somewhere?

It was chilly. Even through her jeans and the old
jumper she had flung on she could still feel the cold
nipping at her.

Deep breath.

She was already taking out the two bin bags she had
brought with her as she pushed through the revolving
door into the foyer where Sam, the guy at front desk at the
weekend, smiled and tried to engage her in conversation.

'Just clearing a few things,' she said chirpily, but her
smile was glazed and her eyes were a little unfocused.

He looked puzzled.

Probably thinks I'm nuts, Lucy thought as the lift
pinged on its way up. Too bad; in half an hour, she'd be
on her way out and that would be the end of that.

She stared down at the ground of the silent, deserted
office as she made her way to Malik's office suite, which
was past the central area with its minimalist furnishings
and its state-of-the-art computers, all now switched off.

She banged lights on as she went. She took a deep
breath as she stood outside Malik's office and then
opened the door and stepped in to a darkened room—
her outer office, where over the years she had accumu-
lated, frankly, the sort of bric-a-brac that her sisters would
fondly have laughed at. There were framed photos, plants,

an array of pens in cases, because who could resist a decent, colourful pencil case? There were some little ceramic *objets d'art* which were great for fiddling around with when she was bored and taking a quick break.

She banged on the light and there was her desk, as clear as she had left it weeks ago...bar the massive wrapped box on top.

It was in silver wrapping with a big red bow.

She stared, frozen to the spot.

What the heck was this and what the heck was going on?

Inside his office, where he had been sitting for the past two and a half hours, Malik vaulted upright the minute Lucy switched on the outside light.

He'd never felt more nervous.

Watch and wait...? See what happened when she opened that box...? No, that felt a little too voyeuristic, although it was cravenly tempting.

He pushed open the door, cleared his throat and then they were looking at one another. Her face was a picture of open-mouthed shock. Her big, blue eyes were wide with absolute astonishment.

'Lucy...'

'What are you doing here?'

'I... Why don't you sit down? Before you fall down.' He moved forward quickly, dragged her leather chair out from behind her desk and rolled it over to where she hadn't moved a muscle since she'd entered the room.

'What are you doing here?' she again demanded shrilly, ignoring the chair. 'Why have you come here? You *knew* I'd be here collecting my stuff, Malik! Why have you picked now to show up?'

'Because…' He faltered to a stop but then nodded to the box on her desk. 'Lucy, would you open the box? It's…something I bought for you…'

'Tripped up at the last minute by a guilty conscience, Malik?' she asked with dripping sarcasm.

Galvanised into action, she strode over to her desk, ignoring both him and the chair, and yanked open the drawers to begin the process of stuffing her belongings into one of the bin bags.

'No need to feel guilty,' she muttered in a driven undertone. 'No need to feel sorry for me. I'm quite capable of moving on from you, whatever you might think.'

'What you said…'

'What about it?' She stopped to glare at him but even in mid-glare she noted that he looked haggard. 'And how the heck did you manage to get here so fast?' she demanded accusingly. 'Last time I saw you, you were about to disappear back into your "find a bride" party.'

Her eyes blurred with tears.

'I didn't disappear back into it for long,' Malik admitted roughly. 'You left me…you walked away… I went to my place in the city centre. You asked how I got here? Private jet. I didn't have the patience to go through the usual channels. I had to get here…had to see you…'

'And now you have. So, you can disappear back to Sarastan in your private jet and pick up where you left off there!'

She was being horrible but how could she help it? How could she be expected to hang on to her self-control when he was standing in the room like her very worst nightmare come to life.

'Did you mean it? What you said…about loving me…'

Lucy stared, livid that he had asked that, livid that he was here and yet unable to deny the truth of what she had told him.

'What does it matter?'

'A lot. The box…it's not a guilt gift, Lucy. Please… would you open it?'

So, she did. She reckoned that she might as well, because the faster she could leave, the better. She couldn't do this. Couldn't be in the same room as Malik.

It was an enormous box and she wondered whether he'd thoughtlessly decided to get her a farewell gift of a new laptop for whatever new job she managed to find. She began tearing off the paper—thick, expensive paper, she couldn't help but notice *en passant*. The bow got chucked on the ground. She could feel his dark eyes on her and, when she quickly glanced up at him, she shivered because she couldn't read what he was thinking, not at all.

And she'd always been half-decent at doing that.

The paper kept coming off, layer upon layer upon layer, and then, just when she was about to give up in tearful, angry frustration and misery, there it was—a little black velvet box which she stared down at without touching.

'What's this?' she asked suspiciously.

'Open it.'

'Tell me.' But she was already flipping open the little box, and there it was—a ring…with a diamond on it. The purest, most beautiful diamond she had ever seen in her life. Not that she'd seen very many, actually.

'What's this?' she repeated, but her voice was hesitant, although she couldn't staunch the rush of excitement that threaded its way through her.

She trembled as he took a few steps towards her until

he was right next to her, so close to her that she could reach out and touch him.

'Will you marry me, Lucy?'

'Sorry?' She blinked and wondered whether she'd misheard or else maybe hallucinated something she *wanted* to hear as opposed to what she *actually* heard.

'I want you to be my wife. Will you marry me?'

'Will I *marry* you? How can you ask that when you're already involved in the process of marrying someone else?'

'Let's sit. This conversation…isn't one to be had standing up, staring at one another with a desk at the side. Makes me think I should be dictating something for you to transcribe.' He smiled tentatively, crookedly, but he didn't move, waiting to see what she would do.

Since her legs were beginning to feel like jelly, Lucy shuffled to the sofa by the wall and fell into it. Her heart was pounding and her thoughts were all over the place. She'd left the little box with the twinkling diamond right where it was on the desk and now she longed to cast another eye over it to make sure she wasn't dreaming.

He sat next to her, not too close but not too far. Close enough to touch, but only if he reached out—no place for any accidental brushing of hands.

They stared at one another.

'You're shocked.'

'Are you surprised?'

'No.'

'The last time I saw you, you were telling me in no uncertain terms just how you felt about me.' Her voice was laced with bitterness and, however much the diamond ring was calling, she wasn't going to pay heed to the temptation to listen to that siren call. *No, sir.*

'Lucy,' he said heavily, and this time he did lean forward. 'I always knew the path I was going to follow. Especially after my youthful…what shall I call it?…*misjudgement*, well, I accepted that love and romance, and all the complications that came with that, were never going to feature in my life.' He sighed. 'I knew what my parents had and I knew that it was a formula that worked—an arranged marriage with no room for misunderstandings. When we…started what we started…'

Lucy stiffened but didn't pull away when he hesitantly reached across to link his fingers through hers.

'Go on,' she said tersely. 'I'm listening. *Just about.*'

Malik smiled. 'Everything about you is so wonderfully unique, Lucy. The fact that I've always thought that should have been a clue as to how I really felt about you.'

'And which is how, exactly?'

Lucy wanted to sound sharp, but instead sounded hopeful, so she glowered to make up for the weakness, which made him smile just a little bit more.

'Dependent,' he said simply.

'Dependent…?'

'I'm in love with you, my darling, and if I didn't have the courage or the wit to see that before then I am happy to spend the rest of my life apologising for the oversight.' He looked at her with utter seriousness.

'But what about all those plans you made? The ball? What about that brunette you spent the entire evening with? I half-expected an announcement to be made by the end of the evening!'

'That was never going to happen,' Malik said wryly. 'It wasn't a fairy tale story to be wrapped up in a few chapters with a wedding at the end. The only woman I had eyes for at that ball was *you*. The only woman's voice

I wanted to hear was yours. The only woman I wanted to spend the rest of my life with… I realised…was *you*. So, did you mean what you said about loving me? I've been a fool, but will you have me now? Will you forgive me my blindness?'

Lucy smiled.

She clasped his hands with hers and leant towards him to brush his cheek with her fingers. That dear, dear face that she knew so well. How could she ever have imagined that what they'd shared could be left behind? He might have been blind to what he'd felt, but she'd been blind as well in assuming that what *she* felt could be contained. Somewhere along the line, attraction had cemented into something solid and wonderful, and she'd chosen to over-look that because she hadn't wanted to admit to it.

So would she marry him—this big, complex, strong, vulnerable guy she'd fallen head over heels in love with?

'Forgive your blindness? I think I can do that… I've been a fool as well for ever thinking that I could get you out of my system. Once you entered it, you were always going to be there for ever. And as for marrying you…?' She dimpled in the way he had fallen for from day one. 'I think there might just be a space in my diary…'

EPILOGUE

'MY MOTHER,' MALIK SAID, turning on his side to look at his adored wife, who was busy reading an interior design magazine, 'Wants to know whether a palace is too extravagant a gift for our son.'

Lucy dumped the magazine on the table at the side of the enormous four-poster bed, which had been their top priority for the house they had bought four months previously 'Our son…has yet to be born…'

She grinned and watched with a burst of love as Malik curved his hand over the swell of her belly.

She was eight months' pregnant and was quietly amused that her husband seemed a lot more nervous about the impending birth of their baby boy than she. He'd made her pack her hospital bag over six weeks ago, even though she had rolled her eyes and told him that he was being over-dramatic.

The past few months had shot past. They had married and the wedding had been wonderful and intimate, with just close friends and family invited. Lucy had fretted that, after the magnificence of what an arranged wedding would have looked like, his parents would be bitterly disappointed. In her usual forthright way, she had aired her concerns with his mother, with whom she had developed a wonderfully close bond.

But not a bit of it. Nadia had confided that she and Ali would have adored something a lot less spectacular, but in the end they had followed tradition and done what had been expected.

Bit by bit, Malik was opening his eyes to what Lucy had gathered pretty much as soon as she had got to know his parents. They might have had an arranged marriage but within that arrangement was a bedrock of love, something Malik had never really seen.

She covered his hand with hers and then shuffled over to kiss him lightly on the mouth as he continued to caress her naked belly.

'I think a toy palace would work very well in due course.' She gazed at Malik lovingly. 'Even though I know your mum and dad are thinking about the real deal.'

'It'll be very hard not to spoil him.' Malik paused and smiled. 'Just as it's bloody impossible not to spoil *you*, when you let me.'

'You already spoil me enough.'

'You refuse diamonds and pearls.'

'I have everything I could ever need.' She stroked his cheek and felt their baby move in her tummy, preparing to join them, to make them a family of three. 'I have you…'

* * * * *

SIGNED, SEALED, MARRIED

ANNIE WEST

MILLS & BOON

A huge thank-you to the ever-helpful Fabiola Chenet.
This story is dedicated to all my French readers,
and particularly Beatrice S and Karine R.

PROLOGUE

'THEY'RE ALL PROMISING OPTIONS.' Adam looked up from his desktop monitor. 'The team's done an excellent job. Thanks.'

His chief acquisitions advisor nodded. 'They'll be glad to hear that, thank you.' He paused. 'Of course, there's a clear winner in terms of potential profit.'

Adam nodded. 'Don't worry, I'll read it thoroughly before deciding.'

The need for profit had driven his endeavours since he was a schoolkid, holding down multiple part-time jobs. Adam had worked like a demon to get where he was, saving, taking calculated risks, and building a commercial empire that had rescued his mother from dragging poverty and put him at the top of Australia's rich list.

Now it wasn't simply about profit. Money wasn't his prime consideration.

Though he'd ensure his acquisition was as successful as the rest of Wilde Holdings. He had the Midas touch and he expected his employees to earn the substantial bonuses and excellent conditions he provided.

His advisor left and Adam settled down to review the options.

An elite champagne house that had been producing fine wines for centuries. An innovative startup promising to revolutionise the sportscar market with genius engineering and gutsy, ultra-modern lines. A cosmetics and perfume company whose name was synonymous with refinement.

He dismissed the couture clothing brand. Having sat through a Paris fashion show with a lover, he'd found the hype over a collection of outlandish designs mystifying.

Then there was the shipbuilding company that made luxurious superyachts for the mega-rich.

The icing on the cake of his success would be acquiring a high-prestige company, synonymous worldwide with luxury.

He was no longer the hungry kid shunned by the establishment families in town while his mother cleaned their homes. But the memory of their contempt lingered.

Money alone wasn't enough. Nor success.

Adam wanted an entrée to the world of old money privilege. That final social echelon that barred brash newcomers. What better way to prove he'd arrived than via a company to which the world's elite flocked?

He'd almost decided to take the shipbuilding company, but made himself open the final file.

The famous House of Fontaine. Established and run by the same French family for generations. Perfumes and cosmetics weren't his style, despite his mother loving its products. But the figures stacked up, or had done until recently when poor decisions had left the company teetering on the brink of disaster.

Nevertheless, he felt his interest waning.

Until he clicked onto a video of a company press conference.

The woman didn't need a microphone to snare his attention. The quality of her silence as she waited for the journalists to settle made him sit straighter.

Her face was arresting rather than beautiful, with flawless skin, well-marked eyebrows and a wide mouth set beneath a strong nose. Her blonde hair was sleekly pulled back and would have looked uncompromising if not for the pearls at her throat and her well-shaped ears. Even a fashion ignoramus like Adam realised her plain black dress had been made for her slender frame.

She had it, that indefinable something he'd never had. *Class.*

The result of bred-in privilege. This was Gisèle Fontaine, acting CEO of the House of Fontaine.

Not that she looked down on the reporters. She waited patiently, exchanging small talk. Her expression betrayed only ease and confidence, her posture perfect as if she hadn't a care in the world, despite what he'd read in the confidential financial investigation.

When she finally spoke, her tone was measured and cool, but with a slightly husky timbre that furred his flesh as each hair on his body lifted in awareness.

Something stirred low in his belly.

Adam blinked, watching her fend off questions with detached politeness and a measured smile that made him wonder what she'd look like if someone dared to disrupt her rarefied, ordered world. She looked as if nothing ever ruffled her. Perhaps it didn't. Maybe her family's wealth had protected her from any discomfort.

The interview ended and Adam reached out to close the recording when the reporter closest to her said something he didn't catch. Gisèle Fontaine turned and smiled, really smiled.

Humour lit her face, making her eyes sparkle. It transformed her demeanour from cultured reserve to gut-punching sexiness.

The recording ended and Adam stared at the screen.

He had that feeling, the tingle along his spine and quickening in his gut that he'd learned not to ignore. Not because Gisèle Fontaine's smile aroused primitive male instincts. But because he sensed this was precisely the opportunity he sought.

Methodically he reread the report, revisiting his earlier assessment.

Then he side-tracked, researching the Fontaine family.

Julien Fontaine, in his early thirties, had managed the company after the death of his grandfather several years ago. Recently Julien had stepped aside, leaving his younger sister Gisèle to act in his stead.

Adam rubbed his unshaven jaw, considering.

He reached for the phone. 'Lien, I need a meeting organised as soon as possible, and a flight to France.'

CHAPTER ONE

THEY MET NOT at Fontaine headquarters in Paris, but on the French Riviera, closer to the company's perfume distillery.

Adam unfurled himself from the sports car and gave his keys to a valet, before a grand Belle Epoque hotel. Self-confident in its domed splendour, it occupied a premier location on the famous Promenade des Anglais, looking over Nice's Bay of Angels. The sun lit its pale façade, a sea breeze made its flags flap and overhead a blue sky enhanced the scene.

It surprised him she'd chosen this place for their lunch meeting.

The hotel was famous and probably sumptuous, but surely an old-fashioned choice for a woman still in her twenties.

She knew his net worth—it regularly featured in rich lists—and must realise it would take more than a famous venue to impress him. Maybe it was familiar ground for her, somewhere her family had come for generations.

Whatever her thinking, all that mattered was that she understood how much her company needed him. Someone with the funds and business savvy to turn around the House of Fontaine.

Adam rolled his shoulders and turned his back to the hotel. On the other side of the road stretched the deep blue, glittering Mediterranean. But the beach below the promenade consisted of rocks, trucked in to make up for the lack of sand. The place was famous, but it didn't excite someone who'd grown up with golden beaches and the endless Pacific Ocean.

He turned back. The hotel possibly had a certain charm but he preferred the less grandiose style of the villa he'd rented along the coast.

Is that what had happened with Fontaine's? Had it stultified under the control of a family that lived in the past instead of looking to the future?

It was time for change and he was the man to see to it.

Besides, the House of Fontaine had something he wanted.

'Just do the best you can, Gigi. If necessary, stall him and call me.'

Gisèle heard the strain in Julien's voice and wished she could reassure him. But there was nothing either of them could do. There were no cards left to play. No lucrative avenues that would turn a quick profit and save the company from insolvency. They, and their financial team, had been over the books too often for any doubt.

'You can rely on me.' Which didn't amount to much. Even if she were in a position to negotiate, she was a scientist by training, more at home in the lab or perfume distillery than wrangling deals with tycoons. 'I'll do my best.'

'I know. It's unfair to put you in this position where you're out of your depth. Maybe I should—'

'Nonsense!' Gisèle looked around the restaurant, glad her table was a discreet distance from the others. The grand room brought back reassuring memories of special lunches here with Grandpère. She lowered her voice. 'Nothing is more important than you finishing your treatment. Not even the business.'

There was silence for a moment. 'I feel so guilty at losing it after it was handed down—'

'I know, I know. From father to son through generations.'

Although their father had never run the House of Fontaine. He'd worked for it but died young. Julien had inherited it from their grandfather and Gisèle was employed there too. The company wasn't just a business. It was a thread running through the lives of every Fontaine for two centuries. It and their employees were like family.

'To lose it under *my* watch, because I wasn't up to the job—'

'That's not true. You were sick. It was natural for you to delegate.'

Unfortunately those he'd delegated to weren't as clever as they thought, taking too many risks that hadn't paid off. The company had embarked on an ill-conceived expansion just as economies around the world teetered on the brink of apparent collapse and sales of luxury goods plummeted.

Guilt bit. She'd been no help, absorbed in her own work, and the extra public responsibilities in Julien's absence, but without the skills to manage the company.

All she'd done was appear as a figurehead from time to time. They both had reason to hate the public spotlight so she could understand her brother's desire to battle his illness privately.

The need for solitude in which to face life's ordeals was ingrained in them both, partly from their grandfather's example and partly as a result of too much press attention early in their lives. She'd done what she could to stand in for Julien publicly, for what was the glamorous House of Fontaine without a Fontaine on show?

'Look, Julien, I should go.' She needed to gather herself. 'He'll be here any moment.'

'Okay. I'll wait for your call. Good luck.'

She could do this, of course she could. It was one more instance of playing a public role. The work for this meeting had been done behind the scenes by people who understood the intricacies of commercial finance, contracts and company law.

Yet her stomach roiled. She straightened, resisting the urge to lift a hand to her hair.

'Don't fiddle, Gisèle.' Her mother's voice was clear in her head. *'Never leave your room until you look perfect. After that a lady doesn't primp.'*

That had been easy for her mother, one of the most beautiful women of her day.

But she'd been right. Poise counted. After Gisèle's early, bruising encounters with the press, she'd learned not to betray uncertainty with nervous gestures.

Not only the press. There was always someone ready to be vocal about the differences between Gisèle and the stunning, petite beauty who'd been her mother.

'Ms Fontaine.'

It wasn't a question, nor quite a greeting, and the deep resonance of that voice made something flutter across her skin.

Gisèle looked up and felt the world fade for a second.

A flash of deep-seated emotion gripped her throat and stole her breath.

She recognised the Australian from her research. She'd even broken her rule and read the gossip rags, seeking as much information as possible about the man poised to rip the House of Fontaine from the last of the Fontaines.

Could they trust him when he said he'd save the company rather than dismantle it? He was a corporate shark, renowned for asset stripping or, occasionally, dragging failing companies into profit with his take-no-prisoners demands.

He looked different to his photos. Those images barely hinted at the energy this man radiated. Energy she felt rippling across her skin and electrifying the air.

Gisèle spoke in English. 'Mr Wilde. How do you do?' She rose, holding out her hand, and discovered that, tall as she was, he topped her by a head.

Stupid to wish she'd worn higher heels.

Moss green eyes surveyed her from under straight black eyebrows. His hair was black too, long enough to reveal it would curl if he let it grow. His nose had been broken and set askew, giving him a tough edge enhanced by his uncompromising, stubbled jaw.

He *looked* like a raider. As if he didn't play by the rules.

His leather jacket and black shirt, open to reveal a V of tanned flesh, emphasised that impression. He couldn't be more different to the suited businessmen she knew.

She guessed he'd be as much at home astride a growling motorbike as in a boardroom.

A shiver skipped down her backbone as his eyes narrowed on her. She kept her smile easy, even when he folded his large hand around hers and that shiver turned into a blast of sensation. Heat and something that made her pulse quicken and thoughts whirl.

'It's good to meet you at last,' he said, as if he meant it.

Because he wants your company. You're simply the means to an end.

Gisèle kept her expression bland as she slid her hand free. Was his 'at last' reference to the fact she hadn't met him in Paris a few days earlier? But there'd been no point until Julien and his team had pored over the proposal.

'Please, won't you sit?'

She was sinking into her seat when she realised that, instead of sitting opposite, he took the chair at right angles to her. His leg touched hers beneath the table.

As if reading her surprise, he leaned in. 'Our discussion is confidential. I prefer not to broadcast it to the room.'

It made sense and Gisèle could hardly object, yet the gleam in his eye told her it was a deliberate manoeuvre at her expense.

She repressed a sigh. How she hated the games some men played.

A waiter laid the place setting before him, offering menus and drinks. It was a relief to concentrate on food rather than Adam Wilde. Yet she couldn't relax. She was far too mindful that, despite his lounging ease, his gaze was keen and, she suspected, his brain too.

Of course it was. He was a self-made man, renowned for his razor-sharp perspicacity. And the ruthlessness needed to build an empire from nothing.

Gisèle ignored her tiny shudder at the thought of Fontaine's at his mercy as she steered the conversation through safe waters. The long flight from Australia. The delights of Sydney Harbour on a sunny day.

Did she imagine amusement lurking in those green eyes? Her hackles rose at the hint of condescension but she didn't react. This wasn't about her, but her family's legacy and the livelihood of everyone they employed.

Wilde waited until the drinks were brought, sparkling water for her and beer for him, before turning towards her. He was too big for this intimate table for two. His knee brushed her thigh, his broad shoulders imposing in her peripheral vision.

But it wasn't just his size. The atmosphere had become charged, creating tiny pinpricks of awareness across her body. Her breathing was too shallow and quick.

Only a lifetime's training stopped her from frowning. Not at the big man who seemed to enjoy discomfiting his opponent in negotiations. That was an old ploy. No, her annoyance was for herself, for reacting to him as a man, not a professional challenge.

The first course was served and as he picked up his cutlery Gisèle spoke. 'So, Mr Wilde—'

'Please, call me Adam. And you're Gisèle.'

He didn't ask permission to use her first name and, for the first time she could remember, Gisèle wanted to insist he use her surname.

Because, she discovered, there was power in a name. At least when spoken in that deep, slightly scratchy voice that stroked at something unexpected inside her.

The sensation reminded her of the time she'd had a massage on a frozen shoulder. The deep probing was intensely uncomfortable but immediately followed by a melting warmth that she couldn't get enough of.

Something like fear skittered through her.

'Unless you prefer Ms Fontaine?'

There was a change in his expression, a tightening around the lips and something hard in his gaze.

She couldn't offend the man who might save the company, even if it meant she and Julien lost everything.

'Gisèle is fine.' She curved her lips into an obligatory smile. 'I was simply going to say that you didn't come all this way to discuss travel and the weather. About your proposal–'

'You seem in a hurry to divest yourself of the company your family built.' He lifted an eyebrow as he took a mouthful of seared scallop and slowly chewed. 'Why don't you tell me about yourself first?'

Incredulity vied with indignation.

She had *no* desire to divest herself of the company! Her heart broke at the idea. It felt like a betrayal of her grandfather and all the staff, to hand it over to a stranger.

Her happiest childhood memories had been made in the flower fields and perfume distillery. Losing the firm would be like losing part of herself.

'You're wrong about that, Mr Wilde—Adam.' Her mouth flattened as she struggled to rein in her feelings. 'We're not in a hurry to have someone take over the House of Fontaine. But we're here to discuss business. I don't see how talking about myself is relevant.'

He shrugged, the nonchalant movement of those impressive shoulders reminding her of the power this man wielded. Everything depended on his agreement. Without him there'd be no deal. The House of Fontaine would cease to trade and its employees would be out of work.

'Humour me, Gisèle. I'm interested.' His expression turned implacable and she glimpsed the iron fist beneath the velvet glove. 'We have plenty of time.'

Gisèle regarded him carefully, trying to work out what he was doing. Other than unsettling her. Not that it mattered what he thought of her. Yet she sat straighter, her expression smoothing as she battled not to betray instinctive hauteur at his probing.

'What do you want to know?'

He gestured to her untouched plate. 'You're not hungry?'

Of course she wasn't hungry. Her stomach was doing somersaults, but it wouldn't do to make that obvious. Gisèle cut a segment from her dainty vegetable flan and chewed mechanically.

'I want to get a feel for the company. Since it's a family enterprise, learning about you will give me a better picture.'

Gisèle repressed a frown. That didn't make sense. She worked hard for the House of Fontaine, but it had been going for generations before she was born. And while she managed an increasingly important section, he must already have sufficient overview.

Adam Wilde watched her as he devoured his scallops. He ate neatly but with a gusto that emphasised he was a big man in his prime.

Not that that had anything to do with their negotiations. But her consciousness of him as a man interfered with her attempts to treat him with impersonal professionalism.

'My brother—'

'I'm interested in your family but your brother can speak for himself.' His eyes glinted. 'Tell me about *you*.'

He scrutinised her so closely.

She was used to being in the public eye and had learned people saw what they expected to see. This man, on the other hand, seemed intent on digging below the surface. As if it really mattered to him what she was like.

She hid an unladylike snort with a cough and reached for her sparkling water. He was amusing himself while he ate.

That he'd choose her as his entertainment rankled. Yet pride couldn't interfere with this deal. So she'd stick to generalities. She wouldn't share anything personal with a man who made her so edgy.

'I was born in Paris. My father worked for the company there.'

'And your mother?'

'She was a model, an American visiting France on vacation after college.'

'That's when she met your father and stayed.'

He clearly knew the story. It was well known, or at least some version of it. People were always eager for details about her tragic father and stupendously beautiful mother. The pair had been glamorous and gorgeous, seen in all the right places with the rich and famous who patronised Fontaine's.

These days the press had to settle for concocting stories about Gisèle and Julien, inventing comparisons between them and their famous parents.

Gisèle took her time, eating another mouthful of the tart that smelt delicious yet tasted like cardboard because she was so tense.

'My father chose her to model in a company promotion and they fell in love so, yes, she stayed. The campaign was an enormous success.'

Her mother had been Fontaine's most popular model, still working on company campaigns after Julien and then Gisèle were born. Before her husband died in a ball of flame in front of the TV cameras at a famous car rally. Before she left her children with their *grandpère* while she searched for someone to fill the gaping hole Gisèle's father had left in her life.

Her relationships with a series of high-profile, extraordinarily wealthy and ultimately uncaring men had provided unending fodder for the media. As had her unexpected death from pneumonia that the press still speculated about.

Gisèle refused to discuss that.

'I grew up in Paris, spending summers in the south.' She glanced up to find Wilde leaning back, his tall frame relaxed but gaze intent. She hurried on. 'The Fontaines were originally farmers but branched into perfume making and then cosmetics. Our main production facility is in the south of France. I'd be down for the lavender harvest, the roses and jasmine. Grandpère taught me about distilling, when essences were taken from the flowers to blend into our signature fragrances.'

Gisèle had been fascinated, and especially by the Nose—the highly talented perfume maker, incredibly attuned to scent—working in his mixing room, devising new fragrance combinations.

'You sound very enthusiastic about it.'

He looked surprised. Why? Had he thought she'd been forced to work in the company?

She remembered his comment about her being eager to be rid of it. Perhaps he thought her job a sinecure. That she was on the payroll as part of the family. Not because she contributed anything useful. The assumption rankled.

But she had too much pride to set him straight. Besides, what did it matter? Soon she'd be looking for work elsewhere. He wouldn't let her and Julien remain. He'd have his own team lined up to manage the firm.

Safer to talk about the company. 'It's fascinating, the magic of blending.'

'Magic?'

Both eyebrows slanted up in disbelief. Perhaps he thought she was romanticising to get a better deal for the company. As if that were possible!

After a short time with him she guessed Adam Wilde dealt only in profits and tangible assets. He wouldn't appreciate the miracles of everyday life. Like mixing essences distilled from mountain flowers to create an utterly new, unique and satisfying fragrance. Like the jewel-studded dark velvet of a mountain sky, away from city lights.

It hit her like a blow to the solar plexus that he wasn't the sort who should be taking over her beloved company. Her family were realists who'd built a famous brand from hard toil in unforgiving, if scenic country. Yet they'd prided themselves on their vision and appreciation of beauty. How else could they have created what they had?

'I think of it as magic.'

She turned from his piercing scrutiny and sipped her water, nodding to the waiter who'd appeared, asking if he should remove her barely touched plate. When he'd gone she turned back to Wilde.

'After school I studied science and eventually joined the company. I've been there since.'

He angled his head to one side. 'But you don't spend all your time here. You're at every important gala event across Europe and beyond, the perfect picture of Fontaine sophistication.'

Gisèle tried and failed to read his tone. His words had a hard edge but didn't sound disapproving.

Instead of trying to puzzle it out she took his words at face value. 'That's kind of you. Julien and I have tried hard to present the right image for the company.'

Despite the personal cost. Even after all this time the sight of paparazzi crowding close, the sound of her name called stridently by a stranger wanting her to turn for the camera, chilled her blood. She'd just become adept at hiding it.

'I'm surprised you find time to work, given your high-profile social life.'

That was *definitely* a dig. It seemed he believed she spent her time drinking champagne at A-list parties rather than working for a living.

Gisèle's blood surged with a rush of anger, but she kept her expression placid. It would take more than a jibe from a man she'd never see again to discomfort her. She'd faced worse than him from a tender age and had learned not to react.

'You'd be surprised... Adam, at what I fit in.'

She almost added that she could even walk and chew gum at the same time, but offending him would be disastrous.

'Perhaps I would,' he murmured.

Gisèle smiled at the waiter who'd brought her chicken dish.

It smelled delicious yet she wondered how she'd eat when the thought of food turned her stomach.

No. Not the thought of food. Adam Wilde. She'd hoped they'd leave the company in good hands. According to Julien they would, but she hadn't seen anything to reassure her. She feared he was a self-satisfied corporate plunderer, one who'd never fully appreciate the House of Fontaine.

The unsettling frisson that zipped through her whenever their eyes met had to be distaste. It couldn't, absolutely couldn't, be attraction.

Gisèle blinked and took a bite of her main course.

'You were eager to discuss the deal,' he said. Surprised, she looked up to see him apparently intent on his fish. 'I have an additional stipulation. One that wasn't in the draft contract.'

She swallowed, thinking rapidly. Any change needed to be examined by Julien and the legal team. But this made her position easier. 'I have an extra condition too.'

Another interrogative lift of that eyebrow. It made him look sardonic, as if ready to find fault with her proposal.

'Go on. What's your condition, Gisèle?'

She put down her cutlery, pressing her fingertips into the tablecloth as if to absorb the solidity of the table beneath it. Her throat was parched but she resisted the urge to sip her water.

'That the current staff are retained.'

'You want a guarantee of employment?'

'You said you want the company to continue—'

'You expect me to give a blanket safety net to everyone, even if they have underperformed? I think not.'

'I'm not so naïve, *Adam*.' She paused, momentarily distracted by the sound of his name on her tongue. 'I can't vouch for every employee but many I've known all my life. We had some underperformers but they've left.' The managers who'd brought them to this situation. 'Our workforce is dedicated and skilled. You won't find better. But,' she continued when he looked ready to interrupt, 'I'm not asking you to accept that at face value.'

'I'm listening.'

'The company has an effective performance appraisal system. Underperformance is monitored and can result in counselling, training and, in rare cases, termination of employment.' She slid her hands from the table, clasping them together under the tablecloth. 'All I'm asking for is an assurance of job security and the continuation of a system that already works.'

'You care about them.'

It wasn't a question but there was something in his tone that sounded like surprise.

And a flicker of calculation in his eyes that made her wonder if he'd somehow use that revelation against her.

How could he? He already held all the power. They both knew it. This meeting was a formality because he'd insisted on meeting a member of the Fontaine family before the deal progressed and Julien wasn't well enough to attend. But that hadn't stopped Gisèle and her brother attempting this one last addition.

'Of course I care about them. And the company.' Her throat tightened as she swallowed emotion.

'You want what's best for them.'

'Naturally.'

'Excellent. That dovetails with my own extra needs. We both know that me taking control is all that's standing between your company and disaster.'

Unfortunately it was true. Yet the knowledge made her sick to the stomach. Julien had said they could probably get other buyers, but not quickly enough, and not with a commitment to keep the company going.

'Go on. What is it you want?'

A smile unfurled across Adam Wilde's face, transforming its hard edges into an attractiveness that clotted her breath in her throat.

'You, Gisèle. I want you.'

CHAPTER TWO

HE HAD TO give Gisèle Fontaine credit. She barely blinked at his statement. Only her pupils' dilation and her sudden, absolute stillness revealed he'd surprised her.

Where and how had she learned such poise?

More than poise. An impenetrable, invisible wall surrounded her. An air, not of snobby superiority as he'd feared when he'd read her Ice Queen epithet, but of control.

As if she'd learned early to hide her thoughts and feelings. Why was that?

It hadn't escaped him that when asked to tell him about herself she'd spoken of other family members. Her life seemed an open book, reported on since birth by a press fascinated by her family, but Adam suspected the public Gisèle Fontaine wasn't nearly as fascinating as the private one.

That made him more determined than ever to proceed. Each moment in her company affirmed that.

So far he'd been unable to read her emotions or thoughts clearly. Only her passion as she spoke on behalf of her employees revealed vulnerability. He'd noted the slight flush across her cheekbones and her quickened breathing. Until, he guessed, she realised she was giving herself away and her breathing evened, leaving only her heightened colour to betray her.

What would it take to ruffle her? Make her forget to be soignée and unflappable? Much as he admired her style, the devil in him longed to see her roused, tousled, desperate. Real. That hint of passion as she advocated for the staff intrigued him.

'You'll have to be more specific. In what way do you want me?'

She faced him with no flicker of expression to suggest she noticed the sexual innuendo in the words.

His admiration strengthened. Or was it satisfaction? Because she was perfect for his plan. This woman wasn't prone to messy emotional demands. She wasn't clingy. He'd bet the last billion he'd made that she'd never have unrealistic expectations of a man.

He'd known exactly what he'd wanted before coming here, but this meeting had confirmed he'd made the right decision.

'I'm acquiring the House of Fontaine, but what would the company be without a Fontaine?' Was that excitement in her blue-grey eyes? No, it was a trick of the light. She revealed nothing but polite attentiveness.

He almost wished they were at loggerheads. She'd make a worthy opponent in a challenging negotiation. In the current circumstances, with him holding all the cards, her agreement was guaranteed.

Almost guaranteed.

Excitement burred under his skin as he sipped his beer and watched her watching him.

He liked that, he realised. Enjoyed being the sole focus of Gisèle Fontaine's attention.

It would have been a mistake to offer for any of the other companies. Fontaine's was definitely the one for him.

'You want me to continue working in the company?'

'Not as CEO. Your skills don't lie in that area. We both know that it was the decisions made in the recent past that brought the company to its knees.'

This time there was no blush at the reference to her poor decision-making. She met his gaze tranquilly.

Adam frowned. Was she really so good at hiding her feelings or did she not care? No, she cared. Her plea for the employees proved that.

A tickle skirted his consciousness. A hint of something to be further investigated. But for now his attention was on securing what he wanted.

'But you represent the company well. You're very decorative.'

There! A narrowing of the eyes and tightening of the jaw. Adam felt like a poker player about to win a fortune after discovering his opponent's tell.

She didn't like being called decorative? She wasn't cut out to lead the business. The company had foundered under her watch.

'I mean that in the nicest possible way, Gisèle. Your company stands for luxury, for distinction. It's a cut above the average. Its name is synonymous with elegance and class. You've got that same air of sophisticated style.'

He wasn't referring to her slim-fitting jacket and skirt of midnight blue, lightened only by the touch of pale grey silk visible between her lapels. Or the gleam of discreet gold earrings. The clothes were part of it but she had such an air, she'd look refined without them.

A sensation low in his belly, like a silent growl, made him blank the distracting image in his head.

'You want me to stay on as a brand ambassador?'

'That's one way of putting it.'

Adam was about to explain then paused, curious about her sudden tension.

She drew a breath then turned her attention to her food, cutting a morsel of chicken and popping it into her mouth, chewing slowly.

Buying time? Obviously. But why?

Adam almost enjoyed the way she drew the moment out. He liked watching Gisèle eat. She wasn't finicky but her movements were precise and, even chewing, that lush mouth made him supremely aware of her femininity. And that he was a man who hadn't taken a lover in months.

'I appreciate the thought and I agree that it would be ideal for the family still to be involved in the company. But I'm not a model. I don't aspire to that sort of career.' She smiled but her eyes remained serious. 'Thank you but I'll have to say no—'

'You haven't heard me out. I don't want to employ you as a model.'

'You don't?'

He shook his head. 'Though I'd expect you to appear in public. You've been the face of Fontaine for some time and I want that to continue.' Because he wasn't just buying the company or the brand, he was buying the idea, the image, and all that went with it. Satisfaction filled him. 'I want you as my wife, Gisèle.'

Fortunately Gisèle had already swallowed that mouthful of chicken or she'd have choked.

Her heart hammered as her cutlery slipped through nerveless fingers, clattering onto the plate.

She waited what seemed a lifetime for him to continue, adding some detail to prove she'd misheard.

Instead he remained silent, watching her as he reached for a bread roll with one tanned, capable-looking hand.

Time slowed as he lifted the roll. She noticed a jagged, silver scar along his thumb. She caught a gleam of even, white teeth as he bit into the bread.

A shiver ran through her from neck to breasts, past her abdomen to her sex. Gisèle swallowed as unfamiliar, unwanted arousal drenched her from scalp to sole.

It was impossible! Unthinkable!

She pressed her thighs together, trying to quell her body's animal response to a man she didn't even like.

It flummoxed her. It was so un-her. She didn't respond sexually to strangers.

Yet it was there, real and unavoidable.

Like the words he'd dropped into the quiet of their secluded table with the finesse of a brick shattering plate glass.

His wife! He wanted to marry her!

She didn't know what to do with herself. She wanted to get up and stride from the room, but that was impossible. She wanted to berate him for playing twisted games. To scratch her skin that felt suddenly too tight to contain all the emotions bursting inside.

It was only as his gaze flickered lower, making her realise the exaggerated rise and fall of her breasts with each constrained breath, that she managed a semblance of control.

He couldn't know that her breasts felt swollen or that beneath her camisole and bra, her nipples were needy points. It was her shameful secret.

'I'm sorry to disappoint you again, Adam.' Her mouth was dry and it took all her willpower not to moisten her lips. 'But I have no intention of marrying.'

She reached for a roll then put it on her plate, realising she wouldn't be able to choke it down.

'I'm sure I can persuade you, Gisèle.'

He lingered on her name and this time his husky voice gentled, turning the syllables into something richly addictive. Like luscious caramel laced with the old brandy her *grand-père* used to savour.

Gisèle blinked, telling herself it was at this man's incredible ego. As if she'd marry a stranger. Yet she had an uneasy feeling her shock was as much about her reaction to him.

Not so ridiculous. He's rich, powerful and intensely attractive, if you like that rough-around-the-edges style. He could probably have most women he wanted.

But not her.

'*I* know you can't persuade me, Adam. But why would you even suggest us marrying? It's so…'

'Convenient? Practical? Advantageous?'

She shook her head. 'It's not any of those things.' Surely even in Australia proposing to a stranger wasn't usual.

Not that he'd proposed. He hadn't asked, merely expressed a wish. As if expecting her to leap at the notion.

'I'm buying an old, respected brand. We both know that while the product is first class, the House of Fontaine is synonymous with your family. The generations upon generations who built it. The glamorous, high-profile family the world knows so well.' He leaned back, eyes holding hers with an intensity she couldn't break. 'You're an intrinsic part of that, Gisèle. Lately you've been the face of the company.'

Actually, a highly paid young woman from the back streets of Marseilles was currently the face of the company. Images of her sensual beauty adorned billboards, glossy magazines and every other form of advertising worldwide.

But, yes, Gisèle had been the company representative at significant events.

'So? You expect me to give up my life as if I'm one more business asset you can buy?'

The gall of him! She'd met plenty of men who considered themselves superior but he was in a class of his own.

'Give up your life? Hardly. Or are you saying you're deeply involved with someone?' He paused as if awaiting a reply. Did he know how unlikely that was? 'In a committed relationship?' Another pause as that damnable eyebrow lifted. 'Or is it just a hot, heavy affair you don't want to give up yet?'

Trust a man to reduce everything to sex!

But he hadn't. His first guess was a committed relationship. If she stopped to think about it that might say something positive about Adam Wilde. But she was in no mood to be positive about this arrogant billionaire.

She gritted her teeth, fighting fury at his spuriously reasonable tone.

'Besides,' he added, 'I'm in the market for a wife. Someone who'll do me proud in public.' He continued as if not noticing her death stare. He should be a pile of smouldering ashes, torched by her fury. 'I want someone poised and perfect. Someone with class who'll never embarrass me or put a foot wrong. Someone who can stand proud in the spotlight. Someone comfortable with the rich and famous, at home in that world.'

Gisèle couldn't believe her ears. 'You think I'm that woman?'

'I know you're that woman. I've seen you in action. Unfazed by reporters, charming yet contained. Elegant, attractive and unflappable.'

At least he hadn't lied by saying she was beautiful.

'You want an excellent PR team if you're worried about your image. Not a wife.'

His mouth twisted at one corner in amusement. 'I know exactly what I want. *You*, Gisèle.'

It was a farce. He didn't know her. Couldn't want *her*.

'I'm not for sale.' Still he said nothing, merely surveyed her with that irritating half-smile. 'I'm not a company asset, included in the contract.'

She reached for her water and took a sip, then another. If it weren't for the many people relying on this deal, she'd leave now. But she had a duty to them. And her family.

'It's nice you think so highly of me.' Nice! It was paternalistic and infuriating. It made her blood boil. 'But as a marriage isn't going to happen, let's return to business and discuss the contract instead.'

A smile was beyond her. Instead she picked up her cutlery and focused on loading vegetables onto her fork.

'Sadly, I see no point.'

She looked up to see him drop his napkin onto the table and fold his arms. The gesture emphasised the breadth of his chest. More like a builder's labourer than a businessman, but according to her research he'd started out working all sorts of jobs, including on building sites.

He wants you to ask why there's no point discussing it.

For thirty seconds she kept silent, not wanting to give him what he expected.

But this isn't about you. It's about the company and everyone employed there.

'No point? You're happy to proceed with the contract as it stands?'

'I've changed my mind. I won't acquire the House of Fontaine. Not without you.'

He couldn't be serious.

He couldn't be...

The fine hairs at her nape rose and she shivered, looking into eyes as cold as a frost-bound alpine lake.

'You actually mean it.' Her voice sounded brittle, but maybe that was because of the blood rushing in her ears, impairing her hearing.

'One thing you'll learn about me, Gisèle, is that I always say what I mean. I'm a straightforward man.'

A deliberately outrageous, devious, egotistical man.

She felt as if the floor of the exclusive restaurant had opened up beneath her and she was in freefall, like Alice in that book her mother had read to her as a little girl.

If only she could wake up to discover this was a bad dream.

She surveyed the luxurious restaurant, almost hoping she was having some strange hallucination. But the murmur of contented voices, the chink of glass and cutlery, the glide of soft-footed wait staff between the tables was all as it should be. The only anomaly was here, where Adam Wilde demanded the impossible.

'You won't find me ungenerous,' he said as if she'd actually agreed. 'There's more than enough money to keep you in the style to which you're accustomed, far more in fact.'

Gisèle was bereft of words. Bad enough he thought her a well-dressed, well-mannered doll he could trot out in public. He added insult to injury by assuming she wanted his money.

The Fontaines had grown wealthy but she'd always worked hard, as much if not more than her colleagues. Besides, lately she and Julien had ploughed most of their personal funds into propping up the company.

'It's not a question of money, Mr Wilde.'

'Ah, now I've offended you. It's Adam, please.'

Gisèle inhaled sharply. Was it possible he hadn't meant to insult her? That he considered her a pawn to be played as it suited him, yet hadn't understood how that felt?

She was no sacrificial lamb. She was a woman with a life and plans of her own.

'I'm afraid you have an unrealistic picture of me.' She couldn't bring herself to use his name. She was too furious, too shocked. 'I'm sure there are plenty of women who present well in public and who'd be eager to take up your offer.'

He shook his head. 'But they're not you, Gisèle. You're the one I want.'

She loathed his arrogance. Almost as much as she hated the part of her, deep inside, that clenched with a dark, inexplicable excitement at the sound of his deep voice saying he wanted her.

Was she so sexually deprived she found that thrilling? It was clear from his bland expression, and his words, that he wasn't speaking sexually. He wanted her at his side in public, the face of Fontaine's, an upmarket accessory.

He had no interest in her personally, despite the deliciously rough edge to his voice when he talked about wanting her. It was a paper marriage he contemplated. A union that looked good in public, but in private she guessed he'd satisfy his other needs with a string of sexy women.

For all the images of him looking severe and businesslike, her research had produced as many of him emerging from famous restaurants and clubs with a range of sultry women snuggled close.

And once in a grainy, long-distance shot, he'd been captured in the shallows of a tropical beach. His companion wore a string bikini and he'd been magnificently bare to the water-line at his hips. The image of his honed, muscled frame, his head bent towards the lithe redhead in his arms, was branded in Gisèle's memory.

No doubt he'd continue pursuing sexual intimacy wherever and whenever took his fancy. He wouldn't turn to a convenient wife for that.

Gisèle *couldn't* be attracted to a man like him. She was stressed, worried about Julien and the company. Her reactions were all out of place.

'Tell me what you're thinking.'

She looked up to find his eyes on her. 'Sorry?'

'You're flushed and your eyes are shining. You look different.'

'Perhaps I'm searching for a polite way to convince you I mean what I say.'

'No need to be polite with me. Feel free to let rip. I want to know what you're thinking.' His gaze was steady, expression unchanged, but his deep voice again held that husky edge that burred along her nerves.

Gisèle folded her hands, resisting the temptation to tell him exactly what she thought of him. It would be momentarily satisfying but too many lives depended on this deal.

'I'm happy to negotiate an arrangement to represent the company for a time. I can accompany you to launches and so forth.' She ignored the shiver of warning rippling down her backbone at the idea of spending time with this man. 'We can amend the contract—'

'That's not enough.' He leaned closer and a drift of subtle scent reached her. Something rich, dark and wholly male. Yet despite her training she couldn't place it. 'It's marriage or nothing, Gisèle.'

'If you take time to think—'

'I have thought. That's why I'm meeting you alone. I assumed you'd prefer we settled this between ourselves.'

This was his attempt at consideration? Suggesting, no, *demanding* marriage in a public restaurant, within half an hour of meeting her? Maybe even *he* baulked at the thought of inserting that particular clause in a commercial contract.

Gisèle struggled to squash a rising tide of laughter, fearing that if she let rip, as he put it, she wouldn't be able to stop.

'That's the deal.' His tone was uncompromising. 'Take it or leave it.'

Her amusement died instantly. There was nothing to laugh at. Only herself for thinking today's meeting would be straightforward. She'd even assumed she might persuade him to guarantee employment for the staff. How naïve she'd been.

Marrying a stranger was impossible. She couldn't do it. But the alternative, sending him packing then watching everything her family had built crumble, was equally impossible.

Her mind blanked. She couldn't think, couldn't plan.

'How long before you need an answer?'

She couldn't believe the words emerging from her mouth but a delaying tactic was good. She needed time to think.

'Before the end of the meal.'

He didn't even have the decency to look smug that he'd put her in this degrading position. They both knew the House of Fontaine urgently needed a saviour.

That more than anything stung.

Fury pierced her brain fog. Her spine stiffened, her chin lifted as she met that moss green stare. Not moss but pond scum, she amended. Slime.

'You spoke as if you intend to represent the company publicly, since you want me at your side.' She didn't wait for him to speak. 'So I need to tell you that while you might be accustomed to making unreasonable demands elsewhere, in my world courtesy and common decency are considered indispensable. It's totally unreasonable to throw out such a demand to satisfy a whim. And to reinforce the fact that you think you have me over a barrel.'

Surprisingly Adam Wilde didn't look annoyed at her outburst. The glint in his eyes looked almost appreciative and this time his smile lifted both corners of his mouth, turning him from saturnine to smack-in-the-chest sexy.

'I knew you were the woman I needed, Gisèle. You've just proved it.'

She goggled. 'Were you...*testing* me?' Her voice was hoarse.

He shrugged. 'Only a little.'

She sank back in her seat, her bunched shoulders easing down as her heart gradually stopped thundering and slowed to something like its normal rhythm. Relief stirred.

It had been a test.

He hadn't meant it!

'I'll give you until tomorrow to agree.'

CHAPTER THREE

ADAM SAUNTERED ALONG the narrow street between old buildings that rose several stories.

Early as it was, there was plenty of bustle. Nice's flower markets were in full swing, buckets of blooms vivid against the cobblestones. Awnings sheltered displays of glossy fruit and vegetables too, prices chalked on small blackboards. Trade was brisk.

He felt that briskness himself though he refused to hurry to the rendezvous. He was eager to cement this deal but arriving early would reveal his keenness. He was too savvy to give Gisèle any option but to agree to his terms.

Gisèle. He felt that familiar clench deep in his body. The flare of heat that had ignited when he'd first seen her in that press conference recording.

He'd felt it again yesterday, entering the restaurant she'd chosen for the meeting. It wasn't the venue that had impressed him or the delicious meal. It was Gisèle Fontaine.

Right up to the moment he walked into the hotel he'd told himself he had the option not to proceed. He'd acquire her company since it fitted his requirements exactly. But as to the other, acquiring her as his wife, he hadn't finally decided. It wasn't as if he *needed* to marry.

But he'd known as he crossed the room towards her that his instinctive decision was the right one.

When she'd parried his deliberately challenging conversation, his certainty had grown.

Her attempt to win a concession for her staff had aroused admiration.

By the time she'd lifted her chin and lectured him on manners he'd been ablaze with impatience for her.

Marrying her was one of his most inspired ideas.

She was exactly what he required. In fact she was more. It wasn't just his head telling him she had the qualities he sought. She'd lit a fire in his belly, in his groin, that refused to be quenched.

He wanted her, as a business asset and as a woman.

Adam couldn't recall the last time he'd had such an all-consuming response to a woman. Insta-lust had been familiar in his youth but these days he was far more discriminating.

Gisèle attracted him on so many levels. She was a rarity. Maybe that's why he hadn't been able to get her out of his head. His wayward libido had latched onto her words about him having her over a barrel.

It didn't matter that she was talking about business. All he could think about was Gisèle, bending forward while he stood behind her, lifting her straight skirt to her hips, spreading her long legs and losing himself in her velvet warmth until she screamed his name, pulsing out her pleasure until he climaxed too.

His step faltered and he paused on the pretext of looking at a shop, allowing his body time to cool. He couldn't walk stiff-legged and aroused to their meeting.

He forced his mind from thoughts of carnal pleasure. And the satisfaction he anticipated when Gisèle capitulated.

It took a while, but focus and self-control were second nature. They were the basis of his success. Those and bloody hard work. And a determination not to be put down by anyone.

He made himself register the warmth of the sun on his shoulders, inhaled the cocktail of smells, damp cobbles, something sweet and a motorbike's acrid exhaust. He'd spent so much time in board rooms and offices, it felt liberating to dawdle along a street during business hours, absorbing the sights and smells.

He'd stopped before a soap shop. Crates supported an artistic display of soaps, some embedded with leaves, some with lavender. Another, judging by the image pressed into it, with honey.

He thought of the House of Fontaine, with its scents and lotions. He imagined his mother's face when he told her he'd acquired it. Her thrill and pride. Her excitement.

Through those tough years after his dad's death, when there was never enough money and his mum worked herself to the bone juggling underpaid jobs, her one treat had been an occasional Saturday off.

She'd take him and his sister into the city with a packed lunch, to the big department store to window shop. Occasionally one of the chic women would do her makeup for free and it was always with Fontaine products. The embossed F entwined with a lavender sprig on those gold bottle tops always made him think of his mum's smile. On those days it seemed as if, for a short time, the weight of worry lifted from her shoulders.

Angela, his sister, still bought Fontaine products for her on Mothers' Day.

Looking at it that way, it was remarkable he'd even bothered to consider acquiring any company other than the House of Fontaine.

Except Adam wasn't given to sentiment. Business was business, to be pursued with rigour and hard logic. He'd never consider acquiring Fontaine's unless he knew he could turn it into something bigger and more successful—a sound return on his investment.

But it wasn't a done deal yet. Perhaps that was why he'd had disturbed dreams, because he knew what he wanted but hadn't yet secured it.

He snapped straighter and resumed his walk, his stride lengthening. It was time to seal this bargain.

She was seated at an outdoor table in a corner of a small square. He'd left the location to her and had again been surprised. He'd expected some chic establishment.

Maybe she preferred the illusion of freedom that came from being outside. But Gisèle was a smart woman. She knew she only had one choice.

Her eyes were on a boy with a red shirt running around a fountain, but Adam doubted she really noticed him. Her brows were drawn down in concentration as she twisted a glass of water round and around.

An unfamiliar sensation fluttered through Adam's chest.

He couldn't be having second thoughts. Ruthlessness was necessary for success. He wanted her company for the profits it would make under his leadership and for the prestige. He wanted her as visible proof that he'd climbed the dizzy heights of social success, and for himself. He'd ensure she didn't lose out from their bargain.

Gisèle stopped twisting the glass, instead running her fingers up then down its length. Every muscle tightened as Adam imagined her hand on him.

Oh, yes, he *definitely* wanted her for himself.

He was digging her and her brother out of a hole, saving their precious company rather than allowing it to be taken over by others and possibly broken up. She'd find him extremely generous. She wasn't selling herself into penury.

Besides, the choice was hers. She could say no.

Except he refused to consider that option.

He marched across the cobblestones, seeing the moment she recognised him and sat straighter, uncrossing her legs and pushing her shoulders back.

One day she'd welcome his approach instead of looking like a soldier preparing to face the enemy. He had a lot of catching up to do but he'd enjoy the challenge.

In high heels, a trouser suit of lilac-grey that complemented her eyes, and another sleek camisole peeping between the lapels, she made his pulse thrum. Her only jewellery were tiny golden earrings and a fine chain with a delicate golden flower that rested in the hollow of her collarbone, emphasising her slender elegance. She turned corporate chic from dull to enticing.

'Gisèle, you're looking charming.'

Her mouth flattened as if his compliment displeased her. She didn't like compliments? Or maybe not ones about her appearance.

'Adam. You look well-rested. Perhaps France agrees with you.'

'I'm sure it does.'

Despite the fractured dreams, he'd woken feeling satisfied with his progress. He'd taken a long run, followed by a hearty breakfast and a conference call to Australia.

His satisfaction dimmed, though, as Gisèle surveyed him. Unlike yesterday, her gaze was openly assessing, trailing from his scalp, over his shoulders and torso, down his legs. He felt that grazing stare like a touch, like fire that ignited under a lover's caress, bringing him to the brink of arousal in mere moments.

Yet there was no softening in her expression, no approval. As if he left her cold and uninterested.

'Please, take a seat.'

She was as gracious as a queen entertaining a stranger. Not like a woman greeting the man who would single-handedly save her business.

The man who intended to marry her.

For a bone-searing moment he actually wondered if he'd been mistaken yesterday, believing she was sexually interested, despite her attempts to hide it.

Then he saw the rogue shimmer of awareness in her eyes as they met his.

Relief punched him. He dropped into the chair beside her, surprised at how disturbed he'd been by the thought his attraction was one-sided. She felt it all right but didn't want to show it. He admired her for that.

Adam was tired of over-eager women. Someone who made him work for what he wanted, as long as she ultimately wanted him too, was a refreshing change.

They ordered coffee and croissants that smelled like they'd just come from the oven, and it struck him that there was much to be said for doing business at an outdoor café on the French Riviera.

'I've thought about your suggestion.' Gisèle sipped her coffee.

'Suggestion?'

'Marriage.'

It hadn't been a suggestion but an ultimatum and they both knew it.

He reached for his cup as if he wasn't eager for her answer. But there could only *be* one answer.

Adam waited, letting her fill the silence. He sipped his coffee, mentally ranking it below what he got in Australia. Angela, his sister, accused him of turning into a coffee snob, but the flaky pastry more than made up for it.

'I had the impression you're after a partner...' Partner, not wife, he noted. Why did she shy away from the word? 'Who's posh. *Really* posh. So you need to know I'm no aristocrat. The Fontaines are working-class stock. I suggest you widen your search.'

Adam chewed the buttery croissant. Gisèle still wasn't ready to accept his terms. He was torn between impatience and admiration at her gumption. It had been a very long time since anyone stood firmly in the way of him getting what he wanted. She was no pushover.

More and more he liked what he discovered.

'You misunderstand. I'm not interested in a title. But wasn't your grandmother a countess? And I thought a Russian princess married into the family last century.'

Blue eyes met his with a stare sharp enough to abrade skin. His flesh tingled and he repressed a smile. A reaction like that from this contained woman was a victory in itself.

It made him wonder how it would be if she stopped bottling up her emotions and allowed them free rein. He looked forward to it.

She shrugged. 'My great-grandmother was penniless but born to a title in a country where they weren't so rare. As for the Russian princess, she married into another branch of the family.'

Gravely he nodded. 'Thank you for the clarification. As I said, titles don't interest me. People do. You have the qualities I want in a wife.' He watched that mask of calm conceal her thoughts. 'So, Gisèle, what's your answer? My legal team is standing by, waiting for me to tell them whether to proceed with the takeover.'

She stared across the square as if lost in thought. 'If I were to consider your suggestion, I'd have conditions.'

Naturally. He was learning this woman didn't give up easily. Her tenacity made him wonder about those poor decisions that had crippled the company. Had she been too headstrong to listen to advice? That didn't sit with what he was learning about her. Maybe the advice she'd received had been flawed.

'I'm listening.'

She turned and there was steel in her gaze. 'First there needs to be job security for all Fontaine staff.' She raised a hand as if expecting him to interrupt. 'I understand your concerns about underperformance, but I want it written into any contract that the current rules will apply.'

'Go on.'

She swallowed, the jerky movement revealing her vulnerability. Adam leaned closer, hit by a wish that they could begin their relationship, not as adversaries but as… What? Colleagues? Lovers?

'My brother, Julien, has worked hard for the company. It's

his life.' When Adam didn't say anything she continued. 'I'm asking you to keep him in a senior management position.'

'To save his pride?'

Gisèle flinched, her mouth tightening. 'It's not about pride, but belonging and caring. He's put his heart and soul into the company. No one knows it better.'

'Yet he stepped aside as CEO and let you act in his stead. I understand he hasn't been to executive meetings for some time.'

The one thing Adam had found annoying and intriguing was his team's inability to access internal company gossip about the siblings. As if loyalty to the Fontaines were inbred into its employees.

No one apart from the press had wanted to speculate on Julien Fontaine's absence yet he'd dropped completely off the radar.

Adam's imagination had run the gamut of explanations from boredom with working for a living, to a breakdown, or an exciting love affair. His experience of people who'd inherited a successful family business was that they rarely had the stamina to succeed.

One intriguing thing about the Fontaine siblings in recent years was their ability to keep much of their private lives private.

It was remarkable considering the hype that had surrounded the family when they were young. At one stage they, and their parents, had been in the press every week. Adam's researchers had uncovered so many media reports it was clear they'd once rivalled European royals and rock stars for notoriety.

Gisèle interrupted his thoughts. 'I assure you Julien's committed and capable. Taking time off work isn't unheard of, you know.'

It was when you were the CEO, but Adam wouldn't quibble. If taking on the other Fontaine and putting him somewhere for a short time where he couldn't do any harm was the price of getting what he wanted, he'd consider it.

'And you, Gisèle? Do you want to work in the company still?'

'You mean apart from being used for photo opportunities?'

She didn't hide her dismissive tone. Adam saw that as progress—her response was genuine, not what she thought he'd like to hear.

Eventually she continued. 'It depends on your requirements. If you want people to believe we're living together I'll need to live where you do. Do you plan to settle in France?'

Still she couldn't bring herself to use the word *marry*. It niggled, but he knew he had no right to be annoyed given how little time and choice he'd given her.

'For the foreseeable future, with occasional trips to Australia and elsewhere. Is that a yes? You do want to work?'

Her eyes rounded. 'Of course I want to work. I have a career I enjoy.'

'There are many people who don't need to work and enjoy a life of leisure—'

'I'm not one.'

'Then we'll find a job for you.'

Gisèle put down the cup she'd been cradling, the chink of cup on saucer loud. 'No need. I'd return to my old one.'

He shook his head. 'It was under your watch, yours and your brother's, that the company failed. You haven't got what it takes to be CEO.'

Impatience brewed. Had she read his interest in her and decided he'd give her whatever she wanted? A chance to ruin the company a second time? She couldn't believe him so foolish.

Surprisingly she didn't look insulted or argumentative. She merely angled her head as if assessing a puzzle. 'Not the CEO role. My job as head of the ethical sustainability unit. I established it and I'd like to continue its work.'

For the first time this morning, no, make that the first time in years, Adam felt underprepared and taken by surprise.

So much for his satisfaction with the report from his acquisitions team. His researchers had missed vital information. Fontaine's advances in ethical research were part of the reason he'd been attracted to the takeover. He'd known Gisèle had worked in the area but imagined her in a minor position, perhaps as a glorified trainee.

But her position hadn't been a sinecure because of her family connection. She really *had* contributed.

He sat back, annoyance at his ignorance vying with excitement. Each revelation about this woman only pleased him more. Even her determination to wrest concessions from him increased his respect.

'You have a problem with me working in a serious job?'

'None at all. So, those are your stipulations? An agreement to follow existing procedure for underperformance, a job for your brother and yourself?'

Her bright gaze held his. He sensed her wariness.

Of course she was wary. But when she knew him better she'd discover the benefits of his proposition. He looked forward to those benefits enormously. His mouth curved in anticipation.

She looked away. 'There's one more thing.'

Her chin tilted higher, leaving him with the impression she was nervous and determined not to show it. He scrutinised her, intrigued. 'Go on.'

She turned and met his stare, her face perfectly composed. Which meant she hid something she didn't want him to read. Every sense went on alert. This, he guessed, meant as much if not more than her other requests.

'If I agree to marry, it would need to appear to everyone that it's a real marriage.'

'It *will* be a real marriage. It would be legally binding and I'll expect you to sign a prenuptial contract.'

She shook her head. 'You know what I mean. If we go to the town hall next week and marry, no one will believe it's anything but a convenient business deal. They won't take it seriously. I assume that's not what you want.'

Adam hadn't given much thought to the logistics of the wedding. He'd concentrated on its benefits. Acquiring the company and having Gisèle on his arm in public would satisfy his immediate requirements.

As for his growing physical needs, he looked forward to pursuing those in private.

But it was natural she wouldn't want to be seen as simply part of the takeover, or as a sharp-eyed gold-digger who'd latched on to him for his wealth. Feminine pride meant she wanted the world to believe she'd conquered the man who'd bought the family company.

'You want to pretend to be in love?'

He'd enjoy having her cosying up to him. It would provide ample opportunity to break down those barriers she erected around herself. Excitement stirred. He had every intention of making this a real marriage.

'Unless you *want* people to believe you bought me as a company asset.' Her eyes narrowed. 'Or because you need someone to gloss over your rough edges at society events.'

His rough edges? He had plenty of those. Usually only his detractors mentioned them and not in his presence. Gisèle used them as a bargaining chip with the insouciance of someone who believed they held a winning hand.

He'd underestimated her and that was rare.

'I don't give a damn about my rough edges. People can take me as they find me.'

But it was intriguing she'd latched onto the fact he'd benefit from having her at his side. Her intuition was good, better than most people's.

Curiosity rose. The more he learned, the less likely it seemed that she could have made so many faulty decisions managing the House of Fontaine. But running a large enterprise was different to running a research unit.

The main thing was that nothing, not her arguments or cool disdain, lessened his determination to have her.

Adam smiled, his mouth curling slowly. His eyes blazed with amusement. She told herself it *couldn't* be approval.

The impact was devastating. Gone was the sharp-eyed tycoon, replaced by a man whose earthy charisma jolted free all her cautious arguments.

Her stomach dropped in freefall. A carnal shiver broke across her skin and she felt a melting between her thighs as if her sex turned to hot butter under that glint of sexual interest.

Or was it appreciation?

Either was problematic. She didn't want to be appreciated by this man. Didn't want him attracted. She breathed out, trying to find her equilibrium as her hands knotted.

You don't like him.

You despise him.

You can't be attracted to him.

Of course she wasn't. Just as she was *not* fantasising about how those big square hands would feel on her breasts. Or whether those sturdy thighs were as iron hard as they looked. What would it be like to sit astride—?

No, no, no. Focus!

'No one would believe the marriage real if it happened too fast. It would be obvious it's a business strategy. Is that what you want?'

Gisèle held her breath, willing him to deny it.

Finally he shook his head the tiniest fraction and a sliver of hope pierced her frozen lungs.

Delay would give her time to come up with an alternative, because being married to a rapacious brute who believed he had the right to mess with people's lives was impossible. Maybe, given time, he'd change his mind. When he got to know her and realised she wouldn't pander to his massive ego. Yet she had to proceed carefully, lest he withdraw the funding that would save Fontaine's.

He looked thoughtful. 'You want a public wooing, is that it?'

'I'll settle for a period of public amity as if we're getting acquainted. Unless you want us to be in the news for all the wrong reasons.'

'You're right,' he said finally. 'Taking over the company will require some time anyway. But…' He fixed her with a penetrating gaze that to Gisèle's alarm seemed to read her like a book. 'We'll sign a separate contract between us, spelling out our obligations. What you'll gain on the marriage—you'll find I can be generous. And there'll be a penalty if you renege after signing.'

She repressed a dismayed gasp. She felt cornered, which was exactly what he wanted. He was even more ruthless than she'd heard, and devious. No wonder he was so successful.

'You don't trust my word?'

He was too clever. Of course he realised she'd be looking for some way out of the deal.

'It's not personal, sweetheart.' Gisèle's pulse thudded at the casual endearment, though she knew it meant nothing. 'The days of doing deals on a handshake are over. I don't leave anything to chance in business.'

There it was, spelt out clearly. A business marriage. Despite everything, relief rippled through her and her high shoulders dropped a little as her tension eased. If worse came to worst and she had to go through with this, at least it was only a business arrangement. There'd be nothing…personal between them.

'If you're drawing up a contract, I want it spelt out that you won't let anyone learn it's a marriage of convenience. I insist on it.'

'Not even your brother?'

Gisèle's heart stopped for a second. 'Not even Julien. This is just between us.'

That was the most important condition of all. She couldn't allow Julien to realise she'd sacrificed herself. He already felt guilty over the company, the weight wearing him down. Which he didn't need if he were to make a full recovery.

Nothing mattered more than that.

The company they loved would be saved. Julien would still work there and once Adam Wilde saw him in action, he'd revise his negativity and give him a key role. Julien would have purpose and his pride and, hopefully, his health.

Beside that, the inconvenience to her didn't matter. She'd work in the area she enjoyed. She'd have to keep Adam Wilde company in public but surely eventually familiarity would obliterate the fizz in her blood she felt around him.

Even if they lived under the same roof, it would be somewhere large enough to give them both privacy. He didn't want her for herself. He saw her as a company asset.

She'd be a trophy, not a real wife.

The idea was anathema. She'd strived all her life to establish a sense of self-worth in a world that had judged her to be less when compared with her glamorous parents. Then she'd struggled to earn respect for her work and abilities.

This man swept that aside as unimportant. Gisèle had never truly hated anyone but she came close to hating the smug Australian.

At least she wasn't in a relationship so there would be no complications explaining her sudden faux relationship. She couldn't even remember the last time she'd dated.

She'd get through this and when Adam moved onto his next project, no doubt he'd be as ready as she to divorce.

He stretched his legs, lounging as if he didn't have a care in the world. But the intent glitter in those mesmerising eyes betrayed that he was no idle tourist.

'I can live with that stipulation,' he murmured. 'You have a bargain. I'll get my team onto the paperwork immediately.'

Gisèle thrust down dismay. Despite the open-air setting she felt claustrophobic. But she couldn't dwell on that. She'd won the concessions she needed. That had to be enough.

'I look forward to reading it.' She'd be searching for loopholes.

'In the meantime, I'll take you to lunch.' His smile had a hungry quality that made her shiver. 'I feel like celebrating our engagement.'

CHAPTER FOUR

CELEBRATING WITH HIM was the last thing Gisèle wanted.

Adam knew it from the way she stilled and the wide pupils darkening her eyes. That hint of fragility snagged his conscience, until he reminded himself she could walk away from the deal if it really bothered her. She wouldn't be a pauper even if the family company folded.

Apart from those tiny signs, her sangfroid was impeccable.

A lesser woman would have found an excuse to be alone. Gisèle did no such thing. She inclined her head, her expression one of calm confidence. 'As you wish.'

As if she bestowed a favour. As if it were she, not he, who'd direct what happened next.

He recalled the articles calling her Ice Queen, partly because she kept her sex life so private the media could find no evidence of a long-term lover. But more often, Adam suspected, because of her self-possession.

No matter what fate or bossy tycoons threw at her, she remained unperturbed.

Except Adam sensed the emotions she reined in. A dispassionate, uncaring woman wouldn't have pleaded for her workforce or her brother.

Not so much icy, he decided, as queenly.

He could imagine Gisèle in an earlier time with a sparkling diadem on her blonde head, her slender neck rising proudly from a jewel-studded gown of rich velvet. Courtiers would bow as she entered her throne room.

Adam's mouth firmed as he blanked the image. He was the last man in the world to indulge in bizarre fantasies. He'd spent his life facing the gritty realities of this world.

Yet the image of his bride-to-be as a medieval queen lingered.

He blamed Angela and the thick historical paperback she'd pressed on him before he left Sydney. *'Take time out,'* she'd said. *'Unwind.'* To please the little sister who fretted about his work-life balance, he'd spent several hours on the flight reading it.

Anger stirred. At himself for letting his mind drift into useless imaginings when he had significant issues to finalise. And at Gisèle for her ability to distract him.

'Excellent.' He stood. 'Let's go, shall we?'

The trip to the harbour was completed in silence in the back of a limo since her high heels weren't meant for walking any distance. Adam used the time to shoot off messages to his minions. By the time they walked onto the marina his brief bad humour had lifted.

Because he was close to wrapping this up.

He assured himself it had nothing to do with the blaze of admiration in his companion's eyes as she took in the large, classic yacht before them. He didn't need anyone's approval. In fact, he'd built his success in the face of closed ranks from the establishment who'd seen him as an outsider, never one of them.

'You enjoy sailing?' He paused on the boardwalk, heat skirling low in his abdomen as he watched her mouth soften.

What other woman had ever distracted him so easily?

He shoved the disturbing thought aside. His desire for Gisèle, and the sexual relationship he anticipated with her, were welcome bonuses. But he'd never allow anyone to deflect him from his purpose. His single-minded focus remained one of the reasons for his phenomenal success.

'I do enjoy it. Julien and I used to go out when we were young. Some of our friends have yachts. How about you?'

Adam shook his head. 'I didn't set foot on one until I'd made my first few million. I didn't have the time.'

Misty blue eyes locked on his. 'You were too busy wheeling and dealing to take time off?'

Her tone was light but there was an undercurrent he couldn't identify. Disapproval?

Adam shrugged. 'It takes a lot of wheeling and dealing to build success from nothing.' He wasn't ashamed of his work ethic. 'Not everyone has a family legacy to help them on their way.'

Not like the Fontaines.

She didn't flinch. 'Julien and I were extremely lucky.'

He liked that she didn't apologise for that luck.

'Plus I had no opportunity to go yachting in the early days.'

A furrow appeared between her eyebrows. 'Yet Sydney is home to the famous Sydney to Hobart Yacht Race.'

Adam inclined his head, pleased that her research on him, like his on her, had gaps. 'I wasn't born in Sydney. I grew up in a smaller, inland town.'

'Ah, no yachts there.'

'No, though some of the boys at the exclusive boarding school down the road came from families who owned yachts. They could afford overseas skiing holidays too, and other things beyond the means of us working-class kids.'

Bright eyes surveyed him. 'You resented that.' She made it a statement, not a question. As if she knew him.

His nape tightened. She thought she could read him so easily?

'Actually, no. I played weekend football with some of them. I suspect a few would have given up all the expensive treats for a decent home life.'

The sort of home life he'd had. His family had been poor but there'd been plenty of affection and support. He wasn't shallow enough to disregard that.

'I've never resented anyone for having something I don't.'

Adam wasn't in the habit of explaining himself but this was the woman he intended to marry. Not that he expected her to become his confidante, but things would go easier if they understood each other better. 'What I can't abide are people who think they're better because they're rich or were born to privilege.'

Gisèle's jaw angled up. 'Yet you want to marry me.'

Adam stepped closer, watching her swallow as her gaze held his. She didn't retreat, just lifted those proud eyebrows higher.

Queenly. Proud. Challenging.

Desire threaded his body, arrowing low. His fingers flexed and he shoved them into his trouser pockets.

'You're saying I've made a mistake about you, Gisèle? That you're a secret snob? That wasn't my assessment and I saw no evidence of it in the investigators' report.'

It had sounded as if she were as much at home with the farmers who grew the flowers used in the family perfume distillery as among the wealthy.

Now she reacted.

'You had me *investigated*?' Her voice rose and the tendons in her neck turned rigid as a flush climbed her throat. Then she blinked and shook her head. 'Of course you did. I should have realised.'

Her beautiful mouth was no longer soft and inviting but dragged down at the corners. Her shoulders rose, hunching under her impeccable jacket.

Adam wished he'd let sleeping dogs lie.

He lived in a world where due diligence often included the use of private investigators to ferret out weaknesses and secrets. It seemed Gisèle, despite her privileged upbringing, wasn't so sanguine about such practices.

He frowned, annoyed that he'd pushed the point. Was he being deliberately crass, hoping to provoke an emotional response?

He felt like a blundering fool who'd told a child Santa Claus didn't exist.

Except Gisèle was no child. Already she stood straighter, that small, perfect smile that didn't reach her eyes curving her lips.

'Well,' she murmured in a composed voice with just a hint of huskiness. 'That will save a lot of getting-to-know-you conversation.'

Maybe he *was* losing his edge, for he hated that dismissive smile. As he disliked her insouciant response, as if she didn't care that he'd invaded her privacy. He'd rather she argued or objected as she had before, fighting her corner for Fontaine's employees.

How was it that he felt wrong-footed when twenty minutes earlier he'd been congratulating himself on his success?

Adam tucked away his disgruntlement. He couldn't fault her for being annoyed or wanting to keep her distance. He'd pushed her into a situation she still barely accepted. It was up to him to show her that, despite her misgivings, she'd find plenty of benefits in their marriage.

Which meant reining in the ruthless corporate shark.

And, what? Charming her into compliance? You're out of practice, mate. Can you even remember how?

Since his successes became widely reported he'd barely had to exert himself to win any woman. They tended to offer themselves.

But Gisèle's not impressed by your success, is she?

Acquiring, and pleasing, a wife was going to be more of a challenge than he'd anticipated.

The trip to Adam's rented villa at Cap Ferrat was one of the strangest Gisèle had experienced.

She didn't like this man on principle. His marriage demand was preposterous. Provoking. Insulting!

Adam Wilde believed she and Julien took their family legacy for granted. As if they hadn't worked all their lives to contribute to it!

Yet, despite her determination to loathe the Australian's swaggering confidence, his prejudices and assumption he'd get his own way, she found herself relaxing and forgetting, for short periods, to be incensed.

It had started when, searching for an uncontentious topic so the trip along the coast didn't pass in stultifying silence, she'd asked about the yacht. He'd admitted he hadn't a clue about sailing. He'd hired the yacht, like the villa to which they were heading. Then he'd asked one of the crisply uniformed crew to take them on a tour.

Remembering his desire to celebrate their so-called engagement, Gisèle had instead expected him to insist on opening champagne and spend the time discussing plans for their farce of a marriage.

It was a relief to find herself inspecting the large yacht, even if Adam insisted on accompanying her.

She should have found his presence claustrophobic. Yet his curiosity about the vessel was...engaging.

She'd assumed that like many people who believed themselves important, Adam Wilde wouldn't admit to ignorance on any subject. Instead he peppered the crew member with questions that showed he might be ignorant about sailing, but had an enquiring mind and a genuine interest in discovering more.

It didn't absolve him from being a manipulative bully but it was hard to stay furious, especially when an admission of an intermittent problem with the motor led to him and their guide, peering at the engine, bonding over mechanics.

Adam had caught her stare and the corner of his mouth lifted, eyes amused as he shrugged. 'Men and engines, eh? It's a cliché but in my case it's true. I spent so many hours coaxing clapped out old motors to work that along the way I found I enjoy it.'

Gisèle had been going to ask him about that when he straightened. She was too slow, disarmed by the warmth of that half-smile that made his eyes crinkle charmingly at the corners and turned him into another man altogether.

Before she could ask her question he apologised for keeping her waiting, thanked the crew member, and suggested they head up to enjoy the view of the coast.

Where was the dangerous corporate raider who'd turned her world inside out? She felt discombobulated.

No wonder he's a force to be reckoned with in the commercial world.

If he kept all his competitors trying and failing to second-guess his moods and intentions, he'd have a natural advantage.

The realisation was a timely reminder as the vessel approached a green finger of land pointing south into the Mediterranean. Saint-Jean-Cap-Ferrat. One of the most exclusive pieces of real estate in the world.

Gisèle had attended a couple of parties here, most recently at the invitation of a tech billionaire who wanted the House of Fontaine to create a new line of cosmetics and personalised perfume for his wife. The first time she'd been a child, arriving with her uber-glamorous parents.

She remembered that day with piercing clarity. The sunlight glittering on an infinity pool looking over the deep blue sea, the tang of fresh mango juice, and inevitable cluster of people around her mother. There'd been a sweet Scandinavian nanny to mind the guests' children. The young woman's eyes had shone with awed excitement when Gisèle's father thanked her for looking after his kids.

Her father had led Gisèle and Julien back to their car, he and their mother laughing as they drove away on that cloudless afternoon.

It was her last memory of her father. He'd died two days later in a car race, the reassuring grasp of his hand around hers, his twinkling smile, gone for ever.

'Gisèle? Is something wrong?'

A gravelled voice broke her thoughts. She blinked and discovered she held the railing in a white-knuckled grip.

'Not at all.'

She turned to find Adam close. Those severe black eyebrows crammed down in a frown and fathomless eyes narrowed on her in a way that made her breath catch.

Because his gaze wasn't just probing. It felt…sympathetic. As if, despite everything, they weren't opponents but were linked by a deeper understanding.

She stared back, transfixed by a feeling this man wasn't the enemy he seemed.

He looked concerned. As if sensing the deep-seated trauma at the loss of her father that she'd never managed to put fully behind her. Because after that, her world had fallen apart.

But Adam Wilde didn't know that. The one skill that had come out of her loss—and it had taken years of painful practice—was the ability to hide emotion. To appear soignée and confident in any situation.

She prayed that ability would allow her to keep the truth about this business deal marriage from her brother.

'You're not seasick?' Adam wasn't convinced.

'On this calm sea?' She gave a huff of laughter as if she hadn't a care in the world. 'Truly, I'm okay. I was just thinking.'

She looked past his shoulder as if taking in the view, noticing a speedboat approaching. Sunlight glinted on its windscreen as it changed direction.

Adam Wilde didn't know her, despite his precious investigators' report. To him she was an asset to acquire then discard when the time was right.

The only way she could disturb him was if she wasn't conveniently at his side as the token Fontaine while he turned her beloved company into something of his own design. But the only way out that she could see was via an inconvenient fatal accident.

A broken laugh that was part silent sob shuddered through her.

She might be desperate, but not that desperate.

She understood the permanency of death and the anguish it created. As if the loss of her parents wasn't enough, her fear for Julien's health compounded that hard-won lesson.

Gisèle pretended to focus on the spectacular view.

They'd stopped opposite a two-storey villa of pale peach. It had a terracotta roof and a white colonnade behind which huge arched windows faced the sea. It looked inviting, secluded in vast gardens, out of sight of other properties. A pool filled the space between the mansion and the sea.

That Adam rented this exquisite place for a short stay, and this superb yacht for occasional use—travelling the twenty kilometres from Nice because he had a whim to sail—reinforced the man's extraordinary wealth.

'What a lovely location,' Gisèle said brightly, collecting her shoes. She'd removed them in consideration for the immaculate wooden deck. Now, at the prospect of putting them on to go ashore with him, her brief delight in the cruise faded.

'I'm glad you approve.' He stepped so close she felt the warmth of his big frame as he moved into her space. She stiffened. 'We could spend time here together.'

'I can't see that's necessary.' She didn't want to be alone with him. Give her crowded squares and busy offices any day. Something about him got under her skin in a way no business rival should.

'But we have a lot to discuss. I want you to fill me in on the company. Plus you want us to give the impression we've fallen for each other. We can only do that by being together.'

He was too close. She took a deep breath and found herself inhaling that elusive scent of his, intriguing and inviting. Immediately her body softened in response. Cedarwood and some deep note. Tonka bean? No, she couldn't place it. Yet the drift of it—warm, masculine and as enticing as fresh honey—sank into her sense receptors.

She'd like to employ whoever made that cologne.

Stop trying to distract yourself! It's not his cologne you're interested in. It's him.

How can that be? He's a brutal, bullying billionaire who doesn't give a toss for anyone but himself.

Yet your body responds when he gets close.

The thought horrified. But there was no denying the zap of tingling energy suffusing her. Threads of heat wove through her limbs, around her breasts and down to tangle in her pelvis.

Gisèle stepped away and found herself against the railing. She swallowed a constriction in her throat.

After a miserable disaster in her teens, she'd decided sexual desire wasn't one of her weaknesses. She was almost impervious to attractive men. Yet standing close to Adam Wilde made her feel hot and heavy in a way that was disturbingly unfamiliar.

'We need to spend time together in *public*. The point is for people to see us together.'

'Precisely.' His voice was a low throb that sounded suspiciously like a purr of satisfaction. Instead of moving back he stepped in, his hand on her upper arm, turning her so they faced each other, side on to the shore. 'That's what we're doing now.'

'If you mean the crew, I don't think—'

'Not the crew. The photographer on the speedboat out to my right. Don't look!'

His breath feathered her hair like a caress and though his hold on her arm was light, she felt its imprint through her jacket.

She didn't look at the speedboat, because strange ripples coursed under her skin, radiating from where he touched her. Her heart did an unfamiliar tumble turn, knocking hard at her ribs.

How could she worry about a photographer when every instinct told her Adam Wilde was far more dangerous to her well-being?

Fear at her unheralded reactions made her voice harsh. 'I've already seen the boat. How do you know there's a photographer? No one knows we're here. In Nice we mingled in the crowd. The chances of a photographer being here as we arrive are slim.'

'It didn't just happen.' His mouth was flat. 'You didn't see the paparazzo at the marina? He was staking out the yacht and didn't make much effort to hide the fact he was taking pictures of us.'

Gisèle opened her mouth to protest that he was paranoid, then stopped. She caught another glint of sunlight on glass. The speedboat had pulled up nearby, closer than seemed normal.

Adam Wilde was a phenomenally powerful businessman. His every move was fodder for the press, both in the business and the social pages. Naturally the media wanted to discover why he was in Europe.

Her heart sank. Had they argued on the marina? What had been their body language?

The last thing she needed was for Julien to see images of them arguing. It would make their supposed romance even harder to explain. Already she dreaded lying about it.

'You didn't think to warn me?' She spoke through gritted teeth.

'Would that have helped?' The lift of one supercilious eyebrow was sheer provocation. 'I can feel the tension in you now. The last thing I needed was for the photographer to pick up on that at close range.'

'Hence this show of solicitude.' She nodded towards his hand, still on her arm.

Now she remembered the conversation on the dock. She'd been surprised at how open he'd been about himself. His admission that he'd never been sailing until adulthood. The detail about growing up in a small town. And the revelation that he despised rich people who thought their money made them special. That had obviously been a hot button for him, which made her wonder more than ever about his reasons for pursuing this marriage.

Had he been pandering to her curiosity, hoping any photographs would show her absorbed in his words?

She felt used. He'd duped her. Then she recalled her reaction when he'd admitted to having had her investigated. If the paparazzo had been photographing them there, he couldn't have missed her outrage.

She was torn. Pride made her long to make Adam's takeover of her business and her life as difficult as possible. But love for her brother demanded she play a woman gullible enough to fall for this man, so Julien would believe in their sham marriage.

'What's the matter, Adam? Are you worried any photos taken in Nice might reveal things you'd rather the press didn't see?'

His eyes glittered and his smile acquired a hungry edge that made Gisèle still.

It wasn't the look of a businessman but a hunter, and it stirred something that might have been fear but equally could have been excitement.

'No. As far as the press is concerned it's early days in our relationship. We're getting to know each other. But it would be helpful—to both of us—if they saw something that hinted at the direction our relationship is heading.'

'What?' She tilted her jaw, determined to show she wasn't afraid, despite her dry throat and the fretful rhythm of her pulse. 'Like me signing a fifty-page prenup? I'm sure they'd find that romantic.'

His laugh, a mellow, dark chocolate chuckle, surprised her. She stared at the strong column of his throat and the angle of his jaw as his head tilted back and his amusement spilled around her.

Why couldn't he have a hyena's laugh? Or an ugly honking guffaw?

Why did the sound fall gently around her, inviting her to

join his amusement? For, she realised as their gazes locked, he wasn't laughing at her but himself.

No, no, no! A single positive characteristic didn't outweigh all the negative. Just because he had a sense of humour…

'I like you, Gisèle. You've got gumption.'

Gumption? What she had was a huge problem. Because she was transfixed by the look in his eyes. Liking it far too much.

'Thank you. I think. But it's probably time we went—'

'In a moment. This is a golden opportunity to start our campaign.'

'Campaign?' Gisèle feigned confusion because suddenly her heart was pounding.

'To convince the world we're attracted.'

Then, damn him, his eyes danced, as if he read her breath-lessness.

As if now his amusement was at her, not himself.

'We only met yesterday. No one would believe—'

'We're the only ones who know that for sure. Besides, people believe what they want to believe, especially when it's right before their eyes. A man falling for a beautiful woman.'

Every muscle in Gisèle's body stiffened at the offhand compliment while something in the pit of her stomach curdled.

Did he actually believe she'd fall for that?

She'd grown up with true beauty. She'd had it hammered into her from adolescence that she'd never meet those high standards. As a result she'd spent years striving to acquire the poise and confidence to present herself as stylish and so-phisticated, despite the press and the self-appointed experts so eager to point out her defects.

She opened her mouth to respond when she realised he'd moved, leaning closer.

His fingers brushed her cheek then settled at the back of her neck, warm and heavy. His face closed in on hers and her thoughts frayed.

CHAPTER FIVE

ADAM MOVED CLOSER, drawn by a force far stronger than the need to feed the paparazzi a story.

Drawn by *her*. The complex woman who made no effort to attract him yet whose every word, every look, made him want more than he'd wanted in years.

Desire was a scratching under his flesh, a flame in his belly, a heavy throb as he watched her eyes flash, her mouth tighten then soften with each mood change.

He couldn't define her allure but it was there, strong and vital, like the sparks where his hand touched her skin.

Those lips, wide and sculpted, seemingly innocent in nude lipstick, drew him like a magnet drew metal.

Slowly he lowered his head, anticipating the sweetness of her mouth flowering beneath his. Until a glance at her eyes blasted his excitement. Huge, dark pupils dwarfed her irises, making her look, for a second, stricken.

Because of him? Did she detest him so much?

Warning bells jangled and he was about to pull back. Except her expression changed, eyelids drooping in lazy anticipation and lips parting as she lifted her face, that second of distress vanishing.

He'd never had such conflicting messages from a woman.

Gisèle leaned in, her warm fragrance teasing him, his doubts undermined as her palm settled on his chest. Her fingers spread as if to absorb his thundering heartbeat.

He heard a sigh, the merest waft of air, but it tangled his thoughts and muffled his doubts.

Adam captured her free hand, their fingers curling together. He closed the space between them. But instead of lowering his mouth to hers as he'd intended, he pressed his lips to her forehead, his kiss as chaste as a brother's.

Since when did he do chaste?

Yet his eyes shut as a rush of emotion enveloped him.

Protectiveness?

Curiosity?

Thwarted desire?

All those. Yet, to his surprise, he felt no frustration at denying himself a proper kiss. Even with the promise of her body against his, every bit as seductive as he'd imagined.

He let the moment expand, feeling her soften against him, her breathing slow, and it felt *right*.

The churning rush of arousal in his lower body eased, the urgent thrum in his blood turning to a heavy but steady beat.

Comfort, he realised. That's what this was. More powerful than the intense excitement of a moment ago. Though desire was still there, a permanent undercurrent whenever he was around Gisèle.

Comfort for her, because he'd hated that moment of dark emotion he'd seen in her gaze. He'd wanted to obliterate it.

But, he realised, stunned, comfort for himself too.

How and why, he couldn't say. And that was unacceptable.

He didn't need or want comfort from a woman. He was perfectly content with his life. Perfectly in control.

Abruptly he pulled back, wondering how a chaste kiss on the forehead could upend everything.

Slumbrous eyes, more lavender than blue, blinked and met his. He wanted, he discovered, to wake up to that warm, hazy gaze on a regular basis. He had the weird notion that even the most taxing day would be easier if it started with Gisèle looking at him that way.

But then she gathered herself, her hand sliding from his, those stunning eyes turning gunmetal grey. As if the savvy businesswoman had returned, determined to fight for the company that, he was beginning to realise, meant so much to her.

Adam was grateful when she stepped away. Though his hand at her nape lingered as if he didn't want to end the contact. Once she'd moved from his reach, his palm tingled at the sense memory of her delicate skin against his and he shoved his hand into his pocket.

She turned so any watcher on the motorboat couldn't see her face. Her words were clipped. 'That really wasn't necessary.'

'We'll have to agree to disagree on that, Gisèle.' Adam let his voice drop and linger on her name, watching with satisfaction as her breath hitched. Not so calm, then. 'It was necessary if we're going to make them believe this is the beginning of a grand romance. I was doing you a favour.'

A frown puckered her brow. 'You think a kiss on the forehead romantic?'

He shrugged. 'I didn't want to overplay my hand. That will show there's…tenderness between us.'

A wry laugh greeted his words. 'It's okay. You don't need to explain that you don't actually want to kiss me. I feel the same.'

He was about to correct her then stopped himself. Of course he wanted to kiss her. She knew that. No woman of her age and looks could be so innocent. She was throwing up words as a barrier.

For he knew, with the instinct that came from years of experience, that she wanted his kisses too. Yet for some reason she denied it. Pride? Or because of whatever had made her look lost minutes before?

'Gisèle. Before this goes further—'

'Yes.' She cut across him as no one else dared, except his family. 'Before this goes further I want to make something clear.'

She folded her arms, the image of determination. Adam

forced his gaze up from where her crossed arms emphasised the curve of her breasts.

'Go on. Clarity, by all means.'

Because the last few minutes had confused the hell out of him. He couldn't believe he'd pulled back without enjoying the promise of her tempting lips. Because of some fleeting expression he'd probably imagined.

'No kissing,' she said firmly. 'No touching. Even for the cameras.'

Adam shoved his other hand in his trouser pocket and rocked back on his heels. 'How do you expect to make anyone believe we've fallen in love?'

Gisèle opened her mouth then closed it. 'By being seen together. Sharing meals. That sort of thing.'

'I share meals with my PA. No one's ever assumed there's a budding romance.'

He watched her wrestle with that, surprised at her vehemence. And her naïveté. The only explanation he could think of was that she was frightened. Frightened of him? Not likely when her laser stare threatened to vivisect him.

Frightened of herself?

It was a curious thought, but appealing. If Gisèle worried she was too responsive, seducing her would be so much easier.

'At the least I need to be able to hold your hand or arm. Even that—'

'Okay, we'll go with that.' She nodded as if he'd agreed. 'No touching except on the arm or hand.'

She drew herself up, and despite his superior height looked at him down the length of her superb, aristocratic nose.

He'd like to tell her how her Ice Queen act turned him on. How, the cooler she grew, the hotter he felt at the prospect of melting her reserve. Of claiming her beautiful body for himself. But she'd find out soon enough. He sensed she struggled to maintain that admirable poise and for once he didn't want to smash straight through his opponent's defences.

Gisèle was far more than an opponent. And it would be so much better when *she* came to *him*, instead of fighting every step of the way.

'You drive a hard bargain, Gisèle. It will be tough, convincing the press based on so little. But I enjoy a challenge.'

Her eyes rounded. 'It wasn't meant to be a challenge.'

'Too late, sweetheart.' Adam felt his smile unfurl. 'That's exactly what it is.'

He paused for her to digest that. 'I solemnly promise not to touch you except on the hand or arm. And definitely not to kiss you.' Her high shoulders dropped and her flattened mouth eased. 'Until you ask me.'

'Until you ask me...'

Gisèle shook her head. Words failed her.

As if she'd ever ask him to touch her, much less kiss her! She'd never met anyone so supremely confident. It infuriated her.

But you like it too. It attracts you, doesn't it? The thought of him kissing you, properly, makes you wet between the legs. You were disappointed when he gave you a peck on the forehead.

The truth was shocking. She tried to deny it but she never lied to herself. Better to face facts, no matter how unpalatable, and deal with them.

And it was a fact that, despite the glowing invitation in Adam's glance, he wasn't really attracted. Otherwise he'd have kissed her properly.

She knew some men liked to prove their dominance. Others liked a challenge and still more saw women as trophies to be won, or stepping stones to wealth or business opportunities.

Skeletal fingers rippled down her spine but she ignored the sensation. The past couldn't hurt her any more. She'd turned pain into a learning experience that made her stronger.

Gisèle was silent as she followed Adam to the other end of

the yacht. Catching sight of the speedboat, she stifled stupid embarrassment that their chaste kiss was fodder for the public.

Because for a moment she'd felt a rush of emotion at Adam's caress.

She didn't understand it. She should have hated it. Yet hate had been the last thing she felt.

She'd wanted him to kiss her!

How could that be? She didn't like him.

His unshakable confidence reminded her of her father. Except her father had been a warm, caring man, reckless in the chances he took, but never bombastic or egotistical.

Adam Wilde wasn't like her father.

Yet something about him drew her.

He challenged her. Forced her onto her mettle, not giving any quarter. Perversely she almost enjoyed that. She'd definitely enjoyed seeing his blink of surprise when he discovered she wasn't the airhead he'd initially thought.

But that couldn't explain how he consistently managed to get under her skin and make her *feel*.

'Let me help you.'

Adam had stopped at the top of a ladder. Below a tender waited to take them ashore.

'No, thanks. I can manage.'

She was grateful she'd worn trousers. Imagine the paparazzi photographs if she'd worn a short skirt.

You don't own a short skirt. Your wardrobe is full of tailored business clothes.

Even the casual clothes she wore in private tended to conceal rather than reveal.

Gisèle's foot slipped on a rung but she caught herself.

'Easy there. You're almost down.' His deep voice came from below.

She took the last rungs slowly, holding on to the ladder as she turned. Adam waited for her. With deliberate slowness he reached out and grasped her elbow as if to steady her, his touch warm and reassuring. As if she weren't already perfectly balanced on the small boat.

It was a solicitous gesture, or would seem so to an onlooker. Only she could see the amusement lighting his eyes, making them glow like sunlight dappling water. 'Okay, Gisèle?'

Her immediate thought was that he laughed silently at her expense, because of the boundaries she'd set. Yet now she wasn't sure. Something passed between them and it felt as if he shared a joke *with* her. As if it were the two of them against the world.

If you believe that you've got rocks in your head!

'Fine, thanks.' Gisèle slipped free and moved away to take a seat.

She refused to fall for his charm. She'd met plenty of corporate sharks, focused on winning at all costs. From what she'd seen, Adam Wilde would beat all of them.

Relaxing in his presence wasn't an option. This was business.

A fact borne out when they reached his villa. As soon as she'd taken a seat in a luxurious sitting room, one of his staff arrived with papers. Contracts.

Gisèle forced herself not to flinch as she took them, though everything inside froze at what she held. An agreement to sell her family heritage to a stranger.

So much for the illusion of a tentative bond growing between them.

She fixed her gaze on Adam as his assistant left. 'I'll need to discuss the details with my brother before we sign.'

If she'd expected to discomfort him, she was disappointed. He didn't look in the least perturbed.

'Naturally. But the second document isn't for your brother. It's a private contract between us. I want it signed before you leave. It covers the matters we discussed this morning.'

'This morning? You've had no time—'

He shrugged and, looking up from her seat, Gisèle saw the

leashed energy in his tall frame. Though it wasn't his physical power that daunted her, it was his non-stop drive to achieve what he wanted in the quickest possible time. He was like a force of nature, unstoppable.

The idea would unnerve her if she let it.

'My legal team was on standby. We already had a contract ready for signature. It was easy to insert text to cover your requirements.'

That was what he'd been doing in the back of the limo. She hadn't known whether to be annoyed at the way he'd ignored her while he was busy on the phone or grateful for the respite.

She'd thought she'd have more time to devise an escape plan before signing anything. But he had her where he wanted her. His reputation for ruthless efficiency was well earned.

Gisèle swallowed, tasting hot metal on her tongue. There would be no escape.

Her breath hitched as if someone wrapped a tightening band around her chest. Not someone. *Adam Wilde*.

'Would you like tea or coffee while you read it?'

'Water, thanks.'

Her throat was desert-arid. Besides, it would give him something to do other than tower over her while she read.

As he crossed the room to a drinks cabinet she gave her attention to the documents but her head swam and the words blurred.

Stress.

Lack of sleep.

The knowledge that she was utterly trapped.

But feeling sorry for herself wouldn't help. She drew a deep breath and tried again.

A glass of iced water appeared in her peripheral vision as he put it on the side table.

'Thank you.' She took a sip and felt her momentary wobble dissipate. She would do whatever was necessary for her family and the company.

Adam sank onto a chair opposite her, picking up his copy of the documents. 'Before we go through our private agreement, you might want to check the sales contract.' He flicked through the pages. 'Page fifteen, subsection C covers your request to keep on current staff.'

Gisèle's brow knitted as she read. The new text gave current employees two months' guaranteed employment and specified that performance assessment would occur in that time.

Her slight unsteadiness disappeared instantly. 'Two months isn't enough. And there's nothing to say what sort of assessment process you'll use. Your team could sack everyone after two months.'

She looked up and found him watching her. But she felt no skitter of nerves as before. This wasn't about him and her. This was about her people. She lifted her eyebrows a fraction. 'Twelve months is more appropriate.'

'Impossible. Three.'

'Three is no certainty at all. Eleven months.'

'And if I find dead wood in the workforce? I don't carry underperforming people.'

'You gave your word.'

Didn't that matter? Gisèle waited, sensing his attitude now would give the measure of the man.

'Six months. And my team will work with yours to review the performance assessment processes and improve them.'

'I want that in writing. And that I'll be part of the team reviewing it.'

After a second he nodded. 'Six months, then.'

Is that what he'd intended all along? He'd agreed more easily than she'd anticipated. Gisèle had the unnerving suspicion he was appearing to negotiate but the outcome was already set. She was surprised he'd budged at all. He was reputedly completely without softness. Success was all that mattered.

'And Julien's role in the company?'

Adam found the relevant clause where Julien was given a

senior management role. Her position as head of the ethical sustainability unit was also included. Her tension eased a little.

'I'll have an updated version made and circulated. Meanwhile let's finalise our private business.'

The way he said *private business* made her skin prickle. Gisèle told herself she was too sensitive. This was another addendum to his business agenda, nothing personal.

Which begged the question she'd wondered since he'd blasted into their lives like a flaming comet. 'Why the House of Fontaine?'

'Sorry?'

For a moment, Gisèle fancied she saw something other than confidence in those strong features. 'What drew you to our business? Your holdings are in engineering, construction and logistics. Why acquire a cosmetics company?'

'An *elite* cosmetics company. A world-recognised brand renowned for quality and exclusivity.' Adam shrugged but she sensed his nonchalance masked something else. 'Diversification is useful. Especially when I see a chance to turn a dwindling business into a highly profitable one.'

'Hardly dwindling!'

'Poorly managed then.'

His stare challenged her to disagree. But what was the point? Some major errors at exactly the wrong time had undone them.

'You're just in it for the profit?'

'I wouldn't take on a business unless I knew I could make a profit from it.'

Which didn't answer her question. Gisèle sensed his prevarication was significant. *Elite*, he'd said. Is that what drew him? Did he want the company as proof of success on another level?

Surely not. Everyone knew Adam Wilde had made it. He had success, wealth and all the power he could want.

Yet the unanswered question niggled.

'If you turn to the shorter contract...'

Gisèle forgot her curiosity when she started reading their private contract. The one in which she promised to marry him within five weeks.

Five weeks! Panic grabbed her throat and made her heart stutter.

There was also a penalty clause that would cost her more than she got from the sale of Fontaine's, more than she could hope to raise from any other sources, if she reneged.

Pain grabbed her chest as her lungs tightened. The terms were Draconian but clear. If she signed this she'd *have* to marry him.

The fact that he'd provide her with an outrageously generous stipend on top of her salary, while they were married, couldn't negate their power imbalance.

She seethed at being put in this position.

He'd realised she'd do whatever it took to preserve her family legacy and used that to his advantage. The contract even specified a minimum number of public events they'd attend each month or host together, at his discretion! The man left nothing to chance.

He's buying your time. Your presence.

At least there'd be no misunderstandings about sharing her body!

He'd even included a promise of strict confidentiality about the nature of their relationship—her condition that no one know the marriage wasn't real. It was the one saving grace in the whole appalling document.

Rapidly she flicked through the clauses listing all the assets she wouldn't have a claim to, should they divorce. *When* they divorced, she silently amended. But why quibble over that when there was so much else to concern her?

'This doesn't set an end date. Just that we'll live together,' she cleared her throat, 'for a minimum of eighteen months.'

Adam shrugged. 'That gives us time to review the situation.' When she didn't respond his eyes narrowed as if with displeasure. 'If you don't like our arrangement then, you can file for divorce.'

Eighteen months. It seemed a lifetime.

'This lists penalties if I renege on the deal. What about you? If we're seen...courting publicly, but don't marry, the press will have a field day.'

She shuddered, imagining the stories, again, about her supposed inadequacies.

'I won't renege. I'm the one who wants this!'

'Nevertheless. I demand a significant penalty if you withdraw.'

It seemed crazy to say it, when she abhorred the idea of marrying him. But she couldn't sign this as it was. He needed to treat her as an equal party.

'Very well.' He scrawled something on his copy and passed it to her. 'Will this do?'

It stated that if he reneged on the wedding he'd pay multiple millions of euros within seven days.

Reluctantly she nodded. He did that so easily. As if *nothing* would deter him from his purpose.

Seconds later he'd added the same text to her copy and had them both initial each version. It felt like he'd closed a prison door on her.

Gisèle opened her mouth to say she needed time for her lawyer to check the details. Except could she trust Laurent, the old family lawyer, not to hint to Julien that the wedding wasn't all it seemed? She couldn't risk that. 'Five weeks is too soon. It's...' Outrageous. Impossible. Terrifying. 'Not feasible.'

Silence greeted her announcement. Her heart sank as she read his expression. This, unlike job security for the employees, wasn't negotiable.

'That's the offer. My original plan was to marry in a week.'

'A week!'

'Take it or leave it. It's your choice. But remember the amendments to the sale, about your brother and the employees, hinge on you signing this, now. Then I'll have a clean version typed up.'

Now the words came, a fluent rush of colourful curses totally at odds with her composed public persona. Not that she voiced them. Her pride and her poise seemed all that were left to her. She clung to them tenaciously, bottling up the scathing indictment of his character in her head.

As if determined to test her limits he reiterated, 'Five weeks.'

Gisèle took out her fountain pen and spared him a glance down the nose she'd spent a lifetime growing into. 'You really think you can convince the world we fell for each other in under two months?'

Adam's gaze dropped to her poised pen.

That fleeting glance told her again that he was more invested in this deal than he let on. He *needed* this for reasons she didn't know. If she understood maybe she could twist that to her advantage and escape.

But she didn't know. So she uncapped her pen and signed on the dotted line, her hand as heavy as lead.

'Don't worry, Gisèle.' His deep voice held that husky note that warmed her chilled body. 'Together, I'm sure we can convince everybody.'

Was that a promise or a threat?

CHAPTER SIX

THE PHOTOS OF her and Adam on the yacht were just the beginning.

Gisèle had faced a barrage of public scrutiny in her younger years but press attention now reached a new pitch of excitement. Because her name was linked with the uber-successful, famously maverick Adam Wilde. A man who set his own rules, daring to do things his way, defying society's expectations.

Sometimes it took her breath away, the level of hype surrounding them in the weeks since those first photos broke. But rarely, because she was busy juggling the expectations of her secret fiancé, the company's employees and Julien.

'I still don't understand it,' her brother said, and Gisèle shifted the phone to her other ear as she selected earrings to wear tonight. 'What have you got in common with him? He's not your type.'

'Since when did I have a type?'

Julien's words bit close to the bone. Despite the male companions who sometimes accompanied her to formal events, there'd been no man in her life for years.

For good reason.

'Exactly,' he replied, making Gisèle grit her teeth at how much her brother knew about her disappointments and disillusionment.

But it was because they were close that she'd go through with this farce of a marriage.

Her big brother had looked after her when their father died and their mother dumped them on their *grandpère*. She'd do anything for Julien, to save his connection to the company he loved. He'd protected her for years. Now it was her turn.

'You go from dating no one,' he persisted, 'to spending all your time with the enemy.'

'Hardly the enemy. You'll be working together, remember? He's saving the House of Fontaine, keeping us and all the staff on. You admitted yourself that was generous.'

Over the long-distance connection from his home near Paris, she heard her brother's mumble of discontent. 'I still don't understand it. He didn't need to do that so why did he agree? It doesn't fit his usual form. In the past he's been aggressive in any takeover, with no sentiment.'

'Sentiment? Fontaine's has terrific staff and excellent products. And you were a highly successful CEO.'

'I doubt Adam Wilde believes that.'

Gisèle put her hand to her forehead, where a headache built. 'Why not accept it as a gesture of goodwill? See how things go when you're back at work.'

There was silence for a moment. 'How are you coping, Gisèle? I feel guilty about not being there—'

'Enough of that! You need this time to recover.'

Though his treatment had finished, his body needed to mend from the trauma of fighting a potentially fatal illness.

'In the meantime he's got you running after him, at his beck and call.'

'It's not like that.'

It *was* like that. But worse, far worse than Julien imagined. Some days it seemed like she spent almost every waking hour with her nemesis.

Then at night he'd feature in her dreams. Disturbing dreams she didn't want to think about. Because in them she enjoyed being with the big, bold Australian in ways that made her blood sizzle and her sex soften.

She dragged in a deep breath and tore her brain away from that sensual, night-time torture.

How smug Adam would be if he knew.

He insisted she accompany him to every meeting at Fontaine's, every inspection of offices and facilities. He'd been adamant and, knowing she had no choice, she'd agreed.

'Being in the meetings has been useful.' She'd been surprised at how much. 'The staff trust me to be honest with them and I understand the work in a way Adam and his minions don't.'

Often she found herself working as a kind of interpreter between the two.

'Adam, eh? That's very chummy.'

Gisèle was about to protest that Adam Wilde would never be her chum. But she couldn't if she were going to convince her brother she was falling for the man.

'You'd hardly expect me to keep calling him Mr Wilde.'

Come on, Gisèle. Surely you can do better than that.

'I find his company…invigorating.'

That's one way of putting it!

She was more stressed than she dared confess. Her nerves were a constant jangle. Not with fear of what he'd do to her precious company—that had abated as she saw him work—but because of his effect on her.

He took her from fury at his bluntness and outrageous demands, to admiration at his insight, and surprise at his rare moments of sympathy when dealing with anxious staff.

Then there was that other thing. The nameless bond that hung, ever-present, between them. It left her quivering and her knees like jelly when his eyes locked on hers and she swore she saw heat flicker there.

Gisèle wrapped her arm around herself.

There is no bond. You're imagining it because for some stupid reason you find him physically attractive. He doesn't feel the same. He has no trouble keeping his distance. The no-kissing, no-touching rule is fine by him.

She hoped he didn't realise how increasingly hard she found it, sticking to that bargain. The fleeting touch of his hand on hers had her yearning for so much more.

'Earth to Gisèle! Are you there?'

Julien's voice jolted her into the present.

Her hand shook and she dropped her earrings. Because she'd just seen herself in the mirror. Her eyes had a dazed, yearning look that terrified her.

Because she'd been thinking, *again*, about Adam touching her.

No matter what, she couldn't let him see her like that.

'Sorry, Julien, I have to go. We'll talk later. I'm still getting dressed and I'm going to be late.'

'What is it this time? Wilde can't have meetings *now*. He has to give you some time off.'

Despite the press's breathless reporting of a supposed affair between her and the Australian, Julien was still convinced their relationship was purely business.

'Actually,' she hesitated, 'it's not work. It's a party. With film people on the coast for the Cannes Festival.'

The silence on the other end of the line seemed to echo with her brother's shock.

Gisèle was about to say it was an excellent opportunity to raise the company's profile, then pressed her lips together. He needed to think it was a real date.

'I see,' he said eventually and, for the first time she could remember, Gisèle couldn't read her brother's tone.

'We'll talk later,' she assured him. 'I have to go.'

She ended the call and sank onto the bed, boneless. She had no one she could turn to, no one to discuss this with. All she could do was try to hold it all together. The business, the charade, and most importantly never letting Adam Wilde suspect her weakness for him.

Easy!

Gisèle's laugh had an out-of-control edge. She'd never felt so out of her depth.

'So it's true. You and the ice lady are an item.'

Adam turned to find his host beside him.

When they'd met a year ago he'd thought Blake, if not a kindred spirit, at least a man he'd consider doing business with. They'd made their billions in similar fields and though competitors in many markets, there could be benefits in a few cooperative ventures.

Now he knew he'd been mistaken.

'Ice lady?' His lethally soft tone had been known to make CEOs quake in their shoes.

Blake made a placating gesture. But his expression showed his delight at Adam's reaction.

Emotion of any sort was a weakness in the world of high stakes corporate transactions. Maybe that was why Blake's relationships were even more short-lived than Adam's. More like a revolving door. The man had come to Cannes in the company of a beautiful Colombian actress, but he'd spent the evening panting after a Norwegian star whose film had received a standing ovation at the festival.

'Sorry, did I get that wrong? That's right. It's Ice *Queen*, isn't it?' His smile widened salaciously. 'But I'm sure the lovely Gisèle melts for you. I bet she's really something when she does.'

If he'd been anywhere else than at a party with Gisèle, who'd fortunately left his side to talk to an acquaintance, Adam would have grabbed the guy by the throat and shaken that smarmy smile off his face. Host or no host.

Acid filled his belly as Blake said Gisèle's name in that snide, knowing voice.

'If you're talking about Ms Fontaine, I recommend you keep your thoughts to yourself.'

He wanted to teach the guy a sharp lesson in respect. But he controlled himself. Not because he'd decided to prove to the world that he was no longer the brash, uncouth outsider many thought. But because he'd brought Gisèle to this party and wouldn't have her name sullied by association with violence.

Blake moved closer, raising his glass in salute. 'She's tamed you? I thought when you acquired Fontaine's you'd beaten us all to a prize. Now I wonder if you've met your match. I never thought I'd see the day.'

Adam couldn't be bothered prolonging this conversation. The evening had turned sour. But he couldn't see Gisèle. Where was she? The party had already been in full swing when they arrived, guests' inhibitions disappearing fast.

Blake wouldn't be the only man attracted to Gisèle. Could she fend off drunken advances if she needed to?

Adam's fists clenched and his muscles tightened as he scanned the mansion's grounds. There were shadows everywhere. If she were in trouble…

'Maybe it's not really attraction,' Blake continued. 'Maybe it's the novelty of a change from the sexy women you usually date. She dresses so soberly. Like a school mistress.' His tone was avid. 'Or a nun.'

Adam saw Gisèle over his host's shoulder, crossing the terrace towards them.

Her hair was swept up, shining like pale gold. It was true her dress was demure. Dark blue with sleeves to the elbow, a high neck, cinched waist and skirt to just below the knees, at first glance it looked modest. Yet it made him desperate at the thought of her naked skin beneath it. The way it shifted and clung as she walked stole the air from his lungs.

She'd driven him crazy from the moment he'd collected her tonight, his skin too tight for the primal urges he battled.

He swung to face his host with a smile he knew held an edge of masculine threat. If Blake so much as *looked* at Gisèle with that hungry gleam, Adam would deck him. 'But such a *sophisticated* nun,' he drawled.

Deliberately he turned towards the pool where some women, including Blake's newest paramour, had stripped to their underwear for a midnight dip. As he watched, one took off her bra to pose in a skimpy thong, ogled by a cluster of men.

'If you'll excuse us, it's time we left.'

He spun on his heel and turned to discover Gisèle had almost reached them. He didn't wait for Blake's response but marched across, took her elbow and hurried her towards the exit.

Damn their agreement not to touch.

He wanted to wrap his arm around her and tuck her close, as if his bulk could protect her from the avaricious eyes of that slimeball Blake. And any other predatory male.

He'd only known the woman a couple of weeks but she tested his limits. Every day as they worked together he was distracted by the sight and sound of her. His brain threatened to short circuit as he inhaled her cinnamon and orange blossom scent whenever they got close.

But never close enough to satisfy what had become a permanent, gut-deep yearning.

Just as well she didn't know what she did to him! She'd use that power to her advantage.

Adam's jaw clenched so hard pain grabbed his neck and the back of his skull. But he couldn't dispel the tension crawling through his body. At the thought of Blake judging Gisèle and, despite his mockery, salivating over her like a greedy hyena.

'But I haven't said goodnight to Mr Blake!' She half turned. 'I did it for you.'

He tightened his grip as they wove through the partygoers. Several tried to stop them. He saw male gazes slide over Gisèle and refused to halt. Even when he realised he'd forgotten to reduce his stride to suit hers, he didn't slow. Something deep inside demanded he get her away immediately.

He'd like to think it was a protective instinct.

Instead Adam feared it was dog-in-the-manger stubbornness. He couldn't have her, yet, and the frustration was like scrabbling claws shredding his veneer of sophistication.

Sophistication! It was a wonder he hadn't punched his leering host on the nose and thrown Gisèle over his shoulder to carry her away to his villa.

He imagined it clearly. Initially she'd be outraged but then she'd melt in his arms, revealing she was as desperate for him as he was for her.

Dream on, mate!

He didn't pretend to know what went on in a woman's mind, but he couldn't miss her stiff posture or darting looks. Needling looks. She didn't want to leave the party.

Why? Had she met someone? A man?

Had he fooled himself, believing he read attraction in her eyes when she let the guard down?

Adam huffed a breath of pure frustration as he guided her through the foyer. It wasn't like him to doubt himself. This second guessing was sending him crazy.

But after seeing momentary hints of stark vulnerability in her eyes, and dealing with her and her brother enough to begin amending his assessment of them, he'd revised his plans. It struck him how furious and resentful he'd feel if a stranger tried to force *his* sister into marriage.

That made him squirm. But if the idea were truly distasteful Gisèle wouldn't go through with it. She might be fighting in a tight corner but she could walk away from the contest if she didn't like the conditions.

Which brought him to the desire heavy and unspoken between them.

His aim was to let her grow accustomed to him. Make her acknowledge what she'd gain from their union. He'd charm her. Not overtly but with patience and consideration.

He'd give her time.

Time! The deadline for their wedding was a few weeks away.

Gisèle tugged free and moved towards his sports car that a valet had driven up. She didn't look at Adam as he opened her door and her thanks were terse.

He got into the driver's seat and accelerated down the driveway. 'I'm sorry to cut the evening short.' He didn't offer an explanation. He'd rather she didn't know about Blake's prurient interest. 'But if you'd like to go on somewhere... A nightclub—?'

'No thanks.' Her head was turned away and she spoke to the passenger side window. 'I want to go home.'

'You're tired? You don't look it.'

He'd felt the energy coursing through her as they walked through the villa, as if he held a live wire. Besides, though he wanted to escape Blake and his cronies, Adam wasn't ready for the evening to end.

'Don't I?' Gisèle's face showed pale in the darkness as she turned. 'Appearances are deceiving. Our first appointment was at eight this morning and it's been a long day. Working in the evening too takes a toll.'

'Working!' He'd taken her to the most exclusive party on the Côte d'Azur. Despite the distaste lingering on his tongue, or because of it—since he'd made her the subject of speculation—his tone sharpened. Or maybe because she classed an evening with him as work. 'Millions would give their eye teeth to attend tonight's event.'

'Millions, but not me. Though I did get to promote our new product range with some guests.'

Adam's hands tightened on the wheel but he resisted the urge to floor the accelerator. She was reminding him her focus was the company, not him.

He told himself not to react. To play a waiting game because he knew—surely he was right—her protests hid an attraction that matched his.

The journey passed silently, Gisèle apparently fascinated

by the nightscape and Adam driving with tremendous care as he battled an uprush of adrenaline and anger.

She opened her door as he pulled into the kerb, but Adam was on the pavement as she alighted. 'I'll walk you to your door.'

'There's no need. It's just there.'

Gisèle had reached her limit. She couldn't bear another moment in Adam Wilde's company.

Sophisticated nun, indeed!

She'd disliked their host tonight from the moment he'd leered at her when Adam wasn't watching. His insult about her dressing like a starchy schoolteacher or a nun didn't surprise her, though his tone had made her skin crawl.

What had gutted her was her companion's response.

You invited it, wearing the most buttoned-up dress you own. Because you didn't want Adam to think you were encouraging him.

Perversely, it had hurt when he'd said sneeringly that she made a *sophisticated* nun, then turned to gawk at the nubile beauties stripping by the pool. He'd made it clear what sort of woman he preferred.

Even while they pretended to be together!

She'd known since puberty she'd never be a classic beauty or stunningly sexy. She'd *aimed* for sophistication, spent years learning to appear that way, pretending her strong nose and eyebrows were assets. Learning to present herself confidently.

He'd made that achievement feel hollow.

Facing her limitations hurt as it hadn't in years.

What did you expect? That he secretly pined for you? His preference for staggeringly sexy women is on the public record. Those melting looks he gives you are an act.

Gisèle knew that. Why be upset when he dismissed her so easily? She should celebrate that he didn't find her desirable.

'What's wrong, Gisèle? Did someone say or do something to upset you?'

Adam stepped before her, blocking her way.

The streetlight showed his frown and a twist to his lips that seemed to reflect the broken line of his nose. He looked... concerned.

'Tell me, Gisèle. I'll sort them out.'

The offer, in that husky growl, stunned her. Gisèle always stood on her own two feet. This offer to act on her behalf was strangely moving.

Some of her indignation melted.

Until she remembered he was the man who'd hurt her.

That was the scariest thing. After continually being compared unfavourably with her mother in looks, deportment, sex appeal and charm, Gisèle had learned to brush off such comparisons. It had taken years to turn herself into a poised, chic businesswoman. Longer to believe in herself so barbed slurs no longer pained her.

But now she felt pain. Because of *this* man's dismissal.

He reached out, long fingers closing around her arm. 'Gisèle? Talk to me.'

He leaned closer and, as if to make a mockery of her fury, his rich, indefinable yet utterly beguiling scent filled her nostrils, making her body soften. She felt that familiar stirring, her mouth drying and nipples budding.

Because, despite everything, she desired him!

Then, as if the universe hadn't dealt enough blows, she saw, in the shadows behind him, a figure with a raised camera.

No wonder Adam was solicitous!

He must have seen the cameraman. His concerned frown and caring tone were props, not real.

His acting now was better than at the party when it had been clear to anyone who looked that he'd rather ogle naked starlets than her.

'You want to know what's wrong? This. Us. Everything!'

Instead of ripping her arm free, Gisèle thrust her head forward, leaning close.

She waited for Adam to laugh off her words. Remind her she'd agreed to this deal and had to go along with it.

That was all it would take to tip her over the edge and make such a scene even the mighty Adam Wilde wouldn't be able to smooth it over.

When he remained silent she whispered for his ears alone, 'What's the matter, Adam? Don't tell me you're going to disappoint the paparazzo? You're doing a great job, pretending concern for me.'

'Paparazzo?' His fingers tightened around her arm. 'That's why you're upset?'

'Why aren't you taking advantage of the moment? I thought at least you'd engineer a clinch. Think of those millions of readers who get their titillation gasping over made-up stories about people they don't know. Maybe we should move into the light. Then they will see us more clearly to comment on what we're wearing.'

Gisèle imagined it easily. Adam's warm embrace, his head lowering to kiss her, only this time not on the forehead but the lips.

When he did she'd bite his bottom lip as hard as she could and stab her high-heeled shoe on his instep. No woman should be forced to sell herself as she was being forced.

But what would happen to Julien then? And the company employees?

A shuddering breath filled her lungs as Gisèle came back to reality with a sickening thud.

You have to do this. You know you do.

Her vision smeared as unaccustomed tears filled her eyes. Tears of fury, not hurt.

The shadowed face before her was unreadable.

They stood close, his body blocking hers from the camera, his hand now lax on her arm. Then to her amazement Adam said in a voice she'd never heard, 'You're right. Go inside, Gisèle. It's late and you must be tired.'

He ushered her towards the door. Neither glanced at the figure hiding at the end of the building.

A minute later she stood in the darkened foyer, the main door closing behind her with Adam on the outside. He hadn't played up the scene for the press. Nor had he berated her.

She didn't understand it.

But that was the least of her worries.

Hurting and furious because Adam made her feel vulnerable again after all these years, she *wasn't* relieved to be alone.

She wished he'd come inside, wrapped his arms around her and seduced her into losing herself in the passion she'd denied herself so long. The passion he alone ignited.

She was in deep, deep trouble! And he was to blame.

CHAPTER SEVEN

FOR ADAM, the period following that party in Nice was fraught with frustration.

Not because there were problems with the takeover. That progressed smoothly. Partly because he'd insisted on Gisèle's presence at every meeting. He'd done it to keep her close. But there'd been benefits as he grew to know her better.

Far from being the society darling who flitted between high-profile social events, or a mere mouthpiece for the House of Fontaine, his fiancée was something else.

Her understanding of the company was solid. She could answer most questions and, if not, always knew where to go for an answer.

The ethical sustainability unit which he'd viewed as one of the jewels in the company's crown was forward-focused and innovative. He understood now that some of that drive came from her.

He was impressed. But every attempt, no matter how mild, to acknowledge her skills was met with stony silence and narrow-eyed suspicion.

Whatever had happened that night had set their relationship back to ground zero.

Relationship! You should be so lucky. She looks at you like you're a snake in the grass. And who can blame her when you're forcing her into marriage?

But Adam refused to heed his conscience. He was in too

deep. Both with the takeover and with her, the woman who kept him awake at night.

Sadly not because they shared a bed, but because they didn't. Adam rubbed his jaw, hearing the sandpaper scratch of stubble.

Is that why she recoiled from him? Because she thought him uncouth? He looked in the bathroom mirror, the sight of his broken nose eliciting a grunt of amusement. Prince Charming he'd never be, despite the perfectly tailored dinner jacket and handmade shoes.

Probably she preferred men with a cultured air.

Or at least men who didn't blackmail her into marriage.

It would take more than shaving to become the sort of man she was accustomed to.

He ground his molars. That brought him back to his reason for acquiring Fontaine's. To prove Adam Wilde had made it to the very top. That there were no doors closed to him now. No exclusive club that wouldn't accept him.

After a lifetime proving himself against the petty prejudices of those who saw him as a brash upstart and did all they could to keep him down, it was satisfying to have the world at his feet.

Except Gisèle. Not that he wanted her at his feet.

Though, considering it, the idea conjured possibilities. Inevitably his body hardened. He was constantly on the edge of sexual arousal these days.

Very soon they'd marry. He should be pleased. Instead he had the sinking sensation that, despite his plans, things spiralled out of control. His plan to seduce her had gone haywire when he'd stepped back from her that night and something, maybe his conscience, maybe her rigid control, made him hold back.

Adam had no taste for an unwilling lover. He wanted Gisèle to come to him.

He'd tried to discover what had gone wrong at the party but

she'd frozen him out. That, he could cope with. But looking into drowned, haunted eyes, as she accused him of fake concern for the camera, had flattened him.

The Gisèle he knew didn't do self-pity. To see her so lost made him feel useless. He'd wanted to make things right. But his concern had been like petrol to flame, only making her more emotional.

The world would laugh at the idea of Adam Wilde as sensitive. But he'd been raised by a single mother, his only sibling a sister. He knew when he'd pushed a woman too far.

Why had he thought Gisèle Fontaine didn't have a breaking point? Because he got his kicks from her feisty responses? Because he saw them as a substitute for the physical passion they had yet to give in to?

What a piece of work he was.

He turned from the mirror rather than face its reflection.

Yet you're going to hold her to the deal, aren't you?

Of course. He'd gone to immense trouble to acquire the company, and Gisèle. He was determined to win through. He couldn't imagine walking away from her. And that had nothing to do with the takeover.

Minutes later Adam stood before her adjoining hotel suite.

He could have obtained a private house for their stay in Paris, especially as they'd spend time in the French capital in future. But he liked sweeping through the best hotel in the city with Gisèle on his arm.

Not because he wanted to show her off to the public. To his surprise, his instinct was to keep her to himself. Instead he wanted to impress *her*.

Adam's raised arm stilled and he watched his fingers form a fist. The realisation stunned him.

You want her to admire you for your wealth, when you hate avaricious women?

No, what you really want is for her to like you. To want you. To have her eyes light up when she sees you.

Fat chance. Unless she acquires Stockholm syndrome and falls for her captor.

His lips twisted against the bitterness filling his mouth and he rapped on the door.

He needed noise, people, distractions. The exclusive charity event promised that and suddenly he looked forward to it as an escape from his thoughts.

The door opened and his hand fell. His sharp hiss lodged in constricted lungs. His semi-aroused groin became a hard-on before he had time to blink.

Gisèle had adopted a new look since the Cannes party. Her clothes still concealed more than they revealed, but she'd abandoned the sedate suits and muted colours.

If he didn't know better he'd think her aim was to seduce him. Or drive him crazy with lust.

Tonight she'd outdone herself.

Adam's gaze locked on the glossy crimson of her lips before dropping to the dark red of her full-length dress. By current standards it was demure, covering her from shoulder to floor. The neckline ran straight across from below the tip of one shoulder to the other. There was no cleavage on show but a wide expanse of pale golden skin that he wanted to lean in and taste. The lustrous fabric cupped her breasts close. Not just her breasts but her narrow waist and the gentle flare of her hips.

She shifted and he caught a flash of pale thigh. His pulse rocketed as he realised the dress was slit over one leg. She moved again and the slit disappeared.

But he knew it was there, felt it with every urgent, masculine impulse he possessed.

'I…' Adam cleared his throat and dragged his attention back up her delicious body. Something flared in her eyes. Triumph? Pity? Excitement?

He wasn't accustomed to being on the back foot. He was always in charge. Now it was all he could do to breathe steadily and not gawk like a fourteen-year-old.

'You look magnificent.' At least now his voice sounded normal. 'New dress?'

Gisèle shrugged and he watched the rise of bare shoulders above lustrous satin. What kept the dress up? What would happen if he caught the edge of it and tugged? Did she wear a bra? Or would her breasts spring free into his palms?

There was a buzzing in his ears and he swallowed jerkily, barely resisting the need to check his bowtie hadn't suddenly tightened.

'New enough. Don't worry, I haven't worn it before. It will still make a statement at the gala.'

Statement! It would make headlines!

'Good. Excellent.'

He didn't care if she'd worn it before. He just wondered how he'd get through the evening without hauling her close and breaking their no-touching rule. Or roughing up the men who were bound to undress her with their eyes when she sashayed into the grand gala.

'You're ready to go?' she asked.

Go? The idea appalled him. He wanted to stay here.

With her blonde hair loose around her shoulders in a fall of glossy waves, and those red, red lips, she looked like a vintage Hollywood star. All gleaming sex appeal and sophistication that made his heart hammer and his blood simmer possessively. He didn't want any other man to see Gisèle like this.

Except those blue-grey eyes surveyed him assessingly.

Would she see his visceral reaction as a tool to use against him? He'd promised not to touch her without invitation, and staying here, alone with her, would make that impossible.

He gestured for her to precede him. 'Shall we?'

Adam didn't take her arm as they left the hotel, or as he ushered her into the grand building that was the venue for the gala.

Gisèle didn't mind. She felt fabulous. The red satin turned

her into a woman she'd never before dared to be. Not completely.

Even better, she'd seen the masculine appreciation in Adam's stare. The way his jaw slackened as his gaze locked on her crimson lips. His survey of her full-length dress had made her skin tingle into sizzling life.

It was the perfect salve to her bruised ego. As were the admiring looks and compliments she received as they entered the exclusive event.

It infuriated her that, at her age, after all the work she'd put in to becoming a successful, self-confident woman, Adam's banter with his billionaire mate had reignited that old feeling of not being good enough.

Maybe because he was also cold-bloodedly acquiring her as a business asset. He didn't see her as a woman in her own right.

Both facts were cruelly designed to undermine someone who'd once battled confidence and body image problems.

Adam had put Gisèle on her mettle and made her want to step out of her self-imposed limits. To attempt something more than the classic elegance she'd strived for for so long.

She'd begun wearing new, bolder outfits for their dates. All, she hoped, with a feminine allure that proved her to be desirable as well as competent.

Until tonight she hadn't been sure she'd succeeded. But Adam's expression whenever a handsome man spoke to her proved she had. He'd move in close, eyes intimidating narrow slits and jaw set. If the man lingered, a pulse would tick at Adam's temple and he'd take her elbow, guiding her away to meet someone else.

Once, to her amazement, she'd introduced him to a European prince he'd wanted to meet, only to have Adam cut short the conversation after the greetings and lead her away. She'd been stunned. Adam was always eager to build contacts with the old established elite.

His murmured explanation was that he had second thoughts

about pursuing business opportunities with a man who ogled her so outrageously.

It was only the dress and makeup that had changed. She was the same Gisèle. But she was human enough to exalt in the ego boost, especially among this horde of beautiful people.

There was one problem. She didn't simply get an ego boost from Adam's response.

It *excited* her. Meeting that glittering stare, feeling the warmth of his tall frame engulf her as they stood together, even the touch of his hand on her arm, made her minutely conscious of him physically. Even more when he looked at her with something in his eyes that made her blood heat.

You're playing a dangerous game, Gisèle.

But for tonight at least, she had no intention of stopping. There would be time for common sense tomorrow.

'Are you ready to go, Gisèle? It's late.'

'Late?'

She looked around the still-crowded room with its rich furnishings and even more richly attired guests. Previously Adam had always been happy to stay late, networking and apparently enjoying the social functions they attended.

His gaze shifted. 'We've an early start tomorrow.'

Of course. Work. Her buoyant mood dipped. She was tempted to say she'd stay and make her own way back. But suddenly the chatter and gaiety seemed claustrophobic rather than invigorating.

'Of course. We need to be fresh for that.'

Tomorrow there was yet another meeting between Adam's team and key staff in Fontaine's Paris office.

She was turning towards the nearby exit when his hand captured hers. Immediately she stilled. In the weeks since Nice, as the press conjectured about a liaison between them, Adam hadn't once held her hand. He only touched her arm.

This felt momentous. She held her breath.

'Gisèle.'

His deep voice was soft, almost lost beneath the conversations and laughter. Yet she heard the cadence like a thrum in her blood.

His fingers threaded through hers as she turned to meet his searing gaze.

There it was. That pulse. That throb in the air. The sound of the crowd was muted and she felt cocooned in a bubble with Adam.

'Thank you,' he said. 'I know I've asked a lot and you've been...magnificent.'

With his sombre expression and serious eyes he wasn't just talking about tonight, she realised. Was this his apology for the devil's bargain he'd foisted on her?

Gisèle stared. Was it possible? Or did she read too much into simple thanks?

'Because I don't look like a nun any more?'

His eyes widened. 'Ah, you heard that. I'd hoped you hadn't. Blake was completely out of line, that's why we left so quickly. It was either that or deck him for his insults.'

She blinked. 'You thought him insulting? But you said...'

'I said you looked sophisticated, and you do. Marvellously so. You've got more class in your fingertip than all the other women at his party put together. And, for the record,' his voice dropped to a marrow-deep rumble, 'I like your severe suits almost as much as I enjoy you wearing something blatantly sexy like tonight.'

Then, to her astonishment, Adam lifted her hand and bent his head, kissing her knuckles, the brush of his lips surprisingly soft. She'd never have guessed any part of him could feel so soft. It belied his appearance of tough masculinity.

The caress left a fiery trail in its wake and she gasped, fingers clenching into his for support.

The world stood still as, mouth still hot against her hand, he looked up under slashing straight brows and their eyes locked.

She'd never seen a more charismatic man. Never felt such

insistent drumming need. Her nipples tightened to thrusting points. Her breath was a silent sigh. Deep inside there was a loosening, a softening that told its own story about her desires.

Despair laced her wonder. At how potent his appeal. He invested a few words and a simple gesture with such irresistible allure that he undid her completely. He hadn't even needed privacy to do it.

A gleam of silver caught her eye, drawing her attention to a woman in a rhinestone dress, raising her phone in their direction.

The unspoken rule of this very exclusive event was no unsolicited photos inside. There were enough on the red carpet at the entrance.

The woman paused when she realised she'd been seen.

Gisèle leaned into Adam. 'Kiss me,' she whispered.

Because they were due to marry in a quiet 'elopement' wedding in a week and Julien still didn't buy their romance. A photo of them kissing would surely convince him.

That was the sane explanation for her invitation.

It was an excuse, because in that moment she finally surrendered. She wanted, needed Adam's lips on hers.

Instead of accepting the invitation, Adam lifted his head, frowning. 'What—?'

'You said you wouldn't touch me without an invitation. This is your invitation.'

Adam was known for decisiveness, yet *now* he questioned! She leaned in, breasts brushing his arm and making her shiver at the delicious contact. 'There's a woman sneaking a photo. It's the perfect moment for a public kiss.'

But instead of complying, Adam straightened to his full height, leaving her stunned and bereft. She'd wanted, *needed* his mouth on hers. She swayed a little on her heels as he turned his head to look at the woman in silver, his features set like chiselled stone.

Gisèle saw the woman wilt under his scathing stare, before slipping her phone into her purse and scurrying away.

'I think not.' Adam's voice was a deep thread of disapproval that jerked Gisèle back to reality.

Had she got it wrong? Was his possessive behaviour merely fodder for the gossips? Cracks splintered her shiny triumph.

She tugged her hand, needing space. But his fingers closed around hers, refusing to release her. Far from stepping away he bent towards her so his murmured words feathered her flushed face.

'*When* we kiss, Gisèle, I'm damned if it will be for the cameras. It will be for us alone.'

He looked grim, with that shadowed marauder's jaw anvil-hard and new grooves carved deep around his mouth. The pulse at his temple thrummed. But his eyes glowed with a green fire that wasn't anger. It was like looking into a mirror of her own feelings. The excitement, the need, the anticipation were all there.

'Do you agree?'

His tone had lost that brandy-laced caramel smoothness. It was almost as ragged as her choppy breathing.

Gisèle's mouth dried and she slicked her lips, swallowing convulsively as Adam's stare followed the movement and his pulse quickened even further. She shivered and he closed his other hand around hers, cupping it gently as if it were exquisitely precious.

Words wouldn't come, not in the face of the hunger of his emerald-green eyes. She nodded. She'd fought to resist him for so long but no more.

A tremor passed through him. As if he'd withstood a mighty force and was suddenly released from the pressure. His tight mouth curved up in a slow-breaking smile that undid her.

'Good. Because when we kiss, Gisèle, it won't end there. Believe me, we'll want privacy and plenty of time for what I have in mind.'

She should have been shocked. Instead jubilation blared through her. Jubilation and excitement.

Their business deal didn't matter. Nor did the media or the crowd pressing close. Only the zap and spark of mutual desire that quenched all caution.

Dazzled, she said nothing as he tucked her arm through his. Moments later they walked into a barrage of light and sound as the remaining paparazzi crowded the red carpet. For once in her life, Gisèle barely noticed them.

The trip to the hotel passed in silence, but a different sort of silence, one loaded with anticipation. Adam held her hand the whole way and insisted that he, not the chauffeur, help her from the car.

She waited for doubts to creep in. The familiar warning that intimacy was dangerous. That it would leave her vulnerable. That he wasn't a man to be trusted.

But as Adam cradled her hand in his, the warning voice was silent.

Long dormant instinct—because she'd given up trusting herself where men were concerned—told her Adam was as desperate as she.

It was there when they stepped into the lift and, with a grimace, he wrenched his bowtie and top button loose, sighing with relief. It was there in the desire-drenched green of his eyes, more compelling, more beautiful than anything she'd ever seen. And in the tiny, almost indistinguishable tremor of his long fingers around hers that belied the formidable power of his tall frame.

Gisèle had no recollection of entering her suite. All her attention was focused on the man beside her and the changes taking place in her own body.

Gentle fingers pried her clutch purse from her grip and placed it beside the long, velvet-covered sofa.

'Gisèle.'

Her name on his lips was pure invitation. Still he didn't

move, just stood, hands flexing as if resisting the urge to reach for her.

He looked as strong and invincible as ever. Except for those restless hands and something in his expression she'd never seen before. Something that made her feel wanted. Safe. Powerful.

An instant later she was on her toes reaching up to cradle the back of his head.

Warmth enveloped her as he wrapped his arms around her and she sighed her delight. Aroused as they both were— for there was no mistaking the formidable erection pressing against her abdomen—he didn't rush her. It felt like they had all the time in the world.

His spicy, sexy fragrance tantalised but she didn't give a thought to its component scents. It was enough to inhale deeply, drawing it in to her lungs—hot, aroused male.

His fingers curled under her chin, thumb pressing on her lower lip. 'I love that red lipstick,' he growled. 'Your mouth is the sexiest I've ever seen. All night I've imagined the taste of it. You've been driving me crazy.'

Heat spun in her belly, circling faster and faster.

She told herself they were just words. The sort of thing said as a precursor to sex. But even that didn't rob them of magic.

Her fingertips scraped his scalp through his hair and he shuddered. 'Stop talking, Adam. You promised to kiss me.'

His nostrils flared and she saw the devil in his eyes as he surveyed her like a pirate about to claim plunder. Then he fitted his mouth to hers and there was nothing else in the world but his kiss.

Gisèle had expected excitement. She got perfection.

Their mouths fitted as if made for each other. They brushed and clung in a dance of exploration and recognition. As if it wasn't their first kiss, but a long-awaited reunion, each knowing instinctively what pleased the other.

He didn't try to dominate. This was mutual. Pleasure racked her when he delved inside, making her lean into him, hands clutching. And when she gently bit his lower lip, his intake of breath and the increased pressure of his erection told of his delight.

Questing hands explored as their bodies melded. Distance of any sort was unbearable as their tongues caressed and passion built.

Gisèle had never been kissed like this. There'd been men on dates who were experienced lovers. But none who read her needs and met them as if it were the easiest thing in the world. As if *she* were all that mattered.

Each touch stoked the fire burning brighter inside, making her want as she'd never wanted in her life.

She was so caught up in wonder and growing urgency that she barely noticed he'd lowered her to the sofa. But when Adam joined her, lying half on his side, half above her, she rejoiced.

This was what she wanted. She arched, silently demanding more contact as she sucked his tongue hard into her mouth. She shivered, senses overloading as she swallowed the low growl emerging from the back of his throat. Her nipples were so hard they ached and the hollow feeling between her legs made her shift restlessly.

A callused hand found the slit in her skirt, smoothing over bare skin. Arousal notched up to frantic.

'Adam!'

He'd lifted his head to watch his hand in the opening of her skirt. The tendons stood proud in his neck and his features were taut. He looked bold, untamed and gorgeous. Now his eyes met hers in a gaze saturated with desire.

'I want—' The jarring ring of a phone interrupted, making him scowl. 'Sorry. I thought it was off.'

He moved to one side, fished out his phone and thumbed it, silencing the call. Then he leaned away and put the phone on the coffee table.

Gisèle watched him turn back to her, eyes ablaze and eager. His hand went straight back to the slit in her skirt, pushing all the way up to her silk panties, wet with arousal. One touch and she couldn't help but jerk her pelvis high in response. It was what she wanted. What she'd craved so long.

Yet it *felt* different. Her body was still a hundred percent willing but her mind was elsewhere.

Drawn by a compulsion she couldn't withstand, Gisèle turned her head. He'd put his phone down but instead of lying flat on the table, it was leaning upright against a box of handmade chocolate truffles, facing them.

Cold washed over her and the swirling heat in her belly turned into a nauseating churn. She went rigid, blood congealing as her fingers clawed his shoulders.

His voice came from far away. 'Gisèle? What's wrong?'

CHAPTER EIGHT

ADAM COULDN'T BELIEVE what he saw. His vibrant, explosively arousing partner froze. Her beautifully flushed face, neck and shoulders turned parchment white above the deep red of her dress.

Her rounded eyes fixed on something beyond him, with the unblinking stare of someone mesmerised by fright.

Swift as thought, he swung his head around, expecting an intruder. His heart pounded and his muscles bunched ready to protect her as he rose above her.

There was no one there, nothing had changed.

'Gisèle? What is it?'

At the sound of his voice she blinked and shook her head but her lips were a crooked line that spoke of pain or distress. At a loss, he turned again. Nothing had altered. The only difference from before was his phone. He reached for it and felt her flinch beneath him.

'I just...' Her voice was a broken whisper unlike her usual confident tone. Or the throaty, seductive voice that had undone him tonight.

Something was badly wrong. Clutching the phone, Adam pushed off the sofa, watching Gisèle watch him. No, not him, the phone. Her expression turned his veins to ice as his brain raced to make sense of her reaction.

Beneath the chill, a kernel of furious heat ignited.

He strode across the room, opened the door to his adjoining suite, and without looking tossed the phone inside then closed the door. By the time he'd returned to her, Gisèle was sitting upright, arms crossed around her waist, bare shoulders hunched. But there were streaks of colour high on her cheeks as she tilted her head to look at him.

Oh, Gisèle.

His chest squeezed hard as he watched her fight for control. As suspicion grew.

Adrenaline surged in Adam's blood, pumping it fast and hard, demanding action. But first he needed to know for sure.

Instead of sitting beside her he hunkered before her, carefully not touching, though every instinct howled the need to take her in his arms.

'Was it the phone?'

Her nod was jerky. 'I'm sorry. I know you wouldn't...'

His suspicion clicked over into certainty and he fought nausea at the realisation.

'But someone did.' His voice wasn't his own.

It wasn't a question. He knew from her body language that they had, even before she nodded again. His hands clenched so hard he couldn't feel his fingers. He swallowed hard, tasting bile.

'It was—'

'Would you like—'

They both stopped. Just as well. Adam had no idea what he could offer that would make her feel better. 'You don't need to explain.'

'But I want to.' Her gaze lifted to his, clear and blue. 'I owe you that after...'

'You owe me nothing.'

But he rose to take a seat beside her. Her smile was crooked and so endearingly courageous he felt a little of his turmoil ease. In its place rose pride and the respect for her that had been building day by day.

Silence lengthened between them but Adam was in no rush to end it.

'It was years ago,' she said eventually. 'I was young and still remarkably naïve.'

'It wasn't your fault!' Nothing could be plainer.

Gisèle reached out and touched his hand on the sofa between them. He wrapped his fingers around hers, relieved and grateful that she didn't shy from his touch. It was clear that tonight had taken her back to a traumatic incident.

Blue-grey eyes surveyed him curiously. 'You're not the man I thought you were, Adam. Or at least not completely.'

Because he'd guessed what had happened to her and was outraged? What sort of man had she thought him?

Don't go there, mate. You don't want to know.

But he had a good idea. Heat singed his skin.

'I reserve the right to some surprises.'

His tongue-in-cheek tone turned the twist of her lips into a gentle smile that squeezed his chest. 'Oh, you definitely do that.'

She drew a deep breath and looked at their linked hands. 'It's not an uncommon story. There was a guy. He was so charming, so caring, so understanding. I was falling in love with him and thought he felt the same.'

She shook her head. 'You'd think I'd have known better given my background.'

'Your background?' Adam didn't want to interrupt but felt he'd missed something vital.

Gisèle shrugged and met his stare. 'You know about my family. Successful and in the spotlight. But it was far more than that. In their time, my parents were *the* European glamour couple. The press couldn't get enough of them. The public loved stories about the Fontaines.' Her voice dropped. 'Especially after my father died and my mother left us with our grandfather.'

She paused. 'Julien and I learned there was no such thing

as a secret shared among friends. Our comments were passed on, sometimes innocently, then twisted and misreported in the press. Everyone wanted the inside scoop on our family. Who we were, what we did, whether we'd measure up to our charismatic parents. It got so that we learned not to trust people outside the family or Fontaine's.'

Adam felt his frown become a scowl, great trenches of anger furrowing his brow at the thought of children being pestered like that.

Absently he rubbed his fingertip over the crooked line of his nose. He'd fought his share of bullies. Even as a kid he'd made sure no one put his family down because of their straightened circumstances.

'Julien and I weren't particularly remarkable, but the media interest continued for years. As a result I tended to…' She looked across the room as if seeing into the past. 'I withdrew. I didn't trust easily. As I said, I should have known better.'

'How old were you?'

'Seventeen. He was in his twenties.'

'Bastard!'

An older man hitting on and hurting a vulnerable girl. Adam wanted to find him and damage him very, very badly. It would be one occasion in which he'd thoroughly enjoy living up to his reputation for being dangerous and too rough to have real class.

Gisèle's head shot up, gaze meshing with his. The painful mix of emotions in her face made him wish he'd been around to deal with the guy.

'As you say.' Her mouth firmed then she continued quickly. 'Anyway, we went to his place. We were on the sofa kissing.'

Adam winced at the similarity to this evening.

'Then…'

She swallowed convulsively and pain tore at his belly, watching her suffer at the memory. He ground out through gritted teeth, 'The jerk used his phone to film you making love.'

'It wasn't love.' Her voice was razor-sharp. 'I only mattered to him as the girl whose private life everyone wanted to know about. He wanted to cash in on my notoriety.'

The look in her eyes was enough to make steam rise from snow. Adam was glad to see that anger. He found it hard to witness her pain.

'I'm sorry, Gisèle.'

He felt ashamed to belong to the same sex as the man who'd abused her.

She shook her head. 'Not your fault.'

'That doesn't matter. I hate that it happened to you.'

Understatement, much?

He stroked the back of her hand. 'Give me his name, Gisèle. I'll make him sorry. You can be sure he'll never make any more secret sex tapes.'

Had he shared them with friends? Posted them online? Adam's flesh crawled and it was all he could do to sit there, pretending to be a civilised man when he wanted to find the perpetrator and—

She turned her hand against his, squeezing, drawing him from his violent fantasy. 'There's no need. I took care of it.'

Adam's eyebrows shot up. 'You did?' She'd been seventeen, abused by an older man.

'And it wasn't really a sex tape. Well, it was but we didn't actually get as far as…'

A rosy blush swept from her red dress all the way to her cheekbones. It made her seem younger and more vulnerable.

Hell! Had the guy been her first lover? The possibility made Adam want to gag.

'It wasn't consummated,' he bit out, needing to cut short the details.

'No, it wasn't. It was…'

Again that pause, and it took all his control *not* to wrap his arms around her and gather her close.

'It was heavy petting. We weren't even fully naked.'

Yet Adam's fingers twitched with the need to wrap themselves around the filthy beggar's throat.

'For some reason, I don't remember how, I noticed the phone propped on the mantlepiece, trained on us. When I mentioned it his response was...off. He pretended it meant nothing but he wasn't convincing. I'd had too many paparazzi snapping unwanted photos all my life so I suppose I guessed something wasn't right.'

She looked at his hand holding hers. 'I reached the phone before him and saw it was filming us.' Fire flashed in her gorgeous eyes as she raised her chin. It struck Adam that he'd never seen her look more magnificent. 'He tried to grab it but in the scuffle I managed to knee him in the groin, hard. Then I pitched the phone over the terrace and into the sea.' Gisèle's eyes sparkled with satisfaction. 'He had a cliffside house.'

Despite the dire story, Adam felt a grin spread across his face. She was some woman! He'd assumed her assailant had kept the recording. He'd probably been bigger and stronger than the seventeen-year-old girl he'd targeted. Nor would it have been surprising if shock had kept her from acting quickly.

'Did you get away safely?'

He could imagine her assailant turning vicious.

Gisèle nodded.

'I'm glad.' The words barely conveyed his relief. He remembered Angela at seventeen. His sister had been a budding beauty but too ready to take people at face value. If something like that had happened to her... 'Give me his name, Gisèle. I know you dealt with the situation. But scum like that need teaching a permanent lesson.'

Adam's voice was gentle, like his hand on hers. But there was no mistaking his fury.

His nostrils flared, his mouth flattened and that marauder's jaw clenched aggressively. With his dark stubble and hair long enough now to be tousled after she'd run her fingers through it, he'd never looked more like a pirate. And his eyes, they glittered wickedly as if envisaging terrible retribution.

The glimpse of his temper was spellbinding. She hadn't told Julien about the event until years later, when Paul was well and truly out of her life. Her brother had been furious, taking what steps he could to ensure Paul never returned to her orbit. But she hadn't felt the deep-seated thrill she experienced now, seeing Adam's elemental protectiveness on her behalf.

Here was a man who'd be ruthless in defending those he cared for. Even those, like her, who weren't dear to him, but who'd been wronged.

She couldn't help but be warmed by his response.

'There's no need.'

Adam raised his eyebrows in query.

'The next morning I visited his aunt. She's a friend of my parents from the old days, someone I've known all my life, and a wealthy, powerful woman. Her nephew was, and I suspect still is, dependent on her for his job, home and prospects.'

Gisèle remembered the lines deepening on the older woman's face as she told her what had happened.

Long fingers smoothed over hers in a slow, reassuring rhythm. 'That took a lot of guts.'

Adam was right. She remembered with horrible clarity her lingering shock and nausea. The shame, even though she'd done nothing wrong. It had taken every bit of strength she had. Would she have dared to if Paul's aunt hadn't been a dear family friend?

'It had to be done. If he did that to someone else later…' It didn't bear thinking about. 'I never saw him again. She said he'd be punished and learn to treat women with respect. I believe if anyone could do that she could. As far as I know, and Julien has checked, he's a better man than he was.'

Adam looked ready to argue.

'I believe he's been punished. I don't want it opened up again. I want to put what happened behind me.'

She thought she had, until she'd seen Adam's phone on the table and the past had rushed back in nauseating clarity.

His hard-hewn jaw flexed, but finally he nodded.

Another first. Adam Wilde pulling back from something he wanted out of respect for her wishes.

If nothing else, tonight was giving her a new perspective on the man she both desired and demonised.

Not much of the demon now, with him stroking your hand as if he believes you still need saving.

How would Adam react if he knew his attempt to comfort her was beginning to affect her in other ways?

Heat trickled through Gisèle, making her shiver. A shiver that had nothing to do with past distress. But Adam didn't know that. She saw concern etched deep around his eyes.

'Would you like to be alone? Should I leave?' He lifted his hand and she was startled at how much she disliked the idea of him going.

'No!' She moistened dry lips. 'That is, I don't mean…' She shook her head, infuriated to find herself having trouble expressing herself. She wasn't a distressed teenager any longer. 'If you—'

'It's okay, Gisèle. I know we won't finish what we started tonight.'

The look he gave her bordered on brotherly.

She respected him for that. It was reassuring. And yet…

'But if you'd like company?'

She nodded, feeling some tension ease from her rigid muscles and relaxing back into the cushions. 'If you wouldn't mind. For a little while.'

Now wasn't the time to consider how the man she'd classed as her enemy was the one person whose company she craved after her emotional upset.

Adam rose and picked up the TV remote control. 'You choose a channel while I call the butler for room service.'

Gisèle wasn't hungry but didn't argue. The idea of curling up on the lounge and watching something to distract her sounded perfect. Strangely, the idea of doing it with Adam at her side was even better.

Something had shifted between them tonight. It had begun when he'd looked at her with such naked hunger and had accelerated with his response to her trauma.

Her feelings had altered.

She trusted him, she realised. In fact, looking back, she had for some time. Adam Wilde was a tough negotiator, and utterly outrageous in his demands, but he'd never once led her to believe he was anything less than honest.

Now, experiencing the heat of his anger over Paul, and his protectiveness, she saw him in a new light.

He was still larger than life, more potently disturbing than any man had a right to be. But that didn't seem as daunting as it once had. In fact, she found it invigorating.

'Haven't found anything yet?'

A soft blanket settled over her knees, plush and comforting. Where had he found that?

Without waiting for a response he took the remote from her to search the channels. He sank onto the sofa beside her, but not touching. She remembered his expression as she'd told her story and knew that was deliberate. He was respecting her space.

Suddenly, Gisèle had a burning curiosity to know all about Adam's mother and sister. He gave every indication of being a man who respected and, to a degree at least, understood women. They'd done a good job with him.

Except he's blackmailing you into a convenient business arrangement of a marriage!

What an impossible conundrum he was.

'What is it about men and remote controls? Julien's the same. He always has to take charge of it.'

Bright, moss green eyes met hers and she felt his gaze like the brush of velvet on skin. Yet there was laughter lurking there. 'Don't you know it's in our DNA? Mastering the remote is a core masculine competence.'

Gisèle stifled a snicker, surprised at how easily he lightened the atmosphere. 'I'm pretty sure DNA predates remote controls.'

Adam shrugged, drawing her attention to the fact he'd shed his jacket. Her gaze diverted to his white dress shirt, the top couple of buttons undone.

What was it about a dangling bowtie that turned a bare, masculine throat into an erotic masterpiece?

There was a rush of something effervescent in her blood as her gaze skated his big shoulders. She'd thought they looked perfect in his tailored, formal jacket. But the thin shirt accentuated the impressive lines of his strong shoulders, arms and torso. Without the extra layer of clothing he looked bigger and broader than before. And from the way he'd felt, lying above her, she guessed he was all hard-packed muscle and sinew.

Adam held out the remote. 'Do you want to choose?'

She shook her head and pulled the blanket higher, more for something to do than because she was chilled. Safer too, to have something to occupy her hands.

'Far be it from me to deny you the pleasure. Just no schlock horror.'

He sent her a sideways glance that she knew wasn't sexual, yet which she felt all the way to her soles.

'Non-stop action? Maybe not.'

By the time the butler arrived with a large tray, Adam had settled on a recent adaptation of a Jane Austen classic.

Taking in her raised eyebrows, he said, 'Is this okay? My sister raved about it.'

So he discussed films with his sister. It sounded like they were close, maybe like her and Julien. The idea intrigued.

'Perfect. Engaging but not too taxing.'

The hero was easy on the eye, but nowhere near as compelling as Adam. She watched him take the laden tray and put

114   SIGNED, SEALED, MARRIED

it on the coffee table. He had a grace of movement that made her wonder if he'd been an athlete before he focused on world domination.

'Here.'

He passed her a steaming mug that smelt of honey and cinnamon. Gisèle cupped her hands around it and inhaled. The smell took her back to childhood, to cuddles and bedtime stories. 'Hot milk and honey?' She'd expected a nightcap.

'Guaranteed to help you relax ready to sleep. My mum swears by it.'

'Yet you're having a beer.'

His eyes danced in a way that made her feel at the same time breathless and reassured.

Gisèle told herself her reactions would make more sense tomorrow, without emotions pumping adrenaline through her bloodstream.

'A man has to fortify himself if he's going to watch historical romance.' He offered her a large bowl from the tray. 'Here, have a chip. You French do them very well.'

'We should. We invented them. And they're called *pommes frites*.'

She bit into crunchy, hot potato, dusted in rosemary salt, and only just managed not to moan in pleasure. She grabbed a few more.

'You like them, then?'

Adam was watching the screen but clearly his focus was on her. For once that seemed neither intimidating nor sexual, but…caring. Amazing how lovely that felt.

'I adore them but rarely eat them.'

The press had been ruthless in her early teens, comparing photos of her rounded features and tummy with her svelte mother, pushing her into a downward spiral of self-criticism and body negativity it had taken years to climb out of.

Now, instead of worrying about calories, she simply preferred eating healthy options. Most of the time.

She sipped her milk and snuggled deeper into the cushions, looking at the screen. 'I expected multi-billionaires to snack on champagne and caviar.'

'Ah, but I'm a working-class guy through and through. As people are very ready to remind me.' Something in his voice caught her attention. Nothing she could identify, yet it made her blink and sit up from her slumped position. 'Relax, Gisèle, or you'll miss the movie.'

He held out the *pommes frites* and she found herself taking a handful.

Strange how relaxed she felt with Adam beside her, recipient now of one of her secrets. She'd spent her life ferociously guarding her private life.

Yet she trusted Adam with that knowledge. Amazing!

Gisèle stifled a yawn and snuggled under the blanket. It was surprising how comfortable it was, having him here.

She woke to find herself snuggled into the warmest bed she'd ever slept on. Cosy but not too soft. Her fingers splayed against the mattress and slowly her sleep-fuddled brain registered it wasn't a mattress. It was a ribcage, gently rising and falling.

Gisèle opened her eyes, trying to decide where she was. Not in a bedroom but a luxurious sitting room, lit by the glow of shaded lamps.

With Adam.

He was asleep, sprawled diagonally along the sofa, long legs stretched out before him, his head on a corner cushion. One limp hand held a remote control and his other arm was wrapped loosely around her back while her cheek rested on his chest.

Experimentally she shifted, feeling the slide of her long skirt against her legs. She, like he, was fully dressed.

The evening before came back in a rush. The excitement. The kiss. The spike of hunger between them. And that dreadful moment of panic when she'd feared the past was repeating itself.

Adam's kindness.

Who knew he could be that way? Each time she thought she knew what to expect he confounded her.

Looking at him now, sprawling and relaxed, he looked even more imposing than usual.

Imposing or attractive?

Both. And more than attractive. Gisèle's gaze traced him greedily. This was the only time she'd had the luxury of surveying him at leisure.

Her pulse quickened as she drew in that familiar, indefinable scent that intrigued her. Then there was his big, hard body, even more imposing up close. Even the sharp angle of his chin and the dark smudge of his unshaven jaw beckoned her interest.

How would it feel to be intimate with him? It wasn't part of their on-paper marriage deal but that was where last night had been heading.

Adam sighed in his sleep and she jerked back guiltily, putting her hands out to lever herself up. One hand planted on the sofa cushion and her other palm landed on his solid thigh, her fingers discovering something equally solid.

CHAPTER NINE

A SECOND PASSED, then another. Gisèle told herself to pull back. To say something, apologise.

But she didn't move. Looking into that searing gaze as his eyes snapped open, she couldn't form the lie. Because it would be a lie. She didn't want to apologise for touching him.

As if her body acted independently from her brain, her hand left his thigh to wrap around that proud erection.

A jitter of nervous excitement registered at his size. But what had she expected? He was a big man.

Heat blasted her cheeks until they glowed. Could he read her thoughts? It felt that way as his long-lashed eyelids lowered to half-mast, making him look even more like a sexy buccaneer.

'I didn't mean to touch you,' she rasped out eventually.

'And yet,' his voice was a rumble that she felt in her womb, 'you haven't let go.'

Impossibly, her blush intensified, burning her throat, ears and breasts. But when she would have snatched her hand away she couldn't, for Adam's hand covered hers, holding her against him.

She shivered at what she saw in his face. At the throb of his arousal beneath her touch. And the aching, edgy sensation that made her lower body hum with need.

Gisèle swallowed then moistened her lower lip, but whatever she was going to say was drowned by a low masculine groan. 'Don't look at me that way, Gisèle. I'm only human.'

He was only human?

'You're the one holding my hand there.' Her voice sounded scratchy.

'You don't want to touch me?'

Of course she did. He knew that. It had been obvious last night when she'd been swept away by excitement. Now she forced herself to think it through. How she'd struggled so hard against him, feeling overwhelmed from their first meeting. And still this moment between them felt inevitable.

'I shouldn't. Considering the devil's deal you've pushed me into.'

Yet she couldn't conjure anger. Her feelings for Adam were too complex for that. Her earlier indignation paled against the visceral need he'd awoken. Then there was his kindness last night. But it wasn't kindness she wanted now.

The pressure of his hand disappeared as he sat straighter, putting distance between them. Deep grooves carved his forehead. 'I would *never* force you into intimacy.'

Gisèle nodded and drew in a sustaining breath. 'I know. This has nothing to do with our business deal. I want you, Adam.'

He said nothing. Had mentioning their differences doused his ardour?

Maybe he regularly wakes hard with sexual arousal.

Maybe it has nothing to do with you.

Maybe last night's kiss was curiosity on his part. Would he really be attracted to you?

The poisonous inner voice sounded so like the one that had ridiculed her in her youth, telling her she was overweight, plain and uninteresting.

But Gisèle wasn't falling for that again. She refused to undermine herself. There were enough people in the world ready to do that for her and she'd learned to ignore them.

If Adam didn't want her he could tell her to her face.

She sat up. 'Nothing to say?'

Her voice wobbled a little. She was putting her pride on the line. She wanted desperately to cuddle up against him. She craved the feeling of well-being she'd woken to.

Gisèle had never told any man she wanted him. It made her both energised and vulnerable.

'What do you want me to say?' His eyes flashed. 'That I want you? Of course I do. You felt the proof of how much.' He paused. 'But I'm remembering last night. Only a few hours ago you were distressed—'

'I'm not distressed now.'

'It would be wrong to take advantage of you.'

Said the man pushing her into a marriage of convenience. The man taking over her beloved family company.

Gisèle gritted her teeth. She told herself she admired his scruples in this at least. Yet it grated that he was concerned *now* about doing the decent thing, but not when he'd devised his Machiavellian business plans. That he wouldn't accept her assurance, but tried to second-guess her feelings, as if he knew them better than her.

Or maybe you're using anger to stoke your courage. Because you've never done this.

That's the last thing she'd tell Adam. He'd take his scruples and leave for sure then.

In one smooth movement she rose. 'Okay, then.'

Was that a flash of dismay across his tightly drawn features? Was he worried she was rejecting him? That pleased her. It would be nice to think Adam felt some of the compulsive desire she did.

Gisèle caught the rich material of her skirt and lifted it as she knelt on the sofa beside him. '*I'll* initiate this. But if I do anything you don't like, Adam, tell me and I'll stop.'

She delighted in his surprise as she moved close. Cupping his bristly cheeks with her palms, she brushed her lips across his. Once, twice, revelling in the deliciousness of it, in her power, the thrill of balancing on the precipice.

On the third pass his lips opened, warm breath escaping on a rough sigh that made the fine hairs on her arms and nape rise. Gisèle changed the angle of her mouth, slicked her tongue along his parted lips, flicking inside to sample the addictive taste she remembered from last night. The taste of Adam. It made her light-headed, swaying closer.

Firm hands bracketed her hips, sliding on the satin then gripping low, the tips of his fingers on the curve of her buttocks.

She stiffened, pelvis automatically easing forward in response. It felt so good when he held her. She wanted to feel his hands against bare skin.

Lifting her head, she looked into gleaming, deep-set eyes. Dark colour streaked his cheekbones and the lines of his face seemed sharper. All that symmetry, bisected by his strong, crooked nose, made a mesmerising whole.

'Not going too far or too fast for you?' Gisèle's voice sounded only a little uneven.

A flash of white teeth gleamed against dark stubble. It might have been a grimace or a grin. 'I think I can keep up.'

Adam's voice was a growling purr as he caressed her through her dress, long fingers applying just the right amount of pressure. She arched as tingles streaked along her spine and around her pelvis. Heat settled at the apex of her thighs and her breasts swelled against the confining fabric.

Gisèle drank in the sight of him. Taking this further would mean stepping off the precipice into the unknown. She didn't know whether *she* could keep up with him. But she'd spent too long running scared from the idea of intimacy.

Now, here, was a man she wanted. A man who made her feel *desire*. She owed it to herself to see this through.

At least she could trust Adam not to sugar-coat lust with the pretence of deeper feelings. Dangerous he might be, but for this he was perfect.

'Second thoughts?' he asked.

'Hardly. I was thinking you're exactly the man I need.'

An expression she didn't have time to read flashed across his features. Then he drew her to him and she toppled into the deep green depths of those fathomless eyes.

This time there was no gentle brush of lips. Their mouths met squarely, automatically finding the most pleasing fit. Gisèle's fingers burrowed through soft curls as she cradled the back of his head, holding him where she needed him. Their tongues met, stroked and delved.

Fire shot through her veins as their kiss deepened, passion flaring bright and hungry.

She wriggled forward, needing more contact, but her skirt hampered her. Adam came to the rescue, pulling aside her skirt as she lifted first one knee then the other to move closer.

Instead of moving back to grasp her hips, his hand stayed at the slit of her skirt. Warm fingers stroked her thigh, higher and higher, drawing the fabric up. She had no thought of stopping him, instead shuffling her knees wider. And all the while that kiss—passionate, seductive and so absolutely what she needed—went on and on, turning her blood to thick honey and sparking fireworks.

She should be exploring his body. Except it was enough for now to anchor her hands against the back of his head, letting their kiss expand and his hand explore.

Fire roared through her as he cupped her mound through lace underwear. His touch was firm. So definite. So perfect.

Gisèle sighed her relief as she tilted into his hold.

Teeth closed around her lower lip, gently biting, and she shuddered, planting her hands on his shoulders, not to push away, but because she needed to hold herself steady.

His hand moved, tugging damp lace and burrowing beneath it, fingers sliding to the place where pleasure centred.

Gisèle gasped as a shock wave of delight raced through her, making her jump. Then his fingertips slid back, circling, teasing, making her forget to breathe. Taking her right to the brink.

'Let go, Gisèle.'

Adam's voice was velvet and aged brandy, smooth yet with a bite. Like the caress of his cheek and jaw against hers, the friction of his unshaven skin delicious.

'I can't.'

She couldn't have reached the brink of orgasm so fast. Because she'd spent her adult life protecting herself so she'd never again be vulnerable to a man. Because the pleasure Adam gave was already so overwhelming, suddenly she feared what would happen if she let him tip her over the edge.

He kissed her again, featherlight kisses across her mouth that teased but didn't satisfy. Kisses on her throat and at a spot below her ear that made her melt and draw tight simultaneously.

He whispered against her skin, pure temptation. 'Let go, Gisèle. I'm here to catch you.'

His fingers moved further, delving. First one in a slow slide and retreat. Then two, and she couldn't help but move, pushing against him as he took her mouth again, tongue sliding deep, filling her, urging her as his hand worked between her legs.

There was an explosion of light behind her eyelids. A detonation of sensation, wild and exquisite, centred at her core and radiating out.

Then she was falling off the precipice. Soaring and floating in another dimension.

Heat engulfed her. Solid muscle. Sure hands. The murmured flow of reassuring words. Soft kisses on her throat, cheeks and lips.

Finally she lay, limp from bliss, as the world reassembled itself around her. She was stretched full-length on velvet cushions, Adam's arms around her, the fine weave of his trousers encasing solid thighs against her legs.

Gisèle sighed and snuggled closer, the movement bringing her against the hard bulge of his erection. But he didn't move, just held her, one arm around her, his other hand stroking her hair lying loose around her shoulders.

'You're spectacular, Gisèle. So vibrant…so combustible.'

Her mouth hooked up in a wry smile. That's what lack of a sex life did to you—made you liable to combust.

'I love watching you climax. You're beautiful.'

Her eyes snapped open. 'No need for flattery.'

'Flattery?' He eased back to look into her eyes. 'It's the truth.'

She wavered, seeing his frown. Maybe he meant it and she was the one with a hangup about the word 'beautiful'. It was the unattainable standard against which she'd been measured. Maybe it was what a man said to a woman during sex.

Despite the sweet lassitude filling her, Gisèle felt nervous. Would she disappoint him? Would her inexperience show?

'Have you got a condom?' she blurted out.

His eyes widened as if in surprise at her change of subject. Then they took on that heavy-lidded look that made her forget she'd just orgasmed. How did he do that? 'Several.'

'Several? Are you always so well prepared?'

'Since meeting you, I'm always prepared.'

She felt her eyes widen at his smug expression. Was he serious?

'You don't believe me?' Adam shook his head as if disappointed. 'Ever since that first day.' He spoke slowly, enunciating every word. 'Every time we've been together I've been prepared.'

She tried to scrounge up indignation but got stuck on amazement.

'You really thought, from that first day, that I'd—'

He pressed a finger to her lips, stopping her words, and she inhaled the scent of sex and Adam and her own climax. She trembled, strung out by the reality of what she'd done and was about to do with him.

Nerves and excitement filled her.

'I don't mean I thought you'd fall into bed with me. Far from it. But I knew what *I* wanted from the beginning. *You*, Gisèle.'

He let that hang between them. 'Of course I've been prepared. I knew eventually you'd recognise what was between us.'

Sex, he meant. Nothing more.

At least this had nothing to do with the business deal. Or the company. Or even the arranged marriage.

Gisèle should be reeling. Instead something inside steadied, realising he was right. This had been inevitable.

Yet she had to reiterate, still stunned. 'You wanted me since *Nice*?'

He nodded. 'You have no idea how much. You turned up at that meeting, so sexy and alluring in that jacket and skirt.'

She frowned. 'My business clothes aren't alluring. They're serious and professional.'

Adam grinned and her heart flip-flopped. 'Your clothes might be serious and professional but they can't hide the sultry woman underneath. I find it arousing imagining what you wear underneath those serious clothes.' His gaze flicked to the line of her bodice. 'Or don't wear.'

Gisèle's breath was a shocked hiss. He was serious, she read it in his dancing eyes.

That excited her. Her as a *femme fatale*? He was delusional but she didn't care. She'd take the compliment and enjoy it.

Right now she was enjoying the way Adam looked at her, with a hungry gleam, as if trying to decide where to start.

A frisson of trepidation made her shiver. She was in uncharted territory. But she liked the idea of being sexy and seductive. Wielding a feminine power that made Adam carry protection, just in case.

She placed her hand on his cheek, feeling the friction of beard growth, a reminder of his potent masculinity.

'Maybe it's time to get out that condom.'

'And it's past time we took this to a bed.'

They deserved more than the cramped confines of a couch. Besides, he needed time to shore up his control. He was close to the edge and didn't want to spend himself prematurely. He'd waited so long for Gisèle, he intended to enjoy every moment.

Watching her come, hearing those soft gasps of wonder and feeling her shudder in ecstasy, had been too arousing. Satisfying too, as if her pleasure were his.

Even if it left him stiffer and needier than ever.

Adam stood and scooped her into his arms. She was all warm femininity and slippery satin. Her throat and collarbone were flushed. Her blonde hair fell in loose waves around her bare shoulders and that slit in her skirt opened over one pale thigh, like an invitation to Paradise.

His belly clenched and his erection twitched as he remembered following that inviting path up her leg to her most secret place.

She was fully dressed but delectably rumpled and more tantalising than any woman had a right to be.

So what's changed?

She turned you on, just giving a press conference. When you saw her in the flesh the first time half your attention was on her body rather than business.

Yet Adam found Gisèle's intellect and character arousing too.

He strode to the bedroom, pausing only to fumble a switch to turn on bedside lights. She felt right in his arms. The only improvement would be if she were naked.

Soon.

Adam set her on her feet beside the bed, taking his time lowering her, teeth gritted against the torture-pleasure of her body sliding against him.

She stood shorter without her shoes, making him more conscious of his size. He felt a flicker of concern that he might hurt her when they came together. Then he met her misty gaze and sense reasserted itself. He'd never hurt a woman yet and Gisèle was as eager as he.

'Clothes.' He was surprised to find his throat constricting. Finally he ground out, 'Time to get naked.'

'You first.'

He'd imagined them undressing each other, but this was better. If Gisèle undressed him he wouldn't last.

Adam shucked off his shoes and socks, kicking them aside. The carpet was thick under his soles as he worked his way down the dress shirt, flicking it open.

Gisèle watched every movement, lips parted. Her intense scrutiny felt like a touch, the trailing of fingers over his bare chest.

'Help me with the cufflinks,' he ordered.

She stepped close, hands deft and head bent, her rich, spice-and-blossom perfume filling his senses. When she was done he peeled off the shirt and tossed it away, watching her eyes widen as she took in his upper body. It made him glad he kept himself fit.

It took seconds to remove the rest of his clothes.

Usually by this point his partner was half naked too. Adam couldn't recall stripping for a woman and was surprised to find he liked it. Not the strip so much as Gisèle's fascinated reaction. As if she'd never seen a naked man up close. Her avid hunger, mixed with awe, was everything he could want.

But he didn't want her awed if it stopped her touching.

Adam took her hand and planted it on his chest. Her fingers splayed as she moved closer.

Better, much better. 'Your turn.'

Holding his gaze, Gisèle reached behind her dress, the other arm crossed over her bodice. The sound of the zip lowering was loud in the silence.

The dress loosened around her waist.

Then with a flicker in her eyes of something he couldn't interpret, she dropped her arm and the bodice fell.

The rush of blood in his ears deafened him. Pain lanced his chest as he stopped breathing.

He'd known she was beautiful, but the jiggle of lush, rose-tipped breasts as she pushed the red dress over her hips... She undid him.

Narrow waist. A sweet curve of hips. Taut thighs.

As she stepped free of the dress, there was only a narrow thong of red lace between them.

Adam couldn't wait longer. He grabbed his wallet, salvaged some condoms and slapped them on the bedside table. When he turned she was already on the bed, eyes huge, breasts swaying with each shortened breath.

She looked utterly desirable, if a little nervous. He understood that. This moment felt bigger than any previous sexual encounter. More intense. Just...more.

He reached for a condom, tore it open and, in a supreme test of control, rolled it on. Gisèle's gaze followed his hands. He saw her swallow and moisten her lips and he couldn't take any more.

Adam kneeled, straddling her legs, hands on either side of her shoulders, and bent to nuzzle her breast. Her skin was impossibly soft there, silken and fragrant. He closed his eyes, kissing his way around the underside, then slowly, in diminishing circles, towards her nipple.

Her thighs opened beneath him, pressing against his legs, and he heard the sweet hitch of her breathing. Urgent fingers grabbed the back of his head, tugging him down. When he lapped at her nipple, then drew it into his mouth, her husky cry of delight engulfed him.

He moved to her other breast, giving it the attention it deserved. All the while the shift of her legs against his, the fractured rhythm of her breathing and the sheer erotic beauty of her turned him from needy to desperate, his groin heavy and impossibly tight.

A movement shattered his fragile control. Soft fingers touched his erection, light as a butterfly's wing. Then they curled around him and his eyes snapped open. Gisèle watched, eyes glittering and lips dark.

'Please, Adam.'

She didn't need to persuade him. Much as he adored exploring her body, he'd been fighting the need to lose himself in her. Now, with her hand around him, it was a question of whether he could last that long.

Shuddering with effort, he rose above her, untangling her fingers and raising them to his lips, kissing her palm before holding her hand against the bed above her head. He captured her other hand and held it there too.

That made her body arch, her breasts tilt towards him. He had to shut his eyes as he nudged her legs wider and settled between them.

Sensation engulfed him. The intimate heat of her body against his. The friction of her smooth skin, the tiny adjustments as their bodies settled against each other, the perfume of sex and flowers and something that was Gisèle alone.

For a second, two, three, Adam held steady, not trusting himself to move. Then, putting his weight on one elbow, he slipped his hand between them, following that inviting cleft to her clitoris, wet with arousal.

Adam grinned, or maybe it was a grimace, for her voice sounded unsure as she said his name.

'It's okay, sweetheart. Just making sure you're ready.'

He stroked her, slow and long, reading renewed need in the movement of her hips.

An instant later he was there, nudging her entrance, falling into her silvery eyes as he thrust slow and steady.

Desperate as he was, prepared as he was, Adam was still confounded by the sensation of their joining. He paused, stunned as Gisèle's impossibly tight embrace tested him. But he couldn't hold back. The temptation was unlike no other. He surged forward, slow and deep till they locked tight.

It was only then that he realised how still she'd become.

How tense. Her eyes were shut and he felt the short pants of her breathing on his face.

Instantly he released her hands, propping himself higher so his chest didn't squash her.

'Have I hurt you?'

Given his size, he always ensured his sexual partners were fully aroused and ready. Dismay rose.

'It's okay, Adam.' Her gaze met his. 'I'm just adjusting. This is...new.'

'New?' He couldn't believe his ears. She couldn't mean...

But she did. The proof, he belatedly realised, was in her untried body.

Heat swept him from scalp to sole. He told himself it was chagrin that he hadn't guessed, hadn't prepared her better. But he feared some of his reaction was excitement. Gisèle was his and he was hers in a way no other man could ever be.

She clutched him, fingers anchoring his buttocks. 'You're not going to stop, are you?'

Adam shook his head. 'Not unless you want me to.'

'I don't.'

He hefted a shaky sigh. 'Good.'

Because he had no idea how he'd manage that. Instead he withdrew slowly, shivering at the exquisite sensation of friction, before gently nudging back into glorious heat.

This time Gisèle was ready, lifting a little clumsily to meet him. Even that tested him to the limit.

He pulled back to kiss her breasts, lavishing more of the attention they deserved, until she gasped and writhed, tugging him higher.

How could he resist her? His body was already moving of its own volition in a slow, building rhythm that would soon send him over the edge.

He couldn't stop. Didn't want to stop, when her eyes glittered up at him, diamond-bright, and she moved with him, eager. He could only try to make it good for her too.

Adam slipped his hand between them, finding her sensitive spot, applying twisting pressure in time with every buck of his hips.

Her mouth sagged on a silent gasp. Her eyes rounded. Her hands dug tighter into his glutes, possessive and urgent, and the friction between their bodies became so beautiful, so intense, he thought he'd die from pleasure.

He felt the change in her. The quickening, that fluttering clench of approaching orgasm. His groin turned to fire, impossibly tight and heavy as a prickle of sensation built at the base of his spine.

With each movement it was harder to believe they were two separate entities. Her tension was his. Her delight. Her building climax.

Then it smashed into them. A wave that lifted them high, catapulting them into the unknown.

Adam saw Gisèle's throat work, heard what might have been his name, and felt a rush of elation and protectiveness as bliss took him.

He wrapped his arms around her, gathering her close as they rode the storm together.

CHAPTER TEN

ADAM RETURNED FROM dealing with the condom and paused beside the bed. Gisèle's hair splayed, tangled, across the pillow. But it was the only hint of their earlier abandonment. She lay neatly on her side, one hand beneath the pillow, her knees slightly bent. As if even in sleep she was self-contained.

As if she didn't need him.

His pulse kicked and discomfort was a wave washing his bare skin. He didn't know why but the idea appalled.

He hesitated. With any other lover he'd slide in beside her and gather her close. There'd be more sex before morning arrived.

He raked his hair, blunt nails scratching his scalp in an effort to get his brain working. But it wouldn't. It was stuck on the fact she'd been a virgin.

A virgin!

The soignée spokeswoman leading one of the world's most elite companies.

The sexy woman who'd stirred his libido in a short film clip viewed half a world away.

The woman he'd lusted after for weeks. Who'd given him one of the most spectacular sexual experiences of his life. Who wore the reddened mark of beard rash on her throat from his stubble. It dismayed him that he'd hurt her, however inadvertently. Yet he couldn't deny secret satisfaction, seeing that mark.

'If you don't want to come back to bed,' said a small voice, 'that's okay.'

Her eyes were misty grey slits in the lamplight. Instantly

Adam sat, brushing her hair off her face, needing to see her expression.

And because he couldn't resist touching her.

With her satiny hair, soft skin and velvety embrace, she was the epitome of femininity. Yet she was strong, her lithe body a perfect match for his, and her mind… She was a woman to be reckoned with.

'I want nothing more than to share the bed with you,' he admitted in a gravel voice. 'But I wondered if you wanted privacy.'

Their eyes met and familiar heat blasted him. He breathed deep and slow, willing away his too-ready erection.

Gisèle lifted the covers and wriggled back across the bed. He got in, gritting his teeth as she snuggled against his side, the weight of her breasts against him, the down at the apex of her thighs tickling his hip when she lifted one smooth thigh over his.

He shifted, trying to distract himself from her innocently arousing touch. Frantic, he turned his brain to the financial implications of another deal he was considering. But profits, losses and turnover couldn't compete with Gisèle, naked and nubile.

She moved her head against his shoulder, her lips brushing his skin and making his molars clench with the effort of not reacting. 'What's the cologne you wear?'

'Sorry?' He was battling arousal and she was asking about colognes?

'Your scent. Is it soap or aftershave? But then you haven't shaved.' Her voice was rushed and breathless and the penny dropped that she was nervous and filling the silence. His heart squeezed. Post-coital small talk was new to Gisèle. He didn't know if that made him pleased or ashamed. 'I've been wondering since we met. I know most colognes but can't place yours.'

Adam stroked her shoulder. 'I don't wear cologne. As for soap, it's whatever I find in the bathroom.'

'It's not a manufactured scent?'

'My mother and sister are the ones who wear perfume. Not

me.' He could imagine the reaction if he'd turned up to work on a building site or in a haulage yard years ago, doused in cologne. He tilted his head, trying to read her expression. 'Is that a problem?'

'Only that I've been going crazy trying to identify it.' Her huff of laughter was warm on his chest. 'You smell…good.'

'Is that a compliment, Ms Fontaine?'

'It could be, Mr Wilde.'

Adam breathed out, some of his tension easing. 'Why didn't you tell me, Gisèle?'

Immediately she stiffened and he turned his head, pressing a kiss to her hair. He disliked it when she tensed. That was when she put up barriers.

'That I was inexperienced? Why do you think? I didn't want you stopping. I thought if I told you, you wouldn't be interested.'

Adam couldn't prevent his bark of laughter. 'For an intelligent woman you don't know much about the male libido. Not interested! Didn't I admit I've been so *interested* I've carried condoms everywhere I go?'

Gisèle shrugged, the movement making her breasts slide against him. His laugh died as he reminded himself she definitely wasn't ready for more.

'It never occurred to me that you had no experience.'

That bothered him. Not only about tonight, but the way he'd pursued her, cutting off her options, giving her little choice but to be wooed by him. If he let himself think about that—

'It's not surprising.' Her voice was light but he heard the strain. 'Given my first sexual experience ended badly.'

'There must have been other men who attracted you.'

Adam's teeth snapped closed at the thought. He hated the idea of her desiring any man but him.

How ridiculous was that, in the circumstances?

'Maybe. But not enough.' She rested her hand in his ribcage. 'You think I'm a coward, don't you?'

He covered her hand with his then lifted it to his mouth, kissing it gently. 'Not at all. You'd had a bad experience.'

'Bad experiences, plural. That recording was just the final straw.' She shook her head, her hair tickling his chin. 'You've no idea what it was like growing up constantly judged and found wanting *in public*. The press loved nothing better than to snap a photo of me with acne or a few extra kilos, or looking awkward or shy. They'd print side-by-side photos of my mother at some glamorous party and me looking fat and frumpy. There'd be columns devoted to my lack of style or how plain I was.'

Adam's grip tightened on her hand, his gut clenching. The dossier he'd read had summarised her early years. He hadn't seen those poisonous pieces. 'That's appalling.'

'That was my life. Judged and found wanting. I grew used to rejection and not being good enough. Combine that with a guy seducing me so he could share a tape of me naked and—'

'I understand!'

Adam didn't need to hear more. He felt sick to the stomach. Gisèle had been abused in so many ways.

Then you came along like a knight in shining armour, didn't you? What right have you to feel appalled, when you're using her for your own ends?

He told himself he'd been upfront with her. She'd had the choice to walk away. He'd been straight down the line with her.

Yet Adam's skin felt too tight for his body. His heart thundered. Every muscle tensed and he tasted metal on his tongue. Regret? Guilt?

He held her close, unable even now to drag himself away and leave her alone.

But there was one thing he *could* do.

'You don't still compare yourself with your mother, do you?'

'Not any more.'

She didn't sound convincing and pain pierced him.

Adam rolled onto his side to face her, wrapping both arms

around her. 'Your mother was a very beautiful woman. If you like predictable sweetness.'

'Sorry? Predictable?'

'Nothing wrong with that. Clearly the cameras loved her. But I prefer a different kind of beauty. Something deeper and more honest than mere prettiness.'

Gisèle struggled to prop herself up on an elbow, looking down at him. 'You're talking rubbish. Is this you feeling sorry for me and trying to make me feel better? My mother was one of the most beautiful women in the world.'

Gisèle's eyes flashed, her cheeks were flushed and her lips formed a pout of disapproval that was the single most alluring thing he'd ever seen. Guilt forgotten, his body reacted with a rush of adrenaline and a surge of blood to the groin.

'I'm telling the truth. You can trust me for that.' He was regularly dubbed brash, rude or a maverick because he favoured blunt honesty to sugar-coated half-truths or downright lies. 'Your mother was gorgeous and so are you. But personally I find a pinch of spice more appealing than a bowl of sugar. Her beauty was real but...predictable. Yours has depth and power. If you don't believe me, pay more attention next time you do a press conference. Look into the eyes of the men there and you'll see what I mean. You're beautiful, Gisèle.'

Beautiful, he'd called her.

Could she believe him?

Something needy and eager had twisted inside her. Even if it had only been an attempt to make her feel good, it had worked. Not because she wanted to be beautiful—she'd stopped fretting over that years ago. But because it showed Adam *cared*. It surprised her how much that meant. How moved she was by his consideration.

Gisèle looked across the conference table to where he sat, listening to the presentation, willing him to turn and smile at her. She wanted to see his eyes soften as they had last night.

But since entering the conference room there'd been no sign of last night's tender lover. No shimmer of admiration in his eyes. He'd avoided looking at her and had taken his usual seat on the other side, surrounded by his team.

She'd never felt the distance between them more.

She told herself Adam was treating her as a professional in a professional situation. Yet it wasn't just in the meeting. There'd been a change earlier.

In the dawn light she'd turned to him, snuggling close and brushing her lips across his flesh, hoping to tempt him into sex again. Their first time had been magnificent and she was eager to try it again.

But Adam had mumbled something and rolled away, leaving her staring at the wide angle of his shoulders and smooth back.

Gisèle had been *sure* he was awake.

A woman more confident in her sex appeal would have shaken him awake, if he weren't already, and seduced him. She'd been tempted, but physical intimacy was so new…

And you still doubt yourself.

It was frustrating but true. It took more than one profoundly beautiful, erotic experience to change a lifetime's thinking.

Later she'd woken alone. Adam was long gone, judging by the cool sheets. He'd left a note saying he didn't want to disturb her and he'd understand if she stayed in bed rather than attending the meeting.

So much for breakfasting together in bed, lingering there for more pleasure.

She'd checked the time, shot out of bed and into the shower. There'd been just enough time to gulp down a croissant and coffee before leaving.

The one bright spot had been Adam's reaction as she walked into his suite on the way to the car. His eyes had lit up and there'd been no mistaking his pleasure or the heat in that brilliant stare.

She'd crossed the room in her tailored suit and kissed him,

sinking into his tall frame and feeling her tense muscles ease as he'd pulled her close and kissed her back with a fervour that made her head spin.

In his arms she hadn't felt like a businesswoman or a commercial asset acquired to enhance profits. She felt desirable and appreciated. Powerful.

Except moments later he'd pulled away, murmuring about the time and the urgent call he needed to make on the way.

They'd spent the drive on opposite sides of the limo's wide back seat, Adam deep in discussion on his phone. Only his long fingers around hers on the seat between them had eased the creeping feeling that something had gone wrong between them.

Now, watching him across the table, the idea intensified. He was so determinedly *not* looking at her.

He turned and their eyes met, and it was like it had been last night. The world fell away and they might have been completely alone. Heat ignited in her pelvis, making her wriggle in her seat. Any pretence that she was listening to the speaker at the other end of the table died.

For long moments their gazes locked. Did she imagine heat streaking his cheekbones? A hungry glitter in his eyes?

Her pulse quickened and her nipples budded against her silk shirt.

'We need to call a break.' Adam looked directly at her so she thought he spoke to her. Then he turned, addressing the others around the table. 'The meeting will resume in fifteen minutes.'

There were surprised murmurs but no objections. Who would dare defy Adam Wilde? People pushed back their chairs and stretched stiff muscles.

Adam leaned towards one of his staff members, saying something Gisèle couldn't catch. The other man nodded, frowning, then took out his phone and strode to the door.

What had she missed? Something had changed as she sat

daydreaming about Adam and what they'd shared. Mentally she shook herself. She'd fought hard for the House of Fontaine, she couldn't afford to be distracted now.

Gisèle rose but, before she could walk around the table, Adam exited the room.

Her way was blocked by her own staff, wanting to check details and propose a compromise approach. By the time she made it out of the room, she couldn't see Adam. Just two of his staff in conversation, their backs to her.

'It's so out of character,' one said. 'He *never* deals with the minutiae. In five years I've never seen him personally manage a takeover at this level. That's what he pays us for.'

The other nodded. 'When he said he was going to attend a discussion on performance appraisal I couldn't believe it. It's not surprising that...'

The woman's words petered out as Gisèle approached.

What wasn't surprising? And why was the Fontaine takeover so different to any of Adam's previous ones?

'Mr Wilde?' she asked.

The Australian pointed down the corridor. 'In the small conference room, Ms Fontaine. I believe he's making a call.'

If that was meant to stop her following, it didn't. She rapped on the door, opening it without waiting for a response.

Adam was on his phone. He watched her enter, his expression giving nothing away. He might have been watching a stranger.

She rubbed her upper arms, suddenly cold. He didn't look like the man who'd taken her to the stars last night. Who'd kissed her briefly yet passionately this morning, then held her hand all the way to their meeting.

He looked like the autocratic stranger she'd met weeks ago.

Adam ended the call and put his phone away. Gisèle didn't wait for him to speak but strode into his personal space.

'What is it? What's wrong?'

'Nothing's wrong.'

Her jangling nerves told a different story. She knew it was sex they'd shared last night, not a promise of lasting devotion. Yet she'd expected at least a shadow of last night's intimacy now they were alone.

He lifted his broad shoulders. 'Okay, not wrong. But something's come up. I need to go to New York today. Now.'

'What about our negotiations?'

Forget the negotiations! What about us?

But a lifetime of guarding her tongue stopped the words.

Was there an *us*? Or had last night been a one-off?

Gisèle backed up a step, arms wrapping around her middle as pain bloomed deep within.

As if reading her hurt, Adam followed, the warmth of his tall frame engulfing her as he moved into her space. Yet she felt cold, for still he didn't reach for her.

'I'm sorry, Gisèle. It's important.'

More important than me? Us?

She bit her lip rather than blurt out needy questions. 'I see. You have important business in New York. And Fontaine's? Our meetings?'

For a long time Adam said nothing. Strangely he looked as tense as she felt. She saw the tendons stand proud in his throat and the rapid tick of a pulse at his temple. As if *he* were stressed. Then his chest rose and fell on a drawn-out sigh and his hands curled around her upper arms, pulling her hard against him.

Gisèle's eyes closed as she leaned into him, drawing in his unique scent and feeling herself relax as his breath brushed her face.

This was what she wanted! What she'd missed.

His hand swept from her nape to her waist then to her buttocks, pulling her closer. Sparks ignited. There was no mistaking his erection pressing against her abdomen.

So Adam wasn't immune. He wanted her as badly as she craved him. It was there in every taut sinew and bunched muscle. In the stream of whispered words feathering her ears. Words of seductive promise and pure need.

The magnate disappeared, replaced by her lover, and she rejoiced.

Gisèle tilted her head up, sliding her hands around his neck, offering her mouth as his head lowered. It had only been a few hours but she'd missed him, missed this intimacy.

Someone coughed behind her. Then coughed again.

'Sorry boss, but you said…'

Adam tilted his head so his forehead touched hers. He huffed a frustrated sigh and muttered what sounded like a curse. His shoulders rose and fell, then he lifted his head, but not before feathering her mouth with his, making her lips tingle.

'I'm on my way.'

The door closed and they stood, both breathing heavily. Adam's arms encompassed her and she felt the ponderous thud of his pulse against her hand at his throat.

'I need to go,' he said finally. 'My plane's waiting. But we'll talk later.'

Adam dropped his arms and stepped away and she felt abruptly cold. How could he do that? Go from heated arousal to businesslike in an instant?

Gisèle's head was spinning. Maybe if last night hadn't been the first time she'd slept with a man she'd be able to switch from business to sex to business too.

She lifted her chin and tried to pretend she was as clear-headed as he. 'And the performance evaluation process? That hasn't been agreed.'

'It was a convincing presentation. I'll instruct my team to accept your recommendation.'

Gisèle stared. 'Just like that?' It had been contentious from the beginning.

Their eyes met and the air sizzled with something that had absolutely nothing to do with business.

'If it works as you say, then good. If it doesn't, we'll scrap it. Now…' he looked at the phone that was once again in his hand '… I need to go.' He met her gaze and something shifted in his expression. 'I'm sorry, Gisèle. I don't want to leave you. But this is…necessary. I'll call tonight.'

She opened and shut her mouth, stunned that he was walking out of these meetings when he'd been the one to insist on delving into every aspect of the company. But it wasn't just the company that concerned her.

'We're supposed to marry in a few days.'

'Don't worry. I'll be back in good time.'

Then he was gone, leaving her bereft and confused. Adam had upended her life into a whirlwind of meetings and glamorous events where the one constant was him at her side.

Heat suffused her as she remembered last night.

Now, suddenly, his priorities had changed.

Had he lost enthusiasm for Fontaine's? For her?

Yet he'd said he didn't want to leave. Said he'd be back for the wedding.

What was the sudden crisis?

How had Adam known about it before he left the meeting? He'd had his phone off. She'd been watching him. There'd been no message passed by a staff member. No whisper, note or text.

Gisèle placed her palms on her churning belly. Was New York an excuse to get away from France and her?

It seemed impossible after last night. But she couldn't shake the idea.

Despite what he said, maybe he was cooling on marriage. Maybe now they'd had sex the novelty had worn off. Her skin crawled and she told herself Adam wasn't like that.

But how well do you really know him?

She tried to summon excitement at the prospect of their marriage of convenience being cancelled. But all she felt was a dull, heavy sense of anti-climax. What was wrong with her?

CHAPTER ELEVEN

ADAM WAS SURPRISED at how tense he felt on his wedding night.

Outwardly, the day had gone well. His mother and sister had warmed to Gisèle, enthusiastically entering into the celebrations, as if their earlier private questions about the rush to marry had never happened.

Gisèle's brother had been civil if standoffish, but that wasn't surprising.

Most importantly, Gisèle had been there.

He'd wondered if she'd show up as promised. Especially as he hadn't had a chance to see her before the ceremony.

He'd returned to Paris to find his mum and sister had arrived unexpectedly from Australia, despite his suggestion they wait for him and Gisèle to visit them in a few weeks. He should have known his mother would insist on attending, even if it was supposed to be an elopement wedding.

So he'd spent last night with his family, unable to track down his bride-to-be. His inability to contact her had unsettled him. He'd spoken to her daily while away, yet yesterday couldn't raise her.

What if she'd decided to renege? He'd been on tenterhooks until he saw her with her brother, appearing mere moments before the short ceremony.

Adam huffed a breath out of tight lungs, remembering his relief. He lifted a hand from the car's steering wheel and raked his scalp. Beside him in the passenger seat his bride was a silent presence.

Even in the dark he knew she wasn't dozing after an evening convincing their families that they were, if not love's young dream, then at least happy to marry.

He recalled the moment they'd been pronounced husband and wife and he'd leaned in for a kiss. Gisèle hadn't exactly stiffened but her lips hadn't moved. Her eyes, a bright accusing blue, had bored into his, and she'd stepped away as soon as possible.

Leaving him regretting his decision to go to New York, knowing he'd erred, yet annoyed that she held a grudge.

Wasn't she glad to see him?

He'd read disdain in that formal kiss and today's cool, distant smiles. In her refusal to carry a bouquet or wear a veil. Even in her choice of dress, not bridal white but a deep, vibrant pink his mother called fuchsia, that looked to him like a declaration of independence.

Gisèle was arresting in the colour. The fitted knee length dress with its deep V neckline was perfect on her. It was fashion as a statement.

Look at me, feminine and powerful, sexy and definitely no pushover. My own woman.

It didn't take a genius to know she wouldn't make this easy for him.

Even if she'd charmed his family with consummate ease. It was his mother's first trip to Paris and Gisèle had been warm and engaging, suggesting excursions, answering endless questions about France.

It was only when she turned to Adam, beside her, that her smile grew brittle.

All evening, as they'd dined in the prestigious restaurant high in the Eiffel Tower, she'd held herself stiffly. Oh, she'd laughed with his family and her brother, but with Adam the curve of her lips was belied by the cool blue of her eyes.

He had a lot of catching up to do.

It had been a mistake, leaving her in Paris. An even bigger mistake not to return until the wedding. But at the time it had felt imperative.

The discovery that she'd been a virgin on top of what she'd faced in the past had been a punch to the gut. A punch of conscience.

For once Adam hadn't thought through his decision. He'd acted solely on instinct that told him to give her space. If he'd stayed they wouldn't have left the bedroom for days. That wasn't the way she deserved to be treated.

More, it was clear he'd done badly, pushing a woman who'd already dealt with so much into what she'd called his devil's deal. He'd felt sick hearing her story of betrayal and sexual predation.

Gisèle might have initiated their lovemaking, but an inner voice told him he should have resisted. She'd been shaken up mere hours before, reliving past horror. She'd been vulnerable.

Adam should have held strong. Better if he'd returned to his suite or hit the pavements of Paris to pound some restraint into himself.

'Where are we going?'

'Out of town for a few days. Somewhere the press won't badger us.' He was sick of paps snapping photos whenever they appeared in public. 'Your luggage has gone ahead.'

He felt her sit straighter. Because he'd arranged it without asking her? If she'd been around to ask he would have. But Gisèle didn't complain. She'd learned to choose which battles she'd bother fighting.

He admired that. Despite the regrettable tension between them, he looked forward to persuading her to forget her annoyance.

'That won't be convenient for business.'

'We'll have a break.'

'A honeymoon?' Did he imagine her voice cracked? 'That's hardly necessary.'

Adam disagreed. But he'd choose his way carefully. He'd made errors and had a lot of ground to make up with his wife.

Satisfaction filled him at the word. Wife.

When he didn't respond Gisèle continued. 'You'll go stir crazy without work. You have meetings, conference calls and reports all day. In the evenings we're always out so you can network or wheel and deal. You never switch off.'

It was true. Adam hadn't built his success by resting on his laurels. But he didn't correct her to say their busy social schedule wasn't all about business. Much of it had been showing off the prize on his arm—Gisèle Fontaine, classy, desirable and socially accepted, the face of his prestigious new acquisition.

'The change will do me good.'

Angela had been at him for ages to take some down time.

'Hmph.'

She didn't sound convinced and he wasn't ready to admit his priorities had shifted. Success was still vital but it didn't hold the same urgency as the need to be with Gisèle.

Adam smiled grimly at the fantasies he'd harboured about honeymooning with his new wife. Gisèle had been a lot more amenable and welcoming in those.

They'd left the city when Gisèle spoke again. 'Tell me more about why you wanted Fontaine's.'

He glanced across to find her twisted in her seat, watching him. Funny how dissatisfying it was that his bride was more interested in business than in *them*.

And wasn't that a change for him?

'I told you. I saw an opportunity for long-term profit.'

'Your mother told me how thrilled she was that you were acquiring it.' Gisèle paused. 'She said when things were tough after your father died, her big treat was a day trip into the city, window shopping. Getting her makeup done for free by a Fontaine's representative.' He felt her gaze on him. 'She said it was a family day out, trying free samples in the stores and picnicking in the park.'

'You think I acquired it out of sentimentality?' He shrugged. 'Perhaps subconsciously that made me consider a cosmetics company instead of dismissing it out of hand. But my decision was based on sound business factors.'

'Was that all?'

Adam started. She couldn't know what had convinced him was the film clip of *her*, arousing every possessive instinct. Making him want.

'What do you mean?'

'You once spoke about it being an elite company. About that being important and I wondered...'

When he didn't respond she turned to stare through the windscreen rather than at him. Much as he disliked being probed, he preferred her attention on him.

'I should have known better,' she murmured.

'What do you mean?'

'You're good at asking questions and demanding answers. But you don't give much away about yourself.'

Whereas she'd laid herself open with her revelations of past pain. Despite her vulnerability, Gisèle had been strong enough to share her trauma with him. But when she asked the simplest question he avoided answering fully.

Because admitting to weakness or pain threatened the image he'd built of himself over the years as capable, able to overcome any difficulty, always successful.

Your success isn't doing you much good now, is it? Gisèle isn't interested in the tycoon, just the man. Which sets her apart from most women you know.

'You're right,' he admitted. He overtook a lorry then changed lane, eyes on the road. 'When my dad died I told myself I was the man of the family, responsible for looking after my mother and sister. I got in the habit of keeping troubles to myself, dealing with problems alone.'

He paused. 'You really want to know what drew me to Fontaine's?'

'Of course.'

Adam's pulse quickened as he let himself remember those early days. The perpetual struggle to prove himself with the odds stacked against him.

'We had some tough years, very tough. Mum didn't earn much as a cleaner and some families she worked for ripped her off, paying less than they should. I told you about the rich kids at the school near our place and that I didn't envy what they had. That was true. But I suppose I developed a chip on my shoulder, dealing with some of them.'

He paused before continuing. 'It got worse when I left school to work full time. I got a job for a wealthy local and worked hard. But he found creative ways to exploit his workers and overcharge his customers. Eventually I left and set up in competition. It was David and Goliath stuff. I wasn't a threat to him, not then. But that didn't stop his son and some mates trying to beat me into deciding to stop when I won a small contract he'd assumed he'd get.'

'Oh, Adam!' The warmth in her voice was all he could wish for. 'Is that when you broke your nose?'

He hadn't realised he'd lifted one hand from the wheel to rub his nose. It was a habit from the old days, one he'd left behind years ago.

'It is. Three against one wasn't good odds. But I'd got some of my startup money as a bare-knuckle fighter and knew what I was doing. They were pampered louts.'

Unlike the aggressors, he'd walked unaided from the scene.

'It made me even more determined to make a go of it. As for the nose… I could have got it reset, but it didn't bother me. In fact, it was a reminder that I could face anything. That was useful every time I took a big risk, or some privileged git tried to put me in my place.'

'That happened often?'

'Enough.' It was surprisingly easy to share with Gisèle, sitting in the dark together. 'In the early days I *was* rough and ready. I didn't try to fit in or play nice. I was too focused on winning at all costs, to help my family and build the company.'

Because he wouldn't rest until his family was safe and his mother could stop the draining hours of menial work.

'Maybe I was too proud, playing up that maverick image rather than trying to fit in with the sleek, self-satisfied oligarchs who dominated the commercial world. I'd go to business functions and hear comments about being uncouth, undesirable, lacking in class. The sort of thing those thugs had said when they tried to beat me into giving up my dream of success.'

His skin burned as he recalled their smug contempt. 'Now my corporation is thriving and I wanted another challenge. I decided this time I'd find something that stood out. Something with a renowned, revered name.'

'Something to show the establishment you'd made it?'

Adam shrugged. 'It wasn't quite that simple. I had a hankering for something different.'

'A perfume and cosmetics company is definitely that. It's nothing like the rest of your portfolio.'

'Variety is the spice of life.'

'Do they still call you that? Uncouth?'

'Still? I have no idea. I don't pay attention to them. I've left most of them behind. But the press like to trumpet my outsider status when it suits a headline.'

The silence extended so long he thought Gisèle wasn't going to say any more.

'So you went to the effort and enormous expense of acquiring a troubled French company to prove yourself to people who no longer have influence over you?'

She made him sound needy for external validation. His mouth firmed.

'Maybe that chip on my shoulder is bigger than I thought.' He hadn't thought of it that way before. 'But the kicker was that their comments reflected on my family too. The first time

I went to a big gala after winning a business award I took my mother and sister. They had to run the gauntlet of deliberately audible snide comments.'

Gisèle gasped. 'That's awful.'

He nodded. 'I vowed never to put them in that situation again. But they were magnificent. My mother, ever the pacifier, pretended not to hear. My little sister turned to a few of them and asked what they'd achieved in the last year that outshone my business acumen and performance. She was seventeen at the time.'

He heard a choke of laughter, swiftly curtailed. 'She's certainly not bashful. Good on her, standing up for you.'

Like Gisèle, ensuring her brother retained a role in the family company. He admired that about her too.

'I like that you're protective of each other,' she continued. 'You seem to be a close, caring family.'

Did she sound wistful? By all accounts her family had been close, until her father's death and her mother's desertion, pursuing one high-profile love affair after another.

Once again Adam felt sympathy and pride for this indomitable woman.

'There was another reason I was drawn to the House of Fontaine.'

Was he really saying this? It went against his mantra of not revealing weakness or giving power to an opponent. Yet he'd just shared what some would call a weakness with Gisèle— his need to show he'd made it to the topmost pinnacle, where none could look down on him. It hadn't felt like weakness. Honesty had its own power.

Besides, she wasn't an opponent. She was far more complex and important.

'Let me guess. You want a cosmetics line designed for your mother. Or an exclusive perfume. It can be arranged—'

'Nothing like that.'

Adam took the exit off the autoroute, heart hammering.

Opening up wasn't easy. This was opening himself as he never had before.

She'd been frank about her past, details she'd kept private for years. It was fitting he be equally as frank. He *owed* her that.

Besides, he wanted more from Gisèle, much more than he'd imagined initially. He mightn't be the most emotionally astute man, but he knew she wouldn't respond to demands.

He didn't want to demand. He wanted her to want him of her own free will.

Which meant ceding some power to her.

If he stopped to think about the implications he mightn't follow through. He plunged on. 'I saw footage of you giving a press conference a couple of months ago.'

'And?'

'That's it. I saw you, Gisèle. And I knew as surely as I know my own name that I wanted you.'

CHAPTER TWELVE

THE CAR PURRED along the darkened road as Gisèle stared at Adam's harsh profile. There wasn't enough light to read his expression but he hadn't sounded like he was joking. In the dimness he looked tense rather than smug.

Her fingers dug into her seat, anchoring herself as the world wheeled.

She licked her lips and swallowed, turning to watch the headlights cut the night as the country road curved. The lights illuminated a pair of eyes in the grass, some small animal transfixed by the vehicle.

Gisèle felt that way, transfixed. Stunned.

'You expect me to believe *I* prompted you to take over the company?'

He'd said he'd wanted her from the day they met but this was something else!

'You think I'm lying?' Adam's hands rotated on the steering wheel as if he tightened his grip. 'You know that's not my style.' He shot her a sideways glance. 'It's fact. I was interested in the company. The figures looked good despite the mistakes that had been made and it met my other criteria. But what tipped the balance was you. Your poise, your smile. There was something indefinable about you, something I wanted.'

There was that word again—want. As if he hadn't acquired her for the continuity of having a Fontaine still attached to the company.

Gisèle's chest ached from holding her breath. Or maybe from the effort of not letting herself be persuaded. Because it was too outrageous.

Yet she wanted it to be true.

Because she'd felt it too, that shocking spark of connection. Attraction. Wanting.

She'd believed it was her own personal weakness. What if she weren't alone in feeling that way?

The idea was too big, too tempting.

Her heart crashed against her ribcage as if fighting to escape, and she had to work to keep her voice even. 'Don't tell me—it was my amazing beauty that hooked you.'

Another sideways glance came her way. 'You *are* beautiful, Gisèle, even if you don't believe it. But it wasn't that simple. There was something else. Your warmth, your animation.' He shook his head. 'I can't put it in words but it was a spark of something I couldn't ignore. Something I didn't *want* to ignore.'

Adam lifted one hand off the wheel and unerringly found hers in the darkness. His touch was warm, familiar and charged. A flurry of sparks burst in her blood, adrenaline coursing, making her sit straighter.

'You wanted me as a family representative. A Fontaine to continue the cachet of the family name.'

'That was only part of it.' When he spoke again his voice was deeper. 'It wasn't all about the business.'

Something potent shivered in the night air between them. Something that made the fine hairs on her arms stand up and the feelings she'd desperately tried to repress stir anew.

'Why tell me this, Adam?'

'I want to be honest with you. We're married. We're lovers, Gisèle. We have a relationship that means something.'

'Does it? That's not how it seems.' Or was she throwing up objections because the idea of their relationship meaning something real raised the stakes too much? It came too close to what she secretly desired. 'You pushed me away. That night we had sex, I turned to you later for more but you rolled away, pretending to be asleep. Once was clearly enough for you so I knew you'd been disappointed. Then in the morning you disappeared so fast your feet barely touched the ground.'

'Oh, sweetheart, you've got it all wrong.'

'Wrong? I was there. Don't say you were asleep. You knew what you were doing.'

Adam took his hand from hers to grip the wheel as he turned between a pair of stone pillars, large iron gates opening as they approached. Ahead lay a long drive under an avenue of trees.

Instead of being curious about their destination Gisèle found herself fixated on the loss of his hand on hers. How much she missed that simple touch.

Anxiety spiked. She'd fallen so deeply in thrall to him! She didn't want to feel this way. She'd rather hang onto the simmering anger that had seen her through his absence, her battered pride giving her the strength she'd needed to face him today.

'I did know what I was doing.' The admission sucked the air from her lungs. 'Not because I didn't want you, Gisèle, but because I wanted you too much.'

He stopped the car inside the gates, turning to her. 'I'd just discovered you were a sexual innocent. What we'd done *whetted* my appetite instead of diminishing it. I wanted to spend the rest of the night inside you, driving you from one peak to the next. Giving free rein to all the sexual fantasies I'd harboured about you for weeks.'

Adam's voice grew hoarse, his breathing choppy, as if reliving those explicit thoughts. 'I was afraid if I took you again I wouldn't stop, but I didn't want to hurt you. You'd been a virgin. I was trying to look after you.'

Gisèle's breathing roughened too, dampness beading her hairline and blooming between her thighs at the thought of Adam wanting to spend the night inside her. Arousal made her shift in her seat, though she knew there was only one way to ease the hollow ache inside.

'You really mean it.'

The discovery twisted what she thought she knew, making her memory of that night shift and resettle into a different pattern.

'I do.' It was there in his gravel-edged voice. 'You were inexperienced so I tried to be considerate. I wasn't sure if I'd already hurt you—'

'You didn't hurt me! It was just...surprising.' More intense than she'd expected, but wonderful. 'I liked it.'

His hand covered hers, squeezing. 'Good. But you were untried. Even if I didn't hurt you then I might have later. My need was...great.'

She shifted again, blood singing at those simple, devastating words. 'So was mine. I'd waited a long time to have sex.'

'I'm sorry, Gisèle. I should have explained. But it seemed easier to pretend to be asleep. Easier to withstand temptation.'

Typical man, avoiding difficult conversations.

But there was no rancour left in the thought. She was too caught in the graphic description of what he'd wanted to do with her. It was a torch flame in the darkness, lighting her up from the inside.

'And in the morning?'

'Much the same. You marched into my room in that tailored skirt and heels and all I wanted was to tumble you onto the bed and to hell with our meeting. But it was more than that.'

He lifted his hand from hers and accelerated slowly down the drive. In profile his features looked sharper than usual. 'That night you revealed how you'd been abused by your lover and it shone an unwelcome light on my behaviour. It made me review how I'd pushed into your world, cornering you into marriage. It didn't make me feel good.'

She'd wanted honesty but hadn't expected this. Adam's words made her head spin. 'You felt *guilty*?'

Though could she really be surprised? She'd seen another side to him at work. While he had no time for incompetence, Adam had surprised with his patience and kindness when dealing with employees worried about the future. And the sweet way he'd looked after her that night, putting no pressure on her, yet caring for her when she had an emotional meltdown...

'I gave you a choice with the contract and you accepted. I don't feel guilty about the takeover.' His words slowed. 'But to hear you'd been abused by a lover...' He shook his head. 'The fact is I wanted you from the first. You got the idea it would be a paper marriage but I never intended to settle for that. Then, the night we began to make love you told me what had happened to you and I felt guilty at having taken advantage of you, pushing you into marriage.'

Her eyes widened. She'd never thought to hear such an admission.

She heard the truth in his words and knew it would be easy to feed his guilt. But she couldn't do it.

For all his ruthless powerplay, Adam was honest, startlingly so. He didn't lie and cheat or demean her like the man who'd aimed to seduce her then share the footage of him taking her virginity.

Adam provoked and badgered her. He'd pushed her into a corner. Yet these past weeks he'd made her feel stronger, better about herself, about *them*. He'd brought her unexpected joy and shown tender consideration when she needed it.

'You behaved appallingly, appearing out of nowhere and making outrageous ultimatums. But it's nothing like what *he* did. You didn't trick me. I *wanted* you, Adam. *I* initiated sex, knowing who and what you were. You're not a sexual predator.'

'That's what I told myself. But I still felt uncomfortable. I needed space to think.'

Her emotions see-sawed. Amazement, excitement, puzzlement. Was he implying he couldn't think around her?

'So you took off to New York.' Her mind was a jumble. 'Yet

you came back for the wedding. Your conscience didn't bite hard enough to forget that.'

He shrugged as he turned a curve and pulled up before a small but perfect château of pale stone. Floodlights glinted off long windows, massed flowers spilled from planters on the stairs that swept up from the gravel drive, and round pepperpot towers at each end turned it into a place of whimsical fancy.

She wouldn't have been surprised to see a pumpkin coach drawn up before the grand entrance. Anything seemed possible tonight.

Adam killed the engine and turned to her. 'I want this marriage, Gisèle. Of course I wasn't going to give it up. I want *you*.' The silence stretched, broken only by the tick of the cooling engine. 'And I believe you want me.'

He was right. There was no point denying it. Yet she hesitated.

Coward. You weren't so reticent the night you demanded sex.

That truth was an itch under skin that grew too tight around her. It was infuriating that what he said was true. Despite everything she *did* want him. She'd been furious and hurt, arriving for their wedding. But never once had it occurred to her not to turn up. To use his absence as an excuse to break their agreement.

Because you want him. You want how he makes you feel. The way he sees you as no one else does.

'Of course you want this marriage,' she blustered. 'You needed a Fontaine—'

'You and I know it's not that simple any more. I want *you*. I've watched you at work, Gisèle, and away from it, and it's been a revelation. It's *exciting* discovering the woman you are, with more depth and integrity than I'd imagined in the beginning. It's *you* I want, not a cipher whose name happens to be Fontaine. And before you say it again, this isn't about the business. This is personal.'

She watched his broad chest rise and fall as if he battled powerful emotions.

Whereas she merely felt as if the earth had fallen away beneath her feet, leaving her tumbling in nothingness.

'It's all about what *you* want, isn't it Adam? What about me?'

His voice was sharp, his words quick and disbelieving. 'You're saying you don't want me?'

Her breath was a sigh. 'Marriage is about more than simple want,' she said finally. 'You didn't give me a choice.'

Adam's words when they came were a low burr that caressed her shivery skin. 'Really? You went through today's ceremony because I held a gun to your head? That's not the woman I know. The strong woman who isn't scared to stand up to me. You could have stood there today before my family and accused me of forcing your hand. Nothing easier. You could have told them what was in that contract you signed. You've met my mother and sister. Do you really think they'd let me get away with forcing you into anything?' He paused. 'Do you truthfully think I want that?'

It hurt to breathe, her emotions a tumult in her breast. Because it was true. Escape would have been so easy.

If she'd been desperate enough.

Within seconds of meeting Adam's mother and sister she'd liked them, known them to be genuine, decent people who loved and thought the world of him.

But she'd discovered he wasn't an unregenerate bully. How often already had she seen his caring side? Seen him change his stance, swayed by others' arguments or needs? He'd been there for her when she needed support.

Yet she couldn't ignore what he'd done. 'What about the penalty clause in the contract you made me sign?'

Even in the gloom she saw his face tighten, his head jerk back. 'You really believe I'd hold you to that *now*, after what we shared?'

'It's a legal contract.'

'One that served its purpose and stopped you running from me in the beginning. But if you really think…'

He shoved open his door, shooting out of the car before she had time to guess his intention. One second he was there, an electrifying presence beside her, the next he was a shadow stalking off into the gloom.

Gisèle ripped her seatbelt undone and stumbled out so fast her heel turned in the gravel. It didn't stop her stomping after him.

'Don't you dare walk away from me, Adam Wilde!'

That wide-shouldered figure stopped then slowly turned, his face a pale blur in the shadows behind the floodlights.

Limping a little, she reached him. 'You can't say something like that then walk away. You should have *told* me where I stood, spoken to me. Not assumed I'm a mind reader.'

Though she exulted in the fact he wanted her for himself. Not because of the company, but for *her*, Gisèle.

The man she'd come to know, who'd been so considerate and passionate, made her want to take the sort of personal risks she'd avoided all her life.

'Why? So you could argue? Run away because you're scared of what we share?'

She frowned, hearing an unfamiliar note in that rich voice.

He shoved his hands in his pockets and straightened to his full, impressive height. 'If that's what you really want, tell me and this ends now.'

'Ends?'

'We'll find a way to end the marriage if you really can't abide me.' There it was again, that curiously flat, almost de-flated note. 'Because I'm not the sort of man a woman like you wants.'

'A woman like me? What do you mean?'

'Isn't it obvious? A man who dragged himself up by his bootstraps.'

Gisèle couldn't believe what she heard, yet there was no mistaking the honesty in that gravelly tone.

The shock of it, that he'd truly end the marriage, and that he believed she found him less than desirable because of his history, made her stumble backwards, her heel sinking into the gravel again.

Off-balance, literally as well as emotionally, she gritted her teeth as she hauled off her heels and tossed them aside, the gravel rough beneath her soles.

It seemed it hadn't just been privileged male competitors who'd looked down on Adam, but some woman or women who'd made him think poorly of her sex. That saddened her. But not enough to quench her ire.

'We've established I'm not a snob. My problem,' she poked his solid chest, 'is you *assuming* I wanted to marry you after I'd come to know you. There was no discussion. No apology. Nothing. What if I was hanging out for love?'

'Are you, Gisèle?'

'No!' Much as she'd adored her parents, she didn't want what they'd shared. 'I saw what grief did to my mother when my father died. She didn't just lose a husband, she lost herself. She didn't even have enough left to share with her children. I never want to be that weak.'

'You could never be that weak.' His hand captured hers, holding it to his chest and something throbbed through his touch. Strength. Reassurance. 'You're a strong woman. That's one of the things I admire about you.'

'Not enough to trust me with the truth. You *herded* me into marriage.'

He inclined his head. 'I should apologise for that. But the truth? You know the truth. I admire you, desire you. I've never wanted a woman more. I like what we share, the spark in you, and I'm not just talking about sex. I believe I can make you happy if you let me try. I respect you, Gisèle. I'll never deliberately hurt you.'

She should pull her hand away but she couldn't. As if something, his energy, his determination, her own inclination, kept her where she was.

Yet marriage was a crazy idea. She should take him up on his offer to end this now.

Except she didn't want to.

For the first time she'd found someone she genuinely wanted to be with, someone who accepted her, cared for her and made her feel special. Someone who at last was being honest about their feelings.

'You don't get off that easily.' She drew in a sustaining breath. 'You say you respect me, but I won't stand for you making decisions for me. I refuse to be with a man who assumes he knows what I want.'

In the darkness his smile was a flash of white. 'And if I promise always to talk things over? To ask? Negotiate?'

Something rippled through her like a great tide, flattening the last vestiges of resistance. 'Then I *might* be persuaded.'

Who was she kidding? The fear that had gripped her when he talked about ending things still reverberated through her.

Adam scooped her up, holding her against his chest, sending excited shivers through her.

'What are you doing?'

'Saving your feet from that gravel and taking you where I can persuade you in more comfort.' His words were a silky caress. 'If you agree?'

Final chance to end this. That would be the sensible thing to do.

But Gisèle didn't want to end it. For the first time she wanted to take the daring, risky, phenomenally exciting option.

'That's an excellent idea.'

Minutes later they were in the château. There were lofty ceilings hung with glittering chandeliers, honey-coloured wooden floors and glimpses of rooms furnished with a mix of beautiful antiques and comfortable modern furniture.

Adam stopped before a graceful staircase. 'We're alone, Gisèle. No staff living in. There's a light supper in the kitchen.' He nodded towards the back of the building. 'Or we could continue this upstairs.'

His glittering eyes made her skin prickle with anticipation. 'I'm not hungry.'

Not for food. Not when he looked at her like that. Even her indignation faltered under the force of longing.

Minutes later they were in an exquisitely decorated bedroom, walls hung with silk and flowers in crystal bowls scenting the air. A vast bed was made up with snowy linens and a profusion of pillows and embroidered cushions, its surface scattered with petals in every shade from cream to apricot and crimson.

It was a romantic bower. Right down to the sheer curtains pulled back on either side of the bed and the ice bucket with its foil-topped bottle and delicate crystal goblets.

'You like it?'

Gisèle slowly shook her head. 'It's not what I expected.' She was in awe. No one had ever gone to so much trouble to please her.

His embrace stiffened. 'You don't approve.'

Surprised, she met his frowning gaze.

This wasn't a love match, yet Adam had gone to great lengths to make tonight special.

'I love it.' She swallowed. 'But one considerate gesture doesn't make up for your behaviour.'

He nodded gravely and lowered her to the floor, their bodies in contact all the way. Her nerve endings hummed with excitement by the time she stood on her own feet.

'I know what I want to do next. But what do you want, Gisèle?'

Excitement sparked. 'To undress you.'

There was no place for false pride here. Negotiations on

their marriage could wait. She couldn't. She reached for his tie, the fabric soft against her palms.

He growled. 'I want to reciprocate.'

Gisèle nodded. Seconds later they stood naked in a pool of discarded clothes.

Adam stroked his palms over her turgid nipples, taking the weight of her breasts, and she felt bliss beckon. His eyes glazed as his voice roughened. 'I want you so badly. But I don't want this to be done too soon. I want to kiss you all over, explore every inch, learn every erogenous zone.' Moss dark eyes met hers and she saw in them the same desperation she felt. 'Would you like that?'

Of course she would. The very sound of it made liquid heat pool between her thighs.

There were unexpected benefits in having Adam spell out his intentions and ask her opinion.

'Only if I can do the same.'

His assent was gruff but his hands infinitely gentle as he nudged her onto the bed.

By the time he'd finished his explorations, she'd found bliss several times under his questing mouth and hands. She should be exhausted. But as he kept telling her, she was stronger than she thought. For as Adam whispered in her ear every new suggestion for delicious pleasure, she found herself agreeing with alacrity.

It seemed she had an unending capacity for the pleasure he gave her. Even her intention of exploring his body in full wavered as he took her from one peak to another.

Until finally the lure of possession was too much. She needed to have him, yearning for something deeper, the union of their bodies.

This time when they came together it felt like there was nothing but raw honesty between them. No filters, no prevarication, no half-truths. Gisèle met his mesmerising eyes and felt like she'd found home.

With infinite care, Adam brought them together. A warm tide engulfed her. A great wave of feeling that was more than satisfaction. More than delight.

For an age they moved slowly, celebrating each wondrous sensation, until it became too much. Their slow dance grew staccato, urgent, reckless, yet beautiful still. And when the explosion hit them simultaneously, Gisèle had never known such joy, wrapping her lover close in her arms as they shuddered in ecstasy.

It felt like the promise of a new beginning she'd never dared believe in.

CHAPTER THIRTEEN

A WEEK LATER they lay in the shade of a huge tree, drowsing after a picnic and the best sex of his life.

Adam grinned. The best sex ever. That was saying something, considering how amazing their honeymoon had been. Intimacy with Gisèle was on a whole different scale to anything he'd known before.

Because she matters to you more than any lover ever has.

'What are you smiling about?'

He turned his head. She lay on the blanket wearing only his discarded shirt, her legs bare in the afternoon heat. Despite the estate being private and protected from intruders, she was still cautious about lolling around naked, unlike him. But she hadn't been prudish when he'd set about seducing her.

Through the fine cotton he saw the thrust of her nipples and the shadowy triangle of hair at the apex of her thighs. He'd never known a more stunning woman.

Inevitably his body stirred. 'You can't guess?'

Her smile was pure cat-that-got-the-cream. 'You're very predictable.'

Yet he didn't miss the sly way she stretched, making his shirt part over creamy flesh. Adam rolled onto his stomach, propping his weight on his forearms, enjoying the view. 'It doesn't look like you mind, beautiful.'

His smile widened as, instead of flinching at the word, Gisèle shrugged. *That* was progress. 'Why should I mind? You're a wonderful lover.'

'And I intend to be an excellent husband.' He revelled in the fact she enjoyed intimacy. But *lover* sounded too temporary for his liking. 'Where do you want to live, Gisèle?'

'I assumed you'd worked that out. You're the one with the multinational business.'

'But we agreed we'd discuss everything.'

He still enjoyed making her blush, describing what he'd like to do with her. Even better was the way Gisèle took that agreement seriously too, voicing her own demands and suggestions. There was something incredibly arousing about this gorgeous woman describing what would give her pleasure, including having her way with his body.

'I have a house in Sydney, and apartments in New York and Singapore. But I thought for now, France. Which would be better, Paris or the south, handy to your research team?'

Gisèle propped herself on one arm, eyes wide. 'Paris makes more sense for you.'

'But the south means you can be with your unit most days. I can telecommute. It's easy enough to get to the capital when I need to.'

'Adam, are you serious? We spent so much time before the wedding out in public. I assumed…'

'That would be our life?' He shook his head. 'It's okay for short stints and I did have connections I wanted to pursue. But mainly I liked going out with you at my side. Now I've got that permanently.'

He couldn't repress his smug smile.

'You're serious!'

'Never more so. I'll still have to travel sometimes. There's a deal I'm looking at in the US and another in Brazil, so I'll need excellent telecommunications. But I can be based anywhere. Whereas it makes sense for you to be with your team. Would you like that?'

Gisèle sat up and wrapped her arms around her bent knees.

'I'd love it. I can do society events when I need to but I'd rather focus on my real work.'

Adam nodded. He had some inkling now of how little she liked the limelight. It was a measure of her dedication to the company and her determination that she did it so well.

'That's settled then.'

Except it seemed it wasn't. His wife chewed her lip, frowning. Adam sat up and stroked a finger over her brow. 'Is there a problem?'

Her gaze dropped to his groin and he stifled satisfaction at her blatant interest. But sex could wait. This was important. He wanted Gisèle to be happy.

'Just when I think I understand you, you pull out another surprise.' Her eyes searched his. 'You said part of the reason for wanting the House of Fontaine was to prove you'd reached a social as well as commercial pinnacle. That you'd made it. But now you don't seem interested in furthering your social position. Even before the wedding you couldn't be bothered cosying up to that prince in Paris.'

The memory made his fists tighten. 'He was overrated. I understand men being attracted to you but he was blatantly ogling. I couldn't work with him.'

Gisèle's frown didn't shift. She covered his bunched fist with her hand.

'You really are the most complex man. It seems so long ago that you came stomping into my life, turning it upside down. I thought I knew you then but you keep proving me wrong.'

Adam kept his tone light despite the heavy thud of his pulse. 'In a good way?'

Her slow curling smile was like a spill of pure sunlight. 'Definitely in a good way. You're not like I first thought. In fact I have hopes for you.'

'Because I'm a phenomenal lover?'

'That could be part of it.' But instead of listing his good qualities she said, 'I think you've been lying to yourself, Adam.'

That startled him. He prided himself on his honesty, with himself and others. 'How so?'

'Don't look stern. It's not an insult.' She stared at their joined hands. 'You wanted to prove yourself to the privileged elite who looked down on you. But you admit you no longer worry what those old enemies think. You've risen beyond them.' She shook her head. 'You're very much your own man.'

Her fingers laced with his. 'I think the person you're *really* trying to convince is *you*. You've carried the memory of being looked down on though no one does it any more. You keep expanding the company, looking for more and more profits. But when will you be satisfied? When will enough be enough?'

Adam wanted to pull his hand free. He'd shared something utterly personal and she was twisting it.

Or was she? Was it possible Gisèle was right?

Something inside stilled as he sifted her words.

For years he'd been so caught up in the need to prove his value that he'd driven himself phenomenally hard.

His family kept telling him to ease back and enjoy the fruits of his success. Yet it wasn't until now, with Gisèle, that he'd allowed himself time off from his frantic striving for more and better.

Heat filled him. Had he used past hurts as an excuse to feed his ego? To drive himself, and others, relentlessly?

A soft palm cupped his cheek. 'Adam?'

'You've given me a lot to think about,' he muttered.

What if the pressure he put on himself, and his high expectations of employees, were because he secretly feared his success couldn't last? That he was doomed to failure and poverty?

Gisèle's eyes turned misty, the way they often were during intimacy. It struck him anew that he'd manoeuvred her like he'd manoeuvred so many business opportunities.

Had she forgiven him for his actions? They'd reached a truce based on mutual need. But was that enough to sustain the relationship he wanted?

'Tell me about Julien,' he said abruptly. It was time to be

totally honest. He couldn't bear any more secrets between them. 'Is he unwell?'

At the wedding her brother had looked thin and drawn.

Gisèle sat back but Adam captured her hand. 'You can trust me, sweetheart.'

She nodded and he felt the pressure on his chest lift. Because she was willing to share this. She wasn't retreating.

See, what you share is far more than sex.

'He was diagnosed some time ago.' She bit her lip. 'The prognosis wasn't good but he's responded well to treatment and we're hopeful.'

'I'm glad he's improving.' Adam squeezed her hand. 'That's why he withdrew from the company and installed you in his place, isn't it?'

Silently he berated himself for not guessing earlier. He'd briefly wondered if a breakdown might have caused Julien's withdrawal. But he'd been inclined to assume it was something more frivolous, believing the siblings had inherited their jobs without the competence to handle them.

What an arrogant fool he'd been!

Just because he'd met some like that, he shouldn't have jumped to conclusions. He'd even felt a self-righteous satisfaction at rescuing the House of Fontaine from the siblings he'd assumed had mismanaged it.

'That's right. Though I wasn't really CEO.' Her smile was wry. 'As you know, I don't have that skillset. The company was managed by some executives who have since left.'

'Because their mistakes almost destroyed it.'

Luminous eyes met his. She nodded.

Nausea stirred. 'Leaving you both in the lurch.'

'Not just us. Everyone who's dependent on it.'

Adam shook his head, sick at the situation she'd found herself in. Then he'd barged in, throwing his weight around, demanding not just the company but *her*.

Would it have changed things if he'd known? He grimaced.

He told himself he'd have been gentler with Gisèle, pursuing her without pushing her into a corner. But he'd still have acquired Fontaine's.

'*That's* why you wanted to convince the world we were falling for each other? To keep the truth from Julien?'

She inclined her head. 'I didn't want him to realise what I was doing. He would have told me to walk away, but I couldn't do that. He supported me through the toughest times. I was determined to do the same for him. You don't know him yet but when you do, you'll discover Fontaine's is his life. His passion. I thought it would kill him to lose the company and every connection with it.'

Adam felt her shiver and drew her close. 'So you'd have done anything to ensure he stayed in the company.'

Even marry a stranger.

His mouth filled with the taste of metal filings. So much for believing Gisèle could have walked away from the deal if she'd really wanted. That secretly she'd wanted him from the first too.

Nor had their deal been about money for her. Her focus had been on family and fear for her brother. Pain sheared through him as the enormity of her sacrifice for Julien hit.

How blithely he'd taken from this woman and how generously she'd acted.

You don't deserve her.

But he wasn't letting go. Incredibly she snuggled close, burrowing against him, her head on his chest. As if *he* weren't the man who'd threatened to rip the firm from their grasp and who'd initially intended to sack them both.

As if she drew comfort from him.

It was remarkable. Adam drew in a shuddering breath and held her to his thudding heart. Things had changed so much between them. It gave him hope for the future.

He vowed to make it up to her. All the stress and worry. He'd do whatever it took to make her happy.

'It's all right,' he murmured, rocking her gently. 'Julien's doing well. He's going to be fine.'

Adam couldn't countenance the alternative, knowing it would tear Gisèle apart. It was clear how much she loved her brother. What she'd done for Julien humbled him.

'I know. Things really are looking up. But sometimes I still worry.'

Adam realised how little opportunity she'd had to be with her brother these past weeks, because he'd insisted on keeping her with him. 'Do you want to visit him? Or have him stay here?'

Gisèle tipped her head back, eyes wide. 'Really? You'd have him here? On our honeymoon?'

Adam had already planned to extend their honeymoon. A week was nowhere near long enough. But he could adapt. His wife needed his support. 'We can have time alone in the future whenever we like. If I'd known the situation with Julien I wouldn't have monopolised your time so much.'

'It's okay, Adam. We have regular video chats. He didn't want me fussing over him in person. He prefers to recover in private.'

Much like Gisèle. Both siblings valued their privacy. How much of that was due to the blare of public interest that they'd faced from birth?

'Nevertheless, I'm sure he'd love to spend time with you. He's based outside Paris, isn't he?' She nodded. 'Why not call him today?'

They stayed on at the château for another ten days. Gisèle had regularly visited her brother, insisting on the third visit that Adam accompany her. He guessed it was to reassure Julien about the man she'd married. Adam hadn't missed the muted but definitely negative vibes from his brother-in-law on the day of the wedding.

The visit had gone well. Even in the time since the wedding, Julien seemed stronger, a better colour in his complexion. After some initial stiffness he and Adam had achieved a level of ease, talking over Fontaine's, finding a surprising amount of common ground.

Gisèle had been right, her brother knew the business and had a quick, insightful mind. He'd be an asset when he returned to work in the executive team.

That visit had also been interesting for the presence of Julien's friend, Noemie, a pretty, kind-hearted woman who clearly thought the world of him. They'd met when he'd been in hospital receiving treatment as had Noemie's daughter, who was now well enough to spend the day with a friend.

Was it Noemie's presence that had made the visit so easy?

Or the fact Gisèle no longer wore the slightly strained look she had prior to the wedding? Presumably Julien had noticed it too, the sparkle in her eyes and her ready smile.

Adam knew that, if Angela wanted to marry, he'd consider no man good enough until he was assured he was decent, honest and intent on making his sister happy.

He didn't begrudge Julien that assurance. In fact he went out of his way to make it clear how much he valued and cared for his bride.

That compulsion he'd felt the first time he'd seen her hadn't dimmed. It had grown, morphing into not just need, but appreciation, caring and a desire to make her happy.

Marrying Gisèle Fontaine had been the savviest move of his career. Not for business reasons but because she made him happy in so many ways.

A month later Adam's life had settled into a new routine. Early morning runs with Gisèle, if they had any energy after dawn lovemaking. Leisurely breakfasts before she left for Fontaine's while he worked from home, rarely needing to be elsewhere to run his enterprise.

After their discussion he'd thought carefully about what drove him and had to concede his relentless push for success after success wasn't necessary. He was trying to reprioritise and take time to enjoy all he had.

Living with Gisèle made that easier. They socialised but enjoyed evenings in, preparing dinner together, making love or watching films. Weekends saw them on the yacht, swimming and lazing in their private garden, or exploring mountain villages in his sportscar.

He couldn't recall ever feeling so contented.

They stayed in the Cap Ferrat villa rather than Gisèle's apartment, but Adam had found a house he thought she'd like. It sat in the hills near the Fontaine premises with magnificent views over the coast. It was a remodelled farmhouse that retained its traditional bones but with modern refinements. Sympathetic extensions provided space for entertaining, an enticing mix of luxury and cosy comfort and, should they need it, space for a family.

The prospect excited him. He itched to show it to Gisèle. If she liked it he'd show his mother too. She'd stopped in after her travels to visit them before returning to Sydney.

'I'm so happy for you both,' she gushed when they were alone, her smile the widest he'd ever seen. 'I had doubts in the beginning about the pair of you and how quickly you married. People from different countries, different cultures, who hadn't known each other long. And at the wedding I thought there was some constraint on Gisèle's part.'

Adam's smile faded. Of course there'd been constraint. Things hadn't been right between him and Gisèle. But he'd hardly admit that to his mother. 'I'm glad you're satisfied now. Believe me, we're very happy.'

He couldn't remember feeling better. Life with Gisèle was beyond anything he'd imagined. As lovers, partners, friends and even occasionally opponents in some argument, they were well-suited.

She made life richer and more satisfying. And she was happy too. He tried hard to be a good husband and she was thriving, being back with her team. Each day their understanding of each other, their respect and enjoyment, grew.

In the early days he'd thought with his libido and his business head. Somehow they'd led him into a relationship that went far beyond sex and work. With Gisèle he felt content. He could be himself and increasingly she let him into parts of her life that had hitherto been hers alone. That was a privilege and a joy.

'I can see that,' his mother said. 'I watch your expression when you look at Gisèle and it reminds me so much of your father when we were together. And I see the way she looks at you. It's obvious that you're both deeply in love. I can't tell you how happy that makes me.'

In love?

Adam struggled to hide his shock.

He'd never been in love. Never even thought about it.

He'd always been too busy. His focus on building success left him no time for establishing a relationship. Instead he'd enjoyed passing liaisons.

Until Gisèle.

It was true he cared for her deeply. But love?

And as for her loving him...

He discovered the idea was strongly appealing. His pulse thudded, a frisson of excitement rippling across his flesh and down to his fingertips.

'Adam?' He swung around to see his mother grinning. 'It's good to see you've finally found someone who can distract you from building an ever-greater commercial empire.'

'There's nothing wrong with focus and hard work.'

'Of course there's not, darling. But some things are far more important.'

His mother gathered her bag and rose from the sofa. 'My taxi will be waiting. Gisèle is finishing work early to help me choose a new outfit for your cousin's wedding. But don't worry, I won't keep her late.'

It was a measure of Adam's shock that he didn't argue about his mother taking a taxi. Usually he'd insist on driving her.

Instead he watched her bustle out, his head spinning.

He had a conference call soon to discuss the American acquisition, but for once business couldn't hold his attention.

Adam drew in a ragged breath and turned to pace the sitting room, trying to digest her words.

Love! Could it be?

An image filled his mind, of Gisèle, flushed and sweating after their morning run, her hair in a damp ponytail, eyes bright from exertion. Gisèle, chewing her lip as she pondered a report she'd brought home. Gisèle standing in the bow of the yacht, laughing as they skimmed over the dark sea. Of her in his arms, hugging him as they took each other to the edge of bliss and beyond.

His heart thrashed against his ribs, so hard it felt like it tried to escape.

He'd been thinking of a family with her. Now he pictured them together through the years, growing older and slower. She'd be as dear to him, he realised, when age wrinkled her skin and greyed her hair. Dearer, because a lifetime's intimacy would only bring them closer.

Adam stood stock still, picturing it, feeling it in every pore of his body.

He loved her.

He'd loved her so long, he realised, but hadn't seen it. Yet once acknowledged there was no doubt. No wonder he'd been single-minded in his pursuit.

How did she feel about him?

Was it possible she loved him?

Or was she making the best of the situation? He shivered in dismay.

He'd known from the first that his behaviour was outrageous. He'd wanted her and insisted on having her, taking advantage of circumstances to get what he wanted.

Adam sank onto a chair, shaky fingers raking his hair as he revisited his actions.

You knew what you were doing, forcing her hand. But that didn't stop you. Even when you discovered she'd been an innocent, and how she'd been taken advantage of before, you didn't stop. Your conscience smarted but you didn't miss the wedding, the chance to tie her to you.

Somehow he'd convinced himself that, because she was happy now, the past didn't matter. She'd forgiven him, or at least decided not to hold it against him because she wanted him as much as he did her.

But it *did* matter. It always had.

Adam loved this woman and he wanted her to love him too. *Of her own volition.* He wanted it to be real.

How could he expect that when he'd used her so badly? When he'd triumphed over her and her brother at one of the lowest ebbs in their lives?

How could he continue to take advantage? Their relationship was built on *his* demands, not mutual feelings.

Gisèle had made him take a hard look at his priorities but he'd only gone so far. He'd refused to take responsibility for his actions.

His skin itched with self-disgust. His triumph over Fontaine's was no triumph at all. Suddenly he saw himself, not as the conquering hero, turning around a failing company, but as someone no better than the smug, privileged people he loathed. He'd wanted, and hadn't given a toss for what anyone else deserved.

Adam shot to his feet to pace. Self-knowledge was a damnable thing.

He'd done so much wrong and it was time to make amends.

He dragged in oxygen, trying to feel relief at the decision, knowing exactly what he had to do. Yet his breath was shallow with panic. His course was clear. But he feared that, once Gisèle was free to choose, she might no longer choose him.

Adam had never been so terrified in his life.

CHAPTER FOURTEEN

'GIGI, IS ADAM THERE? I've been trying to reach him but his phone's off.'

Gisèle tucked her phone against her shoulder as she assembled salad ingredients. With Adam away she couldn't be bothered cooking.

'He's in the US, Julien. He's probably in a meeting.'

Her mouth firmed. She'd grown so used to Adam managing his business empire from home she'd been surprised and disappointed when he'd flown out for a series of meetings in North America.

She missed him. It was the first time they'd been apart since the wedding.

But it wasn't just that. He hadn't been himself for the last week. He'd been preoccupied, almost withdrawn, unlike the confident, teasing lover to whom she'd grown accustomed.

He'd assured her nothing was wrong but she didn't quite believe him. That scared her because whatever else their relationship was, it had always been honest.

Every instinct warned of a problem. Even when they made love it had been with an unfamiliar urgency on Adam's part. But it wasn't just the urgency of passion. It felt different, rooted in something darker than the joy they'd found together. Yet Adam had brushed off her concerns.

Maybe you're jumping at shadows. Julien's illness has made you expect the worst.

'Hmm. That explains it.' Julien paused. 'I don't suppose he said anything to you about the company?'

Something in her brother's voice made her abandon the tomatoes and give all her attention to the conversation.

'We talk about it all the time. What, in particular?' An unnerving silence met her question and her nape furred, the fine hairs there standing on end. 'Is there a problem?'

There couldn't be. Already Adam's changes were turning Fontaine's around.

'No problem. Laurent called. Do you know about that?'

The family lawyer? 'No. What's wrong?'

'Nothing. In fact, it's good news. If it's true.'

Gisèle rolled her eyes. 'Stop talking in riddles.'

'Well, if Laurent's right, and this is what I want to check with Adam, he's signing the company back to us. He'll step aside as CEO.'

Julien sounded as stunned as she felt.

'Step aside?'

'The company is being handed over to us completely.'

'Impossible!' Gisèle braced herself against the counter. 'Adam's committed to Fontaine's.'

'That's what I don't understand. Laurent says he's not even seeking compensation for the money he's poured into it. It makes no sense. He can't simply walk away.'

Ice glissaded down Gisèle's spine. 'It's totally out of character,' she said slowly. 'He wanted Fontaine's badly and he's committed so much into improving it.'

Yet lately he'd seemed preoccupied with other business. Like the US acquisition.

Was *that* why he'd been distracted? Was he turning his attention to the next challenge? She'd believed him committed to Fontaine's for the long haul. Their discussions had left her excited for the company's future.

'That's what I thought. But I don't know him as well as

you. Maybe the American engineering company is more his style than cosmetics?'

Julien's words struck home. Engineering was more in Adam's line. Was it possible that despite his initial enthusiasm he was bored? Did he enjoy the thrill of the hunt, his interest waning once the process of reinvigorating the acquired company was underway? From his staff's comments it wasn't usual for him to be so heavily involved in the minutiae of an acquisition long term.

Was he losing interest?

Instantly she rejected the idea. Until she remembered months ago, telling herself that one day, when the novelty wore off, Adam would move on from the company.

And then he'd have no need for her. She'd be free.

The phone fell onto the benchtop as a wave of pain engulfed her, doubling her over. She clung to the counter, fighting for breath.

The idea was preposterous. Adam had paid a fortune for Fontaine's. He wouldn't give it away.

'Gisèle?'

'I'm here.' She was proud of her even tone. 'It sounds like nonsense.' But Laurent had always been reliable.

'Well, when you talk to Adam, you can clarify it.'

'Of course.'

The problem was she'd had trouble reaching him. Even when he'd gone away prior to their wedding he'd rung every night. Was his schedule so busy now that he had no time for her? Or was he avoiding her?

Nausea swirled in the pit of her stomach.

She'd told herself their convenient marriage had turned into something special. That Adam was the man she wanted, not just in bed but in her life.

She'd never expected to feel this way about any man. Never wanted so much from one.

Gisèle respected his intellect and his ability to make things happen, the way he could turn a failing enterprise into an exciting venture. But more important than that was the man behind the tycoon and the way he made her feel. Desired, and valued, even cherished.

His kindness had been an unexpected bonus. He was forever telling her how beautiful she was. They weren't just words. The way he looked at her, the almost reverent way he touched her sometimes, made her feel beautiful inside. He laughed with her and made the days seemed brighter.

She'd begun to hope that one day he might love her.

Because she was almost sure she'd fallen in love with him. The idea alternately thrilled and terrified her.

Everywhere he went he was popular, as if the corporate shark were a part-time persona. He took an interest in everyone and everything. It didn't matter whether they were wait staff, highflying executives or cleaners.

How often had she found him laughing with one of the staff at the villa or on the yacht? When the housekeeper had received a call saying her son had been in an accident, it was Adam who'd driven her to the hospital in his sports car, then stayed till the boy had received treatment.

Would a man so thoughtful simply drop Fontaine's after so much work? And if his focus *had* shifted to the US, what about their relationship?

Frustratingly Gisèle didn't have a chance to find out for twenty-four hours. Adam called when she was in the shower but when she rang back he was in a meeting. Then she dropped and damaged her phone and had to wait until business hours to get a new one. Only to find he'd switched his to message bank.

Unable to settle, she couldn't face the effort of appearing cheerful for her team. She opted to work from home, giving the villa staff the day off.

So when the front door opened and firm footsteps echoed from the tiled foyer her blood fizzed with nervous anticipation. Adam wasn't due until tomorrow but there was no mistaking his gait.

'I'm on the terrace,' she called, shutting her laptop.

'Gisèle? Are you all right? Why aren't you at work?'

His concern was a relief. Stupid to have been nervous.

Except when Adam appeared he didn't look glad to see her. He looked...wary. Instead of drawing her into his arms he dropped a peck on her head and stood back.

Even so, she found time to admire the way he filled out jeans and a leather jacket, his black T-shirt shaping his solid chest.

'I'm working from home. I didn't expect you until tomorrow. Is everything okay? The US deal's progressing?'

'It's done, wrapped up early.'

Yet there was no elation as he took a chair on the other side of the outdoor table. Normally they'd be in each other's arms. Her body ached with the need to touch him, be held by him. But he kept his distance like a stranger.

Gisèle bit down a rising bubble of distress. Something was definitely amiss. Adam didn't even meet her eyes after that initial, piercing glance. She shivered, reading his body language. This was a man with bad news to break.

She clamped her fingers on the edge of the table, sitting straighter. 'Whatever it is, Adam, tell me. Don't make me try to guess what's wrong.'

Deep green eyes met hers and there was that familiar spark igniting in her blood. But was it in hers alone? He gave no indication the feeling was mutual.

Could it really be that she'd been a passing diversion? She'd been so sure they shared something special and strong.

'Are you really getting rid of Fontaine's?'

That drew a response. Adam cursed under his breath.

His scowl, his shadowed jaw and the delicious tangle of dark hair made him look like a bad-tempered pirate. But Gisèle refused to let attraction distract her. 'You don't think I have a right to know?'

'That's it. I intended to tell you myself.'

Yet he stopped, mouth clamping into a flat line.

She couldn't believe it. 'You're actually walking away from the company?'

He dragged a hand across his scalp in a gesture of frustration or tiredness. Gisèle hardened her heart, refusing to feel sorry for him.

'I'm returning the company to you and Julien. Fontaine's will be run by the family as it always has been.'

Pain banded Gisèle's chest. It was a moment before she realised she'd forgotten to breathe.

So it was true. Unbelievably Adam was discarding the prize he'd been so determined to win. Just as well she was holding on to the table as the world wheeled about her.

'And us?'

'Don't worry, acquiring the company was my decision and I'll wear the costs. You and Julien owe me nothing.'

The pain was back, except this time it wasn't just in her chest. She ached all over as if every muscle and bone drew tight under the most tremendous pressure.

If she'd needed proof, there it was. When she'd asked about *us*, she'd meant Adam and her. But his first thought was the company, her and Julien.

Sharply she sat back, chin lifting in an automatic attempt to hide distress. Yet it took a moment to find her voice. 'That doesn't sound like a clever business decision.'

His jaw tightened. 'It's *my* decision.'

Now he was back, the billionaire businessman who called the shots.

Was the generous lover who'd changed her world a mirage? Had she imagined tenderness between them because she'd wanted it so badly?

Once before she'd thought a man cared for her, only to discover he wasn't really interested in *her*. Had Adam decided that with his interest in Fontaine's waning, he no longer required his French wife? After all, she'd only been an addendum in a business deal.

Gisèle shot to her feet and swung away. She couldn't listen to any more, not yet, not when she hurt so much.

But she had to know. She sucked in a burning breath. 'So your focus now is on the US, yes?'

After a moment he spoke. 'That's right.'

Still it didn't make sense. It was bizarre to go to so much effort only to drop the project. Gisèle stared at the glittering sea. 'And our marriage? Is that over too?'

His chair scraped the flagstones but he didn't approach. 'If you like.'

Her vision blurred and she wrapped her arms around her waist as she stifled a sob. *If she liked.* As if he didn't care either way. Not a ringing endorsement!

Desperate determination was all that kept her standing. 'You want to move on to greener pastures.'

Had it hurt this much when she lost her family? She'd forgotten such bone-deep anguish was possible.

The rush of blood in her ears masked his footsteps, for suddenly his voice came from behind her. His breath stirred her hair, sending cascading goosebumps across her scalp and shoulders.

'What I *want* is for you to be happy.'

His voice was as tight as her bottled-up emotions.

'How very…kind of you, Adam.'

He said something under his breath she couldn't catch. 'Hardly kind. Not after the way I've treated you.'

'Don't you mean the way you're treating me now?' She swung around, an unsteady laugh erupting from her throat. 'Off with the old and on with the new. Is that it? You've found someone in America to replace me?'

Where that came from she had no idea. She hadn't even let

herself think such a thing. But the bitterness consuming her was unstoppable.

Large hands closed around her upper arms. She would have shrugged them off except she looked up and read Adam's shock. He appeared as unhappy as she felt.

His voice was hoarse. 'There's no one else. Only you, Gisèle.'

She wanted to hug those words tight. But actions spoke louder than words, didn't they? 'Yet you want to be rid of me. Like you want to divest yourself of the company.'

'It's not like that. This is *necessary*. I'm trying to right a terrible wrong.' His grip eased, hands sliding around to caress her back. 'I've treated you badly, Gisèle, and I'm attempting to make up for it.'

She frowned, trying to make sense of this, trying to ignore the way her body arched into those sweeping hands.

'What you've done is confuse me. What's going on?'

His mouth ticked up at one corner in a smile so tight it looked like it hurt.

'I wanted you from the moment I saw you. You know that.' Gisèle's needy heart flipped over but she made herself stand tall, waiting, even if she did shuffle a little closer. 'I've never done that before—forced a woman I wanted into a corner. Brought undue pressure to bear.' He shook his head. 'I should have known I was getting in over my head.'

He was in over his head? Gisèle licked her lips and swallowed. She was completely out of her depth.

'I thought I was being canny. It was only later I realised how unforgiveable my behaviour really was. When I found out you were sexually innocent, and how you'd been taken advantage of before, I felt so guilty I couldn't face you. But I came back for the wedding because conscience or no conscience, I had to have you.'

They were so close now she had to brace her palms on his

chest or fall against him. Through his shirt she felt the quick hammer of his heart, as fast as hers.

'Then I discovered you'd had no choice about marrying me. I'd told myself you could have walked away from the deal if you didn't fancy it.' His bark of laughter was harsh. 'My ego told me you fancied me. That despite everything you wanted me. But it turned out you'd been tied because of Julien's illness and had no choice. Even *then* I couldn't let you go as you deserved.'

Gisèle frowned. He didn't sound like he wanted to ditch her. He sounded as tormented as she felt. The ache inside eased a little. Hope stirred.

'What changed?'

Another of those taut smiles as his gaze met hers and she fell into moss green depths.

'I realised what I'd avoided acknowledging. I love you, Gisèle.'

She felt her heart bump her ribs at his admission. It seemed too incredible to be true. But already he was moving on, speaking in a husky voice that signalled deep emotion.

'I'll do whatever it takes to make you happy and make up for my actions. It's not enough to apologise and tell myself you're content now. I need to know for *sure*. I need to make it *right*. I have to give you back the power I stole so you have a choice.'

Gisèle swayed, buffeted by a rush of shocked understanding. He cared for her. *Loved* her. And he was trying to redress past wrongs. Because he wasn't a bad man, merely flawed like everyone else.

Trust Adam to make reparations with the most outlandishly generous gesture! He was always larger than life. With him everything was magnified. The scale of his ambition. The depth of feeling he aroused in her. The magic of his lovemaking. His determination. His sheer, masculine charisma. Even his guilt and contrition.

Gisèle's chest squeezed as the truth sank in.

She leaned into his reassuring heat and strength. 'You're *giving* me and Julien the House of Fontaine so I'll be free to choose whether I want to be with you?'

Adam nodded, his mouth a tight line, a frantic pulse throbbing at his temple.

It was the most extraordinary thing she'd ever heard.

But he was serious. She saw it in his face, felt it in his hammering heart and tense muscles.

'I love you, Gisèle. I want you to choose me. I want to be worthy of you. Nothing else matters.'

For a moment she basked in the glory of that.

'It's not because you've lost interest in—'

'Lost interest!' He gathered her close. 'If you tell me to go, I will. But never, for a moment, think that.' He swallowed. 'I'm trying to be a better man. More self-aware and respectful. More loving.'

She drew a sustaining breath, almost impossible to do when her emotions were a riot of shock and utter joy.

'What if I decide to stay?'

The sudden brilliance in his eyes gave her the answer she needed. Gisèle pressed her fingers to his lips before he could speak. She had no interest in prolonging his agony and she was done with trying to hold in her feelings. It felt like she'd been damming her emotions for a lifetime and finally they were about to burst free.

'You've never been one to do things by halves, have you? You stormed into my world and behaved outrageously. You pushed and demanded but somehow I've never felt stronger than when I was pushing back. Then when I got to know you...' She shook her head. 'The fact is I love you too, Adam Wilde. I want us to build a life together.'

That had stunned her. 'I'd always thought romance wasn't for me.' Not after seeing her mother so lost after her husband's death. 'But now I understand some things aren't a choice. Love is one of them.'

It was a beat in her blood, a tenderness she'd never known before Adam. It was hope and strength and a need to share everything with him.

He lifted her hand from his mouth, keeping it in a firm grip. 'Truly? You love me? You forgive me, Gisèle?'

'As you astutely pointed out, I turned up for the wedding. I could have walked away but didn't. It wasn't about Fontaine's by then, it was about you. The challenging, surprising, wonderful man I want to be with always.'

Next thing she knew, strong arms lifted her and his mouth was on hers, full of tenderness and the sweet promise of love.

When he lowered her to the ground they were both shaky.

'My precious Gisèle.'

Everything she'd never dared let herself expect or hope for was in those three words. Tenderness. Love. Respect. Even adoration. She felt them like a warm tide, filling her to the brim.

'My demanding, wonderful Adam.'

Gisèle stroked his stubbly cheek, enjoying the friction on her palm. But nowhere near as much as she adored his ardent expression.

'I can't believe you love me,' he said. 'It's miraculous.'

'You want proof?' The sudden release of tension made Gisèle laugh as she slid his jacket off his shoulders. 'I can give you proof.'

'It might take a while to convince me. Days. Weeks.'

Adam's voice was endearingly unsteady but his hand was deft as he reached for the zip on her sundress.

Gisèle nuzzled his throat as she slipped open the top button of his shirt. 'How about a lifetime?'

'That sounds absolutely perfect.'

EPILOGUE

'I NEVER THOUGHT I'd say it, Adam, but it was a good day when you came into our lives.'

Adam turned to survey his brother-in-law. 'Don't tell me you actually like me now?'

Julien grinned. 'I've liked you for a long time, *mon ami*, but I had to be sure you'd make my sister happy.'

'That I can understand.'

Adam turned to admire Gisèle, in animated conversation with some guests. She wore a stunning party dress with tiny straps over the shoulders and a froth of skirts. The pale blue material matched her eyes and her delicate necklace of aquamarines and diamonds.

She was so lovely, so dear, she stole his breath.

As if aware of his regard, her gaze met his across the terrace. Her hand went to the necklace he'd given her an hour ago, an anniversary gift.

Julien sighed. 'You two are ridiculously in love.'

Adam raised an eyebrow, following as Julien's attention shifted to the brunette talking to Adam's mum. Instantly, Noemie's head turned and she met Julien's stare with a smile.

'And you're not in love?'

His brother-in-law's mouth turned down. 'It's not so simple. I'm well now, but asking someone to take a chance on that long term—'

'*That's* what's holding you back? Gisèle and I couldn't work out what was wrong. Noemie won't talk about it.'

Julien looked outraged. 'You've asked her?'

'Gisèle did. Her advice was that if you didn't commit soon she should walk away. But your girlfriend refused to push. She said you needed time.'

'She did?'

Adam's mouth twitched at his brother-in-law's expression, the firming jaw and hopeful light in his eyes.

'She did. But we wonder how long she'll be patient. You've seen the way that new advertising exec looks at her, haven't you? You don't want to wait too long.'

Adam knew the executive in question hadn't left Angela's side since the party began. He'd have to have a word to his sister about leaving broken hearts behind when she returned to Australia.

But it was enough to stir Julien into action. He clapped Adam on the shoulder. 'You're a good man, Adam. I'm glad to call you brother.'

Adam was surprised at the rush of warmth he felt at the words. The pair had worked together for a year, though Adam's role in Fontaine's was advisory only. In that time they'd become close, but Julien's hard-won friendship meant a lot. He smiled as he watched the Frenchman cross the terrace to Noemie.

'What are you up to?' whispered a familiar voice.

An arm slid around his waist and he pulled Gisèle close, kissing her cheek.

'Nudging your brother in the right direction.'

'You clever man! I thought he'd never make his move.'

Adam nuzzled Gisèle's throat, finding that spot at the base of her neck where she was sensitive. She shivered and leaned close. He slipped his hand between them, palm to her abdomen, excitement rising.

'Shall we tell them tonight?'

Her eyes locked on his and Adam felt himself fall into those bright blue depths. 'Would you mind if we kept it our special secret for now? You know they'll all fuss.'

'Whatever you like, sweetheart.' Adam wanted to shout their news to the world. But sharing it with the one woman who meant everything to him was the greatest blessing of his life. 'I love you, my beautiful wife. Have I told you that?'

She laughed. 'Frequently. And I love you.'

When she looked at him like that he couldn't resist. His mouth found hers and they kissed with all the tenderness and pent-up passion that characterised their marriage.

Finally Adam lifted his head, aware that the buzz of conversation had quietened. Most guests were still chatting but his mother and sister, and Julien and Noemie, were looking their way, expressions arrested.

He made to lift his palm from Gisèle's flat stomach, but stopped as she placed her hand over his.

She sighed. 'It looks like our secret's out.'

'Do you mind?'

Her expression made his heart roll over. 'How can I mind? I'm the happiest woman in France.'

Adam lifted their joined hands and kissed her palm, drawing in the scent of orange blossom and gorgeous woman. 'And I'm the happiest man in the world.'

* * * * *

MILLS & BOON MODERN IS
HAVING A MAKEOVER!

The same great stories you love,
a stylish new look!

Look out for our brand new look
COMING JUNE 2024

MILLS & BOON

COMING SOON!

We really hope you enjoyed reading this book.
If you're looking for more romance
be sure to head to the shops when
new books are available on

Thursday 4th
July

To see which titles are coming soon, please visit
millsandboon.co.uk/nextmonth

MILLS & BOON

MILLS & BOON®

Coming next month

ITALIAN'S STOLEN WIFE
Lorraine Hall

'I am very well aware of who you are, *cara*.'

His smile felt like some kind of lethal blow. Francesca could not understand why it should make her feel breathless and devastated.

But she had spent her life in such a state. So she kept her smile in place and waited patiently for Aristide to explain his appearance. Even if her heart seemed to clatter around in her chest like it was no longer tethered. A strange sensation indeed.

'I am afraid there has been a change of plans today,' he said at last, his low voice a sleek menace.

Francesca kept her sweet smile in place, her hand relaxed in his grip, her posture perfect. She was an expert at playing her role. Even as panic began to drum its familiar beat through her bloodstream.

'Oh?' she said, as if she was interested in everything he had to say.

No one would change her plans. *No one*. She narrowly resisted curling her free fingers into a fist.

'You will be marrying me instead.'

Continue reading
ITALIAN'S STOLEN WIFE
Lorraine Hall

Available next month
millsandboon.co.uk

LET'S TALK
Romance

Follow us:

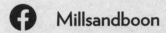

Millsandboon

@MillsandBoon

@MillsandBoonUK

@MillsandBoonUK

For all the latest titles and special offers, sign up to our newsletter:

Millsandboon.co.uk

afterglow BOOKS

Afterglow Books is a trend-led, trope-filled list of books with diverse, authentic and relatable characters, a wide array of voices and representations, plus real world trials and tribulations. Featuring all the tropes you could possibly want (think small-town settings, fake relationships, grumpy vs sunshine, enemies to lovers) and all with a generous dose of spice in every story.

@millsandboonuk
@millsandboonuk
afterglowbooks.co.uk
#AfterglowBooks

For all the latest book news, exclusive content and giveaways scan the QR code below to sign up to the Afterglow newsletter:

Never Date A Roommate
PBO 9780263322897 £8.99
Ebook 9780008938420 | Audio 9780263324860
For publicity enquiries please contact
millsandboonpressoffice@harpercollins.co.uk

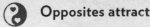

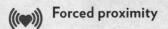

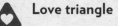

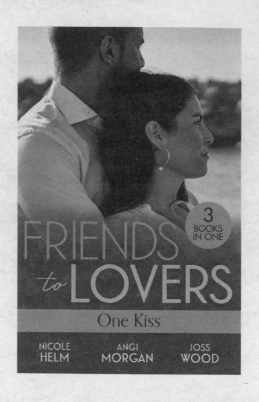